HITLER NEEDS YOU

HITLER NEEDS YOU

a novel by
JACK TREVOR STORY

Allison & Busby, London

First published in Great Britain by
Allison & Busby Limited, 6a Noel Street, London W1

© Jack Trevor Story 1970

SBN 85031 040 7

Printed in Great Britain by
Villiers Publications Ltd, Ingestre Road, London NW5

To my sister and brothers,
Elsa, Peter, Bernard and Olly
and to the memory of my mother

The day war broke out my old woman come to me. She say: ' I'll put kettle on, Amos. We'll have a nice cup o' tea.'

(*East Anglian lore*)

Chapter One

' Tea up ! '

Horace's foolish heart jumped with excitement, his head jerked up and bumped the control bar of the drilling machine, the piece of steel came off the bed and whirled round and he jumped back spurting blood.

' What are you going to do for encore? ' Ernie Trigg asked him. And to Hazel the tea girl he said : ' Look, don't shout like that, dear, when craftsmen are at work.'

The craftsmen, the real craftsmen, all laughed. There was old Ted Wright the instrument maker who built scale-model locomotives for a hobby, Dirty Dick the tool maker who took snuff, Harry Webb a young, crude, newly-married semi-skilled fitter, Mr Roper another instrument maker who never joined in, and Ernie the foreman, a ginger-whiskered comedian. Horace had just joined this élite of the factory, the model shop, as shop boy.

Horace was frightened of all the men and all the machines and in love with Hazel.

' If I don't marry Hazel Springer I shan't marry anybody,' he had already told his mother.

Hazel took Horace to the first-aid room, across in the main radio-production factory.

' Mr Tischler came in crying,' she told Horace.

' Oh,' said Horace.

Her hair was clean and soft as lady-grass. Horace had many dreams, sleeping and waking and walking backwards and forwards to work, in which his lips came very close to hers, her eyes waiting; he had an instinct for life which told him that if their lips ever met it would all be finished and undreamable again. He had not had a chance to break through the tongue-tied shyness of love until today.

In the afternoon when she came round with the tea-trolley again Hazel asked how his hand was and Horace lifted the bandage. The cut was across the ball of his thumb on his left hand and the scar remained all his life.

'Another half-inch,' Hazel said, ' and you'd have got lock-jaw.'

Horace's jaw went stiff; he felt faint and had to sit down on the nearest stool.

Three times a week Horace Fenton went to night school for Electricity and Magnetism.

'Everybody kneel down on the floor with their compasses,' Mr Purdey told them one night. 'We're going to plot the earth's magnetic field.'

It was point-two-two Gauss.

The dream became unbearable cycling home in the dark and Horace made a detour to the house where she lived by the river and stood as close as he dared watching the lighted windows. If she came out he planned to ask her the time. Then he planned to say he was looking for the house of a chap on the transformer line who had promised him some plug-in coils for his wireless building. But she didn't come out.

At half-past ten Horace heard Harry Roy's band from the Kit-Kat Restaurant playing *Bugle Call Rag*. At eleven o'clock he heard a news bulletin about the German army's triumphant welcome into Vienna.

That's what Mr Tischler in research had been crying about today. He had hoped to get his family to England before it happened.

'They're better off where they are, old mate,' Harry Webb told him.

In Germany there were no hunger marchers. In Germany they were building motor roads, factories, houses, cheap motor cars for the workers. All the finest measuring instruments in the model shop were made in Germany. Germany was a hallmark for precision. Working for Siemens or the Todt organisation they would all be getting double what they were getting now, Harry said. He was an AEU man.

'Soon you will be happy,' Mr Tischler had said. 'Soon you will have Hitler here.'

'You're crazy,' Harry Webb told the old German Jew. 'Hitler doesn't want war with England. Germany for the Germans, that's all he wants. I don't blame him.'

'You're safe here,' Ernie Trigg told the Austrian, kindly.

Everybody had told the radio engineer who had helped to put Vienna landessender on the air with a microphone made out of a cocoa tin that he was safe in the Home Counties. Horace would always remember how the old chap turned in the doorway of the model shop and looked back at them.

' Work hard,' he said. ' Hitler needs you.'

Horace did not know what he meant but he felt that it was something other than what was said.

Everybody was up when Horace got home. He thought they were worrying about him and they were, but it was something else as well.

' Was there anybody hanging around? ' Ronald asked him.

' I didn't notice.'

And his mother said : ' Your stepfather's been here.'

' Selling brushes,' said Christine.

' Bloody rubbish,' said Leslie.

' *What* rubbish? ' Mrs Fenton exclaimed. ' *What* rubbish? '

Christine said : ' He didn't mean it.'

' *What* rubbish, Leslie? ' Rhoda Fenton asked again, stubbornly.

Leslie apologised.

' Anyway, it's not rubbish,' she said, mildly. ' I'd recognise him anywhere. Ginger hair, watery eyes, scar on his top lip — smarmy.'

' You married him ! ' Leslie said. She was talking about Leslie's father, Monty Morden. He was a roundabout man from Thurston's fair who had come into The Disabled Soldiers' Club one day and offered to sink his savings into Rhoda's business. What he had done was sink her business into his savings, made her pregnant and when she'd gone into hospital to have Leslie he'd sent all the children next door to a neighbour, sold up the stock and run away with a waitress. Everything bad that had happened to the Fenton family since then Rhoda had blamed on her second husband.

' Besides,' she said, ' this was the only house in the road he called at. I watched him from the window.'

Leslie said : ' He would have said something.'

' He just wanted to see if I was married again.'

11

' He knows you can't marry again.'

She said: ' If I was he'd blackmail me.' And she said to Horace: ' Why are you so late from night school? '

Horace was in no mood for this level of conversation.

Chapter Two

Horace knew a number of isolated things about his family back-ground; this is probably as much as most people know. We are not islands but we are, perhaps, peninsulas.

Horace knew that his grandfather, Sam Dayball, used to tricycle around the village greens preaching. When a friend died, sometimes his tricycle would stand outside the widow's house all night. He was so jealous that he wouldn't allow his wife to see a doctor and she used to drag around with her womb hanging out. He wouldn't allow Sunday papers in the house but kept the *News of the World* under the mat for when his family had gone to bed.

Rhoda Fenton, or Morden as she became for a time, not know-ing whether she was really married the second time or not, had four or five anecdotes about her father. One or two visual images. Going down Ball Plain on a Sunday evening with her friends, all home from service (skivvying), and listening to her father preach-ing. Being bawled out of bed in the middle of the night because her father had found something wrong with the washing-up.

' Rhoda ! ' he shouted up the stairs. ' Pearl ! Edie ! Lil ! '

And another thing he used to say was : ' Pass de winegar, Em.'

This last gave Horace the picture of a very uneducated man, whereas some of the other stuff didn't.

From cross-examining his mother with the object of writing about his grandfather in later life, Horace was told that he was a very fierce man; he had to be, he was foreman at the mill. Hornsmill, that was, the tannery. She conveyed the picture that Sam Dayball strode about skinning things.

' He was very much like you to look at,' she told Horace.

It didn't sound much like Horace to Horace. Horace was more skinned against than skinning. He also learned, since he learned practically nothing about anybody else among his for-bears and therefore Sam was the main rock, that Sam boasted he was born within the sound of Bow Bells which was required borning for a pure cockney and that he finally died of anthrax which could have been caught from an animal skin or from a toothbrush. His wife had been too ill to go to the funeral but she watched the coffin being carried out.

' " Thank God for a bit of peace," she said,' Rhoda told her family. ' He never left her alone,' she added, obscurely; obscurely to Horace who was still a virgin.

Rhoda and her children, being fatherless through the war, talked a lot together and were like cronies. In later life Horace didn't accept that Monty Morden was a complete villain or that the scar on his top lip was pox and not a bayonet wound. Rhoda was a very strong and imaginative woman who suspected the worst about everybody except God. She never fell for that evolution nonsense and was certain that Darwin apologised on his deathbed. She was big-built, big-bosomed, strongly sexed and with a number of chronic ailments.

She was a servant in Finchley when that was a posh area; she attracted the sort of boy friends who got her into bothers by ringing at the front door for her instead of the back. Once she accidentally pulled the tail out of the family parrot, packed her bag and ran away in fear.

This image brought her close to Horace and did away with some of the Forsyte Saga stuff that makes everybody's family the same. Horace was not very good at imagining clip clop; he took *Modern Boy* and was aeroplane-mad like his father.

' If there was an air raid on while Jim was home on leave he would drag us all round the town. " Look, mate, that's a Gotha ! " he used to say,' Rhoda used to say.

James Fenton, Horace's father, had been on the baker's round in Finchley.

' He was half my size. They called him Tich Fenton. He couldn't grow a moustache all the time he was alive.'

Horace's very first memory was learning to walk holding onto chairs and the man in soldier's uniform watching him. Horace would have been fifteen months old. It was his only memory of his father.

' You can't remember being fifteen months old,' people told him.

You can. You'd remember the womb if anything had happened there. There were two last little visuals Rhoda gave the children of their father. One when he came out of hospital in 1918 to go back to France. He had a hole in his arm and was shell-shocked. They walked along by the River Lea at Hartham and he tried to persuade Rhoda to jump in with him but she wouldn't.

' Dad'll look after the kids,' he said.

His father owned a building business in Highgate. That was Rhoda's last memory of Jim. A soldier who came to the Disabled Club she'd started after the war gave her the last memory of all. Bodies that had been the Essex Regiment being carried past on stretchers, all covered in mud.

' That's little Tich! ' he had shouted to his mate.

That was their last visual and not the one they dwelt on. They dwelt on an earlier one. Tich and a pal painting up Florrie Forde's house and her singing them a song, just the two of them. For Horace the picture moved from Forsyte Saga country to The Ragged Trousered Philanthropists. Horace thought in these terms because he spent his Saturday sixpence on little red volumes of the classics with gold print on them in Woolworths. He read himself out of the poverty of their life together, the footed socks, bed bugs, kettle broth and the two-mile walk for a pint of skimmed milk, but kept coming back for the funny bits.

' Do you know what's in this jam? ' Rhoda asked once. She couldn't stop laughing. She was working at a jam factory at that time and had brought a jar home with her; it was the second-grade stuff that went out under a different label. She had seen railway trucks full of mangel-wurzels coming into the factory siding and didn't know why. Then she'd talked to another cleaner who knew about the pips made of tiny chips of wood. ' They call it raspberry jam! ' she said.

They used to roll about at things like that. Just the same she wrote to *John Bull* about it; she used to write to *John Bull* about everything. Like Horace, she loved to see her name in print. And she loved writing letters.

' Now, boys,' Mr Polling said one morning. ' I want you to forget your own problems for a moment and concentrate on a little sympathy for friend Fenton. Stand up, Fenton. I'm going to read the letter I just received from your mother. You feel well enough to stand up, do you? '

' Yes, sir.'

' Yes, Mr Polling.'

15

'Yes, Mr Polling,' said Horace, filled with forebodings.

This was a two-page letter, beautifully slopingly written with all the leisure of a Sunday afternoon, about Horace's tuberculosis, about sending him away to stay on his Uncle Charlie's farm to breathe his own native air.

'You can look at Fenton, boys, but try not to cry,' he said after he'd read the letter. Then to Horace he said: 'How far away is your native air, Fenton?'

Horace didn't know; he had once cycled it and lost his dog which had followed him halfway. It turned out to be forty miles away, which had the whole class laughing. Mr Polling then went into the tuberculosis; did Horace cough, did he spit blood, had he been X-rayed, was he losing weight?

Horace said: 'It's because I look white, sir. Mr Polling.'

'I see.' Mr Polling looked round the class and couldn't say what was in his mind but the thought collected a few sniggers. 'Well, you tell your mother that if she sends you away in the middle of term I shall send her to prison. Is that understood?'

Yes, Mr. Polling, no, Mr Polling.

He was a lunatic. Horace never knew how many boys Mr Polling stamped out in his own mould before this was discovered and he was sent to Fulbourn asylum. One day in the spring of 1930 he called a general assembly; this was done simply by sliding a few partition walls back and discovering other classes suffering different teachers and subjects. Mr Polling brought a wooden chair, put it on top of the grand piano, then climbed it like a mountain, the chords crashing under his shoes and the music teacher tightly shutting his eyes.

'Two of our senior boys,' Mr Polling cried in his pinched voice, 'were walking along Mill Road yesterday with their hands hanging open at their sides. This has got to stop. It shows a loose, uncontrolled mentality. The hands must be closed, firmly but not tightly, like this.'

Mr Polling started walking on the spot on the chair on top of the piano, his closed hands swinging at his sides. You could see that he had had a terrible night, tossing and turning over what he had seen.

About the same time, in Germany, boys were getting similar instruction but which also included how to kick their legs out

16

in front.

Horace didn't know about that.

Arnold Bennett and Frank Harris were in the last year of their lives. Horace had never heard of them. F. Scott Fitzgerald's wife had had her first nervous breakdown. Horace didn't know her. George Orwell was trying to sell stories about his life with the down-and-outs in Paris. Horace was unaware of such a person. Eddie Lang and Bix Beiderbecke were now hack-playing in the Paul Whiteman orchestra. Who were they?

The Prince of Wales continued to break his collar-bone at polo.

This Horace knew.

Chapter Three

On the Saturday afternoon following Horace cutting his hand on the drilling machine an airship called the R101 flew down Mill Road and hovered over Parker's Piece.

Horace was trying to get a model aeroplane to take to the air and failing. It was made of wire and Japanese silk with an elastic motor and was supposed to fly fifty yards or loop the loop twice, but instead just kept crashing straight into the grass and losing its wing.

The appearance of the airship hanging effortlessly in the sky like a big grey cloud made him feel childish and as people gathered, staring upwards, he put his own craft back into its box.

' Hello, Horace,' somebody said.

A pretty girl in a spotted pink frock and with spotted pink ribbon tying her hair in bunches stood there smiling at him.

' Hazel,' she said. ' You know — at work.'

Horace blushed crimson. Of course it was Hazel. The girl he was in love with and couldn't stop dreaming about nearly kissing.

Now he knew who it was he became speechless and clumsy and when she asked him how his hand was and he tried to show her it was better he dropped the box and the aeroplane fell out. He explained that it was a present for his little brother Leslie (already on probation and finished with toys for life) and somehow gave her the impression that he was in a hurry.

' Cheero, then,' she said.

Horace didn't reply because he couldn't think of a word beautiful enough.

Horace Spurgeon Fenton now entrusted his model aeroplane to Alfred, a hare-lipped thin man who looked like Slim Summerville and ran the tea pavilion.

' Wah yah wah ah bah? ' he asked Horace.

Horace told him he wasn't sure. What he planned to do was follow Hazel and perhaps contrive to bump into her accidentally again and make a better job of it. He would say this time, ' Oh,

18

hello, fancy seeing you again. Would you care for a cup of tea somewhere?' No, that would cost money. The four and sixpence he had spent on aeronautics had left him two and ninepence to get through the week. Horace earned sixpence an hour which came out at about a pound a week less stoppages, of which he gave ten shillings to his mother for board and lodging. Just before Radiolympia there would be overtime but that wasn't yet. Therefore he would have to say something like: 'You again! Must be my lucky day. You look very beautiful. Shall we go for a walk over Coe Fen?' Or would that make her think he was trying to get her somewhere lonely?

Then following her down Bateman Street he remembered that you could get into the Botanical Gardens for twopence. Even while he was thinking about it Hazel gave a cry of joy and ran to meet a young man who took her into the Botanical Gardens. Horace was heartbroken. It had never occurred to him that she would go out with other boys.

Whenever he dreamt about her or thought about her she was alone somewhere waiting for him to make up his mind what he was going to do. Under the shock of seeing the pink spotted dress and the purple-striped Perse School blazer walking into the Botanical Gardens, Horace got back to the Catholic Church near the corner of Parker's Piece without knowing how he got there.

'Hello, Horace,' somebody said as he went back into the tea pavilion. The pretty girl, the pink spots, the bunches of lady-hair, pencilled eyebrows, parted red lips, little white teeth.

'Hazel!' she said, exasperated. 'You are funny!'

It couldn't be Hazel. Or else the girl he had just followed for three miles and seen enter the gardens with another chap couldn't be Hazel.

'I saw your little aeroplane on the counter,' she said. 'I thought you'd come back. Would you like a Snowfrute?'

Snowfrutes were water ices made in the shape of long triangular-section prisms wrapped in checker cardboard and costing a penny. You could never get the cardboard off until it was melted and then you had nothing to hold them with (they hadn't thought of sticks, yet, though they had the wheel).

19

' Hazel? ' Horace said. He sat down and looked at her with love and immense relief, forgetting to be speechless. ' I love you,' he said.

Hazel laughed happily. ' I know you do. Harry Webb told me.'

Horace could have wished her to have discovered his love in some more spiritual way.

' He isn't half dirty-minded,' Hazel added.

The thought of Harry Webb saying something nasty to Hazel made Horace boil up inside. ' What did he say? '

' It doesn't matter.'

' Was it about me? '

' No, it was about me. It was that hot day. I had my low-necked blouse on.'

Horace didn't want to hear any more. The dirty swine. He planned to soften all Harry Webb's tools with the blow-lamp while Harry was having his dinner in the canteen.

' Would you like to go out with me? ' Horace asked her.

' Where? ' she said.

That was a funny answer. Going out with someone was an accepted expression, or so he understood. He didn't *know* where.

' Just a tick,' she said.

Alfred was trying to manipulate a tray of teas through the gap in the counter and Hazel went to help, took them from him, carried them with her special flair balanced on the palm of one hand at ear height over towards a table full of cricketers.

' Tea up! ' she cried.

Thank you, Hazel, they said, in different ways. Horace began to realise that she was well known here; that this was one of her regular places. When she came back she confirmed this rather by explaining to him that Alfred's blazer with its gold cricket club badge on the pocket had once belonged to W. G. Grace, the famous old cricketer. From the shabbiness and the size of it it seemed possible.

' Wah yah lah sah tah? ' Alfred asked her.

' No, thanks, Alfred,' she said. ' We're going now.' And she explained to Horace : ' I've got GFS.'

That was nice. That was really nice. His sister Christine used to go to Girls Friendly Society before she met those stable lads from Newmarket.

'Perhaps I may walk home with you?' Horace asked her.

He collected his aeroplane and knocked over several chairs trying to get to the door to open it for her. It made Hazel laugh.

'You are funny. Mr Trigg says you'll finish up cutting your hands off in the guillotine.'

It was a horrifying thought (practically everything he wanted to be in life would require two hands) and yet also intriguing; Hazel had been talking about him with the foreman.

'Do you go to church?' she asked him as they crossed Donkey's Common.

They were walking finger-tip to finger-tip and he wanted to summon the courage to hold her hand.

'No,' he said. 'Do you?'

She said: 'Not since I was confirmed.'

The sheer glory of her having been confirmed (whatever that meant) made him feel dizzy. Horace really hated himself for thinking that Hazel was the kind of girl who would walk round the Botanical Gardens with a chap from Perse School. As they walked, almost touching, through the friendly, smelly slums of East Road, across Maids Causeway and down to Riverside by the gas works (where they took children with whooping-cough), Horace planned that he would confess what he had thought about her after they were married. She would cry and he would stroke her hair. In the dream they had a motor car and plenty of money (though not too much) and were always on the point of kissing. There were fruit trees in the garden and a little ivy-covered house that had everything except a bedroom.

'Cheero, then,' Hazel said.

They stood by the wooden gate set in the brick wall beside her house. Where Horace had stood that late night after night-school, savouring the unattainable. Now here she was a part of his life. After how long? Three days? A week? Was he going to be a fast worker?

'Come for a walk with me tomorrow night. Tomorrow, I mean.' And while she hesitated he got the route in since it seemed to matter to her. 'Down Coldham's Lane, through the tin walk to Cherryhinton and back through the spinney to Teversham Road.'

This seven-mile route march brought a shade of fatigue into her expression, so he suggested they could go and listen to the band on Christ's Piece.

' I've got a date with Charles tomorrow,' she said.

It was like a slap in the face. A chap called Charles had to be at Perse School.

' He's got an eight-cylinder Lagonda with a dicky-seat,' she said.

That was Perse.

Somewhere behind the brick wall a door opened and Horace could hear the sound of washing-up crockery.

' Hazel — is that you? '

' Shan't be a minute, Mum.'

She pushed the gate open with her bottom and Horace could see a face and hair-curlers through the crook in the girl's arm; a smaller and older face than Hazel's.

' See you Monday, then? ' Hazel said.

' All right, then,' Horace said, his heart leaping up again. ' Where shall we go? '

Hazel gave a little shriek of laughter. ' At work, I mean! '

' Oh, yes, of course. Cheero, then.'

' Cheero, then.'

As Horace moved away and before the gate had closed he heard her mother ask : ' Who was that little boy? '

' He's over sixteen! ' Hazel said. ' Isn't he funny? '

Mercifully, Horace did not hear this. His mind was filled with enough confusions without having his morale crushed. And without having the dream polluted by old Charles.

Crossing the river bridge he heard steam-organ music from a fair on Stourbridge Common. The same tunes as ever jerked and piped in the same merry automated way. *Valencia, On The Shores Of Minnetonka, Jericho, Baby Face*; maybe this little boy would go to a Saturday-night hop at the Labour Hall. Or maybe he would put on his brown suit from the Fifty-shilling Tailors, his Petty Cury suit with its double-breasted waistcoat and twenty-two-inch turnups, get a bit tipsy on half a pint of sixpenny beer at the Yorkshire Grey, pick up Jammy Rolls and Neville Hampstead, go to the fair and find himself a bit of hot stuff. Tinnie Lizzie or Ivy Pruer or one of the other machine-

22

shop tarts.

' Who was that little boy? '

Horace Spurgeon Fenton strode through the Willow Walk in his long policeman's stride that had got him through the Scout test at first go. Little boy? He felt like going in the bathroom and giving himself the horn. It didn't pay to be a gentleman. Not if you weren't a grad. Better to run with the wild ones again; spit and swear and pull girls' hair. There were always some good ones at the fair, walking round, chatting and laughing and pretending they didn't know you were following them; then chasing you in between the Wall of Death and the Cakewalk, out of the gas flares and into the grassy darkness.

> *Oh Valencia,*
> *Wave your 'nana to your father bash your*
> *balls against the wall . . .*

Chapter Four

The roundabout man stood by an outer cockerel taking money and giving change without holding on, leaning inwards, beautifully balanced against the centrifugal force. Rhoda watched him with a relic of the same admiration she had felt for Monty. It could have been the same man : a stocky ex-Serviceman in a striped collarless shirt with sleeves rolled up to show his tattoos, braces tied round the waist to keep his army trousers up and yet rebel with the white canvas slippers against the Service life.

' Two for fourpence! Rightcheware! Hold tight! Ta, guvnor! Tuppence for one! Hold tight! '

She couldn't hear him but she knew what he was saying. Knew that when he'd completed the takings on the spinning platform he would swing himself round a twisted steel pillar and drop lightly to the ground without a precipitate step or stumble as though roundabout and world were stationary wherever he touched them. It was with that same careless grace that Monty Morden had sent Rhoda's war-widow world spinning.

' Hold tight! ' he'd shouted on that first rocking night in the brass-balled bed — the one that she and Jim had chosen so carefully at the second-hand shop in Finchley High Road. The spring had jumped off the bedstead and he'd let it stay, rocking and romping and laughing and eating apples till the children came calling at the door, she clinging to the railing above her head for dear life.

She had lost her war pension, her business and livelihood and self-respect with one mad folly. Besides this he had frightened them all to death.

' Come here, Pissie-Lizzie,' he would say, for this was his name for Christine, a gentle girl; ' let's scrape the cinders out of them lug-'oles! '

He insisted on scraping their ears out with the handle of a teaspoon, one tattooed arm holding them helpless, his putteed and booted legs and feet trapped around theirs.

And one dark night on a fairground in Wales he and a crony

24

had killed a black man; tied him in a sack and thrown him in a river. And as though this wasn't enough he had a sister, Sybil, who had suffocated five babies by lying on top of them in the night. Rhoda, coming from a Baptist family, was used to mild anecdotes and she was in a state of shock from the moment of her second husband's first violent revelation.

'What have I done!' she kept crying to herself and the children, whenever Monty was out of the way. 'Thank God little Tich doesn't know!'

Nobody wanted to know. Rhoda's brother Oliver was a Metropolitan Police inspector but he wouldn't come near after what her family considered the disgrace of a marriage outside the Baptist circle.

'You've made your bed, my girl,' Sam Dayball wrote, 'now you must lie on it.' He wrote this on the back of a frantic letter which Rhoda had got Ken, the eldest boy, to deliver one late night after Monty had tried to persuade Rhoda to form a knife-throwing act and then pinned her to the door when she refused.

Soon after this Ken had run away to live with his grandparents and they saw him only once more. This was while they were on the run and hiding out at Burwell in the fens. Ken and his Aunty Pearl turned up on bicycles one Sunday morning; he had come to say goodbye, for he was off to Australia under the auspices of Toc H and the Big Brother movement and they never saw him again.

'That's one thing I'll never forgive Monty for,' Rhoda used to say.

There were plenty of other things she could never forgive him for. He had ruined the Disabled Soldiers' Club long before he ran off with the money and the waitress. Any customers he thought she might like especially, he put chewed tobacco under their mashed potatoes; they seldom came again. He broke into a shop one night and hid the stolen goods in her attic. After that whenever murder, rape or robbery took place she was certain it was Monty. There were nights when she got the children to follow him.

'I want you to fox your stepfather,' she used to say. 'He's just gone down Maidenhead Street wearing his brown suit.'

Horace, four years old, once saw him take his trousers off on

25

the towpath.

' Did anybody see him? ' Rhoda asked, taking their reports. It was her home town; the Dayballs were religious mainstays. She was terrified of further disgrace.

' Oh, yes,' Horace told her. ' There was a woman right next to him! '

For a short while after she came out of hospital with Leslie, Rhoda tried to get the business started again. She took a stall on the market and sold sausage-and-mashed, kept the children busy making ice-cream in the cellar and taking it round on a trolley, changing to fresh fish in the colder weather which she got for seven-and-sixpence a barrel straight from Grimsby, brought by the lorry man who brought the ice.

It was a short, hard-up but happy period. Rhoda took the kids on little outings on the red buses with their heady smells of petrol and dust and bright-coloured tickets. They visited the maze at Rye House, the Great Bed of Ware and Bill Waites Theatre at Hoddesdon where, to the children's astonishment, at the end of the show all the beautiful dancing girls came to the front of the stage and took off their wigs and bosoms — they were all, apparently, Bill Waites's sons.

One sunny afternoon in the unending summer of childhood Horace, Christine and Ronald went for a ride in Mrs Murphy's pony-trap out to Hertingfordbury. Mrs Murphy was an old lady in a black bonnet who lived across the street and had been Rhoda's only friend during her short second marriage. When the children had colds Mrs Murphy brought oranges with a hole cut through the core and sugar lumps inserted. What you did was squeeze the orange and get your mouth underneath the hole.

' She's not married at all,' the children heard Mrs Murphy saying to her Hertingfordbury friends. ' She should go to the police. She could get her pension back.'

What had happened was that Rhoda had had a letter from a girl claiming to have married Monty some time ago and enclosing a picture of herself and the child. Rhoda did nothing about it at that time because if there was one thing more disgraceful than being married to a man like Monty Morden it was not being married to him.

' You must forget that,' Rhoda told Christine when she

26

reported this conversation. ' I've got little Leslie to think about now.'

Horace had already forgotten it. Two things had come out of that afternoon to last him his lifetime. One was that if you bent a piece of grass into a triangle and spit on it the saliva remained clear and shining in the triangle; two, that the girl who had told him this, one of Mrs Murphy's nieces called Nina Vaughn, had given him his first female kiss on the mouth. For some enormously secret and strange inner reason this had excited him like sliding down the stench pole in the Castle grounds. When he said he wanted to do it again she mistook his meaning and licked another piece of grass and held it up to shine in the sun.

' It's a mirror,' she said.

One morning Rhoda came down to the yard to chop the ice and found a dead mongrel dog on the doorstep. To put it there somebody had had to throw it over the back-yard wall and then climb over himself.

' It was Monty! ' Rhoda told the children.

There didn't seem any reason to them why it should be Monty, but they didn't know that Rhoda had started sending them out with Mrs Murphy while she entertained the ice man, a chap called Jack Carter, on his afternoon off. When he buried the dog for her Jack told Rhoda that it must have been strangled with the killer's bare hands.

' I'll have to move,' Rhoda said.

It was the beginning of their moving times.

After watching the roundabout man and seeing that it wasn't Monty, Rhoda walked her brisk walk along the river and across the town to the police station to tell them about this latest visitation, the man with the brushes.

' Who do you usually see, madam? ' the constable asked her.

Rhoda usually saw a Detective-Sergeant Polsworth, but he was not then on duty. He would probably call and see her later that evening.

' I think he's got some news for you at last,' the constable said.

He could not tell her what it might be and Rhoda walked home in a state of excitement, conjecturing. If they found Monty and proved that he was already married when he married her, then she would be due twelve years' back pension and she would be a widow again. Also he would go to prison, which would stop him throwing bricks through their window, setting fire to their curtains, whitewashing obscene messages on their windows and pretending to be a brush salesman — all the things that had kept them on the run all these years through villages and towns and fens.

Also — and this was the biggest also of all — she would be free to marry Captain Cook; if he still wanted her, which he did last week. Captain Cook was the local NSPCC officer who brought parcels of second-hand clothes for the children; and occasionally dresses and underclothes and floppy hats which were scarcely second-hand at all. Last Armistice Day when they were dressed for the War Memorial service, Captain Cook had turned up on his bicycle with his Hawkeye camera and taken photographs of them, one of which he still kept in his purse.

Det.-Sergeant Polsworth came at noon on Sunday when Horace was boning the breast of mutton with his little shoe-mender's knife, ready for stuffing. The detective was stepping over him as Rhoda came to the front door.

'Go straight through,' she told the policeman, remaining to tell Horace: 'You shouldn't do that on the front doorstep.'

Horace said: 'Leslie's just pomped in the kitchen.'

'Oh, my God,' Rhoda said. 'That's his father over again. My Tich used to go to the very end of the back garden to do that.'

Horace knew he did; Rhoda was repetitious about saintly things.

There was one of Christine's cultural set-pieces going on in the front room of the council house when Rhoda, having opened all the windows and sent Leslie outside, finally went in to talk to the detective. Christine knelt yoga-fashion on the rag-piece rug listening to Dame Clara Butt singing 'I know that my Redeemer liveth' and watching Ronald sculpting the King's head in blue gault with his fingers, sometimes dipping them in a pudding basin of water. Detective-Sergeant Polsworth stood in the little bay window as though afraid to breathe and with a very off-duty look in his eye for Christine. Christine was wearing a little Grecian-cut nightie and was holding both her breasts with cupped hands

28

as the music came and the head grew and seemed to be possessed with some kind of religious fervour.

'Chris! Get yourself properly dressed!' Rhoda told her.

Rhoda was ignored until the song had ended and then Christine said: 'Mother —' when she said 'Mother' like that Rhoda knew she was out to impress somebody — 'Mother, this is Stan. Stan — my mother.'

Rhoda said: 'But this is my detective-sergeant. He's come about Leslie's father.'

Chris said: 'Yes, I know that. But we're old friends. We met at Sid's. You know, who runs the hairdresser's up East Road. It was Stan who overturned the car at Six Mile Bottom.'

'I had no idea she was your daughter, Mrs Morden,' the young policeman said, 'her name being Fenton — oh, and by the way, I've got some bad news for you —'

'You've brought me home often enough,' Christine said.

'Ah, but never sober!' laughed the young policeman.

Rhoda, unnoticed, had sat down to wait for the bad news. Ronald, who had wanted to be a jockey but was a call-boy at the Pitt Club, seventeen years old and already partly bald, was putting the finishing touches to the clay head which was destined to be a Royal doorstopper in the family for the next ten years.

In searching for Monty and for documentary proof of his bigamy the police had discovered that he was a deserter on the run from the authorities and had changed his name several times, often using the last geographical location of whichever fair he happened to be with.

'Morden is a place in Surrey,' Det.-Sergeant Polsworth told Rhoda when she had dragged him away from her daughter. 'Your real name is Whateley.'

Rhoda sat stricken; Horace and Leslie came in to listen, sensing drama.

'Legally,' the detective said, 'you are Mrs Bernard Whateley.'

'Bernard?' Rhoda cried. 'His name is Monty —'

She was interrupted by a crash and a scream as Leslie threw Ronald's sculpture of the King's head across the room for the first time. The scream was Ronald's rage as he hurled the basin of water at Leslie. They grappled and Horace tried to drag them apart.

'What's the trouble?' Sergeant Polsworth asked Rhoda.

'You should have waited until I was alone,' Rhoda told him. 'That poor little wretch keeps getting his name changed. First it was Morden, then I changed it to Fenton when I thought the marriage illegal, then back to Morden when you couldn't prove anything — now he's Leslie — what is it?'

'Whateley,' Polsworth told her.

The fight suddenly subsided. Horace was lying on his back on the floor clutching his throat and dragging his breath in and out as though through one hole of a mouth-organ. His voice box, as it was later discovered, had been crushed back into his windpipe.

Rhoda had the fatalistic conviction that Horace would die within the hour; she had killed her first child, Oliver, by feeding him green apples while he was on the pottie; she had pulled the tail out of that parrot in Finchley; and now a third disaster was overdue. She stood in the bay window watching the road, rocking Horace in her arms, all sixteen years of him, shaking her head hopelessly at the other children (Polsworth had gone for the doctor) and unaware that Horace was watching her, fighting for his breath and unable to talk.

'If anything happens,' she told Ronald, 'you'd better say that you did it. Leslie's already on probation.'

The boy died, but the man was born complete with lifelong asthma, an Adam's apple which clicked out of joint if he yawned or sneezed carelessly and had to be pushed back with his fingers, and a voice an octave below the lowest norm.

Chapter Five

Hazel Springer was dead.

In her place, when Horace got back to work in the model shop on a Monday morning five weeks after his accident, was a woman called Mrs Jenkins from the canteen. She didn't even shout 'Tea up!'

'What happened?' Horace asked Harry Webb.

Harry had been marking out a chassis on a piece of sheet steel but now he turned right round from his bench and looked at Horace.

'What?' he said.

'What happened to Hazel?'

'What happened to Hazel? What happened to you!' Harry shouted to everybody no matter what they were doing: 'Come and listen to this!' And to Horace he said: 'Say something.' And when he couldn't think of anything: 'Go on, *say* something! Horace has got balls at last!'

It was very embarrassing for Horace. Mr Tischler was there; Driscoll and Jones from the drawing office setting up a new radio-frequency attenuator project. And besides all these and besides the instrument-makers Harry had shouted so loud that even the research engineers through the glass-windowed wall had turned from their whistling beat-frequency oscillators and flashing oscilloscopes to stare through the glass at Horace.

And worse still, Mrs Jenkins on the trolley, who was a woman, was staring at Horace and smiling at Harry's rude remark.

Horace until now had a high voice and had sung boy-soprano in Trinity Church choir. He had been mistaken for a girl when carol-singing at doors, and had sung solo at the musical festival for the county, representing his school, St Mary's in the Fen:

> *My father died and I do not know how,*
> *He left me six horses to follow the plough,*
> *With a wim wam waddle-O,*
> *Jack's lost his saddle-O,*

31

Jackie boy, bubble-O,
Under the broom!

This same Horace Spurgeon Fenton now said in a deep basso-profundo :

' My brother punched me in the throat and knocked my voice box back. What happened to Hazel? '

Everybody laughed or was amazed and Harry Webb, who was proud at having discovered the new Horace, said :

' You're going to have to grow a moustache and beard with a voice like that! '

Other people started chiming in with witty suggestions about what he could now do, naming such things as drink, tobacco and girls; but Horace was shocked that they could be making jokes when he had asked how Hazel Springer had died. Ernie Trigg, who was really a comedian and whom Horace could have forgiven as one would a professional for plying his trade, was the only one sensitive to Horace's feelings about the girl and as soon as he could he took Horace aside and explained the tragedy.

Hazel had been found dead in her cold bathwater, killed by a faulty gas geyser.

' It was in the *Daily News*,' Ernie Trigg said. ' There was an inquest two weeks later.'

There had been a collection and a beautiful wreath from the firm and she had been laid to rest in Newmarket Road cemetery. Hazel was all over. The shock to Horace was not because he had been in love with her, or thought he had, or had experienced the excitements of love because of her, but because she was a person who had been evidently alive like himself and was now evidently dead.

Hazel was Horace's first death. His first intimation of mortality. He had not been aware of his father getting killed and the baby Oliver had died before Horace was born. The closest he had come to death until now was the pilot of a Blackburn Blue-bird who had plunged into the ground at two hundred miles an hour during Sir Alan Cobham's Air Circus on Coldham Common. Horace had been sitting near when it happened and had got to the wreckage as quickly as anybody, but then had hung back when he saw that the pilot's head did not move; he believed he had seen a dead body.

' The joystick's through his stomach,' somebody had said.

Horace had stopped trying to get into the Royal Air Force. Because of this, that unknown dead pilot almost certainly saved Horace's life during the war to come.

Horace at this time was not aware that there was a war to come. He was not interested in war. Wars were mainly in *Triumph* and *Champion*, whereas Horace preferred *The Magnet*, *The Gem*, *Modern Boy*, *Boys' Magazine* and *Funny Wonder*.

' Stan wants to see you,' Christine told Horace.

' Just a minute,' Horace said.

He didn't hear what she said, for he was straining his ear against an almost new beautiful Blue-Spot moving-coil loudspeaker lying on its back amid a tangle of wires on a TRF four-valve breadboard radio hook-up which was all lying there as dead as a doornail. Not even humming. Ah, something wrong with the power pack.

Horace Spurgeon Fenton checked the connections on the mains transformer primary winding, wiggled the mains adjustment tappings; checked the connections on the 350—0—350 secondary HT winding with its centre-tap to — yes, nicely earthed to the frame and chassis-wire; checked the 4v rectifier LT and the 4v main valve-heater circuit; checked the full-wave rectifier valve connections, shook the valve, held it up to his bedroom window to inspect the innards; checked the smoothing circuit — one 20-henry choke, one $8 + 16$ microfarad electrolytic condenser with no hot wax bubbling out of it; checked all connections on dropping resistors and de-coupling condensers to each valve anode; checked all valve grid couplings; checked all cathode automatic bias circuits; checked right back stage by stage from loudspeaker to output pentode through two audio amplifier triodes to the tuned-radio-frequency pentode input with its regenerative circuit and its band-pass aerial coupling.

Everything was perfect and it was as dead as a doornail. Last night, Roy Fox crisply playing *The Girl In The Little Green Hat*; tonight, nothing. Typical. Horace lay on his back on his shaky little iron frame bed and got back to Harry Wharton and the Famous Five in *The Magnet*.

Billy Bunter dodged round the table. Across that article of furniture he eyed Wharton warily through his big spectacles.

' I say, old chap, don't be stuffy!' he gasped. ' What's the good of getting shirty, old fellow? Have a smoke!'

' You fat, frabjous, fat-headed frump, I'll be —'

' Be a man, you know,' said Bunter, encouragingly. ' Like me! Look here, I've got lots of fags — that's a box of twenty-five. They're good, you know — Smithy always has expensive smokes — I mean, I got those smokes in Court-field this afternoon. I never found them in Vernon-Smith's study, you know —'

Horace stopped reading because quite suddenly it seemed silly. Horace became thoughtful; how strange. The Famous Five had never seemed silly before.

Footsteps on the stairs, a ' Bother!' as Rhoda pulled out the banister from the wall and then came in.

' You shouldn't try to read in this light,' she told Horace, and then, worried : ' Why do the police want to see you?'

' Who?'

' Christine said Stan wants to see you. It's about the factory. Have you been doing anything?'

Of course Horace hadn't been doing anything. Leslie did things, Horace didn't do things.

' They've gone to the Festival,' she said. ' You'd better see him when he comes back. He keeps calling me Mrs Whateley. I don't feel like Mrs Whateley.' She switched on his light and nothing happened. ' I'll put a sixpence in.'

When she'd gone downstairs and put a sixpence in the electric meter the valves on the breadboard started to glow and soon London 5XX came belting through the Blue-Spot loudspeaker at more than two watts undistorted.

' Turn that down!' Rhoda screamed up the stairs.

Herr Hitler, the German Führer, screamed back. Hitler, Horace Kenny, Kenway and Young, Nat Mills and Bobby, Henry Hall, Nosmo King, Hutch, Doris and Elsie Waters, Mussolini, Horace thought, twiddling the spindle of the two-gang tuning condenser to find something more entertaining. Daventry 5GB on long wave

34

with Radio Paris — they were certs. Luxembourg, Fécamp and Normandy could be relied on after dark —

Horace suddenly realised why he was wanted by the police. The almost new Blue-Spot moving-coil loudspeaker belonged to the firm and he had been caught by the gatekeeper bringing it out. He had made the usual excuse that it was wanted for experiments at home — which research people were allowed to do — and gave Mr Tischler's name as guarantor. What you were supposed to do was get a chit signed by a senior engineer. Anyway, he thought it had been accepted but now it looked as if it had been reported.

Now he would have to avoid the police until he had seen Tischler and explained and got a pre-dated apparatus chit.

Horace did not want a conviction, even though the probation officer's club in King Street was the best one in town. Leslie had got himself elected by throwing bricks through the port-holes of cabin-cruisers on the river.

When Detective-Sergeant Stanley Polsworth brought Christine home from the theatre, Horace was out.

' Where would he go at eleven o'clock at night? ' the young policeman asked.

Rhoda said : ' He's behaving very strangely since his voice changed.' She thought it best to get it in early in case it had to be explained to a magistrate later.

' Oh? ' Stan was investigating the last hours of Hazel Springer, and this was just the sort of thing he was after. ' What sort of things does he do? '

Before Rhoda could get properly launched into a recital of Horace's eccentricities, Christine came in with the coffee and began talking about the play they had seen at the Festival Theatre. Although stuck in the same jam factory where Rhoda had once worked, Christine was intent on bettering herself in her spare time. Cambridge was a town where the highest culture was available to the slum-dwellers once they had mastered the art of making a living.

' Sarah Churchman was marvellous,' Christine said.

' Not Churchman,' Rhoda said. ' Churchill. Her father was an admiral in the war.'

' Horatio, isn't it? ' said the young detective.

35

' No, that's Bottomley,' Rhoda told him. ' He runs *John Bull*.'
' And Flora Robson,' said Christine.
' She must be his secretary, then,' Rhoda said.

But Christine was still talking about the play. She was glad that Stanley had worn his new plus-fours.

Chapter Six

Twenty-four hours after Chancellor Adolph Hitler, unarmed, had had Roehm, chief of the Brown Shirts, riddled with bullets by the Black Shirts, Horace Spurgeon Fenton smuggled the Blue-Spot moving-coil loudspeaker back into the model shop and replaced it in the accessories box.

'Horace.' Ernie Trigg came up while he was doing this with something important to say which, however, was suddenly replaced by a song which had just occurred to him. 'Listen,' he therefore said. He sang, doing a little tap-dance in the meantime and pretending to play a ukelele :

> *' Met a girl name Sadie Green,*
> *Sweetest gal in New Orleans,*
> *She could dance, she could sing,*
> *She could do 'most anything! '*

He now started playing the 'spoons' on his knee with two matching aluminium sides of a multi-vibrator chassis; his men, not yet settled to the hard facts of the day, paid him attention. Astonishingly, Mr Roper the instrument maker who never joined in, began to make a rhythmic 'boom boom boom' sound like the bass man in the Mills Brothers.

> *' Now de other night down at de hall,*
> *When de band did play,*
> *She got on dat dancing floor and dis is what*
> *   she say: — '*

'Trigg ! '
The shout, loud but distant, muffled by several rooms and doors and corridors and a flight of stairs yet still recognisably the chief engineer, W. B. Barclay, BA, was repeated several times by intermediaries : 'Trigg ! ' 'Ernie ! ' 'Trigg ! ' And finally by the chief draughtsman Mr Green putting his head in the door :

37

' Mr Trigg — Barclay! '

Ernie Trigg put his hands above his head and wiggled the palms like Al Jolson: '*How'm I doing, Hey Hey!*' And to Horace he said: ' He doesn't want me, he wants you.'

This startling information did not at first register with Horace, who was feeling thankful that Ernie's singing had covered the quiet replacing of the stolen speaker in the accessories box.

' I've got to talk to Mr Tischler,' Horace replied, rather surprisingly. Everybody looked at him, for he had gone deathly pale. He had a pleasant, good-humoured, nothing kind of face, the best feature being girl's cupid lips which now went oddly with his deep gravel voice. The point was it was a cultured, modulated and almost academically distinguished voice now and irritated people with better jobs who hadn't got one like it. It was to be a boon and a bane to Horace for the rest of his life. Whoever had accidentally punched him in the throat had done him a lifelong favour. Rhoda blamed Monty.

When Horace had gone scuttling off to find Tischler, Ernie Trigg said to himself, deeply: ' I've got to talk to Mr Tischler.' It pleased him and he tried it several more times.

' Mr Tischler? ' Horace said in the electronics research laboratory. Mr Tischler was not there. He was also not in the glass-blowing department, the drawing office or the stores.

' I think I saw him go into Barclay's office,' the storekeeper said. This was a stoop-shouldered, sunken-chested man with bad asthma called Charlie. ' By the way, Fenton,' he said, as Horace was rushing out, ' it's not *Mister* Tischler, it's *Doctor* Tischler.'

Horace looked back at Charlie through the steel-mesh cage in which Charlie seemed to live.

' I know that,' Horace said.

' How do you know? ' Charlie said. Horace was already off and he had to call again: ' Here. Fenton. How do you know? '

But Horace didn't hear him and Charlie had to go on puzzling. He had just been called into the chief engineer's office and asked how he knew that the old Austrian or German Jew was a Doctor of Science; and several other very obscure things. Charlie had been asked to say nothing of this questioning to anybody, but he was in the unique position of meeting everybody who came with their requisitions to the store. And they had to stay on good terms with him or he would say he was out of stock.

So far that morning W. B. Barclay and Tischler and little brilliant Carl Brockelberg the chief physicist had had Mr Green in for questioning and Passion Flower Driscoll, Jones and everybody from the labs, and now they were working their way through the model shop.

' Doctor Tischler? ' Horace had popped his head in the chief engineer's door; it was a big office and also the company boardroom and it seemed to be full of people, though at first, because Horace was so intent on wanting Tischler to back up his larceny of the Blue-Spot speaker, he did not notice them. ' Could I talk to you? '

' That is what you are here for, Mr Fenton,' Doctor Tischler said.

It was the first time anybody had ever called Horace ' Mister '; he put it down to his new voice.

' Who's this? ' W. B. Barclay was asking Carl Brockelberg.

Tischler told the chief engineer that it was Trigg's new shop boy.

' Well, come in, boy,' the chief engineer said. ' That is, if there's any more of him than a head and a voice.' He had the habit of throwing off witty asides.

W. B. Barclay was one of the persons Horace intended to record for posterity when he got back to his writing. His writing career to date had been desultory. Mr Covell, his schoolmaster under Mr Polling, had encouraged him in essays and tried to get him a job on the *Daily News* and even lent him an old enormous typewriter which he had dropped. He had tried a number of short stories in which you didn't know it was a cat (mouse, bird, chair) talking until the last syllable, practically. These had not gone down very well except with his brother Ken in Australia. Then the appearance of a new magazine *The Thriller* offering £100 for a story had given him fresh incentive which died out on the twentieth page. Lately he had had a rather brusque note from the Regent School of Journalism replying to a sample story he had submitted and telling him that they could not even accept him as a pupil.

It was this that had driven him back to night school and

Electricity and Magnetism.

The chief physicist, who was very young-looking, exceedingly kind and reputed to be religious and only have one lung, told Horace to sit down; but W. B. Barclay stopped him.

' Boys don't want to sit down,' he said. He was inclined to roar things. He was a big man who had a comic moustache; he looked like uncle Joe Stalin and sounded like the comedian Harry Tate, his voice always rising at the end on a squeak of incredulity. ' Three dayees! ' was one of the things Ernie Trigg would say, copying him. Now he said : ' I didn't sit down all the time I was a boy.'

Nobody really took these extravagant claims as the literal truth, but they knew what he meant.

He now proceeded to warn Horace the questions he would ask might appear meaningless but Horace had to do his best with them. Also he was not to repeat anything he heard in that room. By this time Horace began to realise that this had nothing whatever to do with his unauthorised borrowing of the loudspeaker. There was a period after this inquiry when everybody went around the factory not repeating anything they had heard in that room; the result was they were asking each other the same apparently meaningless questions. Viz :

' What is the exact time? '
' I don't know.'
' Haven't you got a watch? '
' No.'
' Have you ever had a watch? '
' No.'

W. B. Barclay was asking the questions while Doctor Tischler and Carl Brockelberg seemed to be there to watch Horace's face and judge if he was lying, though once Brockelberg said in his precise scientific way :

' May I interject? '

Horace prized that phrase all his life and once used it in a county court with such timing and delivery — a small-town solicitor was making him look irresponsible and feckless, leading two lives with two wives — that he won his case and had the judge (Macmillan) warmly commending his integrity to the court.

' Has anyone approached you and asked questions about anyone in the factory?' W. B. Barclay now said; then before Horace could reply he replied himself: 'I refuse to ask such stupid questions in the cause of obscurity. I'm going to tell you what we're after, Fenton, you being an intelligent chap with a deep voice. Doctor Tischler is a refugee from the German Nazis. There are thousands over here now. They are being victimised and terrorised and sometimes their relatives still in Germany are being endangered by pro-Nazi organisations in this country. Has anybody ever asked you questions about Doctor Tischler?'

'No,' Horace said, after all this.

Doctor Tischler said to W. B. Barclay: 'I think you have said far too much. If my fears are rootless we shall draw attention to me. This boy must be sworn to secrecy. Perhaps on the Bible.' To Horace he said: 'Have you a religion?'

'Girls, I should think,' W. B. Barclay chuckled. 'Look at his white face. Don't worry, Tischler, I can judge my staff. Now then, Fenton, have you ever seen this book before?'

'May I interject?' Carl Brockelberg the chief physicist said again. And to Horace he said: 'Do you know what this book is?'

'Ah, yes,' W. B. Barclay said. He excused himself and went into his private lavatory off the boardroom, stood peeing with the door open, splashing loudly with just the front part of himself out of sight, keeping his face and attention on the meeting. His secretary, a very sophisticated young woman named Mrs Bowrie who was married to Alexander Bowrie the service manager, just went on with some typing in one corner of the room; she was in fact keeping the minutes of the interrogation direct on her Underwood to save shorthand notes.

Horace said: 'It's a textbook written in German.'

'What sort of textbook?' Brockelberg asked him.

Horace thumbed a few pages of the thick old book, saw that there were circuits and diagrams and formulae, recognised reactance and resonance, impedance and aerial array field-strength diagrams. He said:

'Radio communications.'

Doctor Tischler said: 'Who do you think it belongs to?'

'You?' Horace asked.

Tischler said: 'Have you ever seen it in my laboratory?'

41

'No,' Horace said.

'Have you ever seen anybody else with it?'

'No,' Horace said.

W. B. Barclay came back doing up his fly-buttons, for there were no zips in those days. He said, cheerfully: 'I think we can safely assume that Fenton is useless. Who else is there to come?'

'Just a minute, sir,' Carl Brockelberg said. And to Horace: 'Turn back to the beginning of the book.'

Horace did so.

'What do you see?'

'Corner of a page missing.'

'Do you know what was written on there?'

'The price?'

'Not the price,' Brockelberg said, patiently.

Horace suddenly knew. Whether it was the shape of the missing triangle of paper or the yellowing colour and texture or the way the edge looked as if it had broken with over-folding rather than been torn or cut.

'Name, address and date,' Horace said. Then, more specifically: 'A word like München. A date with a funny seven with a cross across it — yes, 1927.' And as they were staring at him, W. B. Barclay and Brockelberg brightly as though an experiment had come off, the German with some fear, Horace said: 'I swept it up. It stuck on the boards and I couldn't shift it with the broom. I picked it up.' And to Tischler: 'It didn't have your name on it. It was another name.'

'Do you remember what it was?' Tischler said.

'No,' Horace said.

'Good,' said the refugee from Hitler. 'Now you must forget the word München and the date and anything else that was on that paper.'

'Yes,' Horace said.

W. B. Barclay said: 'Well, there's one little mystery cleared up. You see, Tischler? You're safe here. It fell out of your book. It got swept up. Nobody stole it. All right, Fenton, you can go. You've done very well. Thank you.'

The chief physicist, Carl Brockelberg, said: 'I would like to ask Fenton one more question.' He asked it: 'Do you know what München means?'

' Yes,' Horace said. ' Munich. Hazel told me.'

' Come back,' the chief engineer said.

Horace had got to the door but now he came back.

' Hazel? ' W. B. Barclay said.

Not only were Brockelberg and Tischler listening to Horace now as if he were a very faint watch, but also Mrs Bowrie had stopped typing to listen.

' The tea girl,' Horace said. ' She was there when I picked it up. She thought she had dropped it.'

Brockelberg said : ' You mean she noticed you pick something up and thought it might have dropped out of her pocket? '

' Yes,' Horace said.

' But it hadn't? ' Tischler said.

' No,' Horace said.

W. B. Barclay said : ' And then she threw it away? '

Horace said : ' I expect so. I don't know. I forget.'

Doctor Tischler said : ' You gave it to the tea girl and that's the last you saw of it? '

' Yes,' Horace said.

Doctor Tischler said : ' Bring her here.'

Mrs Bowrie said : ' She's dead. He's talking about Hazel Springer — Mr Green's office girl.'

' I remember,' Doctor Tischler said. And as if to himself, he murmured : ' She was gassed.'

They all looked at him. Horace had that same feeling he had had when Tischler told the model shop : ' Hitler needs you ! ' The feeling that other things were intended.

Carl Brockelberg gave Horace a little nod and Horace went out.

Chapter Seven

' Wotcher, Horry ! '

Horace looked up from his gardening too quickly and got dizzy and had to stay bent for a moment. Neville Hampstead came into the front gate of the council house.

' I've started shaving,' he said.

' Oh? ' Horace said.

' You haven't got a bit of two-by-two, have you? ' Neville asked. ' Wood,' he added, at Horace's blank look.

' Come and sit down,' Horace invited. Still bent, he went and sat on the front doorstep.

' Where's your bike? ' Horace then asked.

It was a town where everybody rode bicycles with baskets on the front.

' Aston's got it wired into one of his hook-ups.'

' I wouldn't allow that,' Horace said.

' You know what Kapitza said? It's the first time anyone won the Nobel Prize on a bike ! Have you got any wood? '

Horace Spurgeon Fenton forgot his dizziness and became narrow and alert. ' Kapitza? Is he a foreigner? '

' Russian,' Neville said. ' He's got a Lagonda.'

' Lagonda ! '

' Why? '

' Nothing,' Horace said. ' Is his first name Charles? '

' No. Peter. He's mad. They all are.'

' Any Germans? ' Horace asked, casually.

' Dozens,' Neville said. ' Gott, Mohr, Geiger — why? '

Horace said : ' Have you ever heard them mention a girl called Hazel Springer? '

' Hazel Springer? Let's see. . . . No, I don't think so. What's the time? What about that old bedstead? That's about two-by-two, isn't it? '

' Or Doctor Tischler? '

' Tischler? Who's he? '

' It doesn't matter,' Horace said. Then he thought of something else that had come out of the meeting in W. B. Barclay's office. ' Have you got any political affiliations? '

' I don't think so,' Neville said, ' but you can have those old Admiralty Handbooks.'

Horace didn't pursue it as he didn't know what it meant either; they went through to the back garden to look at the broken bedstead.

The reason Neville didn't know about Hazel was that Horace had loved her too much and too secretly for a lot of chat. He had barely mentioned it to the girl herself. As well as this was that Horace and Neville had drifted apart since they stopped being errand-boys; Horace had gone into the radio factory and Neville was a lab boy in Free School Lane. Once they had been close; had played truant together, shot pellets at each other, created a dog called Dog Thumb which you got by drawing round your crooked thumb and adding different hilarious expressions. They had run with a fine crowd of kids in a slum part of the town known as Red Romsey, playing ' Offs ' which was practically gang warfare and letting off bombs by spitting through a small hole in a tin containing a small amount of carbide and then trailing a fuse string into it.

Their parents had been either London and North Eastern Railway employees or college servants. They were fed on long crusts of bread from the college kitchens with margarine and sugar on them, good allotment vegetables, offcuts of meat, chitterlings, pigs-fry, fish and chips. Their special pleasures were The Kinema on Mill Road, fairs on Midsummer Common, swimming in The Snobs, picnicking at Byron's Pool, scrumping, gleaning and horse-leading, and standing outside and shouting in storms. The shout was a long warble breaking octaves in the throat; it could be heard across the fens from Isleham to Prickwillow, Meldreth to Burwell. If you couldn't do it you weren't a Romsey Red. Everybody had to have a bicycle.

Horace Spurgeon Fenton saw himself as *A Child Of The Jago*, by Arthur Morrison. Lamplighters came round and lit the gas lamps with long poles in the evening, Knockers Up came round and banged bedroom windows with long poles in the early mornings, girls played hopscotch, boys got birched and

45

sometimes people got drowned in the river. Everybody, it seemed to Horace, in those days and in that place, just outside the giant's castle wall, within smell of the kitchens and within sound of the May Balls, was happy and excited and there was enough unemployment to go round.

'Queen Mary's in town buying antiques!' Rhoda would tell the children.

There was always something to heighten the day.

'They were right in the middle of splitting the atom and they run out of bits of wood,' Neville Hampstead grumbled as he sawed up the side-members of the old bedstead.

'What do they want to split it for?' Horace said.

Neville explained: 'It produces rays. You bombard the nuclei with Alpha particles and you get rays.'

'What, death rays?'

'No! Alpha, Gamma, Beta — and X-rays. They go right through you.'

'Don't they hurt you?'

'They don't know yet,' Neville said. He didn't feel too happy about some of the work. He didn't like the way Mr Crowe kept asking him if he felt all right. 'These bits of wood hold up the cyclotron.'

'What's that — Hercules or Raleigh?'

'Don't be a chump,' Horace's friend told him.

Neville could explain anything, for he had been errand-boy for Bowes and Bowes, the university booksellers. This is why, straddled on his bike up Trumpington Long Road or deep in the lushy meadows of Madingley Road, he had come by a lot of book-learning and finally the job in the lab. He was the cleanest boy Horace had ever met, his face Lifebuoy-shone, his hair watered down and stiff daylong and he was reputed to shine his shoes every day — though this was only hearsay.

Horace's own technical education had come in the first instance from a set of give-away cigarette cards in BDV brand cork-tipped. His holes and blind spots were the cards he could never get hold of; the practical advantages of single sideband transmission would niggle and worry him all his life because the card seemed unobtainable. He had a great secret fear of going to the grave with a bit of half-knowledge. Even Mr Sochaki, a defecting scientist whom Horace went to work for out of school hours, had been unable to explain it to him except in some obscure form of cosmic phenomena which he called sunspots.

'Listen, boy,' he would tell Horace.

Horace would listen raptly to a buzzing crackling background from a huge speaker mounted in a skylight over the shop doorway.

'This is your sunspots,' Mr Sochaki would tell him.

'Ah,' said Horace.

'Ah' from Horace meant precisely nothing.

'There goes that poor Mr Sochaki,' Rhoda used to say.

His little radio repair shop was at the top of their street in Red Romsey. He was a big, bony, gaunt man in small shabby acid-holed suits. He strode past delivering accumulators for wireless sets; worn-out shoes, trousers at half-mast, dark anarchist eyes behind bifocal glasses held together with insulating tape. He was said to be a conscientious objector from whatever was going on in the radio laboratory at the university. He had forsaken a professorial chair and a string of degrees and honours and opted for the simple useful life in Red Romsey, keeping wireless sets working and batteries charged and running a fetch-and-deliver service.

'There goes that poor Mr Sochaki's awful family,' Rhoda would also say.

Horace had first been attracted to Sochaki's shop by the noise. The loudspeaker over the doorway sounded like a fairground. It was fed, Horace discovered, by what was known as a breadboard radio. That is an immense palpitating circuitry of components and wires and valves as big as beer bottles all spread out on the top of an old kitchen table. It was so powerful that even if you disconnected the loudspeaker — which Mr Sochaki would only do if you had something important to say — you could still hear the music buzzing in the laminated intestines of the output stages.

'Listen !' Mr Sochaki would tell Horace.

Horace would listen intently to the sounds coming from the amplifier with no loudspeaker connected.

'Sunspots?' he would hazard.

But it was only *Minnie the Moocher*.

The awful family lived in the room behind the shop. Mrs Sochaki was a shabby, bottle-blonded, hard-faced woman who lived in a long brown fur coat, popular with the students, a second-hand raccoon moulted by sulphuric acid which was puddled everywhere. She fought from morning till night with about a dozen children of all sexes and ages. The girls were only distinguishable by their crudely-cut dresses made from advertising banners with words like Mazda, Ferranti and Osram printed on them. They all got electrocuted from time to time and had sores and scars and patches of hair missing. On the street, with their broken-down pram and push-chair they looked like a horde of marauding Berbers looking for crusts.

'They say they don't wear any knickers,' Rhoda would say.

Horace was able to reassure her. They did wear knickers, they lived on jam sandwiches and pork jowls and fish and chips, or huge bags of scrumps from the bottom of the fish-fry pan and every night was bath night for some of them. Amid the noise and the affray of the Sochaki household Horace learned how to build his own wireless set and he took his wages in the form of second-hand radio components, reels of wire, solder and flux.

'One day you will build a great wireless like mine,' Mr Sochaki used to tell him.

Before this happened, however, the Sochaki marriage seemed to fall apart. Horace came in one evening with two heavy accumulators which he had carried two miles from Blinco Grove and found Mr Sochaki kneeling behind the counter crying on the lap of an attractive young woman who was stroking his hair. No words were exchanged for Ambrose's band was blasting everything within a three-mile range, but a few weeks later the music stopped and when Horace turned up for work the shop was shut for good.

'He's gorn orf,' Mrs Sochaki told Horace.

She had managed to break the loudspeaker wires but didn't know how to switch the set off and Horace showed her. It was the first time he had heard her voice. It transpired, once the noise had stopped, that the blonde woman was not Mr Sochaki's wife at all, but his mother; the children were his half-brothers and sisters by a second marriage.

'It's always a mistake,' Rhoda Fenton told her children.

Chapter Eight

At the end of a long, tiring day Rhoda Fenton (or Morden or Whateley) walked home the interminable lengths of the council acres in her same brisk and businesslike style, stopping only to correct injustice amongst quarrelling children or hoist her truss.

Tonight she was walking a little faster, for she had stolen two onions for her family. That was the dramatic way she thought about such things. She thought about Horace breathing his native air and stealing onions for her family. She also thought a good deal about pulling out the parrot's tail in Finchley as a girl. She had what she described as an ' obsession ' about it.

' It's not " obession ", Mother,' Christine told her recently. ' It's " obsession ".'

' Are you sure ? ' Rhoda said at first; then the more she thought about it the more certain was she that she had been wrong all her life. The thought horrified her. ' People must have thought I was ignorant. People must have thought I was another Mrs Murphy. How awful ! '

Mrs Murphy, with the pony and trap opposite the Disabled Soldiers' Club, had mispronounced words and used them in the wrong place. You couldn't be like that when you were in business.

Tonight, all the way home on the works bus, she had been afraid that people could smell the onions; could smell that they were stolen.

' I'm going to make you a kettle broth,' she told the children. Each was cynical after his or her own brand of humour and she said : ' I don't know why you sneer. It's full of goodness.'

The essential ingredient in kettle broth was raw onions; after that it could be anything remaining in the cupboard — scraps of cheese, bread, marge, cold scraps of meat or fat, tag-ends in tins of beans, all with plenty of vinegar, salt, pepper, mustard, and covered in boiling water from the kettle.

' Rattle your knives and forks,' Rhoda would tell the boys if Christine had Stan in the front room or the neighbours were outside the window.

' I'd like to try this on Lord Cecil,' Ronald would say, having spent his day in the quiet splendour of the Pitt Club.

By this time Ronald's gault head of the King had been thrown across the room seven times, mostly by Leslie. It was now beginning to harden.

On this night of the stolen onions Detective-Sergeant Stan Polsworth came into the kitchen looking for Horace, who wasn't there.

' He's putting the garden tools away,' Rhoda told him. ' What do you want him for? '

' Just a bit of information, Mrs Whateley.'

When the young detective had gone out into the back garden Rhoda found Christine looking thoughtful on the sofa in the front room.

' If he calls me Mrs Whateley once again,' she told her daughter, ' I don't want him to come here any more. Find somebody else.'

' I can't,' Christine said. ' I think I'm going to have a baby.'

Rhoda drew herself up to her full businesslike height and all Sam Dayball's evangelistic wrath came into her face.

' What have you been doing! ' she cried.

Christine said, mildly : ' You know very well what I've been doing, Mother.'

That's funny, Stan thought.

He stood just outside the back door looking around the Fentons' garden. It was a long garden divided from similar long gardens by a wood stake fence. At the end of the long gardens of Green End Road were the long gardens of the council houses in Kendal Way. You could see fifty back gardens and back doors. Outside many of the houses you could see what the occupants did for a living : decorators' trash, errand-boys' bikes (Eaden Lilley, Blott, Sainsbury, Winton Smith), mechanics' overalls hanging on lines; it was a kind of open prison with no privacy allowed.

What Stan thought was funny was that Horace must be hiding in the tool-shed. There was nowhere else you could possibly hide in a new council house garden. It wasn't funny exactly, it was frightening. What was it Mrs Whateley had said about the boy?

50

He does strange things.

Detective-Sergeant Stanley Polsworth knew a few strange things people did; especially to policemen. Police-Constable Gutteridge had been shot through both eyes trying to stop a lorry over Fordham; that was a strange thing. Inspector Newly calling all innocent and unsuspecting on that young grad up Hawthorn Way who'd failed his exams; both of them shot dead: that was another strange thing.

Stanley played it cool, admiring the garden and gradually working his way towards the shed. It was a funny sort of garden. A lawn near the house with an immense grave-shaped mound of a flower bed in the middle full of lilies. There was a heavy roller made out of an oil-drum filled with cement with a steel rod through the middle. The vegetables started with a double trenched row of celery, banked up to bleach the stalks, and then a great wilderness of asparagus partly in tall fern dotted with purple and red splashes of anemones; vegetables and flowers all mixed up, and all along the garden path little sandcastles made of cement tipped out of a seaside bucket as though a child had been playing.

'That's pretty,' Stan said. He said it as though he could have been talking to himself, but he had already heard Horace's asthmatic breathing inside the shed — the door was just ajar (Horace had claustrophobia through being locked in a refrigerator at Winton Smith's).

'Not bad, is it?' Horace said.

'Oh, are you there?' the detective said. 'I didn't know you were there.'

'I'm just watching this spider,' Horace told him.

Stan pushed wider the tool-shed door and looked in. 'You like spiders, do you?'

Horace had a feeling he was being humoured. He came out.

'Going to cut some grass, are you?' Stan was looking at the grass-hook in the boy's hand; it was a nasty weapon.

Horace put it down.

'Do you mind if I ask you a few questions?' Stan said. 'Sort of unofficially?'

They started walking the length of the garden having an unofficial talk, watched by fifty or sixty people.

'Christine tells me you knew Hazel Springer?'

51

' Yes. It was terrible, wasn't it? She was our tea girl.'

' According to my information you were rather fond of her? '

' Oh. Yes, I was. I liked her.'

' Apparently you were going to marry her? '

Horace laughed; it seemed silly now. He passed it off as a family joke. Seventeen years old and earning a pound a week and getting married. ' What's the trouble, then? ' he asked his future brother-in-law.

' Well, she was supposed to have been alone in the house when she died. But it's not certain. There might have been somebody there. Perhaps a boy friend — her family were over St Neots visiting. You know, Sunday afternoon.'

Horace said : ' If he was there, why didn't he save her? '

' Ah ! ' said the detective; going on : ' Now, then — did you ever go out with her at all? '

' No,' Horace said, promptly.

' Ah,' said Stanley again, but in a different way. ' Then if somebody said they saw you with Hazel Springer on Parker's Piece the day before she died they'd be lying — or mistaken, of course.'

' Was that the day before she died ! ' Horace exclaimed.

' Then you admit that you were with her? '

Admit? Horace thought. What *was* this?

' Of course you don't have to say anything if you don't want to,' Detective-Sergeant Polsworth told him. ' You have a perfect right to see a solicitor first.'

' Do you mind if I sit down? ' Horace asked.

They had come back to the lawn and he sat down on his home-made roller. The back door opened and Christine looked out :

' Tea up ! ' she cried.

It gave Horace the shivers. He had read this scene a thousand times. The cross-examination, the sly tricky question, and then the sudden re-enactment of the drama, tricking the murderer into thinking his victim was still alive and ready to incriminate him. Surely his own sister wouldn't co-operate in a thing like that? And who had seen him with Hazel? Who had gone to the police? He betted it was old *Wah yah bah lah dah gah* in the tea pavilion.

' So you were seeing her? ' Stan persisted, having waved Christine indoors.

' No. I bumped into her.'

' Bumped into her? '

' Accidentally.'

' I see,' said the policeman.

Horace said : ' I was flying my aeroplane. Hazel came up and spoke to me. I didn't even know who she was at first.'

' Flying your aeroplane? '

Horace told him about his model aeroplane that wouldn't take to the air. Told him about the R101 airship coming over.

The detective-sergeant said : ' You realise that the R101 crashed after that on its maiden flight with the loss of all lives? '

' But that was over France, wasn't it? ' For an insane moment Horace thought he was being accused of shooting it down with his aeroplane.

' Where did you go after that? ' Stanley asked.

' What? '

' You bumped into her accidentally on Parker's Piece — yes? '

Oh God, Horace thought; suppose somebody saw him following Hazel all those miles; if it was Hazel, which it wasn't.

' I just walked home with her,' he said.

' And didn't you make a date with her for the next day? '

' No ! '

' Didn't you go indoors with her? '

' No ! '

' Did you kiss her or anything? '

' No ! I didn't even hold her hand. There was nothing like that. She was the tea girl, that's all. I just said " Cheero " and walked on. I didn't even go right to her house — it was broad daylight on a Saturday afternoon.'

' You know where she lived, though? '

Oh Christ, Horace thought. ' Not really,' he said. ' Somewhere down by the river near the gas works.'

Stanley just watched him in silence, which unnerved Horace, who added :

' That's what she said. Anyway, her mother was there — '

He'd done it; he'd done the complete Billy Bunter. Instead of jumping on him Stanley Polsworth smiled, relaxed, offered him a Robin, lit one himself.

'All right, Horace — so you were sweet on her?'

Horace nodded, not trusting words any more.

'And did you write this to her?' Stanley was holding out a piece of paper, turning it both ways but not allowing Horace to touch it.

It was a works requisition for a dozen one-inch 2BA countersunk screws and a new No 33 drill signed by Ernie Trigg and receipted by Charlie in the stores. On the other side was written:

> *Sweetheart, if you should stray*
> *A million miles away,*
> *I'll always be in love with you.*

'It's a song,' Horace said. 'I was just learning the words.'

His future brother-in-law was taking a sad but kindly attitude now. 'Horace, you must have known the words or you couldn't have written them down. This is on one of Chris's Woolworths' records — Jack Payne's band.'

Horace nodded. He said: 'I was going to slip it into a tea cup when she wasn't looking.'

'That's better,' Stanley said, cheerfully. 'That's got the ring of truth about it.' And then quite suddenly he said: 'Now where were you on the Sunday?'

'Eh?' Horace said.

Stanley said: 'Where were you between 3 pm and 5 pm on Sunday the 23rd? Now take your time, Horace. Think about it.'

Horace thought about it, then said: 'I was lying in the front room with my throat bashed in — you were here.'

Detective-Sergeant Stanley Polsworth's face went perfectly blank for a moment; then he said: 'Well, I'm blessed — was that *that* Sunday? So it was! Well, that's all right, then. Now you can do just one more thing for me, then I'll scrub you off the list — okay?'

'Okay,' Horace said.

Stanley said: 'I want you to think very deeply about this. You give a straightforward, truthful answer and I'll get you off the hook.'

Horace nodded; it seemed a fair exchange. He didn't want to

54

go through that again. *All you've got to do*, he'd made one of his murderers say in one of his stories, *is keep calm and stick to your story*. Well, it wasn't as easy as it sounded; not even when you were innocent.

' I want you to tell me this,' Stanley said, lowering his voice : ' Has your sister Christine been with any other chap in the last six weeks? '

' What? ' Horace said. He thought they were still on the Hazel Springer case.

' Don't repeat a word of this,' Stanley warned him. ' This is the Official Secrets Act. Has Chris been out with anybody else lately? '

' Not that I know of,' Horace said.

' Has she had anybody here? Think carefully.'

' No. Nobody.'

' Have you heard her so much as mention anybody else? '

' No.'

' Where did she go last Thursday night? ' Stanley now asked. ' Don't forget I'm going to take your name out of the case.'

' Last Thursday? '

' She said she couldn't see me last Thursday. Did she go out? '

' That's my Maths night,' Horace said. ' I was at night school.'

' What time did you get home? '

' Ten o'clock.'

' Try to remember if she was here when you got home.'

Christine looked out again : ' Your tea's getting cold, darling.'

' Coming,' Stanley said. ' Nearly through.' And to Horace : ' Can you remember? '

' Yes,' Horace said. ' She was here.'

He didn't remember at all but he got the sure feeling that this was the answer required. He was right.

' Good lad,' the young detective said. He put his arm around Horace as they went in. ' Made you sweat a bit, did I? Well, that's my job,' he added, rather proudly.

And family unity, Horace thought, *that's mine*.

Chapter Nine

Due to the comfortable boredom of factory life (school life, life itself, routine living), Horace thought, composing another literary idea for some future use, the least exciting things attract a crowd (attention, comment). For instance, if a dog walked across the playground during a geography lesson the class was happily disrupted; if it actually peed it made the whole day. Now what was this?

Crowd around the works notice board, watching it. Watch, he thought, that's a good word too, instead of looking at. As though perhaps it was moving. *He sat watching the book*, Horace Spurgeon Fenton thought, as he joined the throng.

FOR THOSE ABOUT TO DIE — READ THIS

This was a green chalked headline above a blow-up ammonia duplicate of a typescript which itself was a quote from a recent speech in the House of Commons by a Mr Winston Churchill. It was also war-mongering communist propaganda, as Harry Webb had already explained to Horace and the model shop (who, engrossed in instrument making, were inclined to be a-political).

WRITE TO YOUR MP AND DEMAND RE-ARMAMENT BEFORE IT IS TOO LATE

it said in yellow chalk.

Then the speech:

> I dread the day when the means of threatening the heart of the British Empire should pass into the hands of the present rulers of Germany. We should be in a position which would be odious to every man who values freedom of action and independence, and also in a position of the utmost peril for our crowded, peaceful population engaged

in their daily toil. I dread that day, but it is not, perhaps, far distant. It is perhaps only a year, or perhaps eighteen months distant. It has not come yet — at least, so I believe or I hope and pray; but it is not far distant. . . .

— Winston S. Churchill speaking
in Parliament last week

' Does this mean there's going to be a war? ' Horace asked. He was asking nobody in particular but as it happened Dirty Dick was there.

' There's always going to be a war, boy,' he told Horace.

He was a man of about forty who wore a gaberdine raincoat and rode a very upright bicycle. His face was clean though always unshaven, and his snuff habit tinged his top lip and his fingers, though because of the sneezing his eyes were clear and his brain alert.

' We're not looking at that,' he now told Horace. ' We're looking at this.'

What everybody was looking at was a photograph of a young man. Underneath the photograph was written :

HAVE YOU SEEN THIS MAN?

It went on to say that anybody who could identify the young man or give any information about him should speak to their chargehand or foreman.

' Who is he? ' Horace asked.

' That's what they want to know,' said Dirty Dick.

' What's it about? ' asked Horace.

It was about Hazel Springer. Dirty Dick didn't know this. Some of the girls on the front row of tables in the canteen knew it. By the time it reached Horace it was murder. The photograph on the notice board was a copy of one that Hazel had framed next to her bed. Nobody knew who it was, not even her parents.

' She'd have to tell her mum and dad,' one of the girls said. ' If it was next to her bed.'

' I bet he was married, that's why,' said another.

On his way out of the canteen Horace took another long look at the face on the green baize board. His heart gave a tug; he almost recognised it and then didn't. Was it the chap in the Perse blazer, the chap at the Botanical Gardens — Old Charles, perhaps? There was something definitely familiar about that thin, pale face, the old-fashioned suit, the dedicated fanatical eyes. It was not like somebody he'd ever known but more like a picture in some old murder case — Crippen or Thompson and Bywaters perhaps; or even an ad for Kruschen Salts or the ' Let Me Be Your Father ' figure in the Bennet College advertisement.

The face on the notice board, in Horace's mind, had a strangely public quality. This was because, though nobody had yet realised it, it was a face the whole world knew when it was some twenty years older. The young man on the notice board who had been Hazel's pin-up was none other than Adolph Hitler at the age of twenty-two. It was the portrait of The Führer as a young artist in Vienna.

' Rotten swine,' Horace muttered to himself.

There were tears near to his eyes, thinking of the girl, and he vowed that he would bring this chap to justice if he got time.

One night, sitting on their bicycles just where they had met at the corner of Chapel Lane and Chesterton High Street, Horace Spurgeon Fenton and Neville Hampstead went deeply and at great length into the business of life and its various spiritual and material values. There were many little two- and three-way conferences of this nature in the days when people rode bicycles with baskets on the front for their books and comforts and shopping; they were, as it were, already at home : and yet, unlike inside a car, available and sitting down.

People had been known to enter into the promises of marriage sitting on bicycles.

' I'm never going to get married,' was one of the things Neville said, out of something that had happened during his day at Free School Lane laboratory (The Cavendish).

' Why not? ' Horace asked him. Horace had already fallen in love several times and looked forward to the next time. Falling in love was really more exciting than being in love. The very first time her eyes held and registered your interest. The way she then instantly tugged her skirt down; it was as instinctive as a dog turning round before lying down and probably had a sexual reason too deep to be known now.

It was Neville's opinion that a chap had to earn too much money if he was married. This would make him put finance before the proper considerations of a job; would interfere with his career.

' I don't think so,' Horace said, partly for the sake of argument; his Brooks saddle was very comfortable and kept the skin surfaces of his anus apart to relieve the itching. ' You could get married comfortably on three pounds a week.'

' Five pounds a week,' Neville said. ' Professor Wood has worked it out. For a house and car and enough to eat and dress yourselves and keep up running repairs you need five pounds a week. You want to vote for him.'

Doctor Alex Wood the scientist was standing for Parliament, though neither of them was old enough to vote yet.

' His wife's nice,' Horace said. ' They live in St Barnabas Road. I used to deliver their meat.'

' I never want to earn more than four pounds a week,' Neville said. ' Give my mum a pound.'

Horace said : ' A skilled instrument-maker can get three pounds a week. Ted Wright gets that, so does Mr Roper and Dirty Dick. Harry Webb gets two pounds ten but he's semi-skilled. His wife goes out to work.'

' I wouldn't want that,' Neville said.

' Nor would I,' Horace said.

' But I wouldn't want to be out of work, either,' Neville said.

' No, nor would I,' Horace said.

He had no need to worry about that; he left school on the Wednesday at Easter 1931, started work on the Thursday and never had a single day out of work in his life.

' Here comes old Holiday,' Horace said, suddenly. ' You see the way he rides. Wotcher, Holiday ! '

' Wotcher,' Holiday called back. He had a large white face which, because of his hump back, seemed tipped upwards like a plate.

' What's the matter with him? ' Neville asked.

' He's got a chassis up his shirt,' Horace said. ' It's not his, it's Bert Claydon's. Only nobody stops Holiday because of his hump. He dropped his glove the other day and couldn't bend down to pick it up because of the sheet of aluminium inside his pullover.'

'That's stealing,' Neville said. 'I don't think that's right.'

Horace said: 'It's only for work. I'm making a five-metre transceiver now.'

'You can bend Beta rays with a magnet,' Neville said, getting the conversation back to his own field of nuclear physics. 'That's how you tell the difference between one sort and another.'

'I may join the Air Force after all if they bring Queen Bees in.' Queen Bee was the first radio-controlled aeroplane now being experimented with. 'That's if I can't get my stories printed.'

Neville Hampstead said what many others were to tell Horace in the fifteen years it took him to get into print: 'You can't be a writer unless you go to college. You want your BSc with honours, BA, MA and Doctorate. Lots of our fellers write books.'

What had taken Horace's train of thought to the Air Force now took his depressed thoughts into the air again: a squadron of high-flying fighter planes were buzzing in tight formation high over the town; compact little Hawker Fury 1s with twin synchronised Vickers guns and powered by Rolls-Royce 525 hp Kestrel engines, capable of high speeds and alarming aerobatics. Horace had been watching them ever since school playground days. Now at this moment astride his bike at the top of Chapel Lane with what Neville had just said, they seemed to epitomise the impossibility of doing anything without an education. BDV cigarette cards were not enough.

'For instance,' Neville said, 'do you know Einstein's theory of relativity?'

'What?' Horace said.

'$E = mc^2$,' Neville Hampstead stated. 'It's the relationship between energy and matter.'

'Oh?' Horace said. His arse started itching and he moved gently; his ignorance did this very often.

'Sometimes when you split an atom,' the lab boy said, 'you lose an electron. It's turned into energy. The isotope of plutonium — that's 235, of course, not 238 which is normal — could release enough energy to blow the universe apart.'

'I didn't know that,' Horace said. And he said: 'We've done the earth's magnetic field. It's 0·22 gauss up Mill Road.'

'Of course,' Neville said, 'you have to know the speed of

light — that's the c^2 component of the equation.'

'Three hundred million metres per second,' Horace said, coming into his own BDV field again. 'The speed of light,' he added, at Neville's surprise. ' It's the conversion factor — wavelength into frequency in radio communication. F. J. Camm thinks nobody will talk about wavelength in the future. It'll be all frequency. Last week in *Practical Wireless* they showed you how to play tunes on a rod in a tuned oscillator circuit.'

Neville Hampstead thought about this for a moment but it didn't seem to fit in with anything they were doing at Free School Lane at the moment and he gave it up. But it was in this still moment that Horace decided to entrust Neville with his murder problem.

' I'll think about it,' Neville Hampstead said, when Horace had outlined the facts surrounding the tragic death of Hazel Springer.

Typical, he thought to himself. It was typical of Horry Fenton to throw some unrelated facetious element into a scientific discussion. When it came to science generally Horace was a bit of a dilettante. He was inclined to start whistling just when you thought he was trying to concentrate and engage his mind. He talked intelligently enough and seemed interested in everything, yet he was always whistling as though whatever impression he might want to give, his head was really stuffed with jazz and pop tunes which kept leaking out when the conversation died away. He seemed to have some sort of jazz rhythm going on instead of an ordinary pulse. Now it was murder stories.

' I can't go to Perse School and search for this chap,' Horace was explaining. ' I can't even go to Perse School. You go to Perse School, Nev. Isn't that where you got your bike? '

Neville turned red. What was this — blackmail? Not that taking a bike was considered stealing; everybody's bike was taken from somebody. And if you ran out of bikes all you had to do was go down the police station and pay two bob for one. New bikes cost three pounds ten and people didn't have that sort of money except on HP.

Horace was saying: ' I thought if I gave you the photograph you could have a look round there? '

61

' I don't know,' Neville said.

Horace said : ' He may have a Lagonda.' And he added : ' Or wouldn't they let you in? '

' Of course they let me in! ' Neville Hampstead exclaimed. ' I'm always at Perse. They've got better lab equipment than we have. Half our instruments came from Perse — of course we train their chaps. Some came in today to look at Wilson's original Cloud Chamber.'

' Well, then,' Horace said.

' Where is it? The picture? '

Horace spun his pedals round ready to ride and his loose chain rattled on the frame. ' We'll go and get it off the board. You can come in with me. They'll think we're working overtime.'

Neville said : ' I'm in a bit of a hurry tonight.'

They had been standing there for an hour and a quarter. Sitting there.

' They've got lovely bread and dripping for overtime. Two slices for a penny,' Horace said. ' I'll buy you some.'

The two boys circled tightly in front of a big green double-decker *Ortona* bus which skidded to stop.

' Sail before steam! ' Horace shouted back at the driver.

Wobbling, they cycled off down Chapel Lane, gradually turning it into a race and standing on the pedals.

Chapter Ten

Why is it always, reminding me of, a love dream that never could be, Horace thought, singing, orchestrating, playing every instrument and putting in the counterpoint and pedalling at the same time, *Sweet moon song, that wasn't meant for me. It came riding on a moonbeam gliding to my heart from up above.* . . .

That lasted him from the Public Library in Corn Exchange Street to Victoria Bridge. After that he went through *Darkness On The Delta,* and *It's a treat to beat your feet on the Mississippi mud* by association and then : *You're A Heavenly Thing, Misty Island of the Highland* and through the trickier Four Aces version of *I Got Rhythm* and home. There was nothing he could do about all this; it sometimes wore him out.

In the big sagging wicker basket in front of his handlebars were William Blake's *Songs of Innocence* and Dean Swift's *Polite Conversation.* Since his total rejection by the Regent School, Horace had set himself a course of reading from the masters; not only reading but copying out long extracts in longhand to see if he could find out how it was done. Nothing had happened yet except that of all the writers he had tried William Blake had struck something in his heart and he didn't know what. It was going to take William Saroyan to release it and another ten years before he found that brilliant American Armenian writer and learned how to get himself onto the paper with all his faults and shortcomings intact.

' Stan wants to see you,' Christine told Horace when he got in.

Well, Horace didn't want to see Stan. He himself had a perfect alibi for poor Hazel's death since he was almost dead himself at the time. And he now had a scientist working on the case, against whom Stan stood little chance. W. B. Barclay had stated the case in the office the other day :

' If it's political the police are no good. All they understand is robbery and r-a-p-e — ' he had spelt it out in deference to Horace's age. He had been trying to reassure Doctor Tischler that he was still perfectly safe in the Home Counties; that his wife and children were perfectly safe in Austria at the moment; that he would not bring the attention of the police to the missing name and address torn from the book nor link it with the dead girl — who obviously had no connection with the Nazis in Britain; that they would do nothing to attract attention or publicity to the Jews working in England. The most he would allow was the posting of the photograph of the unknown young man on the works notice board. 'It's obviously a young married man she fell in love with — hence the mystery,' the chief engineer had said, as though quoting an infallible equation.

'I'm on the point of making an arrest,' Detective-Sergeant Polsworth told Horace later that evening, holding him firmly by the shoulder.

'That's good,' Horace said.

'The murderer was seen hanging about outside her house late at night watching her window,' Stanley said.

'Oh?' said Horace.

Rhoda said: 'It's a wonder you didn't see him, Horace. You come that way home from night school, don't you? Just fancy!'

'What else?' Horace said.

'You remember that picture of the suspect — that she kept beside her bed?'

'Yes,' Horace said.

'It's been stolen from the works notice board,' Stanley said.

'You see?' Leslie said; it had turned into a family conference. 'It's what I said. It's somebody from your works.'

Rhoda said, thoughtfully: 'The fair was here that week, wasn't it?'

The young detective now said to Horace: 'Did you know that Hazel Springer kept a diary?'

Horace didn't know. Horace was a little fed up. He knew it wasn't her fault, but her death was impinging on him far more than her life had ever done. All he could clearly remember her saying to him now was: 'You are funny!'

'She mentions you in it,' Stanley Polsworth told him.

Horace was beginning to perceive that Stanley unconsciously or not was doing his best to keep Horace connected with the crime; or rather with the suspected crime. Nobody had proved that any second party was involved in Hazel's death. At the inquest an open verdict was returned. The pilot light on the gas geyser had gone out. When Hazel, probably with soap in her eyes, reached out to turn the tap fully on for more water, she did not notice that the gas came up without being alight. It had happened before; it was one of the most well-known accidents in the home. And, of course, there was always the query why the pilot light had gone out. It could have been blown out by the draught from the flap of the towel, say; or it could have been put out by someone in the kitchen turning off the gas at the main and turning it on again.

And the only clue that there might have been someone in the house besides Hazel was that the bathroom window was open when the girl was found. The Springer family couldn't remember opening it; they were certain they didn't. Hazel might have opened it in her dying panic. But if so, why didn't she also open the door and get out?

' " Horace made me laugh again today ",' Stanley Polsworth read out from a little green Woolworths' notebook.

' Oh, really? ' said Horace, with a pretence at being good-humouredly interested.

Christine said : ' What sort of things did you use to do? '

There was a note of complaint and surprise; he seldom made his own family laugh. The reason for that was that like doesn't find like very amusing. Whatever oddness Horace had, they probably all had it. They only made outsiders laugh; and only that when they were being particularly earnest about something as Horace had been earnest about Hazel. It was his stuttering inarticulateness that had made her laugh.

' She was a pretty hot number by the look of it,' Stanley said, scanning through the diary again. ' Perhaps you'd like to have a look through these initials and see if you recognise any? She had a different chap every night of the week! '

Horace could not believe this, but he took the diary and scanned it.

' First of all look at all the Mondays,' he told Horace. Then to the family, as one who does an unusual job : ' That way you get the pattern of behaviour — or POB.' And to Horace again : ' You notice how ABL occurs on Mondays? '

Horace wished he'd bloody well shut up.

Here now in his hands were Hazel's thoughts; the story of her days. Written in such a way that he could hear her calling again: 'Tea up!' For the first time since it had happened Horace felt like crying; it had taken all this time for it to hit him. 'Horace loves me, Harry said' was one entry. Another explained something she'd mentioned on Parker's Piece: 'Harry said something wicked about my bosom. He wants me to see him.'

Horace looked up, lost in thought.

'Who's ABL?' Stanley urged. He had noted Horace's emotion and tacked it onto his list of things about Horace.

Horace said: 'Did you read this about Harry Webb — asking her out? He's a married man. He used to annoy her.'

'He was only joking,' Stanley said. 'He told me.'

Horace had another startling thought: 'Harry's always on about Germany. What a hero Hitler is —'

'Well, he is a hero,' Leslie said. 'Our schoolmaster said so. A 90·3 per cent solid vote in the Saar —'

'What about Doctor Dolfuss getting killed and King Alexander?' Christine said. 'That was Hitler. What about all those Jews being kidnapped and killed —'

'Never mind all that,' Detective-Sergeant Polsworth said, impatiently. 'Who's ABL?' he repeated to Horace.

'Must be home for ABL' was one Monday entry. Another read, astonishingly: 'ABL in bed tonight — smashing!'

Horace refused to believe it and would not read it out.

'Look at the Tuesdays,' Stanley now requested. 'Who's J.J.?'

Monday was ABL, Tuesday was J.J., Wednesday was S.K., Thursday was L.S., Friday was H.R. and Saturday was AMB. She seemed to sleep with most of them.

Stanley said: 'Her family say they've never heard of any of those people. I think they're shielding somebody — person or persons unknown, that is.'

Rhoda said: 'Why would they do that? With their daughter dead?'

Stanley said: 'With all those names it looks to the Superintendent — and to me, of course — that the Springers were using their daughter for an immoral purpose. Now they're trying to cover it up. Her father's on the dole,' he added, as though in

66

sufficient explanation. ' He used to work at the gas works but was caught stealing coke.'

' Who's R.C.? ' ' Horace asked now.

' Where's that? '

Horace showed him : ' Sundays.'

' No, no, that's not a person, that's the Rhythm Club — you know, over Millers in Hobson Street. She always went. Got a stack of records. All rubbish of course.'

Christine suddenly knew on this moment that she hated Stanley and was going to have to go through with a horrible marriage for the sake of the child. It was a combination of things. It was his insensitiveness to Horace's distress about the dead girl; to Stanley she was just a job. It was his butting into her recital of Hitler's atrocities with a ' never mind all that ' and it was his dismissal of Hazel's gramophone records as ' rubbish '. She saw that anything he didn't understand would always be rubbish. She realised now that the man she was going to marry was unintelligent.

' You don't know any of these people, then? ' he was now asking Horace.

Horace was secretly deciding that he would go to the Rhythm Club next Sunday and look for old Charles.

' The strange thing is,' Stanley said to Christine, ' the girl was *virgo intacta —* '

' That's a lie! ' Horace burst out, being able to take no more slanders against someone who could not protect herself; and in tears he stormed up to his room. ' That's a beastly rotten lie! ' he shouted back down the stairs.

Chapter Eleven

On the Friday morning of that week a new, experimental cathode-ray tube exploded, killing and injuring several flies.

Horace was in the model shop receiving instruction from old Ted Wright when it happened. Ted was showing Horace what he believed to be the basis of all engineering — how to file precisely square a piece of steel. As in playing golf, the whole thing rested on your stance, the angle of your elbows, your mental attitude to plane surfaces and finite angles; your relationship with God, in a way.

'You see this set of squares?' Ted had said to Horace in his early days at the factory. 'I made those the week I came out of of my apprenticeship at John Brown's — that was in 1897. They still look like new, don't they?'

They looked like jewels lying in their baize-lined case. The tinest one, no more than half an inch each way, true in its angle and surface to within one-ten-thousandth part of an inch, the same as the largest; each one blue-tempered and oiled and nesting within the other: the whole set in its cedar-wood box ready to be used as a reliable tool in the making of precision instruments.

'Now the smooth file,' Ted Wright told him.

Horace started with the smooth file, but Ted immediately stopped him.

'You've lost your rhythm, haven't you?' he said.

Horace admitted that he had.

'Now, be calm, rest a moment, take your time. Let the thumb of your right hand press down for a moment on the blade of the file. It takes its parallel from the surface. You see? Now start that steady straight arc. A new file wants to rock. Don't let it. A new file wants to change your thoughts. Don't let it. If you master this you'll master your writing.'

'What writing?' Horace said. Horace had never said anything to anybody in the model shop about his writing.

'Because if you master this you master yourself,' old Ted Wright told the boy. 'It comes from the senses and the instincts.

Inner balance. In a word — control.'

And he said other things that surprised and impressed Horace for life. He said that in engineering, with all the marvels of machinery and instruments and new devices, the humble file was really the foundation because it was closest to a man's hand and mind.

'It's like a violin in a vast orchestra, Horace,' old Ted said. 'Or better still a guitar. Do you know what Beethoven said about the guitar? He said it was a whole orchestra in one instrument.'

You would never have suspected that old Ted knew what Beethoven said. It was this remark, coupled with what happened the following Sunday at the Rhythm Club, that took Horace to the guitar. But he was never going to achieve perfection with his hands — or at least not consistently. There was something missing in his hand-to-brain co-ordination that would always cause the odd last split-second dither : make his music reading too slow, cause a buzz on a chord, jump the letters in his touch-typing. It happened now with the filing.

'That's all right,' old Ted said. 'Throw that bit away and start again. Practice makes perfect.'

But it doesn't; practice only makes perfect in your own craft.

The bang when it came was muffled like thunder in a shoe-box.

'Aye aye!' Harry Webb shouted. Skilled men and even semi-skilled shouted a lot, made noise in accordance with their status; threw things on the floor — they were signs of autocracy which Horace admired and would later try to imitate. 'Heil Hitler!' shouted Harry from his work at a lathe. 'He's here, mates! Black shirts and double-pay for everybody!'

What seemed like seconds later there came the tinkle of glass. Ernie Trigg was already running for the door leading to the labs.

Uncle Tom's Cabin was a general-purpose soundproof cabin in the electronics lab upstairs; it was made of thick hardboard and lined in its cavity walls with sawdust and wood shavings. Later, papier-mâché egg-boxes were to become popular for soundproofing.

When Horace was called in to clear up the débris there was nothing left of the cathode-ray tube which Doctor Tischler had

69

been working on. There was the glint of buried glass in walls, floor and ceiling; the last tinkle of sound had been the gun of the tube (the neck, containing the heavy hardware of cathode, accelerator plates and magnetic deflecting coils) shooting through the double wall, across the lab and out by way of a large pane of glass of the lab window to land on the concrete below.

'Har, har, har!' W. B. Barclay was roaring with delight.

Apparently the explosion (or, rather, implosion) had proved one of his theories; he held extravagant theories quite extraneous to the accepted canons of engineering or applied science. Over this one Carl Brockelberg was giving him two and sixpence in settlement of a bet.

'Baird was right,' the chief engineer cried, delightedly. 'They should have settled for the mirror drum. Once they get these things into domestic television families will be wiped out all over the country — bloody funny. Har har har!'

Doctor Tischler, who had been tending the tube two minutes before it blew up (or, blew in), was not terribly amused. He sat by the bench sipping warm sweet tea and held his feet up for Horace to sweep underneath.

'They'll put a piece of bullet-proof glass in front of the screen,' Brockelberg surmised.

'Ye gods!' W. B. Barclay said. 'What a way to be entertained!'

The accident was due to the temperature and humidity inside the cabin. While Horace was still picking bits of glass out of the walls with tweezers, Ernie Trigg was called in to arrange some kind of ventilation.

'Just a hole in the ceiling, a fan, a pipe across the lab, down through the plating shop and into the open air — that's all,' W. B. Barclay said.

It was his style to design anything for anything in five seconds.

'I'll get Harry Webb on it,' Ernie said.

'How long?' the chief engineer asked. It was his favourite question.

'Oh — three days,' Ernie said; it was his favourite answer.

'Three dayeeeees!' cried W. B. Barclay in his famous Harry Tate voice.

It echoed through the building and sailed out over the zigzag

roofs of the factory acres and across the churchyard into Chapel
Lane and kept Horace's world smiling and happy.

'That old Jewboy should've been blown up,' Harry Webb
told Horace, bitterly.
'Why?' Horace asked.
They were working for Tischler and Harry objected to it;
they were running the ventilation pipe across the plating shop
and out through the wall.
Harry said: 'Don't you know? No, of course you bloody
don't. Long as you get your quid a week. Bloody yids. For every
quid you make they make five. That don't worry you, does it?
I tell you what Doctor Bloody Tischler is — he's anti-Nazi.'
'Are you sure?' Horace asked. It sounded ugly.
'Another thing is his name's not Tischler.'
'Oh?'
'It's something else. Hazel noticed that,' Harry said.
'Hazel Springer?' Horace said.
Harry Webb turned from sealing a join in the pipe with
Bostik. 'You go up to him, sudden like, and say: "Doctor
Tischler!" — like that. He turns round to see if somebody else
is there. He always does it. Hazel noticed when she took his tea
up. He's stolen that name from somebody else. The real Doctor
Tischler.'
Horace said: 'It's probably to protect his family. They're still
in Austria.'
'Mind the acid bath,' Harry said, walking carefully on the
duckboards around the big tanks. 'Don't breathe the fumes.'
'You going to be long, Harry?' one of the platers asked. 'I've
got to swill this floor down.'
Horace was pondering what had been said about Hazel. Did it
mean that Hazel and Harry used to have political conversations
together? Did it mean that Hazel did steal that bit of Tischler's
book with — yes! That was it! It had his real name and address
in it. Anybody knowing that could inform the Germans and have
his family arrested. No wonder the old boy was upset. But Hazel
wouldn't do a thing like that. Harry would, though — if he
thought Tischler was anti-Nazi.
'It was the Jews who stabbed the German Army in the back

71

in 1918,' Harry was saying now. ' Sold 'em out to the Russians and the Allies. Do you know what for? Money — what else? '

' Gosh,' Horace said.

He knew what Nazis were, but what were anti-Nazis? Something far worse, surely? And what about ABL and J.J. and H.R. and all the others in Hazel's diary — which side were they on?

And where did they meet?

Horace was becoming increasingly certain that Hazel had been murdered.

Saturday afternoon Horace went again to Parkers Piece. Did it take a possessive apostrophe or not — he never knew. The neat and big square of grass in the middle of the town held many associations for Horace. Skipping on Good Friday mornings, for instance; not just kids but the whole town, parents, dignitaries, university dons. He'd seen Jack Hobbs and Duleepsinji batting here in the corner by Warkworth Terrace. He'd played cricket here with Neville and Jammy, Leslie Smith, Dusty Miller; he'd flown innumerable model aeroplanes with varying success and always alone — it was a solo business, for most of the spectacular flights and stunts were in the mind.

He left his bicycle by the railings, the green railings which were to go for war material and never be replaced. He walked from Gonville Place across to the centre lamps and then on to the tea pavilion by the University Arms Hotel. A few children playing, a few dogs playing, a few people lying on the grass. No real crowds, no airship, no cricket, no old Charles or Perse blazers — no girl in pink spotted ribbon. *Hazel! You know — at work!* Horace sniffed at the memory. It was jolly sad.

My life a hell you're making, he thought. *You know I'm yours for just the taking. . . .* And the Coleman Hawkins tenor bit.

Horace followed the ghost again through the town : Regent Street, St Andrews Street, Petty Cury, K.P. (Kings Parade), Trumpington Street, Lensfield Road, Hills Road, Bateman Street. *The Botanical Gardens . . .*

Nothing.

Just a blister on his heel where his swollen bursa rubbed on the sock gathered together with cotton. When he got back to Gonville Place his bike had gone.

Oh no, it hadn't gone! There it was, somebody had just shifted it to the other side of the tree, changed it from a Hercules to a B.S.A. with a Sturmey-Archer three-speed and a different sort of front basket. He rode it away quickly with somebody shouting after him either from the Piece or from his guilty mind.

Sunday.
' I say! Excuse me! '
Two girls going in, looking back.
' Is this the Rhythm Club? '
It was; upstairs over Millers music shop. Where they were going. Ah, yes, well, thanks. He wouldn't go in just yet. For instance, how much did it cost? He should have asked them. He went back into the street. Couldn't hear any music. Lots of bikes across the street by Christ's wall; basket to basket to basket. Few cars; Morris, Trojan, Austin Chubby, Lagonda — blinking millionaires' sons. Lagonda?

Horace crossed the street to look at the Lagonda.

Is this where Charles brought her before taking her home and killing her? No, that wasn't right. The timing was wrong. They had gone for a spin on the Sunday afternoon, then he'd taken her home for some tea. Hazel had popped up for a bath. . . .

Horace went into the Rhythm Club.

' There's that chap with the nice voice,' he heard a girl say from somewhere behind him as he was buying a sixpenny ticket.

' That includes tea and a scone,' the young fellow told him. ' Hazel will get refreshments in the interval — '

' It's not Hazel now,' somebody said. ' Gertie and Stella.'

Of course! *Tea up!* She used to do it here as well.

Horace took a vacant chair next to a Chinese girl in the back row. She smiled at him, then looked towards the front again. It was a long room with about a dozen rows of rush-seated chairs facing a little dais. There was a jazz drum console on the dais covered in oilskin. An Eavestaff mini-piano with the lid down in walnut. There was a big radiogram with a young man fumbling inside it, his expression strained. Everybody was watching him.

' Get on with it! ' somebody called.

' Hurry up, Charles! ' cried a girl.

So this was Charles?

73

The Chinese girl smiled round at Horace: ' It's always doing this.'

' Oh? ' said Horace.

She wasn't Chinese at all. Surprising how many girls looked Chinese in a university town. Pretty as a doll, black short hair, white face, dark almond eyes, tight skirt with a little split up the side showing her leg, four-inch-heel red shoes. She wasn't with anybody, either.

' Cigarette? ' Horace asked her.

' Sorry,' she said. ' Haven't got any.'

Horace blushed; too shy to correct the question. Then she smiled at him again :

' Charles will have some.'

Did this mean she was with Charles now?

Horace wanted to smoke but couldn't very well now without looking mean.

Suddenly the loudspeaker crackled and a great burst of noise as of needle scratching across a record.

' Fuck ! ' said Charles.

Horace could have gone through the floor. He dare not look at the Chinese girl, who was suddenly polishing her long pointed nails. The room had gone as quiet as a dentist's waiting-room. Charles now stood and faced his audience, his long face carved by a self-conscious grin.

' Frightfully sorry about that. Well, anyway, good evening. My name is Charles Baldwin, as some of you have good reason to know — '

Laughter and clapping and the tension easing as he got his audience with him. Horace was astonished. Charles Baldwin? He was the Prime Minister's son ! Surely he couldn't be an anti-Nazi? You couldn't even expect him to be a Nazi. As for gassing Hazel, that would soon be hushed up once they knew who did it.

Well, they wouldn't hush Horace up. From what he had pieced together from Hazel, from W. B. Barclay, Brockelberg, Tischler, Sergeant Polsworth and Harry Webb, Horace planned to go home and, working through the night, write a full-length and fearless exposé on the death of Hazel Springer; like the one running at the moment in *Passing Show* on Jim Mollison and Amy Johnson. Tea and scones, fast Lagonda cars, rhythm clubs, anti-Nazis. And right in the very last line reveal that it has been written by a talking cat, like Saki's *Tobermory*, who saw and heard everything.

He worked it all out in his mind, sent it off and had it rejected practically by return of post.

Charles Baldwin was saying:

' Parlophone have just issued this fine album of Red Nichols' Five Pennies — the finest of the lot in my opinion being *Bugle Call* backed by *Backbeats*. Listen to the absolutely spiffin' clarinet solo by Jimmy Dorsey. I've just scratched it to bits with this rotten soundbox of yours.'

Laughter and shouts of ' Hard luck.'

' I'm going to play that side first,' Charles went on, ' then tell you a little about the line-up. Perhaps by the time you've heard it you'll be able to tell me something about it — but no cheating. Anybody who read Leonard Feather in the *Melody Maker* last week — just keep quiet. Okay? '

Charles put on the record, then stood back and closed his eyes.

The Chinese girl leaned towards Horace and whispered: ' Eddie Lang and Joe Venuti are in this! '

' Who? ' Horace said.

Charles opened his eyes and rapped: ' Chloe! I heard that! '

The needle was still on the bit before the music starts; everybody turned round and looked at them, laughing. Chloe covered her face with her hand in shame. Then suddenly it began — brass reed and string and percussion in solid ensemble playing with an off-beat rhythm. It was music like nothing Horace had ever heard before; it did to him even in the first few bars what William Blake had done with his writing; it started his heart beating faster, stirred him into a strange kind of involved sadness. The players as they took their inspired solos, Miff Mole on trombone, Red Nichols on trumpet, Eddie Lang on guitar (it might have been Carl Kress), coming to life as people, their instruments things of real brass and wood with the light gleaming on them and spittle running down. What could have put such sad, beautiful, exhilarating thoughts into their minds and how could such individual and wayward voices combine and mingle and interlock with the single glowing spirit of the piece?

These were not the words in Horace's mind at that moment

75

for he had not got words yet; what happened happened in his blood. As through a trance he heard the records being played and sometimes Charles's voice.

' For jazz is a genuine thing and genuine things have fallen on evil times. Real jazz, which you are hearing now, is the human spirit in revolt against poverty and despair. It rides highest where the human condition is lowest. . . .'

Yes, yes, Horace was thinking. Yes, yes, yes. It was music and rhythm that touched his Red Romsey roots and perhaps something much more distant than that; something among his ancestors. In the discussions that followed the music with the scones and tea, Horace began to learn something about the background and the people of jazz; began to search for some secret hidden affinities with the slums of Chicago and the smells of Storyville.

' You're enjoying it, aren't you? ' Chloe said as they sipped hot tea together with *Riverboat Shuffle* as accompaniment.

Horace couldn't reply because, once again, he couldn't think of a word beautiful enough.

' You're not going across the common, are you? ' Chloe asked him as he got her coat for her at the end. ' I hate walking across that common in the dark.'

Horace left his bicycle where it was; he could find another one tomorrow. He would not find another Chloe tomorrow. He would not feel tomorrow the way he felt now. What the boys had been talking about for years was now going to happen. For the first time in his life Horace wanted a woman and he wanted Chloe. He had been sickening for this ever since his voice dropped and now it had happened.

His physical need had already communicated itself to her and the jazz had taken down the barriers.

' Shall we have a little rest? ' Chloe asked as they passed a small railed-off section of the common reserved for children.

They lay in the grass in the pitch blackness by the swings and they could see traffic passing along Victoria Avenue.

' I'll do it,' she said, helpfully, when his hand wandered under her clothes.

As the Catholic clock struck a quarter past eleven, Horace became a man. ' Oh my God, oh my God,' he kept saying as it happened. 'This is wonderful. Oh my God.'

Chloe was crying happily, as she always did.

Doctor Tischler was sitting, also crying, with a Ham Radio friend in Milton Road, G5KO, who had recently read him a coded message from a friend in Germany to the effect that his wife and two children had been sent to a concentration camp at a place called Dachau.

'It's probably a kind of Butlin's,' the friend said.

Chapter Twelve

There was a moment in the mornings when the Fentons met briefly in the kitchen. Rhoda came down first, put the gas oven on and made a cup of tea in peculiar style : six spoonfuls of tea in the hot pot, then three inches of boiling water to make a kind of concentrated essence. After three minutes she put in the rest of the water. Her tea was so strong that the others could use an inch of it in the bottom of their cups filled with boiling water and it was still strong tea. They'd all been brought up on Brooke Bond tea; they had had it in their bottles while Rhoda was busy in the Disabled Soldiers' Club.

This moment of togetherness enabled them to swap cryptic information about themselves.

'We're going to get married in October at Arbury Road Baptist Chapel,' Christine told them.

'The Probation Officer's homosexual,' Leslie told them. He was right about that; Horace had to fight a rearguard action later, though the officer was much liked and was good with the boys. He used to abbreviate their names; Horace was Ho Fen to him and Leslie was Les Mor (later Whate).

Horace said : ' I had sexual intercourse last night.'

Christine said : ' None of my friends, I hope? '

And Rhoda said : ' Is your winkle all right? Your father had terrible trouble with his winkle. Because he wasn't circumcised.'

' I'm going to be a famous guitarist,' Horace said then, hoping for a better response.

Ronald had his usual enclosed expression as he ate his bread and milk; you never knew whether he was stupid or absorbed.

' Does that mean you won't be doing any more writing? ' Rhoda asked. When Horace had his writing spells she had to sit up half the night translating his handwriting into her businesslike strokes before it went off to Collins for typing at twopence a thousand words. There was a tea-chest full of it in the tool-shed, gradually being eaten by mice.

Rhoda was in fact quite relieved that Horace had a deep voice now and had started going with girls. There was a time when she was worried about him and had written to *John Bull* for advice. This was after she had been up to the compost heap to empty the teapot and caught sight of Mr Goodchild next door at his bedroom window watching Horace sunbathe in his swimming trunks on the lawn. Also his tuberculosis seemed to have cleared up since he stopped locking his bedroom door.

Ernie Trigg responded more encouragingly than anybody else to Horace's musical ambitions. Later, when Horace Spurgeon Fenton played with the University Quinc Jazz Band at the Arts Theatre Jazz Concert, Ernie Trigg and old Ted Wright were there in the expensive seats clapping his one four-bar break. Ernie, being a frustrated entertainer, was particularly anxious to inspire Horace to do what he had failed to do.

' You don't want this humdrum engineering life,' he told Horace. ' You're not cut out for it. Look at this — ' He picked up Horace's first proud attempt at a blue-steel set-square like the ones Ted Wright had showed him; he had spent hours perfecting it. ' Rubbish,' Ernie said, throwing it across the model shop into the scrap bin as if it was the greatest compliment he could pay Horace. ' Confidentially,' he went on, lowering his voice, ' it's taken all my persuasion to keep you working in here — Barclay wanted to put you into production. You get a guitar and I'll give you some lessons. Even your face is good — people laugh just looking at you.'

' Can you play the guitar, then? ' Horace asked.

' I should think so,' Ernie said. ' I can play the uke. Shouldn't be too difficult.' The work was piling up and people were calling for him but Horace had fired all his enthusiasms for show business again; he kept signing requisitions without looking at them and giving people short answers and permission for time off without even listening to them. ' We could form a quartet. The Ernie Trigg Blue Four — remember the Eddie Lang/Joe Venuti Blue Four? '

' Do you know about them? I didn't know you knew about them. Eddie Lang went round accompanying Bing Crosby — all the singers used him. He and Joe Venuti used to play on the doorsteps for the neighbours when they went home to Phila-

79

delphia. Of course, they were famous then.'

' Pity he died,' Ernie said.

' Who? '

' Eddie Lang — two or three years ago. Overwork, pneumonia, one-night stands.'

Horace didn't know he was dead. He felt immeasurably depressed. He had already planned to include Eddie Lang in the texture of his life and times when he got back to his writing; when he'd discovered the elusive trick. Eddie Lang was dead and he'd only discovered him last night. It made Horace more determined than ever to get a guitar and learn to create the same blue joy.

In his Red Romsey boyhood the only place for musical instruments had been The Wild Man From Borneo at the top of Thoday Street. It wasn't a real shop; it was the front bay-windowed room of a yellow-brick terraced house, well coated with LNER smoke. The window was a mixture of yellowing sheet music of *Monastery Garden* vintage, ancient violins without strings, old mandolins, piano tutors and miscellaneous musical rubbish. A big black-and-white cat sat in the middle of it all, looking out at passers-by.

The Wild Man was a big old man with a hooked nose and deep-set eyes, his hair just a fuzz sticking out at the sides, bald on top. All that kept him in touch with the thirties was a stock of gramophone needles, though Horace had also bought from him things like jews' harps and kalamazoos — things that you buzzed through as with tissue paper and a comb. Once in the shop, however, the old man would keep you talking for hours if he could.

' Now you see that? That is a three-string bass. It used to be played in a church. It's worth £300. How old are you? Ah, well, this was before your time, but when I conducted the orchestra in Boston — that's in America, you understand? — we once performed before the last Red Indian chief to hold office. I suppose there were fifty of us. In the middle of — oh, I forget what it was we were playing — this Red Indian chief came up onto the rostrum and started banging the tympani. You know what a tympani is? He was sending a message! Like borrowing the

80

telephone. How old are you? '

He would always make certain that you were not old enough to contradict him.

' A guitar? What sort of guitar? ' he said when Horace came in with his request. ' Do you know how many different kinds of guitar there are? Now let me show you something. How old are you? '

Horace realised that he had made a mistake coming back here. He managed to get out after half an hour, narrowly avoiding the purchase of an old stringless mandolin which he had almost been talked into buying when he was eleven.

' Now that's the instrument you must learn to play. With a mandolin you can lead the orchestra — did you know that? How old are you? ' Oh yes, and he said, which nearly did the trick, so flattering was it : ' They're not guitar fingers. You've got mandolin fingers there.'

On Horace's second visit to the Rhythm Club there was a live concert featuring with the club band two star performers, Duncan Whyte and a coloured pianist Gerry Moore (not to be confused with Gerald Moore the great accompanist). Charles was this week organising the tea and scones in the annexe room.

'Mr Baldwin? ' Horace said.

Charles turned round quite slowly, seemed to think about smiling before smiling; and then having smiled folded his arms as though to wait. There was something very satirical about him which amused Horace.

' Charles,' said Charles. ' Everybody calls me Charles. My old man hogs the Baldwin bit.'

So he *was* the Prime Minister's son! Or was the Prime Minister Ramsay MacDonald?

' I heard your recital last week,' Horace said.

Charles's face lit up with unrehearsed pleasure : ' *Did* you! How jolly nice. Out at the King's Head? '

' Where? ' Horace said.

' Girton? My poetry thing? *God let me pack and take a train I'm fed up with this fucking rain!* It was a take-off of the Golden Boy — '

' I mean here,' Horace told him, apologetically. ' Red Nichols'

81

Five Pennies.'

'Oh, *that*. I've gone on to the Duke now — I suppose you don't want ten perfectly new Parlophone records?'

'Wish I could. Can't afford it. I'm taking up the guitar —'

'Do you mind if I sort of split these scones while you're talking? Do go on.' He seemed to use his whole great lanky body over the breadboard, writhing about over each scone in turn, his big face coming round now and then: 'Where're you at?'

It struck Horace that Charles thought he was talking to a university man; better to mention night school than the wireless factory.

'Tech Col,' Horace said, taking a leaf from the Probation Officer's book. 'Elec and Mag.' And improving as he went on: 'Horace Spurgeon-Fenton.'

'Oh? Hyphers! Good show.' Then Charles's broad good humour closed into a thunderous cloud of thought: 'I say! Not little Horry Fenton? Weren't you a friend of young Hazel?'

'Oh,' said Horace. 'Yes. I did know her. Slightly.'

'She always thought you were *terribly* funny,' Charles said, giving Horace a fresh glance to see why. 'What a sad, tragic, abysmally awful thing to happen!' he said, splitting open a scone on each adjective.

Horace had forgotten all about Hazel until now.

He said with, therefore, more compassion: 'Yes, it was. Horrible. She was a jolly nice girl.'

'Pity she got caught up with that BUF rabble.'

'I thought it was GFS?'

'That's what she told people. I blame those rats at Leys.'

'Not Perse?' Horace said. No, of course it was Leys! He realised now that blazer at the Botanical had been Leys. Now he'd sent Neville to the wrong school with that photo. Not that anything had come of it.

'No, no. Perse are all right. I was at Perse. Leftish, most of us.' He had grown thoughtful as he cut the scones, as though pondering something; now he turned to Horace, the point of the knife almost going into his chest: 'Did you have anything to do with poor Hazel's death? I shall have to stab you if you don't tell me the absolute jolly truth.' His face had gone darkly red and the knife was trembling.

82

'What?' was all Horace could think of to say. The quintet had started up in the main room and there was little chance of rescue.

Charles said, bringing the knife to press into Horace's Fifty-Shilling suit: 'You kept trying to take her somewhere. Cherry-hinton or some such place. Through the tin walks and so on. Up the Spinney — why?'

'Only for a walk! Just for a walk!'

'Oh, splendid,' Charles said, and he got on with slicing the scones. 'You must forgive all that. I've been checking up on everybody.'

'So've I,' Horace said. 'I thought it was you!'

Charles stopped slicing and looked at him. 'Well, I'm jiggered,' he said.

'Do you know about the photograph?' Horace asked him.

He told Charles about the unsigned picture by the girl's bed and his efforts to discover who it could be.

'I'll get it published in *The Review*,' Charles said. 'I'm some kind of editor there,' he added, vaguely.

The girl who last week had commented on Horace's lovely voice now popped in, holding a cigarette in a long holder: 'Charles, are you coming or aren't you? Oh, hello,' she said to Horace.

'Take over here, Horry — do you know Claire?' He gave Horace the knife. 'I'm on the bass tonight.'

'I'll butter for you,' Claire told Horace.

And then they were alone together, Horace feeling happy and domestic and rather excited. The boom boom boom of the string bass joined the lower harmonies of *My Baby Went Away*.

'Ta,' Claire said, taking another scone.

Horace, having rehearsed something at last, said: 'And where do you work?'

'I'm at Newnham,' she said. 'I'm going to be a doctor. What about you?'

'Writer,' Horace said, off-handedly.

It was the truth. Schoolboy, office-boy, butcher-boy and shop-boy — he had always been a writer.

'What will you write about me?' Claire said.

She smiled at him and wiped a wisp of hair off her forehead

with the back of her hand because she had margarine on her fingers. Horace fell desperately in love with her.

He didn't reply because he couldn't think of a word beautiful enough.

' By the way,' she said. ' Chloe told me to tell you her fiancé's here tonight — whatever that means.'

' Oh? Right-o,' Horace said.

And he could tell that she knew what it meant; knew that he was a man. And he thought : *Fiancé!* Do people really do that sort of thing to other people? And with strangers too. It made him feel very sad. Claire misinterpreted this in relation to her message.

' Coming back for a waffle? ' she asked him.

' For a waffle? '

' I'm very good at it,' she said. ' Charles's place. Jesus Lane. He'll probably give you a lift.'

' I've got my bike,' Horace said.

He now had a Humber with butterfly handlebars.

And she said : ' Has anyone ever told you — you have a very attractive voice.'

Horace was at first modest about it but then, remembering that she was a medical student, told her about the accident.

' Oh dear,' she said. ' Can I feel it? '

She grasped his Adam's apple and wiggled it a little.

' Hello, what goes on? ' Charles had come back, the number over. Doctor and patient ignored him.

' You know,' Claire told Horace seriously, ' that could turn to cancer in later life.'

' What later life? ' Charles said, taking and munching a buttered scone. ' We're all going to be killed in Hitler's war.'

Although smiling, his long face had a strangely knowledgeable look which didn't go with buttered scones or long cigarette holders or waffles.

84

Chapter Thirteen

' What's BUF stand for? ' Horace asked Ernie Trigg.

' Buff,' said Ernie. ' This is a buff.'

It wasn't that buff. Horace had used that buff to polish the brass of a beautiful toasting fork he had made with an also beautifully turned and buffed ebonite handle which now hung beside the fireplace at home.

Horace said: ' I think it's some kind of organisation. Something you belong to.'

' He means The Buffs,' Dirty Dick called across. ' It's a regiment in the Army.'

Horace didn't think it was that, either; he couldn't imagine Hazel belonging to that.

' You're ignorant,' said Ted Wright, meaning the whole model shop with the exception of Harry Webb who was still ventilating Uncle Tom's Cabin for Doctor Tischler. ' The Buffs is a Rotary club,' Ted said. ' Short for The Buffaloes. The Ancient Order of Buffaloes. Anybody seen my three-eighth reamer? '

As Ted went round the shop knocking things flying and crashing to the floor, which was the accepted ritual when a missing tool was holding up some skilled piece of work, Ernie Trigg came over to Horace's bench.

' Why? ' he said.

' Oh, nothing,' Horace said.

' You're not writing again, are you? You know that's no good without a college education. What about this guitar? '

Horace, who had a kind of obligation to Ernie now to make good in show business, told him the difficulties. The only way he could get a decent guitar was on hire-purchase.

' You should have said,' the foreman told him. ' I'll tell you where to go. J. A. Davis — that's where I got my ukelele banjo. Eleven and ninepence altogether — I paid a shilling every fortnight.'

' They're no good,' Horace said, though he didn't want to hurt Ernie's feelings. ' Not for guitars.' He knew J. A. Davis — who

85

didn't? They advertised in *The Magnet* and every other boys' magazine. The cheapest decent instrument he could get was the lowest-priced Epiphone from Moore's in Bridge Street. It was the Olympic at twelve pounds — nearly three times as much as a new bike. 'A pound a month for twelve months.'

Ernie said : 'You could get a Gibson for that.'

You couldn't get a Gibson for that; a Gibson cost more.

'Eddie Lang played a Gibson,' Ernie Trigg said. 'You ought to have a Gibson.' He wanted Horace to have the best; he could see a little five-piece outfit down at The Barn at Fen Ditton, sounding something like Django Reinhardt et le Quintette du Hot Club de France. 'Listen to this,' he said then, his imagination soaring again : 'What's this?'

He had picked up a length of gas-piping which Horace was fashioning into an instrument rack and he played a very soulful trombone rendering of *Confessin'*, reaching high with the imaginary slide for the high notes and digging deep for the low notes.

'Trigg!' W. B. Barclay had the endearing habit of shouting a name and then turning away and scratching his behind so's not to see anybody doing anything they shouldn't.

'Yes, well, get these pipes unblocked,' Ernie told Horace. 'We'll talk about the other later on. I've got a good idea.'

He did a little soft-shoe shuffle across to the chief engineer, undulating his hips like Step'n Fetchit.

Ernie Trigg survived the war and the last anyone heard took a boarding-house on the North Sea coast at Cromer. There is a talent greater than other talents and that is the talent for enjoying talent and impersonating talent and carrying talent to those who are unaware of it. Ernie's fate as an hotelier was not the happiest but not the saddest either, for he was content with a small audience.

Ernie's good idea involved Horace in three nights a week overtime on a capstan lathe in the machine shop to pay the instalments on the new Epiphone guitar and for a weekly lesson with Miss Fiske in St Barnabas Road. But once again Horace had come to the wrong place.

'You don't use a plectrum on the guitar,' Miss Fiske told him.

'To use a plectrum on the guitar is sacrilege. If you want to use a plectrum you must learn the mandolin.'

Horace felt he would be very lucky if he escaped being a mandolinist. She was an elderly, whiskered lady who taught the piano and violin as well. She insisted that Horace held the guitar in the classical manner — this is sitting up straight on a low stool with the knees apart and holding the fattest part of the instrument between the legs so that the neck and fingerboard project far away to the left — it made it impossible, with the Epiphone, a compact, punchy instrument with a long, rakish, slightly curved fingerboard made for slogging in a dance band held upright or tucked well back under the right arm, even to reach the lower frets with the left-hand fingers.

'That is not important at this stage,' Miss Fiske told him. 'For the first two weeks we shall concentrate on open-string exercises.'

And to show him how he could, with hard practice, be playing when he was as old as she was, she played him Mendelssohn's *Spring Song*.

It depressed Horace.

'Wotcher, Horry!'

'Wotcher, Nev.'

To avoid getting off his machine, which is something you didn't do until you actually went to bed, practically, Neville Hampstead had cycled up onto the pavement and come to rest with one foot on each gatepost.

'Off that,' Detective-Sergeant Polsworth said, sternly. 'That's an offence.'

Neville couldn't take this in, so he said to Horace: 'I've got that photo back.'

'Not here,' Horace said.

He was so anxious to get Neville away quickly that he walked up the road carrying a garden rake and a handful of twitchweed. Neville rode along in the gutter by moving his pedals to and fro in little jerks, just enough to take up the chain slack and keep the bike in motion.

'Who's that?' he asked when they were at a safe distance. 'Not your mother's second husband?'

Horace was dropping the twitchweed on a drain by the kerb and trying to push it through the slots with his shoe, but it wouldn't go. He explained to Neville about Stan marrying Chris and coming to live with them in the front bedroom. Stan was already organising his prize chrysanthemums and Horace was having to clear out his rather original arrangement of asparagus, anemones and purple-sprouting broccoli. Stan thought he was mad putting vegetables in the front garden.

' They're not vegetables,' Horace told him. ' It's a pattern.'

' I sent you to the wrong school,' Horace told Neville now. ' It was Leys.'

' He doesn't go to either,' Neville said. He took the photograph from his pocket and gave it to Horace. ' I've had it identified.'

' Well, go on ! ' Horace told him.

' It's Frank Lacteen,' Neville said.

' Oh? Is he an anti-Nazi? '

' He's a Hollywood actor. Plays these mad killer parts. You remember — *The House Without a Key?* '

Horace remembered; gosh, that was an old film. They'd been living in Burwell. It's where the brick had come through the window late at night and Rhoda had trailed them all down to PC Wray's house in The Causeway in their night-clothes. *The House Without a Key* was a serial run at the Gardiner Memorial Hall Saturday afternoons; they put the projector in the men's lavatory and shone the beam through the hole in the wall.

' That was a silent,' Horace said. It was a South Sea Island drama; Frank Lacteen had paddled about the lagoons at night in an out-rigger canoe. Some people said he looked like Ronald. ' Why would he want to kill Hazel Springer? ' Horace said then. ' Perhaps he's out of work now with talkies? '

The lab boy found nuclear physics less baffling than Horace Fenton. Soon, they wouldn't see each other any more. Horace was already whistling something, his interest in the picture waning.

Neville explained : ' It's a pin-up picture. Girls send away for them and put them beside their bed. My sister's got one of James Cagney. It's signed : " With love to Dorothy from Jimmy ".'

Horace said : ' This one's not signed.'

' Well, it's him, anyway. Danvers-Walker recognised it. He's the president of the Perse Film Society. It's definitely Frank Lacteen. Hazel must have written to Hollywood for it.'

Horace gave the picture one more glance before putting it away. It was a pale, thin, intense face, clean-shaven, dark hair smarmed down; somebody too serious and too occupied to want anything as frivolous as a picture taken of himself. It was the face of a failed artist.

Had one wealthy Austrian Jew bought one of the young and dedicated Hitler's paintings, it might have saved ten million lives.

Chapter Fourteen

Odd that Neville had mistaken Stan Polsworth for Rhoda's second husband, because quite suddenly Monty Morden (or Bernard Whateley) turned up.

Rhoda always knew he would.

' When you're all old enough to earn he'll come on us and expect us to keep him,' she used to say.

She hadn't said it lately because even with them all earning there wasn't enough left over to keep a cat. The increasing cost of living kept accurate pace with every extra penny that came in; the subsidised council house rents had recently been adjusted upwards to eight shillings and ninepence a week.

' What do you want? ' Rhoda said.

' I'm Monty,' Monty said.

' I know you're Monty,' she said. ' You're not coming in.' She called over her shoulder : ' Horace ! '

' How's little Horace? ' Monty asked, warmly.

In twelve years he had not changed by so much as a grey hair or a wrinkle; he stood there in all his brutish army cleanliness, boots polished, khaki puttees gathering a pair of old brown left-off trousers from knee to ankle, a leather fairground jacket, face pink and optimistic, hair cropped, ears spooned out, his body leaning back against the spin of some imaginary merry-go-round; on a stationary doorstep there was a tendency to overbalance and he had to grasp the doorpost for a moment.

' Are you ill? ' Rhoda asked him.

He said, swift as ever : ' I ain't eaten for three days, gal.' It was an East Anglian voice; Leslie was getting it.

' I'll get you some kettle broth,' Rhoda said, ' then you must go.'

She had forgotten how uneducated and uncouth he was; forgotten how desperately she had needed a man's hardness, no matter what. How ignorant and innocent and wanton she must have been. No wonder the Dayballs had cut her off.

Monty was a gypsy !

They all met him and looked at him and listened to him and exorcised the twelve years' haunting. They were all, with the exception of Ronald, as big as or bigger than Monty was and the power was on the other foot. They could very nearly feel sorry for him. Especially when Rhoda began cross-examining him on the list of atrocities.

'What were you doing in Burwell in 1925?'

Monty was in prison in 1925; she had been saving the threat of prison to force a confession from him about the bigamous marriage, but he had already been caught and had served two years for that old robbery.

'What about that black man you murdered in Cardiff?'

'What? Oh, that. That were old flash, dear. I like to see you all agog — rare pretty you were. And still are.'

He had his arm round the back of her chair and had one smoky finger rubbing the nape of her neck, which had always worked before.

'Don't leave me alone with him,' Rhoda told the children when Monty had gone out to 'slash' as he called it.

'Stan's coming at seven,' Christine said.

'Perhaps we can get him to arrest him,' Rhoda said.

Horace said : 'What for?'

'We'll think of something,' Rhoda said. And she said : 'What about knocking you off your bike? Couldn't you identify him?'

Horace had been unable to identify himself for weeks. The job at Winton Smith's, the butchers and cooked meats shop, had not only given him the head trouble, the awful dizziness and sickness any time his head came off the pillow while he was asleep, but it had also given him lifelong claustrophobia; he had been locked in the refrigerator with Miss Nightingale. It was his job to take all the unsold meat from the shop on Mill Road to the factory refrigerators in East Road; it was Miss Nightingale's job to stay late and check it in. Somebody had slammed the door on them and the light had gone out. After incurable damage had been done to Horace's psychology Miss Nightingale had the bright idea of taking off one of her high-heeled shoes and banging the ice pipes.

'What happened in there?' everybody wanted to know.

'She missed him and hit the pipes,' Mr Barlow said, pretending that Horace was capable of attacking a woman.

Mr Barlow seemed to hate him; hate his pretty lips and high, musical voice and sensitive ways; hated that Horace was inclined to weep if grumbled at. He gave Horace all kinds of ugly, dirty and miserable jobs. If it was a bright, sunny day, just right for a ride out to the country with Mrs Bagley's Wednesday chops, he would send Horace down to the dark, dank stone cellar to make a brine for the beef and pork in the stone sinks, mixing the salt and saltpetre and water. If it was a pouring wet day he would send Horace pedalling seven miles out to Barrington with cat's lights.

'And move those feet round, fuck-pig,' he used to say. He always called Horace ' Fuck-pig '.

To the customers he smiled and when they asked him how he was always said : ' Not too bad for an old gentleman.'

But he didn't consider himself an old gentleman. On Thursday afternoons, which is not early-closing in cooked meats, he was visited by two prostitutes; he would sit in his little office at the end of the counter with them and eat cream cakes which Horace had to go out and buy; then he took them down the brine cellar onto a bed of dry ice and sawdust sacks. It was the only time he allowed Horace to serve behind the counter.

One day he sent Horace to a house in Great Eastern Street with a letter. It was a very scruffy, smoke-blackened house backing onto the main railway line and the back door was open. As Horace stood there awaiting a reply to his knocking he saw mice running backwards and forwards along the water pipes in the scullery. It was one of the prostitutes who answered the door and read the letter and then angrily slammed the door in Horace's face at his polite inquiry as to whether there was any reply.

'They've given me a dose,' Mr Barlow told him when he got back.

Other errand-boys had told Horace what a ' dose ' was and had also explained to him about prostitutes; particularly Bentley's boy from the butcher's next to The Playhouse cinema.

' If it wasn't for women like that,' he said, in one of their bicycle conferences, ' the world would be full of sexual criminals.'

It was one of the things Horace was going to try to remember to write down somewhere.

' Do you know what they did to me? ' Mr Barlow said to Horace after he'd been to Addenbrookes Hospital. ' They tied me down and shot hot mercury up my cock.'

Horace was appalled; he never mentioned any of this to his family.

They gave Monty a drink at the Yorkshire Grey, then took him down to Drummer Street and put him on a bus to join Thurston's fair at Soham.

' I'll come back end o' the season, ol' darling,' he promised Rhoda.

' We'll have to move! ' Rhoda told the children that night.

Chapter Fifteen

' Fran! I say, Fran! Over here! '

Pock! Pock! Pock! Pock!

The barking of a dog, the sound of distant geese, the chiming of a church clock, a gramophone passing on a punt and Jack Buchanan singing *Goodnight Vienna*. A multitude of summer voices, men, women, girls, children, in grassy confusion, wind in the willows above, the council cutter chuffeting away again, the splash of oars.

Pock! Pock! Pock!

' Peregrine! '

Peregrine? Horace thought. God almighty.

He was floating in the water with his eyes closed. Floating on his back, the sun and sky, the low willow fronds, the muscular things he did with his eyeballs making coloured patterns shift around, making tiny spots dance, shooting little bullets in the blood this way and that.

' Mind that chap with your punt pole — '

No, Horace refused to open his eyes until his head touched the opposite bank; that's what he had promised himself. And he was dying to know what the pock pock pock was. The pattern changed to purple tinged with yellow as the sun completely emerged, fell warm on his face, belly, toes. He was good at floating but he could not swim. If he moved a muscle he sank. He had pushed himself off from the side and wanted to see if the momentum would carry him across.

Quite suddenly a hand grabbed Horace's ankle and pulled him down.

' Let go! ' Horace cried.

Next instant he was under, sniffing in horrible water, threshing to regain his feet and then to his horror discovering that he was out of his depth. The hand had gone and so had the world. For a moment his face came above the surface but he saw nothing through his water-logged eyelashes. A moment later he was going down again, his feet cycling desperately to find something solid. Then somebody yanked him up by the hair.

'Stop struggling!' a girl said. 'Stop it or I'll let you go!'

Pock! Pock! Pock! Pock!

He heard it still, choking, rubbing the water out of his eyes, feeling now gravelly mud under his feet.

'All right?' the girl said. She was standing next to him and the river came up to her chin. It was Claire. 'I thought you could swim,' she said.

This led Horace to believe that she had pulled him under for a joke and he forced himself to laugh. Water came out.

'Come out and lay on your belly on the grass,' she said. 'You're full of dirty old Cam.'

They got out of the river and onto the grass and nobody noticed the incident, yet it was quite serious. Horace could not talk coherently for ten minutes. Even then the water behind his nose was an agony until the sneezing started and mucus and water streamed over his hands.

'Use this,' Claire said. 'You'll be all right.'

She was offering him her bathing skirt. And as he used the wet blue cotton to blow his nose on she said :

'Good job I was here!'

That was a funny thing to say, he thought. If she hadn't been here it wouldn't have happened.

'Claire!' A girl was trying to heave herself out of the river by bouncing up and down, holding the wooden platform.

'Collect my things,' Claire called. 'I'm taking Horace home.'

'What about the canary?'

'Fuck the canary,' Claire called.

Horace said : 'I'll have to get my clothes.'

'Gertie'll get them for you. You remember Gertie and Stella.'

Two wet girls were smiling down at him. Both wore daring swim suits and rubber hats; one had a freckled familiarity which he associated with the Rhythm Club.

'Find his label,' Gertie said.

'There it is,' said Stella. 'Pinned on his trunks.'

Claire unpinned the locker label from his trunks and then put her arm around him, helping him to rise.

'I feel a bit dizzy,' Horace said.

'He was floating,' Claire explained to her friends. 'Suddenly he went under.'

What a bloody liar, Horace thought. And fancy using that word; swearing like a navvy. You could go off people.

Horace said: ' I'm not going through the streets like this! '

' Chaucer Road, silly,' Claire laughed. ' Over there.'

They were now walking across the bathing green, avoiding the bodies. Horace thought she lived in Jesus Lane but then remembered that that was Charles.

' It wasn't Charles either. I don't know where Charles is. Charles is a mystery.'

' Oh? ' Horace said. ' Where did we have the waffles, then? '

He remembered a big Victorian room full of chatting undergrads, a crippled chap playing a zither and a lot of boring talk about history, politics, music, theses, tripos, badminton, new French films and agricultural research. Horace had pinched one of their bikes and hurried home to write down as much as he could remember for posterity but would probably never use it.

' You didn't take Peregrine's bike, did you? '

' What? '

' He thought you took his bike,' Claire said.

' I walked,' Horace said. ' Over the common and through Banham's boat yard.'

' I told him your father was a policeman,' Claire said. ' That shut him up. That lot don't like the police.'

So she also lied, Horace thought. Horace couldn't bear liars. Then he thought: What lot? And then he thought: Peregrine? Where had he heard that name recently?

' Or was it your uncle? '

' What? '

' Who was a policeman? '

Horace had not told Claire anything about his family. He hadn't had time.

' Or perhaps it was Charles warning the others,' Claire said.

Mind what you say in front of Fenton, Horace thought. His father's a detective. His brother-in-law's a policeman. His uncle's a magistrate.

' They were smoking opium again,' Claire said. ' That was really why.'

' Ah,' said Horace.

96

' And you kept refusing it, if you remember.'

' So I did,' said Horace, dryly. What opium? Where? When?

' That always makes them suspicious. I mean if you don't participate. In Berlin everybody participates.'

' Yes, I know,' Horace said.

Berlin?

' I expect Chloe told you.'

' Chloe? '

So she knew Chloe. Of course she knew Chloe. *Chloe's fiancé's here tonight.* . . . No wonder Claire knew all about him. He had practically disembowelled himself to Chloe on the grass that night.

' She was Franz's first girl friend when he escaped from Heidelberg,' Claire said, chattily. And she said : ' Don't walk on the gravel in your bare feet.'

They had left Coe Fen bathing place, walking tip-toe as people do in bare feet and holding hands; now they crossed the grey gravel and headed for the rougher grass where the horses fed. Beyond were the heavy trees of Chaucer Road and pointed conifers rising from secret gardens. Mansions stood in Chaucer Road and only a select few of those. Exiled kings lived there, or so it was reckoned. Occasionally Horace glanced round hoping for a sight of Gertie or Stella or his trousers.

' You'll like Franz,' Claire told Horace as they entered a laurel drive.

Horace was exceedingly doubtful about liking anybody while he was dressed in blue striped bathing drawers and with his head aching from the river water. Also he didn't like the way they were approaching the front door. Horace was more used to trades-men's entrances. The road itself threw a scare into him. It had *Private Road* and *No Way Through* signboarded at the Trump-ington Road end. As small kids Christine had brought them past many times on the way to their picnics at Byron's Pool. Some-times Leslie, who had an instinct for crime, would run into the road and run out again just to make Christine shout at him. Now here was Horace walking up to a baronial front door almost naked.

' Come on, Horace. What are you waiting for? '

' I can't see the girls with our clothes.'

' You don't need clothes now, we're home.'

She was fitting a key to the lock.

' Is this your house then? '

' Of course not. We share a flat. Stella's father bought it for her. Just for term time.'

They were inside now. It was not built on the scale of a council house with every cubic inch doing its job. You could have driven a pony and trap into the tiled hall. Most of the windows had stained-glass pictures of pilgrims on them.

' Franz! ' Claire called. Then she said : ' Go through that door and introduce yourself. I'm going to put something on. He's rather excitable. At the sight of flesh, I mean. Tell him to give you a drink.'

She vanished through a white door. Horace hesitated for a moment, decided to do a bunk, got halfway back to the front door and was riveted by a voice behind him.

' Don' moof! '

' What? ' Horace turned round and found a young man standing near an open door holding what appeared to be a black revolver. ' I say, now look here,' Horace said.

' Don' moof or I shoot! '

' I'm Horace,' Horace said. ' You must be Franz? '

He had moved and the gun came up, the safety catch came off, the finger tightened on the trigger. It was ridiculous; like something out of *Modern Boy*. The young man was, too, with his skull-like face, owl-glasses, hair cropped almost to baldness like a Martian interrogator.

' Franz! ' Claire's voice came gaily from the part-opened door she had entered. ' What do you think of him? '

Franz swiftly slipped the gun into the pocket of his jacket just before the girl emerged, now wearing a pink-flowered kimono, smiling at the two of them.

' Horace is a writer. Franz is crazy about Goethe,' she explained in mutual introduction.

' I've never spoken to Gertie! ' Horace exclaimed, thinking he had fathomed the reason for the gun. ' I've only met her briefly once before.'

Claire laughed joyously. ' Goethe, not Gertie. He's terribly funny. He's always saying things like that. Gertie and Stella are

98

bringing our clothes. I rescued Horace from drowning. I'll make you some tea.' She was taking them through into a large living room where the floor seemed to be covered in cushions and gramophone records.

Throughout the tea and the social pleasantries and Horace remarking on paintings, sculptures and the view from the window, the gun remained silently bulging between the two young men. Horace had realised that the German student had been unaware of Claire's presence in the house; so who did he think had broken in? And was it a real gun with real bullets? Part of Franz's forbidding silence was forbidding Horace to mention it to Claire. *Excitable*, she had called him. She might be in deadly danger. Whether to warn her or wait and tell Charles about it.

' I think the girls are coming! '

Claire's observation coincided with an outburst of fierce dog barking from somewhere in the gardens. He had heard nothing upon their own arrival.

' And Walter must be back,' she added, as if to explain this. ' Sir Walter Laddick,' she added to Horace. ' Emeritus Professor of Russian. It's really his house. He's ninety-six. That's him up there.' It was a dark oil painting of a pale, wraith-like young man in cap and gown, holding a book. She said : ' I'll show him to you if he's in the garden.'

She made it sound as though Walter was a statue.

' You can change in my room,' Claire then told Horace. ' Just move some of my things.'

She went out and they heard the other girls coming in.

' He is a damn Stalinist! ' Franz now said.

' Are you sure? ' Horace exclaimed.

' He should be shot,' the German youth said.

It gave Horace a chance to mention the gun. ' Is that a real gun? '

' Parn? '

Horace pointed to his pocket. France was wearing an African type bush jacket and the pocket was no longer bulging.

' Your gun,' Horace said again.

' I haf no gun,' Franz said.

He turned his pockets out. He had no gun.

' You've hidden it.'

99

' Parn? '

And then the girls were in the room.

' Come on, Tarzan,' said Stella. ' Get your knickerbockers on.'

As Horace was doing this in Claire's bedroom he overheard the girls recounting what had happened.

' One minute he was floating,' Claire was saying, ' the next he went under, feet first. I had to dive in after him.'

' You should get a medal,' Gertie said.

Horace looked at himself in a gilt-framed Regency dressing mirror. It had only just come to him that it was not Claire who pulled him under at all. It was somebody else. The thought made him giddy and he had to sit on her bed for a moment.

So there was all this for Horace to dwell on. All the pieces for the jigsaw but no idea what the picture might be. Supposing for instance they were all in it? Charles, Claire, Chloe, Gertie — Horace listed them in his story ideas book. Franz, Peregrine and the Jesus Lane Opium Eaters. There was probably no end to them. And who was The Canary?

' What about the canary? '

' Fuck the canary. . . .'

The Master Mind, perhaps? It began to sound more and more like William Le Queux. *Don' moof! Don' moof or I shoot!*

' What are you on about? ' Rhoda had come into his bedroom. He must have spoken the words aloud. ' What about your guitar practice? '

' I've got an idea for a story.' If he told her one small element of what was on his mind she would send for the police. She would also write letters to Hannen Swaffer, *John Bull* and the *Daily Chronicle* at least. At *least*. Horace no longer believed somebody had tried to drown him on Saturday; it was more reasonable that one of the underwater swimmers had been having a lark. Horace knew that he was not guilty of anything. For the most part people liked him.

' Who are those flowers for? '

' What? Oh, a girl. A young lady I know.' This was not going to be enough. ' Claire. I met her at Rhythm Club.'

' All those flowers for one girl! What's she going to do with them — make wine? '

100

Horace had picked all the anemones before Stanley had a chance to dig them in. There were about two hundred blooms ranging the blue to scarlet spectrum in the scullery sink.

' I hope you're not going to get her into trouble.'

' Oh no. No, it's not that one, Mum. This one's a doctor. At least, she will be. She's at Newnham.'

Horace should not have mentioned this. He received a fifteen-minute lecture about going out with girl undergrads. She was not worried about him, she was worried about them. Rhoda had a built-in duty towards the upper classes.

' You could ruin her whole career. Does she know what you do for a living? Where you live? I ought to write to her father.'

' It's nothing like that. I'm helping her at St Thomas's Hall tonight. It's a club for the mentally handicapped. The flowers are for the hall.'

Rhoda's face was full of new alarm. ' Do you mean up Histon Road? They're lunatics! '

' They just play ping-pong.'

Rhoda said, fervently: ' Don't turn your back on one, Horace! '

When Horace had gone out with the flowers cramming his bicycle basket she walked up to the phone box and laid on a squad car to meet him out that night. The terrors in her mind included lunatics, Jews, Negroes, tramps, cripples and gypsies; she had tried to keep her family safe from them all her life.

' He's got a very weak chest,' she explained to the Duty Sergeant.

' We know he has, madam,' said the sergeant.

' Oh, how absolutely thrilling! ' everybody said about the anemones.

' Horace grew them himself,' Claire told them.

' That's the kind of husband I want,' Gertie exclaimed. ' One who'll grow me oodles of lovely flowers.'

What at first amazed Horace was the number of his old school chums who were now mentally handicapped. Organising the games, singing at the piano, swinging skipping ropes with Claire, Horace kept on being mildly embarrassed by the people who hailed him as an old friend. ' Wotcher, Horry! ' ' Hello, old mate. When did you join?' He caught Claire laughing at his confusions.

' Which school was this, then?' she asked him over the tea.

He told her about his mother getting him sent to a special school because of his tuberculosis.

' I didn't know you were tubercular?'

' I wasn't,' Horace told her. ' But she wouldn't let it rest. Took me to see Doctor Phillips eleven times. In the end that's where they sent me.'

Claire said: 'That's not a health school. That's for the retarded. That's why they're all here!'

' Good God,' Horace said.

The thing that shocked him was that in all the time he was there he had never noticed that anybody was dim. Horace had not even been top of his class. A further shock awaited him at going-home time when a driver came in to collect the group. It was Mr Sochaki.

' Hello, Horace, nice to see you. How's the radio?'

' Not bad,' Horace said.

' It's all these sun spots,' said Mr Sochaki. ' They can't get through.'

Mr Sochaki had not run away to get married at all. The girl upon whose knees Horace had once seen him weeping in the little shop was his house mother — she was there tonight, taking the girls to wee-wees and stopping the boys thumping each other. Mr Sochaki had been sent back inside.

' Don't be upset, Horace.'

' I admired him more than anybody,' Horace told Claire. ' He was the first scientist I ever met. They said he was from the university.'

' His father was a Polish prisoner of war. His mother was in the Land Army. That's how they met. I've got all their case histories. I'm going to specialise in psychiatry.'

They were walking, handlebar to handlebar, along Histon Road before mounting. The police car followed twenty yards behind. It quite suddenly came to Horace that he was another case history for her. In the same moment, because it was meant, because they were right for each other, it also came to her that this is what he thought.

'Will you hold my bicycle?' she asked him.

Horace held his own bicycle with one hand, her bicycle with the other. Claire now put her arms up around his neck and kissed him all over the face before coming to rest on his mouth.

'I love you!' she kept muttering angrily. 'I love you! I love you!'

'Now, look here, just a minute, I say,' Horace kept saying, trying not to let the bicycles fall. 'I believe somebody wants me —'

'Are you all right, Mr Fenton?' the policeman called.

The bicycles fell with a clatter across the pavement as the police car drove away.

'Take me where you took Chloe,' Claire instructed him. 'Quickly . . .'

Pock! Pock! Pock! Pock!

Horace sat up in bed. The sharp sound had been in his head; in his dream. He had heard it at the club tonight. Of course: the sound of ping-pong! He had heard it when he was floating and when he was drowning. Ping-pong . . . Now his memory caught it, two suntanned people playing bat and ball on the grass by the river.

Peregrine!

Horace had stolen Peregrine's bike, Peregrine had had his own back. Nothing to do with Hitler. Nothing to do with what Hazel knew or didn't know. Nothing to do with Dr Tischler. Phew! What a relief. It had been pocking away in his sub-conscious all this time.

'Horace?'

Rhoda stood in the doorway in her night-dress.

'You were late home,' she said.

'We walked by the river,' Horace said. 'I love her. She's wonderful. If I don't marry Claire I won't marry anybody.'

'You can't marry a doctor, son. You're only sixteen. You'd better say your prayers. Gentle Jesus meek and mild, look upon a little child . . .'

Horace held his balls, comfortingly, reliving it, moving his lips against the pillow in the darkness. I love you! I love you! I love you! he said, angrily. And if you were married you could do it

103

all your life whenever you wanted to. Oh Claire! Oh Hazel! Oh Chloe! Skirts, legs, breasts, tossing hair, biting mouths moved across his inner eye like the colours of sunlight in the blood.

Chapter Sixteen

Catastrophe struck Horace when he'd paid three instalments on the guitar and had three more lessons from Miss Fiske, mastering three scales and the nine related major chords. His overtime money was suddenly stopped by an anti-armaments strike at the factory.

It was the Monday morning after Monty's sudden appearance and after he'd discovered that the picture beside Hazel Springer's bed was Frank Lacteen (Hitler); Harry Webb came up to Horace in a rage.

' Do you know what this is? ' He was holding a turned brass bush under Horace's nose.

Horace knew only too well what it was; he had turned out more than four thousand of them in the past three weeks on the capstan lathe. Horace had dreamed about them.

' It's a turned brass bush,' he said.

' Do you know what it's used for? '

Horace didn't know and didn't care.

Harry said : ' It's bloody war work. It's part of an aeroplane bomb release assembly.'

It gave Horace a feeling of some importance which was short-lived.

' Don't you read your production cards? '

' What? '

' Hanging by the machine. If not, how do you know what the piece-work rates are or if you're getting the right rate for the job or what the operation time is? Look.' He showed Horace a complicated-looking card covered in squares and figures and with the title of the part across the top two inches high : ' Bomb Release Assembly A435 — Turned Brass Bush A/B 765329.'

' Oh,' Horace said.

Harry said : ' Don't you listen to Mr Baldwin? Mr Mac-Donald? Mr Chamberlain? This is the very sort of thing that's going to make Chancellor Hitler angry — no wonder he's getting ready to defend himself. There's the country crying disarmament and there's you making bomb releases — bloody lovely, init? '

Horace felt really guilty. He'd only done what he'd been told to do.

' That's an old answer, that is,' Harry said, scathingly.

Old Ted Wright came up. ' Leave the boy alone, Harry. He's only trying to make a few bob for his music lessons.'

' Oh yeah? ' Harry said, bitterly. ' That's nice. He fiddles while we burn. Bomb releases! '

Dirty Dick rallied round — he'd taken to giving Horace sniffs of his snuff lately. ' It's not him,' he told Harry. He pointed upstairs : ' It's them.'

' Yeah, it's always them,' Harry said. ' Well, let me tell you something.' He got hold of Horace's cowgown collar : ' It's chaps like *this* that makes *them* possible. Where's Ernie? I'm getting everybody out on this one. . . .'

Very little had been seen of Ernie Trigg since last Thursday when W. B. Barclay had come down to enlist his aid in a special job. Since then he had been up in the soundproof cabin, locked against acoustic intrusions, calibrating a new audiometer and checking it against the acuity of the typing pool, one by one.

Horace had heard of sit-down strikes but this was his first experience. An odd, embarrassing experience it was too, sitting with tools to hand and the work in front of you and doing nothing with the bosses strolling around and saying nothing. In fact if anybody picked up a screwdriver or a chisel they were shouted at. They were not in the model shop but had gone over to join the production in the main assembly shop; it was as though the more people there were seen to be doing nothing the more effective the protest against the armaments.

First of all came an explanation from Mr Stanton, the general manager, apparently — though Horace had never seen him before. The bomb releases were not a part of the factory's normal work schedule, he said, but merely a sub-contract carried out on available machinery to help the Handley Page aircraft factory at Radlett.

' Shame! ' shouted Harry Webb.

And ' Shame! ' shouted many others.

There followed speeches from the works manager, Mr Bones,

106

and from W. B. Barclay himself; himself, so far as Horace was concerned, because he was the most important of the lot. Horace always saw him as a possible Prime Minister with Ernie Trigg as Home Secretary, keeping the country in stitches.

' You all know meeeeee ! ' the chief engineer shouted, his voice rising up.

' Good old Harry Tate ! ' somebody shouted.

' Beeee that as it mayeeee,' W. B. Barclay went on, ' I want to draw your attention to a member of my engineering staff — to wit, Doctor Tischler whom God preserve of Vienna ! You are objecting to the strengthening of this country's defences — how many of you would object if the Nazis came and took your families away to concentration camps? '

' Rubbish ! ' shouted Harry Webb.

And ' Rubbish ! ' shouted many others.

W. B. Barclay then played his trump card : ' Don't tell *me* it's rubbish ! ' he shouted. ' Tell my friend Tischler — ' Doctor Tischler now rose to his feet from behind a chassis cradle, his face white with emotion. ' It might help to cheer him up if you are so sure that his wife Elke and his two children Hans and Mette have not been murdered. But first let me tell you — they were carried away from his brother's house a week ago and his brother was killed — bayoneted if you want the details — trying to prevent it.'

Tischler stood there for a moment with tears flowing and nobody said anything. Gently, W. B. Barclay sat the scientist down again.

Then Harry Webb called : ' Unfair tactics ! '

' Ah, shut up, Harry,' somebody said.

Horace was resolving yet again to find out who killed little Hazel Springer and whether it was connected with the betrayal of Doctor Tischler.

He had been thinking altogether too much about his own affairs. The first thing to do was try to find old A.B.L., J.J. and H.R. He couldn't believe that Hazel had been sleeping with them but he was certain that they were all members of the Buffs. Whoever they were.

Horace was relieved to see that he was not the only one dabbing his eyes. Mr Stanton had got to his feet again.

107

'Now then,' he said. 'We shall stop overtime on this project
— we were stopping it anyway — but I want work to start within
two minutes from now. One more demonstration like this, and
you're all out of a job. As it is I want — ' he glanced at a list
'— Mr Harry Webb, Mr T. Driscoll, Mr H. C. Tomlinson, Mr
Whitby — ' he went on reading out the names of men engaged
in union activities, then finished : 'To report to the wages office
for their cards forthwith — they are sacked. That's all.'

The meeting was dismissed, the executives were going, the
workers were scrambling for their posts.

'Comrades! ' Harry Webb shouted. 'Just a minute! '

'Fuck off, Webby,' somebody said.

He was pushed aside; the university was the only authority in
that town. Later, in the model shop, watching Harry collect his
tools and shake hands with everybody, Horace felt sorry for him;
felt that it was partly all his fault through wanting the Epiphone
when he could have made do with a Giuseppe.

'Good luck, Harry,' said Ernie.

'Sorry to see you go,' said old Ted Wright.

'Good luck in your next job, mate,' said Dirty Dick.

'Ta, mate,' Harry Webb kept saying; he didn't seem to have
accepted it yet. He seemed dazed. When he shook hands with
Mr Roper, he said : 'What about the Instrument Company?
You've got a brother-in-law there, haven't you? '

'They're putting them off,' Mr Roper said. 'There's no work
about.'

'Bloody marvellous, isn't it? ' Harry said.

'You want to try Krupps, mate,' old Ted Wright said.

Harry swung round, all fire again, for he would never learn
his lesson. 'I would, too. Bloody right. If I could get there. Or
the Skoda works in Czechoslovakia — Hitler's got them working
full pelt.'

Ernie said : 'You say that — yet Horace can't make bomb
releases? '

Harry said : 'You lot don't understand. I don't think you
know anything about politics. Hitler's not arming against us.
Hitler's stated his aims clearly in *Mein Kampf*. The fair and
just reclamation of German territory, the repatriation of German
minorities, the removal of the stigma of Versaille — '

The two-pound hammer caught Harry in the middle of the back; he fell forward with a ghastly breath-exhaling grunt. Doctor Tischler, whom nobody had heard approach, jumped on him and tried to retrieve the hammer to finish the job. The men seemed idiotically paralysed and unable to do anything. The Jewish scientist was bringing the hammer down for a death blow when W. B. Barclay's voice stopped him.

' Tischler ! '

They all looked round; even the injured Harry looked up from the floor where he was still lying on his face. W. B. Barclay now had his back to them and was scratching his behind and waiting for some decent kind of order.

Ernie provided the astonishing aftermath to this unpleasant episode at the end of the day when he came to Horace's bench.

' Well,' he said, ' it worked.'

' Oh,' said Horace. Horace's ' Oh ', in case anybody is wondering, was an expression of polite interest combined with the hint of a partial knowledge of what the other party was talking about.

' From tomorrow,' Ernie said, ' you're a semi-skilled fitter at elevenpence an hour — you've got Harry's job.'

' Gosh,' Horace said.

' I've done my bit,' Ernie said. ' Now it's up to you.'

Horace could not any longer pretend to understand what Ernie was talking about. Ernie was talking about having leaked the bomb-sight information to Harry to produce exactly the results which it did.

' I see,' Horace said. ' Don't you believe in rearmament, then ? '

' Jesus,' Ernie Trigg said. ' I'm not talking about rearmament. I'm talking about our band. You've got fivepence an hour rise — that's nearly a pound a week. You can have double lessons and pay off your guitar — and that's not all. I've found a pianist — Edna. She plays in the canteen sometimes.'

Horace said : ' Is that the pretty blonde on the laminated iron core line ? '

' Do you know her ? '

' I think I worked behind her once,' Horace said.

He'd been sent home for the day for holding her hand.

109

'There's just one thing, Horace,' Ernie Trigg said, and it was obviously going to be something that he didn't like saying, especially to somebody he liked. 'Mind you, it's not me,' he added.

'Oh?' said Horace.

'They'll want your birth certificate. All the skilled men have to show their birth certificates — you know, just to prove we're not bastards like the management.'

'What's a birth certificate?' Horace asked, with genuine interest.

Ernie laughed. 'That's what I like about you, Horry.'

If it was something everyone knew, then Horace didn't, was what he meant. It was the secret of genius.

One of the things Horace didn't know was folded inside an envelope in Rhoda's shoe-box. On the envelope was written in his mother's handwriting: *My Mental Make-up at 50, RW or M or F.* Inside was an astonishing letter written, apparently, to herself. Horace, sitting up in his bedroom, felt that he ought not to be reading it. This is what it said:

Notes on Myself

All my worry has brought me no sense of truth and less of reality. I wonder what one must experience to find that. In the self-pity which comes to me I seem incapable of being sure of anything except my own depression. The question arises — what can I do now to escape from added suffering? To think, to feel, one must suffer. But I am unable to escape the thraldom of imaginative flights of fancy, and am quite ashamed of my habit of day-dreaming and the strange and weird stories which I weave for myself. I look on it rather as a drug-taker may look on his drug — as something which is wrong but too pleasurable to be denied. But it is strange that I cannot put down in writing or express verbally those things which I see so clearly and so vividly in my mind.

I can see things happening. In my case, a struggle against overwhelming odds. In my mind I live it and identify myself with it. But like a musician without hands. I can find no medium of expression.

Another strange experience is that I suddenly realize at the age of 50, although my body has grown older my mind seems to have remained stationary, my intelligence and outlook that of a much younger woman. I cannot believe that youth has really passed.

I simply feel that I have passed through a deep experience which has brought me no happiness and from which I have learned very little and that I have been stunned, as though my experience of life has given me concussion.

Now I will try to waste no more time on regrets. Surely there is still some time left in which even I may find some sort of reality.

Signed : R. Fenton
(Whateley, Morden)
August 1935

' Jesus,' Horace said. He really felt like crying. No mention of him for one thing — just herself. And where did she get that vocabulary? Horace did not know that his mother had this sadness, but more than that he did not know that she could write like that. He couldn't imagine Jammy's mother or Neville's mother writing like that. Or feeling like that.

' Horace! Have you found it? ' Rhoda was calling up the stairs.

' Not yet,' Horace called.

What he was looking for was his birth certificate. He knew that she kept her personal papers in this shoe-box but he had never been interested enough to look in it before; a broken white cardboard box with Freeman Hardy and Willis on the side. She was always popping things into it and taking things out or browsing through it.

' When I'm dead look in here,' she used to tell the children; not morbidly, but as part of their family conspiracy. ' I've put down everything I want you to have. That little table's for Ronald's sculpting.'

They didn't listen to her.

Nobody really listened to Rhoda. You don't listen to your own mother — for one thing you've heard it all. Or have you heard anything? Horace found his birth certificate, then went down and made his mother a cup of tea.

'I don't want a cup of tea. I've got heartburn.'

'You can have some McLeans powder first,' Horace told her.

The astonishment, Horace thought, looking at her now as she sat by the window re-reading her Patience Strong poems, was that she was secretly unhappy with her life. She was the one who was always happy. Whatever happened. She never stopped laughing and singing and jollying them along. Of course he realised that she was not the merry raving lunatic he made her out to be in his literary thinking, any more than W. B. Barclay was a red-nosed clown; Rhoda was really a jolly tragic and heroic figure, as women went.

'What's got into you?' Rhoda asked him when he gave her the tea.

'Nothing,' Horace said. 'I thought you'd like a cup of tea.' And as she sipped it rather self-consciously — for Horace had sat down to watch her — he said : 'Now is there anything you want to tell me?'

A musician without hands? he was thinking.

'You haven't done anything wrong, have you?' she asked him, suddenly.

'I'm not sure,' Horace told her, profoundly. And he added : 'How are your piles?'

But she didn't seem to want to talk about them.

Among Rhoda's chronic ailments were bleeding piles, foul varicose veins (her leg was like a beetroot) with great suppurating ulcers which put her in agony and which she had to drag out miles to work with; there was what she called indigestion, she practically lived on McCleans Stomach Powder and there were little drops of it everywhere and white rings on tables (at her death they found she had a ruptured diaphragm for half her life which nobody had diagnosed), shocking constipation for which she took masses of senna tea, Beecham's Pills and herbal rubbish with the result that when she went to the lavatory it sounded like Niagara Falls, though she was quite unaware that lavatory doors are not soundproof. These were only the beginning.

She had skin rashes, particularly after Monty, which had her face and throat weeping and scarlet; she would lie in the window

112

with the sun shining on the irritation (this is the real God). Among the milder things which were no less painful were her enormous bunions; shoes, which usually had to be second-hand, crippled her — and she was a heavy woman who spent her life on her feet. Besides all this she had bumps that formed on her scalp which she used to dig out with the point of the scissors.

' Do you think it's dangerous? ' she used to ask the children afterwards.

Rhoda was also a hypochondriac. You're inclined to think that hypochondriacs have no real illnesses; this is not so. Your best hypochondriacs are riddled with diseases and complaints and miseries and it is these that compensate for not having the really deadly things like cancer and Parkinson's Disease.

But she had more than this to compensate her, she had her second husband. Once they were all pea-picking out at the remote fenland farm somewhere between Wicken and Clayhithe (Slate Farm); they used to get something like sixpence a sack. Rhoda suddenly stood upright against that enormous sky. She said nothing, she just stood there; she'd lost her business, her pension, her Jim; she was suffering a million agonies and there was nothing to go home to but the beginning of another back-breaking day like this one; the beginning of another long pain-wracked McCleans night.

The next moment she was pea-picking again.

Sometimes Rhoda would collapse unconscious on the floor with all of the children frightened, working to bring her round. Everything just combined and got her.

' I'm all right,' she used to say, when she sat up.

Apart from this she used to worry about everything that was happening in the world and she used to worry about the Royal Family, whom she thought weren't really happy. She would write to all the papers and magazines about various injustices she had encountered (she wrote fifty-three letters to Hannen Swaffer). She also wrote many business letters suggesting, for instance, that she could start a Joe Lyons Nippy restaurant in places like Wisbech; and to umpteen wholesalers asking for credit. She started sweet shops in several villages, expanding to teas and bringing in slot machines — this is what had first brought Solly Joel's stable lads to Christine. She wrote letters for the gypsies and sometimes absent-mindedly signed them with her magnificent sloping signature, Rhoda Morden. And, for a time : Rhoda Whateley Morden.

But even in spite of all this Horace was shocked to discover that his mother was secretly in despair about her life. She kept up a brave pretence. She sang all the time she wasn't in actual pain (there was her rupture and her truss); she sang *Roses of Picardy, Beulah Land, Three O'Clock In The Morning, Sullivan* (he's the son of an Irishman), *Pack Up Your Troubles* and some of the more recent pops like *Red Sails In The Sunset*. She had a good, strong, rather corny soprano voice.

In the end her children never did the things for her that they wanted to do; they were loaded with too many responsibilities of their own.

Fortunately, the debt of love is more important than its repayment.

Chapter Seventeen

Horace Spurgeon Fenton's first significant piece of writing came out of an evening at night school. It had nothing to do with electricity and magnetism, however, but was a lesson in compassion that came from a boy named Ronny Atkins whose father had just been killed in the Spanish civil war.

' Two minutes' silence for Ronny's father,' said Mr Purdy.

The two minutes was an agony for the class. Not the agony of Ronny's father gone forever and never coming back, but the agony of holding your breath; the agony of the doctor's waiting room, of hoping your stomach won't rumble. The agony of trying to keep a solemn face. The agony of trying to get involved in somebody else's personal tragedy and failing.

' Fenton ! '

Mr Purdy, propped against the cross-section drawing of a dynamo, was frowning angrily at Horace; others in the class turned and stared.

' No whistling ! ' said Mr Purdy. ' Now let's start again.'

Horace turned bright crimson, shocked and shamed. He had not intended to whistle; he had been borrowing sadness from the twelve-bar blues. *Went down to St James's infirmary. Saw my baby lying there* . . . Others were having difficulty with sustained grief. Bagley had started his tank going under the lid of his deck; a notched cotton reel motored by twisted elastic, its power stored in slices of candle which allowed a matchstick to slowly turn. Horace had now fallen back on Rupert Brooke, a trick he'd taught himself for Armistice Days. *Oh! Death will find me, long before I tire Of watching you; and swing me suddenly Into the shade and loneliness and mire.* . . .

At its best it actually brought him to tears.

However, this was not the lesson.

' What do we mean by the molecular theory of magnetism? ' Mr Purdy was asking a little later. He was a homely though serious man who, through taking adult evening classes and explaining things to people who had long forgotten the funda-

115

mentals, always looked as though he was about to be struck.
' You, Horace.'

' What, sir? '

' The molecular theory of magnetism,' said Mr Purdy.

' Oh — I like it,' Horace said.

He liked everything about night school. First because he didn't
have to be there. He could go home if he wanted to without his
mother being sent to prison. Also the spirit of the other pupils,
all there to learn because they wanted to learn; because there
was now something they wanted to know. Horace had been hung
up for a time on the multiplication of fractions. He refused to
believe that a half multiplied by a half equalled a quarter.

' You can't multiply something and make it less,' he had
explained to Mr Purdy on that early occasion. ' Multiply means
to increase. A half times a half must be more than a half.'

He was so convincing that students who had finished with
simple arithmetic when they were ten now began to have doubts.
It had disrupted the class until finally Mr Purdy had told Horace
that he would just have to damn well accept it. Having accepted
this Horace found the rest easy; having accepted the impossible
then the molecular theory of magnetism became a matter of
common sense. In fact he preferred it. Of *course* soft iron became
magnetised when you stroked it with a magnet or subjected it to
the lines of force associated with an electric current in a closed
circuit. If a half multiplied by a half was a quarter, then anything could happen.

But this was not the lesson either.

' Before you go I have an announcement,' Mr Purdy told the
Elec and Mag class that night. There was to be a motor-bus
excursion to the engineering works of the Marconi Wireless
Telegraph Company at Chelmsford on the following Saturday.
Anyone interested to write their names on the Projects Chart.

' May I borrow your pen? ' Horace asked Ronny Atkins.

Ronny had just written his own name on the chart and
screwed on the top of his fountain pen. ' Use Bagley's pencil,' he
told Horace. But Horace knew instinctively that it was wrong to
write your name in a public place in pencil and he insisted on
borrowing the pen. Ronny insisted on refusing to lend it to him.
It was the last present his father bought him. He didn't lend it

116

to anybody. And anyway, he couldn't get the top off again —
it was stuck.

' Let me do it for you,' Horace said.

Using his engineering knowledge, Horace managed to break
the pen in half. Ronny Atkins took the pieces back and without
crying walked away. Riding home that night Horace cried;
without the blues, without poetry, he had become involved in
somebody else's personal tragedy.

This was the lesson.

From this lesson, a few nights later, he wrote the following
short story :

THE BOY WITH THE DEAD FATHER
by : Horace Spurgeon Fenton

IN THE MORNING they told Uncle Cuthbert to take me for
a walk.

They gave him sympathetic looks. ' They ' were the rest of
the relatives who were staying in the house. Uncle Cuthbert's
wife — Aunt Joan — and several other aunts and uncles and
cousins.

I could see he didn't want very much to take me for a walk,
and I was hurt, because we got on rather well. Next to my father
I liked him best of everybody. He bought me my first grown-up
book, which was about a dog. Also he didn't hold my hand when
we walked but let me put my hands in my trouser pockets like
a man.

It wasn't a nice morning at all, for there was a bit of fog and
I had to wear a scarf that Aunt Joan had knitted and which
scruffled my neck, and gloves that brought the lining out of my
pockets every time I took my hands out to blow my nose.

Uncle Cuthbert seemed worried. When he was worried he
pulled his nose when he spoke to me and said ' Aaaar ' in front
of what he wanted to say. He was a big man and rather plump
and usually he was very jolly.

We walked into the park and went towards the pond.

' How old are you now, my boy? ' he asked me when we got
by the water.

He didn't usually ask silly questions like that. He never missed

117

my birthdays. I suppose it was because he didn't have a boy of his own. I told him I was seven.

' I — ar — want to talk to you,' he said. ' I want to tell you something, Peter; there's something I want to say, my boy.'

We were near the boat shed then, and he watched me ' cut bread-and-butter ' with a flat stone on the water. I couldn't imagine what he wanted to say. One of my stones skipped three times and then disappeared into the mist. I heard the faint splash when it fell. This seemed to give Uncle Cuthbert an idea.

' I would like to tell you a story of what happened to me at this very spot when I was about — aaaar — mmm — yes, about your age, Peter. Round about your age.'

This was more like Uncle Cuthbert.

' I lost something that was very dear to me,' he said. ' And it broke my heart. Very nearly. There was a toy shop in the High Street, and one day there was a fine sailing ship hanging across the window on strings. A really fine sailing craft, with square tops'ls. It took me twelve weeks to save up my pocket money for that ship. Twelve weeks and some extra errands for my father to get the last two shillings. Then she was mine.

' I shall never forget her maiden voyage — her first voyage. The first time she went into the water.'

We continued walking round the pond.

' You brought it — her — here? Every day? '

' That's the sad part about it, Peter,' my uncle said, and he really looked very sad indeed. ' I only brought her down that one time.'

' She sunk — '

' No, no,' he said. ' She didn't founder. She was a fine ship. Her balance was perfect. She rode high in the water and sailed close to the wind like a true British Sail of the Line.'

I looked at the water and kept quiet. This was one of the best stories he had ever told me. This was a tale of the sea, and Uncle Cuthbert was a grand old salt.

' I came down here to the pond with my Aunt Celia and the dog,' he continued as we walked. ' I left my aunt back there on the grass and I went across the gravel foreshore on my own and let the ship down into the water. I was the master and pilot and the crew. There were many other craft out on the water, and white, brown and red sails bending and bowing in the wind as far as I could see. The wind was stiff and coming from Lensfield Road — from the north. I set her at fifty degrees into the wind and let her go.'

' What — what happened to her? '

My Uncle Cuthbert gazed into the north. ' I never saw her again,' he said. ' Nobody ever saw her again. She sailed out and never came back. It very nearly broke my heart.'

' You looked for her.'

My uncle sighed again. ' The whole park looked for her. The boat-keeper looked and my aunt and all the people who were sailing that day. We went out in a boat and looked for her, and the boat-keeper used a telescope, but she had gone. Disappeared. Vanished.'

I said nothing. I felt there was nothing to say. I shared my uncle's sadness. Twelve weeks of saving, with extra errands for his father, and then nothing. No ship. No more adventures. Just holding her and launching her and then watching her sail away for ever.

' I came to the park every afternoon for three weeks,' he said. ' I haunted the pond. I worried the boat-keeper.'

' It broke your heart.'

' Yes. Very nearly. Until I realised what had happened.'

' You did? You knew where she'd gone? '

' Not where she'd gone, but why,' he said. ' Let's sit down on this bench, and I'll tell you.'

I took a handful of stones and sat by him on the seat. He got out his pipe and continued his story.

' As I saw it,' he said, ' that ship was waiting for me to come along and buy her.'

' Waiting for you? '

' Yes. Why else should a craft as fine as she hang unbought and unlaunched in dry-dock for twelve weeks while I saved up my sixpences? She was waiting for me. She was meant to be afloat. And I was the one to launch her. She had no intention of returning. She wanted to get away from land. To sail on, free, for ever. That's the way I saw it.'

119

'But what happened to her?'

'Nothing,' he said. 'She is still sailing on over the water. Never touching land. Never making port. A fine ship with tall masts and a square tops'l.'

We both looked very hard into the mist.

'I didn't mind so much then,' he said. 'I felt that I was aboard her. That she was mine. That she would always be mine. Much better than seeing her scratched and storm-broken and finishing her days in the bottom of the toy cupboard.'

'Yes! Oh, yes!'

My uncle looked at me. 'You see how I felt?'

Indeed I did. Again we stared into the mist. There might easily have been tall white sails gliding quite close by the shore. I stopped throwing stones.

'Now that you see,' my uncle said, 'I want to ask you something. Would *you* feel the way I felt if something you loved very much sailed out of your life and never returned?'

I said, 'Yes.'

He said, 'Or — somebody?'

'I — yes. I think so.'

'How would you like to come and live with Aunt Joan and me?' he asked.

'I would love to.'

'Then — aaar — ' this was the first time he had said 'aaar' since he started the story — 'how would you feel if my brother — your father — sailed away for ever like that ship? And never came back?'

He was being silly again.

'He couldn't!' I said.

He put his hand on my shoulder.

'I'm sorry, Peter,' he said. 'You must be brave.'

'But he *couldn't*. You know he couldn't, Uncle Cuthbert,' I said. 'My father is dead. You know he is. You know that you all went yesterday to his funeral, so how could he sail away like that?'

My uncle pulled me gently to my feet and he ruffled my hair. He didn't look worried any more.

He said: 'I think we are going to get on very well.' And he smiled.

And when he smiled he looked so much like my father that I
wanted to cry.

It was Horace's first significant piece of writing because it was
not written by a bird or a chair but by a boy.

'This is a nice little story,' Rhoda said as she translated it into
English.

Little? Why was it little? Horace's brother Ken, writing about
it from Riverina in Australia where he had now forsaken sheep
farming and joined a travelling burlesque show, said: 'Great!
These should sell like hot cakes!' Then he went on to advise
Horace not to give up his job for writing until he was certain
that he was head and shoulders above the rest.

Head and shoulders? Why head and shoulders? The editors
of seventeen magazines and newspapers and journals all said:

*The editor regrets that the enclosed submission is unsuitable
for publication in this magazine. However, thank you for
your offering and rest assured that all manuscripts receive
careful consideration.*

Regrets? Why regrets? *No remorse, no regret,* Horace thought,
cycling here and there, *we'll just part, exactly as we met — easy
come, easy go.* . . .

121

Chapter Eighteen

Captain Cook's great discovery came one wet June afternoon just when Rhoda needed it most; it was one of those days when she felt that she couldn't go on. Nothing had happened except the results had come out of a *John Bull* Bullets competition and she had not even won a half-crown target prize. Her entry: *Desperate times — need cheerful clocks*, was so much wittier than the one that had won £500 for someone in Worcester. Such unfairness seemed to symbolise the unendingness of everything. She had seen the children off to work, Leslie off to school, but had been unable to face the walk to the jam factory bus.

She was lying upstairs on her bed when she heard Captain Cook chaining his bicycle to the front fence. Bad as things were, she thought, she could never marry a man who did that — or carried his money in a purse.

' Mrs Fenton ! '

' Coming,' she called.

' Glad you're in,' he cried, spreading his hands with gladness. ' I was just going to leave you a note — ' he scribbled on invisible paper. ' But then I saw your note to the insurance man.' For this he placed his hand like a piece of paper pinned to a door. His miming came from dealing with stupid people on his NSPCC child welfare round. ' I've got some good news for you — ' This was arms raised like a sun-worshipper, followed by ' I think you'd better sit down while I tell you,' in which he pulled her a chair and invited her into it.

He was a bright, clerkish little man with a small Charlie Chase moustache and he was dressed in the navy uniform and silver buttons of the Society. Horace could take him off perfectly; practically anyone could.

' That girl,' he said, when Rhoda was sitting. ' Did she wear spectacles? ' For this he shaped his fingers like binoculars and put them to his eyes.

' What girl? ' Rhoda said.

' The one who wrote to you. The one you thought your second

122

husband was married to already? '

' Oh. Yes, I think so. Yes, she did.'

Captain Cook said, dramatically : ' They're living in a caravan at Isleham. They've got four children. One older than your boy. Do you see what that means? '

' Are you sure? '

' Positive. They're on our books — the Newmarket office deals with them. I just happened to make a few inquiries.'

' Is it the same name? ' Rhoda at that first moment of possible freedom was worried that she might have to break the news to Leslie of yet another name.

' Butters,' Captain Cook told her. ' Look, I've got it written down here. Jack Butters.'

Rhoda could not bring herself to look at it. Butters!

' Now get that young detective onto it,' Captain Cook urged her. ' This is your chance.'

' I don't know. I can't tell Leslie he's illegitimate! '

' And you can't tell him he's now Leslie Butters,' Captain Cook said, for he knew her greatest fears. ' Besides, there's fifteen years' back pension to come — nearly two thousand pounds. You could buy a house and have enough to last you the rest of your life! ' All of these enormous possibilities turned him into a windmill of movement and excitement.

' I'll have to ask the boys,' Rhoda said.

' Just think,' said Captain Cook, tapping his forehead, ' you could go to France and find your husband's grave.'

' My husband's grave is in Westminster Abbey,' Rhoda reminded him.

' If you couldn't find it in France then you'd know for sure,' he said. And he added : ' You could even get married again. If you felt like it.'

Rhoda often felt like it. It was one of the things that distressed her most.

' And don't forget,' Captain Cook said in parting : ' If you want any legal help come to me. We'll do it through the Society.'

Rhoda thanked him and offered him tea which he hadn't time for, and after he'd ridden away on his bicycle she went down to the telephone box with twopence to phone the police station.

With the ending of overtime Horace got back to night school just in time for the exams — National Certificate First Year Electricity and Magnetism, and Radio Communication City and Guilds. He struggled with the first paper for half an hour, finding nothing in it that resembled anything he had been studying. He felt somebody looking at him and turned round to find Charles Baldwin pulling faces two desks away; he was also holding up the test paper to bring it to Horace's attention.

Horace was in the wrong place again; he was trying to pass an examination in architecture — Buildings and Materials. Too late now to get into the right room, Horace had missed his first year exams and would have to go the same course again. Charles had indicated that Horace wait for him, so he did.

Horace said, when Charles came out of the big iron gates : ' I thought you were at college.'

' Good,' Charles Baldwin said. ' Now about young Hazel. You were going to give me a picture for *The Review*? '

Horace told him that it had turned out to be a film star.

' Oh, pity,' Charles said. ' You see, I've uncovered a rather nasty little plot — I may get MI6 onto it. Those fascist bounders at Leys. They're betraying refugees to the Jerries — people are getting killed.'

' I think I may be able to help,' Horace said. He took out the list of initials which had come from Hazel's diary. ' I got these from the police,' he said. ' She was probably in their clutches or something.'

Charles studied the list of initials for some moments, then his face lit up with a happy smile. ' Thank heavens there are still people like you in the world, Horry old chap,' he said. ' She was in their clutches all right — dance-band mad. Used to rush home and turn it on in bed.'

A.B.L. on Mondays was Ambrose's Blue Lyres from the BBC studio. J.J. was Jack Jackson from the Dorchester. H.R. was Harry Roy from the Kit Kat. She had a date every night with a different band on her radio.

' Gosh,' Horace said.

' Give you a lift home in the old Lag? ' Charles offered.

Once again Horace abandoned a perfectly good bicycle for something better.

' Who's the BUF, then? ' Horace asked, as Charles roared up Jesus Lane. ' The Buffs? '

Charles told Horace it wasn't the Buffs; it was the British Union of Fascists. ' Mosley's lot. You must know them? '

Horace had never heard of them; things like that didn't penetrate the Giant's castle.

' They keep having punch-ups with the Communists in the East End,' Charles said.

' Which are the anti-Nazis, then? ' Horace asked, feeling that he was really getting clued up at last. There was no answer and he looked sideways; Charles was just looking at him, although still keeping an eye on Victoria Avenue. ' Harry Webb said Doctor Tischler is an anti-Nazi, though he seems all right.'

' Ah, Tischler, yes, Tischler — it seems to want a rhyming word, don't you think? Tell me about him.'

' It's jolly sad, really,' Horace said.

He told Charles Baldwin all about Tischler — the torn page, Hazel, Harry, the family in Germany, the concentration camp, W. B. Barclay's warning about foreigners. It lasted them right into Green End Road.

Listening, Charles had gone very quiet indeed; grave is really the word — a kind of Peter Cook face in its most crusading mood. As if what Horace had been saying added onto something he already knew and amounted to something else. Also, though heaven knows it's hardly fair to say so, as if it would be useless discussing it with Horace Spurgeon Fenton, anyway.

' Gotcha ! ' Detective-Sergeant Stanley Polsworth cried, slamming the front door shut and grabbing Charles Baldwin's arm; the detective had been hiding behind the front door as Horace pushed it open and took his friend in.

' 'Straordinary fellow ! ' Charles exclaimed. ' Is this your brother? '

Horace tried to push his future brother-in-law away.

' Don't do that ! '

The family was waiting in the living-room; had been waiting ever since Stanley called from his position in the front bay window that Horace had just come up in a Lagonda.

' What have you been up to? ' Rhoda fired first.

' Do you mind, Mrs Whateley? ' Stanley said.

' Say that again,' Charles requested; ' by Jove, I think I've got it. You're a bobby! You're that chap who stopped me — ' then darkly to Horace : ' Is this a trap? '

Horace, very irritated for he'd wanted to make a good university-type impression on Charles, said : ' Only for my sister. They're getting married soon.'

Christine burst out laughing and drowned whatever grumbling Stan was doing. She said to Horace : ' You're very witty since you started at the Rhythm Club. Must be the company you're keeping.' You could see that she was very smitten with Charles.

' Company is right,' said Stan, for it was a favourite form of expression; and to Charles : ' I see you've still got that stolen car — '

' Not stolen — borrowed. I gave you the particulars — '

' All false,' Stanley Polsworth said, speaking in that steady, fair, but convicting way that policemen have. ' Lord Brocket's never heard of you.'

' Nonsense. In one of his moods, I expect — '

' Perhaps you'd like to tell me where you live again? '

Horace said : ' 93 Jesus Lane.' It was a good address; a good flat. Horace had had waffles there. Not to mention opium.

' No, in fact,' Charles said, ' no. Not really.'

He had become a little embarrassed at involving Horace in a lie; at involving the innocent. Police didn't matter.

Stanley was now consulting his little book : ' Now. I'll tell you where you live. Coronation Street — up Hills Road. Number 62. Your father's a wheel tapper.'

Horace was astonished, but not disappointed.

Charles said : ' I am not ashamed of being a proletarian.' And to Horace : ' Nothing about politics.'

Stanley's head came up : ' What was that? '

' It's warm tonight, isn't it? ' Horace said.

Stanley said to Charles : ' I'm going to take you into custody.'

Christine said to Charles : ' Isn't the word " proletariat "? '

Rhoda said : ' What about that photograph? '

She was talking to Stanley Polsworth, who now remembered why he had been waiting for Horace and produced the photo-

126

graph which we now all know portrayed Hitler at a little-known time of his life.

'You stole this,' he said to Horace. 'It was hidden in your room. Why?'

Horace was furious; is this what having a policeman in the family was going to be like? He said as much.

Stanley said: 'You know who this is, don't you?' And to the family he said: 'This is to do with the death of that little girl. It might be a murder case.'

'You told us all that before they came,' Christine said.

'Now he's mixed up in it,' Stanley said, meaning Charles Baldwin, 'it looks very serious indeed.' And to Charles he said, bluffing: 'Politics, is it?'

Charles, looking at the photograph and recognising it as a copy of the same picture he'd seen adorning Joyce's wall at Leys last night, thought it must certainly be politics, but he said nothing at this stage.

Detective-Sergeant Polsworth moved them towards the door. 'I want you both to come down the station for questioning.'

'And I'll be at the Dorothy dancing,' Christine said.

She was striking a blow for their freedom; and it worked. Stanley at first allowed the tension to drop by suggesting that Charles called at the station tomorrow and then got defeated by a belated but effective ball from Ronald who, with Leslie, had been content to listen until now.

'Lagonda?' Ronald said. 'What's the number? ER 775? That's Lord Cecil's.'

'Oh! There!' Charles exclaimed. 'Brocket sold it to Cecil.'

Ronald said: 'He keeps it in Marshall's garage in Jesus Lane.'

Charles said: 'He keeps it there when he's not using it, I keep it there when I'm not using it — they know me well, naturally.'

Naturally; he was a mechanic at Marshall's.

Christine was saying to the policeman: 'I hope you're not going to go upsetting all our friends!'

'Stanley's been to see Monty.' Rhoda had used Captain Cook's information to set wheels in motion. She said to the detective: 'Tell them what you told me. I wasn't going to tell them.'

Leslie had turned pink. 'It's not another name, is it?'

127

Rhoda put her arm around him but he threw it off. She said:
'You're my son. Your name is Fenton like the rest. I always said
it was, didn't I? Yes, I did.'

Stanley said: 'He was already married.'

'I'll kill him,' Leslie said.

'You mustn't do that, Leslie.' Rhoda got between her youngest
son and the door. 'He's got four children.'

'They live in a caravan at Isleham,' Stanley said. 'They were
married in 1919. Two years before he met your mother.'

Ronald said: 'But can you prove it?'

'That's my job,' Stanley said. 'And I've done it. You're all
going to be rich.'

'And I'm going to be a bastard,' Leslie said.

'You were always a bastard,' Christine told her brother. And
as he flew at her and Stanley held him in an official grasp, she
laughed: 'Well, you were, weren't you? Why don't you laugh
it off —'

'I'll buy you a motorbike,' Rhoda said.

'I don't want a motorbike!' Leslie said. 'I want a car.'

Stanley said: 'You're not old enough to drive. I'll tell you
what you're going to have — a new father.'

'I am forming rather an alarming theory,' Charles said. 'Tell
me this. Is Doctor Tischler the kind of man who would chase
after young bits of skirt — like I do, for instance? By the way,
how did you get on with Chloe? If you don't want to tell me I
shall understand. Perfectly. Or is he one of those professors who
wouldn't know a nipple from a whitehead?'

They were up in Horace's tiny back bedroom that builders
make when they've got a bit left over. Horace had shown Charles
his guitar and played his nine chords and now they were discussing the case. Horace now knew the picture was Hitler and about
Hazel's catering connection with the BUF. It was his opinion
that Doctor Tischler was only interested in his own family.

'Then why did he follow Hazel home from work?'

This was news to Horace; practically everything was.

'I'll tell you why,' Charles Baldwin said.

It was a day when Doctor Tischler had shouted at the girl for
tidying his books. It was the day she had seen him weeping; it

was the day Hitler went into Vienna.

'He probably thought she was prying. Not for herself. For somebody else. He wanted to find out who it was — does that make sense?'

Horace thought it made sense.

'He found out where she lived,' Charles said, 'and he started watching her house. Remember what the neighbours said?'

'But that was me,' Horace said. He had to explain himself and Charles was deeply touched.

'Her death must have hit you rather hard,' he said, compassionately.

'Gosh, yes,' Horace lied.

Charles pointed out that it didn't spoil his theory; Tischler could have watched the house in Riverside too.

'That Sunday afternoon,' Charles went on, 'he saw me drive away in the Lagonda — a foreign car. That clinched it for him. He went into the house to question her — but found an easy way to make sure she wouldn't pry again.'

'Good Lord,' Horace said.

'The gas mains switch is in the kitchen,' Charles said. 'Up here on the meter over the sink.' He put his hand up onto Horace's bedroom wall. 'Who's this?' he asked.

It was a glossy photograph of a beautiful girl wearing just a few beads; Ronald had given it to Horace in exchange for helping him to scrape gault from the banks of the river by the Iron Bridge.

'Lilian Gish,' Horace told Charles.

'After that,' Charles said, 'he just crept away.'

'Mind yourself on the wall,' Horace warned him. He had used an orange water distemper which came off in fine powder. 'What shall we do?'

They decided to take the theory to W. B. Barclay. Horace had described W. B. Barclay rather well, from his Joe Stalin appearance to his 'Three dayeeees!', and included that the chief engineer, whether entertaining top executives or lecturing to the student apprentices, very often wore no socks.

'Marvellous,' Charles said. 'He sounds a very authoritative fellow.'

Stanley and Christine were on the point of going out when

they came down but it was quite obvious that the detective was almost rupturing himself to know what was going on between the lads.

'Don't go out, Horace,' Rhoda called. 'I'm cooking your chitterlings. Perhaps your friend would like some.'

Charles declined and Horace put them in abeyance; the whole house already smelt like crisp cooked bowels.

'Just a minute, sir,' Stanley said. He was blocking their path to the front door and looking at Charles. 'Where do you work, exactly?'

Charles said: 'I don't work. Exactly. I'm studying architecture. One thing they're going to need after the war is a lot of buildings.'

'What war?' Stanley Polsworth said. 'Are you another of these warmongers? Did you hear Winston Churchill last night — stirring it up?'

Christine said, with some tiny measure of hope: 'Do you really think there's going to be a war, Charles?'

Rhoda came through from the kitchen with a piece of hot chitterling cap on a fork, very cross: 'There's never going to be another war!' she said. 'My Jim made sure of that. He's the Unknown Warrior,' she explained in an aside to Charles. 'The Great War was the war to end wars. They made a land fit for heroes to live in.'

Charles looked at them in wonder. 'How can you say that? Germany's been building up since the middle twenties. Even when they were in the League they were evading the Versaille conditions by disguising military aircraft as civilian. They've had a whole army of highly-skilled staff officers in bowler hats for years.'

Horace said: 'I didn't know that!'

'You don't know anything,' Charles told him, cheerfully. 'It's what I like about you. You probably will be a writer — everything comes fresh to you.'

Ronald had now come out into the hall with Leslie, interested in what they had been overhearing.

'There's not going to be a war,' Ronald said. 'Hitler has signed a pact with Mussolini — it was on the wireless. A non-aggression pact.'

Detective-Sergeant Polsworth confirmed this: 'It's only the League of Nations that wants war,' he said. 'Hitler doesn't want war.'

Charles smiled at them, enviously. 'Do you really seriously believe that? What a happy life you must lead.'

Hitler needs us, Horace thought as he went out with Charles. That's exactly what Doctor Tischler meant.

'He's not a Varsity man,' Stanley told Christine when they'd gone, aware of her brighter eyes and that she'd done her hair a different way while the boys were upstairs. 'He's a townie. I can smell 'em a mile off.'

'That's the chitterlings,' Christine told him.

They made love every night now on the sofa, simply because the cow had gone and the gate was open.

They had driven to the big mock-Tudor villa four miles out of town in the long Queen Edith's Way and spoken with Anne Barclay, the chief engineer's wife. She had recognised Horace and tied the dog up.

'You're the little boy who cut the lawn, aren't you?'

It had been a short-time period at the works before Horace moved into Research; Ernie Trigg had come looking for somebody in the coil shop who wanted a half-day's work. This is really how Horace had got his move, for he'd got on well with Ernie.

'I can see you wield real influence with this company,' Charles said as they waited for Mrs Barclay to try to reach her husband by phone.

'My voice used to be very high-pitched,' Horace told him, lamely.

Charles laughed. 'I know what you're trying to say.' Then he said: 'I say — she's rather dishy.'

A very pretty little blonde girl put one eye around the doorpost and studied them. Funny to think of W.B.B. as a dad; but then it wasn't. He was a dad; at home wherever he went with no pretences or formal faces. It was because he had the confidence that goes with a brilliant mind.

At the Gog-Magog Golf Club they went ranging over the course and finally found him. Back at the club he bought them beers, spreading everything out of his pocket for the bartender to choose what he wanted. Horace was to notice all these things, for later on the chief engineer moved to another company and Horace was one of the people he took with him, moving him up the ladder, sending him to automation and servo-control courses and taking him around the country investigating problems of industrial control.

' Now who do you say you are? ' W. B. Barclay said again as he handed Horace his beer. ' Oh yes — I remember. The chap with the voice. I thought I told you not to mention Tischler or anything else that was said? '

Charles stopped Horace's apologetic stuttering by giving the chief engineer a clear résumé of the story so far; he seemed to talk the same kind of confident British language, using words like ' goff ' and ' orf ' and braying loud ' har har hars ' when it was appropriate. Horace listened and admired them and liked them, sipping his brown ale. One day, he would be like that.

' As a theory, I like it,' W.B.B. was telling Charles, ' but it's preposterous. Tischler couldn't hurt anybody.'

Horace said : ' He tried to kill Harry Webb.'

' Ah, yes, that's a good point,' the chief engineer said.

He tapped his fingers on the table for a moment and started humming *You'd be so nice to come home to*. Charles and Horace waited. He said at last :

' I'd like to bring Brockelberg in on this but he's out at Madingley and there isn't time. Hugh ! ' he called to another member across the bar, a man with a red beard, who looked round. ' Know anything about schizophrenia? '

' Not my bag, Bill — sorry.'

W.B.B. now took out a small comb-sized case from his inside pocket and extracted a slide-rule on which he proceeded to do a long and careful calculation. ' My God ! ' he said at last. It made up his mind. ' All right then. We'll go and find Tischler — anybody know where he lives? '

' Hertford Street,' Charles said, ' up by the Rendezvous.'

Funny, Horace suddenly thought as they drove down the long chalk hills. *How does Charles know where Tischler lives?*

He didn't question it because he didn't want to find out anything unpleasant about Charles; he seemed a good chap. In the

132

Lagonda mirror Horace could see W. B. Barclay following them in his little fawn Austin Ruby, the golf clubs sticking out from the sunshine roof. They turned into Queen Edith's Way and waited outside in the car while W. B. Barclay went in to make dinner arrangements. When he came out he was running; stopped for a moment to talk to them — well, to Charles, really.

'Tischler's dead,' he said. 'Phone message. The night watchman just found him in the cabin.'

'Gosh,' Horace said.

It was almost as though Doctor Tischler, having learned of the fate of his wife and children, had built his own gas chamber in order to share their suffering and their death. Against the suicide theory was the fact that he was wearing the audiometer earphones and the cable-jack had jerked out of the panel as he fell to the floor.

'I find it hard to accept that it was accidental,' W. B. Barclay told a police inspector who had taken charge. His name was Jarvis and he had Detective-Sergeant Polsworth — brought out of the Dorothy ballroom, since he was already engaged in the Hazel Springer investigation — working with him. Stan was at present down in the plating shop trying to find out why the ventilation pipe had fallen back from the wall opening and dropped into the tank of carbon tetrachloride — used as a metal degreaser.

'One would need a number of required conditions to make Tischler's death accidental,' the chief engineer said, in his lecturing voice. It was not that he was indifferent to the Austrian's fate; just that problems took first place in his mind.

Horace, sitting on Tischler's stool at Tischler's work bench, listened to all this and made his own conjectures. The pipe could have fallen of its own accord, since it was indifferently fitted by an indifferent workman.

That old Jewboy should've been blown up, he could hear Harry Webb saying again.

'Then again,' W.B.B. said, 'carbon tetrachloride fumes would be detectable and would first of all produce a feeling of elation, of intoxication — it is an hallucinatory drug. We played with it in high school. That is,' he added, 'unless Tischler was smoking.

133

If he was smoking then the effect would be more rapid and unpredictable.'

' He was smoking, sir,' Inspector Jarvis said.

' Ah,' said W.B.B. with some satisfaction.

' May I interject? ' Horace said.

They turned round, seeing him for the first time; Horace, self-conscious now, had surprised himself. Nevertheless, his sudden thought blurted out: ' If the fan was going, how could the fumes have gone into the cabin — it sucks the wrong way.'

The inspector went away to investigate and W.B.B. nodded to Horace, pleased with him. ' A good point — Fenton, is it? Are you studying anywhere? '

Horace told him. Charles came up from the plating shop with Polsworth and Inspector Jarvis returned from Uncle Tom's Cabin. The fan had been turned round; instead of sucking it was blowing.

' Then we must go back to the suicide theory,' W.B.B. said.

Charles said : ' I'm afraid I must contradict that, sir.'

' Yes, of course,' Barclay said, evenly. ' I shall contradict it myself soon. I suggest that we all sit down and get somebody to make some coffee. Fenton, try to get Brockelberg on the phone — I'd very much like him here.' He looked at the police inspector : ' Perhaps you'll send your man to fetch him.'

' Yes, sir,' said the inspector.

' And whatever we decide,' W. B. Barclay said, taking out his slide-rule again and starting to calculate on it, for it kept his mind working, ' poor Tischler has been murdered.'

' Murdered, sir? ' Inspector Jarvis was now looking at the slide-rule. This was quite new to him in criminology.

' By the Nazis,' W.B.B. said. ' The Gadarene herd. The animals of Europe. . . .'

Chapter Nineteen

The bicycle rider in Burwell Fen yodelled his happiness at leaving a boy and returning a man and having a woman there to prove it.

' Do it again,' Claire said.

Horace did it again, the noise breaking octaves in his throat.

' Now listen ! ' Claire said. She had stopped pedalling to listen. ' There ! It's coming back ! '

Very faintly, from some directionless source beyond the meadows of the Lode and beyond Devil's Dyke, someone was yodelling back.

' That's funny,' Horace said. ' You'd think they'd all be grown-up by now.'

Claire laughed at him and started pedalling again; she saw things in him that other people didn't see and it pleased him. She'd seen things in his writing that even he didn't see. She called it his ' X ' factor. She couldn't explain to him what it was but she said :

' Take that title, " The Boy With The Dead Father ". When you're middle-aged and successful, look at that again and remember me. Remember what I say. You'll find that you can't improve it. You'll be lucky if you're doing as well.'

' I can't sell it,' Horace said.

' They can't buy it,' she said. ' That's the way to look at it.' She meant that the people who wanted it didn't know where it was. Horace had not found them yet. And she told him that if he wanted to write more stories like that he must look into his own life, examine his own roots. ' You are really the boy with the dead father,' she said.

' Which way ? ' she called now.

Horace told her the way.

This was his first road. On this road he had ridden in his first motor car, the taxi that brought him, as star boy soprano, to the Musical Festival. This quiet low country road, metalled with brown chippings and verged with grass, reed, poppy, mallow-marsh and warpbinder, ditched and hedged and following the Doomsday routes between fields of corn, beet and clover, joining

135

the Swaffams with Burwell, Lode and Stow-cum-Quy and sending its dead-end drifts and lanes down to the bridgeless Cam and
the black fen dykes, this was the first of some twenty roads that
would join Horace to life, fame, love and finally the grave.

'Oh look! Stocks!' Claire exclaimed as she dismounted
by Pound Hill. 'Are they genuine? Did Oliver Cromwell use
them?'

Horace had used them. Horace had been locked into the
stocks by a boy called Dicker Docker and had had his own collection of rotten unblown birds' eggs thrown in his face. Dicker
Docker was smaller than Horace but he was built like a fist. He
came from an underprivileged motherless farm-labouring family
which included two brothers, a sister Shirl, a huge father who
sat all day on a little wooden chair in the High Street watching
people and horses pass by, and a rotation of pigs who lived in
the side yard. In the course of the five years the Fentons lived
in Burwell Dicker Docker attacked Horace many times, beating
him up with his fists in a sixty-minute marathon fight along The
Causeway, locking him in the stocks, almost knocking his eye out
with a cudgel and actually shooting him behind the knee with
a *Diana* air gun. It had broken Horace's nerve so that he would
hide if he saw Dicker Docker coming. Something about Horace
infuriated this nut-hard fen boy.

'It's your "X" factor,' Claire told him. 'You either love it
or you hate it. I love it.'

Horace's 'X' factor had to do with avoiding the cliché
wherever he found it. This means the avoidance of accepted
behaviour, attitudes, laws, food, patterns, ethics, punctuation,
death, jokes, sex, clocks, smiles, tears, taste, funerals, weddings,
christenings, parent/teacher associations, friends of multiple
sclerosis and oranges. He was not old enough yet to know what
trouble this would cause him.

'That's Mr Macbeth the chemist,' Horace told her as they
cycled down the long crooked village. 'He used to bring dead
cats to life with cayenne pepper.'

Horace had earned a shilling a week from Mr Macbeth for
travelling round the villages on Mitcham's little red bus collecting live cats in a basket. This was Parsonage Lane where he had
been trapped by a horse and here was Spring Close, site of the

136

Norman Castle, where Horace had been stuck up a tree for three hours.

'You had a lousy boyhood,' Claire told him. 'Are you sure you wouldn't rather go somewhere else?'

It hadn't seemed lousy at the time. There had been picnics on Devil's Dyke, walks across the heath to see the Cesarewitch run at Newmarket, blackberrying, bird-shooting with a torch at night for blackbird pies, corn-gleaning at harvest and horse-leading in the holidays.

'This is where I used to bring my cows,' Horace said as they wobbled by the thistled field on the Reach Road.

'And still do,' said Claire.

Memories sprang at him. *What d'you do wid all y'r fedders, Leslie?* The little Irish boy whose mother used to cook with a dew-drop on the end of her nose. The window the brick came through at dead of night. *You can like, a ukelele lady, ukelele lady like me.* . . . The Warrens, Jenkins, Adams, Thurstons, Games, Hurrels, Badcocks and Claydons. Dicks and bums behind the haystacks on Ness Road.

In Toys Lane Claire again dismounted.

'What are those people doing?'

'Drawing water from the well,' Horace said. He used to do that, carrying it home on a two-bucket yoke around his shoulders.

'My God,' said Claire. 'Twelve miles and we're in mediaeval England yet. In Golders Green we have taps.'

'We've got a tap now,' Horace said.

She laughed at him again; the more sophisticated Horace wanted to pretend to be the more he became a village simpleton. This was the 'X' factor too. Detecting this from her laughter, Horace said:

'We'll go home through Bottisham and I'll buy you a drink.'

'Push me, Horace,' Claire said. 'I'm tired.'

She put her sandals up on the front mudguard of her bike and Horace pedalled hard, one hand in the middle of her back. They passed the church hall where Horace was a scout until he'd lost his uniform for not being able to keep up the sixpence a week. They passed the barn in which a troupe of mummers had been massacred and the front room of a condemned shack into which the Fenton family had finally dwindled in the pea-picking times, leaving their furniture in Cooper's second-hand shop, the remnants of Jim's honeymoon home and the draughtboard tables from the tea shop. They passed the war memorial where on November elevenths they had stood for two minutes' silences, remembering the dead, and they passed the meadow behind the tithe barn where each Mayday Horace had danced around the maypole.

He stopped mentioning these things, however, because he did not want Claire to think of him as a boy any more.

' Boy ! '

The cry was so close and so clear and so loud that Horace slipped on his pedal and almost pushed Claire off her bike.

' Boy ! Over here ! Quickly ! '

Two funny little old country women were running the long length of a flower-bordered garden path waving their arms at him.

Claire said : ' I think they mean you.'

Horace was of a mind to push on but Claire had blocked his path and was half off her machine, one foot on the ground. The two women in their long dresses came clucking shrilly towards them like scared hens.

' 'Tis a matter of life and death, boy,' one of them told him. ' Do you know Doctor Hanton's? Ride like the devil and give him this note ! '

' Like the devil ! ' cried her friend. ' Do 'ee stand up and ride and don't stop till you get there.'

' And there's a sixpence for you, laddie,' said the other.

Claire said : ' What is it? An accident? '

' 'Tis our Beth afore her time,' said one of them. ' The poor child be nearly born ! '

' Well, don't worry,' Claire told them. ' I'm nearly a doctor.' And to Horace she said : ' Ride like the devil, laddie ! ' He could see that she was greatly amused and enjoying it. This was the emergency she had always dreamed of, with her the shining hero. ' I'll want plenty of hot water,' she was saying as Horace rode off. ' A ball of garden twine and a pair of shears — or something like that.'

Horace rode like the devil, standing up over the crossbar and bearing all his weight down on the pedals, all pretences gone.

Horace Spurgeon Fenton! he thought, each word driving the pedal down, *Writer, artist and year book!*

' Hard, bony boy, panting, unsure, searching for his mother in the nearest whore.'
' What are you saying? '
' Piece of poetry I just made up.'
' I'm not a boy.'
' But you are, Horace. I love boys. Young boys. Virgins. Didn't Charles tell you? Yes, he did, he's a sod — oh! Careful! '
' Sorry.'
' Not sorry, Horace. Be rough.'
' I can't do it.'
' You're trying too hard. Think of something else. Be yourself, not yourself lying on top of a Jewish girl in tall ripe grass. *Natur, natur! Nichts so Natur als Schakespears Menschen.*'
' What does that mean? '
' It's Franz's Goethe. Put your Gentile foreskin to my lips.'
Don' moof! Don' moof or I shoot!
' Now, while it's hard. No rush, no hurry. Oh, my God, that's beautiful. Slowly now, please, very slowly. And stop. And slow. And quick quick, stop. Again. Don't you talk? '
' You're not really Jewish? '
' Yes, I am. Second generation Golders Green.'
' Are you anti-Nazi? '
' Not so's you'd notice. Don't talk *too* much.'
' Your lot stabbed the German army in the back.'
' So you're complaining? '
' I'm going to finish — '
' Don't finish! Don't finish. Think of something else.'
' Who's The Canary? '
' What? '
' The Canary. Fuck the canary, you said. By the river. To Gertie and Stella.'
' That's wonderful. Can you keep doing that? It was just a canary. It got out. We chased it down to the river. Don't talk now.'
' Franz had got a gun.'
' Believe me, Franz *needs* a gun — Gun! Gun! Gun! Yes,

yes, yes, yes — oh, my lovely fucking goy . . .'

Writing that night he tried to describe her as an exercise. What made her so full of sex was her bum. It moved under her tight skirt so it looked from behind as if she was a thin girl riding a dainty pony.

Chapter Twenty

Ronald came back from the Pitt Club one day and made an announcement, which wasn't like him.

' I'm going to be a milkman,' he said.

Rhoda was overjoyed. ' That's the first time I've ever known you to show any real ambition! ' she exclaimed.

' Neville Hampstead's just had his arm off,' Horace said.

' Whatever happened? ' asked Chris.

Rhoda said: ' They're a funny family altogether. You see, they'll get a pension for him before I get mine back.'

Mrs Leah Munnings was now fighting the case. Mrs Leah Munnings was headmistress of Horace's old school for the mentally retarded (now The Lady Adrian) up Milton Road; she was also a well-known socialist Member of Parliament. In Horace's day it was known as the Fresh Air School and they had admitted him to the curriculum of good plain food, no mental work, plenty of football and lying in fields on stretchers. He had made six painted fretwork firescreens, ten chased leather bridge-scoring books, four beaten pewter pots. One night he had got in the driving cabin of the double-decker school bus and started it going while the driver was getting the kids and teachers aboard. The bus overturned onto some allotments amid a dreadful panic, and at a later inquiry a teacher got the sack. Horace had been returned to his old school at Red Romsey.

' What's your little boy doing now? ' Mrs Leah Munnings asked Rhoda when she came about the pension.

' Do you know who the Wander Bug is? ' Leslie said. This was another of their family liaison sessions. ' Captain Cook.'

' It's because I turned him down,' Rhoda admitted, not without pride.

' Well, it's better than shooting himself,' Christine said.

' Just,' said Horace.

And Ronald continued: ' At the Stetchworth Dairies in Tennyson Road.' He was still talking about his ambitions.

The Wander Bug was going to cycle round the world for peace. Captain Cook, now wearing his Salvation Army uniform, being photographed on Parker's Piece. His bicycle, donated by Ward's of East Road, laden down like a mule with survival contributions from Eaden Lilley's, Joshua Taylor's, Laurie McConnell's, Winton Smith's, Page's, Robert Sayle's, Bodger's, Herbert Robinson's, Waite's (arctic wear) and enough others, including a Bible from Heffer's, to fill two columns in the *Daily News*.

' I want to thank my sisters and brothers,' Captain Cook cried over the Tannoy, his arms semaphoring brotherly embraces, ' and take the word of peace to our brothers and sisters in distant places. To the Africans, to the Asians, to the Europeans — '

' To the Jews! ' cried a voice not far from Horace.

' Fuck off, Webby,' somebody said.

Captain Cook, pushing his heavily-laden bike, headed the procession across the Piece towards his kicking-off point at the Scott Polar Research Laboratory. Following him came the citadel band blazing some militant love march.

' I thought you had your arm off? ' Horace told Neville.

A band of basketed cyclists followed the crowd, getting ready to escort the famous peacemonger as far as Royston.

' It wasn't me, it was Mr Crowe and it wasn't his arm, it was another finger,' Neville said.

A boy called Foster, an old Romsey Red bully with a cropped head, riding a Royal Enfield, swore a string of alliterative obscenity about scientists in general, starting with ' feeble '. A Salvation Army girl marching just in front of his wheel did not turn her bonneted head. After this he said :

' They should be thinking of something to stop Hitler, not messing about with atoms.' His father had read something like this in a Stafford Cripps quote from the *Daily Worker*.

' Hitler needs us,' Horace said, with just the right amount of bitterness.

The boys fell silent, working this out. Just behind them Jammy Rolls had his cigarette cards trapped in his spokes, ready for blasting off; at top speed he sounded like an outboard motor.

Outside the town the cycling cavalcade passed five abreast along the Trumpington Road, narrowing to three as they forked right at The Old English Gentleman at Harston. It was on this road that Horace had lost his dog while cycling in search of his native air.

'She slowly dropped behind,' Horace told Neville, as they sped along, side by side, a green Rudge Whitworth and a black Raleigh.

'I still say it was a rotten thing to do,' Neville Hampstead said.

'I wouldn't do it now,' Horace said.

Horace had improved in many ways.

'Hello!' Claire was edging up between them on a broken-down Girton-type bike with a sloppy basket dredged down almost onto the front wheel with books. 'Mind if I come between you?'

Neville Hampstead's eyes had crossed slightly with nerves; it happened whenever he met girls. But the girl was smiling at Horace, her head ducking down to meet her rising knees as she kept pace with them.

''Tis our Beth afore her time!' she panted.

A high-flying squadron of Hawker Furies went over at right-angles to the road and vanished behind the combined smoke from the three tall chimneys of Barrington Cement Works.

In the broad fields the last harvest of peace awaited the gathering.

Foundations of Progressive Education

Foundations of
Progressive Education
The History of The National Froebel Society

Joachim Liebschner

THE LUTTERWORTH PRESS
CAMBRIDGE

The Lutterworth Press
P.O. Box 60
Cambridge
CB1 2NT

Copyright © Joachim Liebschner 1991
The right of H.P.J. Liebschner to be identified as
the author of this book has been asserted by him in accordance
with the Copyright, Designs and Patents Act 1988.

First published by The Lutterworth Press, 1991

British Library Cataloguing-in-Publication Data
Liebschner, Joachim
    Foundations of progressive education: the history of the National
    Froebel society.
    I. Title
    372.21

    ISBN 0-7188-2835-6

Printed in the UK by
WBC Print Ltd., Bridgend, Mid Glamorgan

Contents

Für Ingeborg Gurland

Acknowledgements

At the time of my retirement the Trustees of the National Froebel Foundation suggested to me that I write the story of the Froebel Movement in Great Britain, based on the minute books of the Foundation. At first I shied away from a task which involved the skills of a researcher and the gift of a writer, neither of which I possess. On reflection, however, it occurred to me that someone ought to make the effort to record the achievements of a movement, which, as the reader will see, revolutionised educational practices in our schools. And even if no one else were to profit from the writing, I certainly would benefit from the study of the people whom I had so long admired.

I would never have completed this task without the encouragement of Molly Brearley, the former Principal of the Froebel Educational Institute and Kay Davies, the former Principal of Wall Hall College who have guided me patiently and wisely through every chapter. Without their counsel and encouragement, the book would never have been written. I also received help, especially with corrections, from Terry Fursland, the wife of the former Headmaster of Strand-on-the-Green School and from Margaret Turner. Josie Ashton Mauro and Jill Leney typed and re-typed the manuscript at least twice. Juliet and Peter Norris put me on the trail of *The Idiot Teacher* and the little Froebel School in Sompting. Jane Read, the archivist of the Early Childhood Collection at the Froebel Institute College provided helpful advice, and Jill Redford, the Principal, and the Governors of the College who gave permission to reproduce the pictures in this book. To all of them, I wish to express my warm thanks. I am also grateful to the Trustees of the National Froebel Foundation for their helpful comments and support over many years. I only ask the reader not to place the responsibility for any mistakes or shortcomings at their feet. It is entirely mine.

And finally, there is Ingeborg Gurland, the Froebel teacher, a German Jewess who lost her loved ones in a concentration camp and then used her small savings to provide the former German prisoner-of-war with the means to study in this country.

Foreword

This is the story of a handful of young women who changed British education. These women were members of a society which tried to implement the educational philosophy and practice of Friedrich Froebel, the German schoolmaster who believed that a child's intellectual, spiritual and physical development came about by the child's own actions. In Froebel's schools, adults would carefully observe the children in their care and then suggest and guide rather than prescribe and dictate. Froebel's interest in the very young led to the creation of the Kindergarten with its emphasis on play as a means of education.

The idea that children needed to be listened to before one could teach them; that children at play were children learning; that children's active and creative living provided a more lasting education than the one provided by adults telling children the answers to questions they had not asked; All this was so contrary to prevailing belief and practice that it needed much time and skilled practitioners to persuade ordinary men and women, teachers and principals, administrators and politicians before the new education became common-place. But how were the young women to acquire the knowledge so essential to their task?

The Prussian Government, mindful of its own precarious position after the 1848 uprisings, viewed Froebel's educational ideas with increasing suspicion. To educate children by encouraging them to probe, to investigate, to pose their own problems and find their own solutions rather than unquestioningly accepting the knowledge and ideas of others, seemed to the Government to be nurturing future revolutionaries. In 1851, the year before Froebel's death, it issued the Kindergarten Verbot. This edict, which closed all Kindergartens without exception, was based on the view that they were anti-Christian and anti-social institutions. A hard judgement on the man who said on his deathbed that all his life he had striven to bring people to a knowledge and love of Christ and whose practices in the classroom emphasised the social responsibilities of each member in the room.

The teachers at these schools, mostly women trained in Froebel's school in Keilhau or his training institute in Marienthal, had now to choose between giving up their profession, teaching in state schools and thereby negating their ideals, or going abroad and carrying Froebel's philosophy and their own enthusiasm with them. Within twenty years of the closure of Kindergartens in Prussia, Froebel's teachers were working in countries as far afield as Russia and America and as close at hand as Ireland and England.

The first Kindergartens thus formed in London, Manchester and Dublin soon attracted the attention of teachers, especially those concerned with younger children.

X

There was also a growing awareness that more needed to be done for children below school age and that conventional methods of instruction were of little value when applied to children of the younger age-range. Thus, in 1874, the Froebel Society came into being with the express purpose of promoting the Kindergarten system. To do this, members of the Society had first to inform themselves more comprehensively about Froebel's theory and practice. Books, written in English, were not available and few of the members had mastered the German language. At first, members of the Society had to rely on their German friends and on their German-speaking members to provide them with lectures, courses and translations of articles and pamphlets.

The more members expanded their knowledge, the more they changed their classroom practices and the more questions parents asked. The Society therefore arranged public lectures as well as exhibitions. Requests from teachers for more information about the new education led to courses for practising teachers and the establishment of the first Kindergarten Training College within the first few years of the Society's existence.

Even though the Society experienced many serious set-backs over the years, its work eventually not only provided for the training of Kindergarten teachers and the dissemination of Froebel's ideas through summer courses, lectures and exhibitions, but in setting up its own inspectorate for the inspection of Kindergartens changed pre-school education from a child-minding activity to an educational venture.

Just before the First World War the Society also introduced a course especially designed for those who were involved in the training of Kindergarten teachers. As only a small number of those who were selected for the course ever completed it successfully, the diploma had the standing of a university degree, and gave holders of the diploma easy access to work in training colleges. Thus by the 1930s and 1940s many colleges were employing Froebel-trained lecturers in their education departments whose enthusiasm for child-centred education was carried into primary schools by their students.

Though not many people realized how the changes in our primary schools from a formal, subject centred and three-R-based curriculum to a creative-activity and child-centred education came about, the Plowden Committee with its mandate 'to consider primary education in all its aspects' more than hinted at the cause. Its report *Children and their Primary Schools*, published in 1967 recorded:

It was rare to find teachers who had given much time to the study of educational theory even in their college days. Perhaps the strongest influence was that of Froebel, mediated through the Froebel Training Colleges.....

Not many schools or colleges can be found, either in this country or abroad, which carry Froebel's name. Yet, most of those countries where Froebel education has been introduced still maintain pockets of educational endeavour where his philosophy is kept alive. Several educational institutions in the United States, for example, especially around Chicago, are running courses for Kindergarten teachers on Froebel lines. In Japan, Froebel's Gifts, a seriated collection of wooden building bricks, were produced as late as the 1920s and the present Froebel schools enjoy a high reputation. In Ireland, a two-year part-time Froebel course for practising teachers is regularly over-subscribed. In East Germany, Froebel was used to support an educational system which emphasised the importance of teaching children to work together for the common good, while in West Germany he was equally successfully quoted to support a system which placed the emphasis on the needs of the individual child. The educational system of the newly united Germany is thus likely also to be in his debt. English universities introduce their students to Froebel, together with Rousseau and Pestalozzi as the founders of progressive education.

The story here told is based on the records of the Froebel Society's minute books. The Society's offices were based in London and old Froebelians from other parts of the country, especially Manchester and Bedford may feel that insufficient attention has been given to their efforts. While it is true that there were many pockets of active and enthusiastic Froebelians in other parts of the country during the hundred years of the Society's existence, the main thrust, which eventually affected educational thinking on a national scale, came from London. A more detailed examination of Frobel's ideas is provided in the forthcoming book *Freedom and Guidance in Play* by the same author.

So as to provide the reader with some idea of the scale of differences between Froebelian ideas of the treatment of children and those generally prevalent at the time, reference has been made to historical records and educational documents. Summarising such reports and records entails simplification which often lead to falsification. Every effort has been made to avoid this, though, no doubt, grey areas still remain. Whatever the shortcomings of this book, and there will be many, the author hopes to have succeeded in creating a fitting memorial to all those Froebelians who spent their lives in the service of children.

Introduction

The influence of the Froebel Movement has been tremendous in this country, so why is it, the reader may wonder, that people have scarcely heard of its existence. After all, Montessori schools are well known and can be found in most parts of the country while Froebel schools have disappeared except for the one in Roehampton. Those who do know about Friedrich Froebel will say that much of what Froebel proclaimed is now common practice in our schools so that, in a sense, all schools have become Froebel schools. It is certainly true that even when major innovations had been observed in a school, the observers often failed to inquire why and how these new ideas and new ways of teaching children had been brought about. At the same time the teachers who were responsible for these changes did not find it necessary to proclaim the source of their inspirations. Take for example the revolutionary activities which were going on in the little village school of Sompting in Sussex, at the turn of the century - activities which influenced teachers and school inspectors for over half a century and about which historians have written ever since.

In 1952 (Reprint 1977) Gerald Holmes published *The Idiot Teacher*, the story of Teddy O'Neill's school in the heart of industrial England, early this century. Gerald Holmes, a school inspector, provides us with an account of a Lancashire school which had been made into a workshop so that its headmaster could claim 'that these yards and buildings are educational laboratories'. It was an open school, a school where parents were made welcome, where adults were encouraged to learn with the children and where the community at large used the school during the day-time as well as during the evening hours. Class lessons were rare and if they did take place, they were used either as a means to stimulate research and provide the means for finding out or to confirm and order the knowledge acquired. The teacher was seen as an enabler, stimulating 'the ability to find out and the desire to do', rather than being the provider of knowledge. Children were encouraged to work together, to help each other and to devise strategies for solving problems corporately. Competition was not known and individual time-tables demanded an integrated day. In short it was a typical Froebel school and yet there is no mention of Froebel anywhere in the book.

The author tells us that at the time when Teddy O'Neill attended his teacher training college, he came across a book by Edmond Holmes, the then recently retired Chief Inspector for Elementary Schools, who had acquired a thorough understanding of the workings of the country's educational system, first as an Inspector of Schools from 1874-1905 and then as Chief Inspector. The book, entitled *What is and what might be*, gave a very critical account of the school system as he knew it. He described the work done in England's elementary schools as repressive and destructive of children's mental and spiritual powers. Unfortunately for him, he says, he had not realized until late in his career that what he was witnessing and inspecting each year, had little to do with educating children. Now in his retirement he condemned the prevailing method of spoon-feeding children and the teachers' inabilities to encourage independence of action and thought. He writes:

> ...the aim of the teacher is to do everything for the child; to feed him with semi-digested food, to hold him by the hand, or rather by the shoulders, when he tries to walk or run; to keep him under close and constant supervision; to tell him in precise detail what he is to think, to feel, to say, to wish, to do, to show in precise detail how he is to do whatever may have to be done; to lay thin veneers of information on the surface of his mind; never to allow him a minute of independent study; never to trust him with a handbook, a note-book, or a sketch-book; in fine, to do all in his power to prevent the child from doing anything whatever for himself.... (Holmes 1911:4)

But Holmes' book also provides a solution to the problem. He says that late in his career he had been fortunate enough to encounter a school in rural England, where 'Egeria', his ideal teacher, was surrounded by ceaselessly active children whose bright and happy faces gave evidence of the value of self-motivation and creative activities.

> And the activity of the Utopian child is his own activity. It is a fountain which springs up in himself. Unlike the ordinary school-child, he can do things on his own account. He does not wait, in the helplessness of passive obedience, for his teacher to tell him what he is to do and how he is to do it.... If a new situation arises, he deals with it with promptitude and decision.... His initiative has evidently been developed with his intelligence; and the result of this is that he can think things out for himself.... (Holmes 1911:154-156)

'The function of education is to foster growth', says Holmes at the beginning of the book. He talks of 'the development of latent powers' in children and 'the unfolding of their latent life'. These are all Froebelian terms, but there is no mention of Froebel.

We know that Edmond Holmes' eye-opening experiences took place in a small country school where 'Egeria' held court. Hyndman tells us that the school was in Sompting in Sussex and that 'Egeria's real name was Harriett Johnson[1]. We are not told who Harriett Johnson was and why her school should have been so different from all the other schools Edmond Holmes had been visiting for forty years. But if we take the time to visit the school and care to look through the School Log Book, we will find the following entries:

> 10th December 1897   Commenced new Kindergarten Gift with children this week. Stitching geometrical patterns.

> 8th May 1898   Practice during lesson of Kindergarten Songs etc. for May-Day celebrations.

> 23rd June 1899   The children have learned a new Kindergarten game 'The Railway Train'.

In Harriett Johnson's own book *The Dramatic Method of Teaching*, we read:

> A child learns, and retains what he is learning, better by actually seeing and doing things, which is a guiding principle of Kindergarten. There is not a very marked difference

between the ages of the children who enjoy learning by Kindergarten games and of the so called 'older scholars'. Why not continue the principle of the Kindergarten game in the school for older children?   (Finlay-Johnson ND:19)

A.T.Ternent in his unpublished biography of Harriett Johnson states:

There can be little doubt that Miss Harriett Johnson was a most enthusiastic disciple of the great German educationist Friedrich Froebel ... her fundamental assumptions are: That the function of education is to foster growth. That the business of growing must be done by the growing child and cannot be done for him by his teacher or any other person. That the whole being of the child - mental, moral and spiritual, as well as physical - is making a strong and spontaneous effort to grow; in other words the child has great potentialities which are merely wanting to be realized.... That the teacher, in his attempt to foster the growth of the child, ought to follow these lines, that the school life ought to be, in the main, a life of play, but play taken seriously; play systematized, organized, provided with ample material and ample opportunities, encouraged and stimulated in every way. (Ternent 1971:51)

Harriett Johnson was a Froebel teacher and yet neither Edmond Holmes, who was forced to re-examine his life's work when he met this woman, nor the historians who wrote about Holmes' influential book refer to the origin of these educational changes, refer to Friedrich Froebel. Indeed Armytage, who considers Holmes' book *What is and what might be* 'the manifesto of the English progressives'[2], even states that the inspirations had been gleaned from the ideas of Madame Montessori. Other authors of books on the history of education mention Holmes's book as one of the few books which greatly influenced educational thinking at the beginning of the century[3]. Curtis and Boultwood believe that the two outstanding teacher-writers MacMunn and Caldwell Cook were greatly 'encouraged and invigorated' by Holmes' book and mention is made of their discipleship to Montessori and Rousseau[4]. There is no mention of Friedrich Froebel.

Gordon and White in their book *Philosophers as Educational Reformers* allocate several pages to Edmond Holmes, pointing out how the book took the educational world by storm when it appeared in 1911[5]. How in his theory and philosophical idealism he placed 'self-realization' as his highest aim and how it could be achieved in the classroom. They provide 'not surprising' reasons for his philosophy. After all Holmes had been to Oxford where the philosophy of idealism became rapidly dominant. Several other philosophers, authors and professors are mentioned who might have influenced Holmes. There is no mention of Froebel. And yet, by Holmes' own admission, all his studies in Oxford and all his readings about Buddhism, his contact with Thomson Hill Green made not the slightest difference to his life's work. He inspected school after school, as an instrument of the prevailing system, until his eyes perceived things differently because of his encounter with a Froebel teacher. Gordon and White allocate several pages to Edmond Holmes in a book on educational reformers. Friedrich Froebel is referred to in three sentences.

Mary Borser's book *Willingly to School; A History of Women's Education*, published in 1976 does not mention the Froebel Society nor the man who created the first women's teacher training college in Europe, probably the world. However there are writers who do acknowledge that Froebel's ideas 'formed the basis for the reinterpretation of infant and junior teaching that was central to the new education movement' even if they do not mention the Society which was instrumental in bringing about the new education.[6]

Froebel teachers and the Froebel Movement in general may be held responsible for not spreading the name as much as the philosophy and activities so closely linked with that name. But then, this is not really surprising when one knows that Froebel himself was never eager to create special Froebel schools. He believed that his ideas were neither new, nor revolutionary, nor special but grew out of the universal truth that a child is an essential member of humanity and as such needs the adult's respect, attention and care. This was not merely a matter for children in a special Froebel school, but an essential for all children in all schools, everywhere. Froebel believed that it would take three hundred years before all his ideals had been accepted by parents and teachers. Two hundred years have passed, Froebel may have been too optimistic.

Now that links between Froebelian philosophy and activities and present-day educational theory and practice have been more clearly established, authors of books on the history of education may find it difficult to continue to ignore the man and the movement which together probably influenced English education more than any other educator and certainly more than any other educational movement. They will at last have to acknowledge the debt of gratitude the nation owes to all these young teachers, mostly women, who with gentleness of manner, modesty of spirit and love for their children, so unobtrusively brought about the changes which have revolutionised children's lives in this country.

1. Hyndman, 1978, p44
2. Armytage, 1970, p227
3. Van der Eyken, 1973, p144
4. Curtis & Boultwood, 1962, p234
5. Gordon & White, 1979, pp194-198
6. Lawson & Silver, 1973, p283

Michaelis Kindergarten, 1908. Circle Games.

Chapter 1

Friedrich Froebel 1782-1852
The Man and His Ideas

Every human being, even as a child, must be recognised, acknowledged and fostered as a necessary and essential member of humanity. Friedrich Froebel

Among the Froebel manuscripts in the archives of the Naturwissenschaftliche Universität in Berlin there is an account of Froebel's last days, recorded by his second wife, Luise. At the end of the report are some pencilled notes, now very faint, which describe Froebel's last encounter with a child. Its concluding sentence sums up Froebel's philosophy in a few words. The record, in translation, reads:

> On the Sunday before Froebel's death, one of the children brought some flowers. Froebel greeted the small messenger with great joy. And though he already found it difficult to lift his hand, he held the child's hand and put it to his lips. Froebel now asked us to look after the flowers, saying:'look after the flowers and spare my weeds, I have learned much from both of them.'

Flowers and weeds, when carefully observed, provided equally important information and were, therefore, of equal importance to Froebel, just as intelligent and slow-learning children, conformist and non-conformist children demanded equal respect. Froebel's belief that beneath every human fault lies a crushed human virtue led him to accept even the least intelligent and most difficult children as essential and important members of the community. Yet, these were not the only reasons why children in his school felt happy and secure. Lessons under Froebel's guidance were based on children's own experiences and their own lives. Topics studied were interrelated, referred directly to the children's environment and took account of their different levels of understanding.

Such an educational institution was quite different from most of the other schools functioning in Europe at the time. Froebel lived in a century when children were considered something apart from adults, something to be tolerated, something to be filled with knowledge and moulded according to adult's wishes and demands. John Wesley, for example, gives the advice:

> ...make him do as he is bid, if you whip him ten times running to effect it. Let none persuade you it is cruelty to do this, it is cruelty not to do it. Break his will now...
> (Hyndman 1978:2)

Such a view of the aims of education was repudiated only by minorities. The prevailing attitudes and practices led to violence, arson, revolt and mutiny from those children who had the strength to object. The uprising of the pupils of Winchester School in 1818 had to be suppressed by two companies of troops with fixed bayonets. In the same year, the boys of Rugby School set fire to their desks and books and then withdrew to an island which had to be taken in an assault by the army. In 1783 scholars in Eton revolted against the headmaster, pillaged rooms and smashed windows. The last mutiny occurred as late as 1851 in Marlborough. Schools in the rest of Europe were no different. In France, Italy, Germany, Austria and Spain, adults were at a loss as to how to tame the hordes of unruly youngsters in their care.

Yet, at the same time, an inspector who had been called to report on Froebel's school in Keilhau, because of rumours that pupils there were undisciplined, had long hair and too much freedom, wrote at the end of his inspection:

> I found here, what is never and nowhere shown in practical life, a truly and closely united family of some 60 members, living in quiet harmony, all showing that they gladly perform the duties of their various positions.
>
> A family which is held together because of its strong bonds of mutual confidence and because every member seeks the good of the whole, everything - as if of itself - thrives in happiness and love.
>
> With great respect and hearty affection all turn to the Principal. The little five year-old children cling to his knees, while his friends and colleagues hear and honour his advice, with the confidence which his insight and experience and his indefatigable zeal for the good of the whole, deserve.
>
> While he has bound himself in brotherliness and friendship to his fellow-workers as the support of his life's work, which to him is truly holy work, that this union - this brotherhood - so to speak, among the teachers, must have the most salutary influence on the instruction and training and on the pupils themselves is self-evident, the love and respect in which the pupils hold all their teachers find expression in an attention, and an obedience, which render unnecessary almost all disciplinary severity. (Hanschmann 1875:136)

While in the rest of Europe children suffered the indignities of third-class citizenship, in Froebel's school they were respected as people in their own right, and of equal value to any adult in the community. Because lessons taught were matched to children's levels of understanding, discipline was not a problem. In all of Froebel's writings we do not find one article on discipline and punishment. It was not an issue which needed discussion. But how did such a transformation of attitudes towards children come about?

Froebel was a natural scientist by self-education and vocation. His observations as a child in the parsonage garden, as a forester in the woods and as an estate manager on the land convinced him that the growth and development of man was similar to the development of plants and animals. All development was a matter of mediation between opposites, between plus and minus, day and night, male and female, positive and negative. This idea is frequently expressed in Froebel's writings but especially in his essays on the Spherical Law. Froebel believed that, as nature and man proceed from the same source, they must be governed by the same laws. Just as nature mediates between man and God so the spirit mediates between man's inner and outer life. The laws of nature are also the laws of life, and the laws of life are the laws of education. There was unity in all things. Froebel had observed it, and the philosophers had said so too.

When Froebel entered the University at Göttingen in 1811 he wrote to his brother that he did so, not for the sake of outward recognition, but in an attempt to find out more about himself and how to live. This search for a way of living in harmony with oneself, God and one's neighbours probably originated in the Evening Hours of Reflection held at Yverdon when Froebel was working with Pestalozzi.

That such discussion should have permeated society in those days is not surprising in the context of the writings of the great thinkers of the time. German transcendental philosophers of the nineteenth century, like Fichte, Schelling, Hegel and Krause had been creating philosophical systems which were all-embracing, taking account of God, nature, man, the All and reconciling the arts, the law, morality, the sciences as having one source and one foundation. Hegel called it the Absolute Spirit, the Will. They also acknowledged obscure metaphysical elements in human life which were not directly available to human experience, but which man surmised to be part of reality. In England, poets like Wordsworth, Keats and Shelley were expressing similar ideas, emphasising unity.

In 1817, the same year Froebel opened his first school in Keilhau, Beethoven was writing the major parts of his last symphony. For the first time ever, he introduced the human voice into a symphony to let it mingle with the instruments of the orchestra, thus united, creating some of the most powerful and glorious sounds ever produced. The ninth symphony is today being used by the European Community as its anthem to express unity.

Musicians, poets and philosophers were all busy demonstrating how things belonged together, and so too were the scientists. Close analysis of oxygen, hydrogen, carbonic acid and nitrogen was leading to the organic theory. Cavendish, Priestly and Scheele were demonstrating how a limited number of elements (carbon, hydrogen, oxygen, nitrogen and some metals) were used by nature to build up a vast store of organic compounds, thus confirming the philosophers' theories.

Yet, the teaching and learning which was taking place in schools in no way indicated a unified whole. Not only was knowledge separated into different departments, but each department also had no connection with life outside school. Froebel writes about his own schooldays as follows:

We repeated our tasks parrot fashion, speaking much and knowing nothing, for the teaching of a subject had not the least connection with real life; nor had it any actuality for us, though at the same time we could rightly name our little specks and patches of colour on the map.... I received private tuition also in this subject. My teacher wished to advance further with me and so took me to the Geography of England. I could find no connection between that country and the country where I dwelt myself so of this instruction I also retained but little. As for actual instruction in German, it was not to be thought of, but we received direction in letter writing and spelling. I do not remember with what subject the teaching of spelling was connected. I do not think it was connected with any. It hung loosely in the air. (Lange 1966:47)

This lack of connection between subjects also worried Froebel in his university days. In his diary he records how he was beginning to search for order and unity in his studies, in his own life and in life in general. Froebel came to the conclusion that everything functions in relation to the Creator, the total unity. And yet he also knew that every man, woman and child was uniquely different. How were these two great opposites to be reconciled? Froebel writes:

> Here then budded and open to my soul, one lovely bright spring morning, when I was surrounded by nature at her loveliest and freshest, this thought, as it were by inspiration, that there must exist, somewhere, some beautifully simple and certain way of freeing human life from contradiction, or as I then spake out my thought in words, some means of restoring to man, himself, - at peace eternally, and that to seek out this way should be the vocation of my life.

Froebel searched for this unity, or at least for the theoretical justification for this idea, all his life. However difficult it may prove for us to understand the meaning of this subject in his writings, we will have no difficulties in observing and understanding the connections of his educational theory as seen in his practice. Here is but one example, namely the role of women in Froebel's education.

Froebel's mother died ten months after he was born. His father, a stern but fair and hard-working village parson, had little time for his children. He married again and Friedrich Froebel's relationship with his step-mother was quite satisfactory until she gave birth to her own child. From then on, the relationship became cooler and cooler until it was like the meeting of two strangers. He never really knew what mother-love meant, yet the mother figure became central to Froebel's concept of education.

Caroline von Holzhausen, the thirty-one year-old wife of an aristocratic landowner, awakened in Froebel the idea of the importance of the mother in the education of children. Her marriage to a man who cared more about his social life than the needs of his family compelled her to look for a private tutor for the education of her three boys. Froebel, aged twenty-three, was recommended and after his first meeting with this sensitive, caring and intelligent woman, accepted without hesitation. Her serious concern for the education of her children on Pestalozzian lines together with Froebel's sustained efforts to reconcile the parents' demands with the children's needs, created a relationship between Caroline von Holzhausen and Froebel which lasted for decades. Froebel very soon considered her to be the ideal mother of her children and had no hesitation in showing his admiration which the neglected older woman gladly accepted. She, in turn, became a warm and compassionate listener when Froebel talked about his own childhood and the kind of love between mother and child which he now witnessed but had himself never experienced. Such mutual trust led Froebel to see in Caroline von Holzhausen a person who not only gave freely of her love and affection to her children but who at the same time became the child's first and most important educator. She became his symbol of ideal motherhood.

The mother in Froebel's subsequent writings was not only the person who cared for a child's physical and emotional needs, but one who also provided for his intellectual demands. It is she who plays the first games with the child, talks to him and provides the first words, encourages him to take his first steps and guides his observations to differentiate between like and unlike.

Froebels ideas about mothers + parents.

Because a child's first impressions are also the most lasting ones care has to be taken that the child's first instructions are sensitive and appropriate. The mother being the most important person in a child's life needs, therefore, to be educated accordingly. To achieve this, Froebel created women's organisations which, in their weekly meetings, discussed their children's development, listened to lectures and disseminated educational literature produced by Froebel and the Keilhau community. So that parents would know how to teach their children at home, Froebel made sure that they had access to the Kindergarten all through the day in order to watch the teachers at work. Parents were also encouraged to participate in the games and the play activities carried out with the Gifts, a carefully graded series of wooden bricks which could be used for building houses and stables, for making beautiful patterns or for learning the multiplication tables andsolving mathematical problems. In the playground some of the benches were especially reserved 'For parents and friends of children'. Education was a joint venture between parents and teachers. There was unity in all things.

It was probably also this concept of unity which brought Froebel to the realization that all was not well in schools as long as they were staffed by male teachers only. 'We will never succeed in our educational endeavours until we involve the other half of humanity,' he used to say. When putting this idea to a teachers' conference, and we have to remember that this was an all-male conference consisting of teachers, principals, inspectors, ministers of education and university professors, the audience continually interrupted the proceedings with comments and questions. One of the university professors asked; 'Does Herr Froebel mean that eventually we will also have women university professors?' The minute book records that the audience 'collapsed with hilarious laughter'. The Fool of Blankenburg, as Froebel was known in some educational circles because he played with children, had done it again. Women teachers! Whatever next?

To Froebel the issue was not a matter for discussion as the solution was self-evident. He always maintained that a good school was like a good home. Just as one needed a mother and father and children at home, so one needed male and female adults and children to create a harmonious school.

When the government ignored Froebel's suggestions for the creation of a women's training college, he founded such a college himself, three years before he died: the first women's training college in Europe, and probably in the world.

But let us return in time to the days when Froebel was not at all sure what kind of profession he would take up eventually. His childhood experiences, with no playmates nor a mother to spend his time with, led him to an appreciation of nature which deepened the more he dwelt on it. Confined to the garden between the parsonage and the steep hill behind the house, the young Froebel's observations of the flowers and the weeds, the spiders and the birds, the sun and the rain started a life-long interest in nature which found further nourishment and support when, at the age of fifteen, he entered an apprenticeship as a forester, learning about the care of animals and plants and their dependence on each other for growth and survival. Very much to the consternation of his father, Froebel did not complete his apprenticeship. After two and a half years Froebel believed that he had gained as much knowledge from his rather idle master, as he would ever do, and left to take up his studies in the natural sciences and in mathematics at the university. He eventually ended up at Berlin University, concentrating on the most recent discoveries in the field of science and studying crystallography under Professor Weiss, the leading expert in this field at the time. Froebel must have been a diligent and intelligent student, for when the Swedish Government asked Professor Weiss to recommend a curator for their newly opened Mineralogical Museum in Stockholm, Weiss suggested Froebel.

Froebel, however, had begun to realize that a mere academic occupation where theory is rarely tested against real life could never satisfy his inner life, and, therefore, refused the offer of a secure job. More than ever before, he was looking for the means to put his educational ideas about unity, into practice. The opportunity presented itself when his younger brother Christopher, a parson, died unexpectedly. Froebel considered it his duty to become father to his brother's young children, and left Berlin to join the family in the parsonage of a small village in Thuringia. Another two of Froebel's nephews joined the family and the first lessons recorded took place in the woods, in the village stream and on the meadows. Books were used to verify observations. Direct experience and learning by discovery were paramount in Froebel's educational activities from the beginning.

Within the year, Christopher's widow had to leave her former home. Fortunately sufficient money was available to buy a small farm nearby in Keilhau. Froebel and the five children moved with her and it was here in Keilhau, that Froebel's first Educational Institute got under way. In less than ten years, by 1825, fifty-six pupils were attending the Institute.

In the meantime, Froebel had married Henriette Wilhelmine Hoffmeister, a highly intelligent and cultured lady whom he had met in Berlin. She was the daughter of a First Secretary to the Prussian Ministry of War, who refused to give his daughter her dowry when he heard about Froebel's low social standing. Undeterred, she supported Froebel for almost thirty years. She, like Froebel, was extremely fond of children. What sorrow it must have been to them both never to have experienced the joys of parenthood. At the beginning of the marriage she put all her energies into managing the domestic affairs of the community, but towards the end the partnership had grown in harmony and mutual respect to such an extent that Froebel consulted her on educational matters, especially when developing The Gifts for the first Kindergarten. Wilhelmine died in 1839, thirteen years before Froebel.

Life in the Keilhau community, imbued with the spirit of respect for others regardless of age or sex, was simple and spartan. The rules by which the members of the community lived were the same for adults and children alike. From the first days of spring until the first days of winter, boys wore short trousers and so did their teachers; swimming before breakfast applied to pupils and staff alike and Saturday morning's cleaning of stables, yards, gardens and classrooms was shared by all. When the extension of buildings was considered, children were involved in the planning, and, of course, helped in the execution of the project. Froebel's dictum that 'Life educates' could not be demonstrated more convincingly than when every member of the community made his individual work-contribution towards the well-being of all. Living and learning, in that sense, were synonymous.

But the day's work also included 'lessons' in the school building. The classics, poetry, languages, mathematics, geography and history, biology and the sciences, were all taken care of. Here again the starting point for each of these subjects was life itself. A geography lesson might start by sitting on top of a hill in order to draw a map, or walking along a river-bed to check an existing one. History lessons became more realistic when children and staff watched over the camp fires on a chilly hill-top before dawn broke to commemorate a battle. Walks through Germany and as far afield as Switzerland and Austria, of four week's duration for the older children and one or two weeks for the younger ones, gave experience of conversing, eating and living with people from different social strata when the party stayed in a castle on some days and in a hotel or tavern on others. Pupils learned to eat from silver plates with the aristocracy as well as from tin pots with journeymen and tramps. Though drama, poetry and music were largely written and composed by the staff and pupils themselves, there were annual visits to the State Opera Houses in Dresden and Frankfurt.

Froebel, the architect of it all, provided the inspiration throughout the challenges and made sure that all the different activities made one unifying whole. He did little direct teaching in those days, but would often present children in the playground, or in the classroom, with a problem and leave the children to solve it in their own way. Whatever the answer the children eventually produced, Froebel would accept the solution, provided the reasoning was sound. Everything was directed to make children think for themselves. Woods, hills, streams and mountains around the Institute were given new and more appropriate names, some of which are still in use today.

The growing popularity of the Institute in the early 1820s demanded the addition of new buildings and the extension of the old ones in order to accommodate the growing number of pupils. Yet the funds to carry out such large projects were never sufficient. Towards the end of the 1820s, the community was heavily in debt and, because the craftsmen employed could no longer be paid, work came to a standstill. There were also disagreements among the staff, with Froebel accused of being dictatorial and self-seeking, while Froebel himself charged his staff with faint-heartedness and not believing strongly enough in the crusade. At the same time the community suffered one fatal accident which led to accusations of carelessness. Numbers of pupils dwindled from sixty to five within a few years.

Set-backs, however, only seemed to fill Froebel with greater energy to drive his life's work forward. The Duke of Meiningen had asked Froebel to give him his ideas for the reorganisation of the school system in his principality. While events in Keilhau moved from bad to worse, Froebel, quite unperturbed, worked unceasingly on his ideas for an educational system which would provide opportunities for learning from the cradle to the grave, irrespective of ability, sex, social class or race. The Helba Plan, as it became known, envisaged a three-tier system, starting with the 'Development Institute' for the 3-7 year-olds. Froebel believed that the common practice of not accepting children into schools until they were six or seven years of age led to missed opportunities, hard to rectify later in life. Children in this Institute were not 'schooled' but would be provided with opportunities to develop freely using their gifts by means of self-activity and creative work. At the age of seven, children would move either to 'The Institute for Art and Crafts' or 'The Institute for General Knowledge' according to their abilities and inclinations. Once maturity had been reached, the former would enter the 'University of Self-Education' and the latter any of the usual universities. Neither Institute nor University was considered superior to the other all combining the 'doing' with the 'thinking' which were leading to 'ability and understanding' Because life itself educated, all pupils would share in the running, maintenance and development of the Institutions, looking after gardens, live-stock and buildings. Artefacts produced were to be utilitarian in design yet incorporating aesthetic qualities.

At a time when a school, per se, with its concentration on academic subjects was considered the only sphere of pedagogical concern, we are confronted with a plan which provides educational opportunities for people from all walks of life, of any ability, for both sexes from earliest childhood into adulthood. And if some children/pupils/adults were weak in some areas, Froebel suggested group-work so that people could learn from each other, learn to co-operate and work for the common good. Competition was not a feature of the Helba Plan.

Froebel's ideas, however, were never put into practice. The Duke's Minister of Education, afraid of losing his job, succeeded in persuading the Duke not to accept the plan. Froebel was badly shaken by this unexpected rejection, especially as the Keilhau Community, then fighting for survival, provided no support or encouragement to the idealist, who seemed incapable of facing reality. Froebel believed that the time had come to leave Keilhau, and in 1831 departed for a lecture tour in the western part of the country.

Frankfurt, the centre of German liberalism at the time, was the obvious starting point. It was also the place where Froebel contacted his old friends, the Holzhausens who introduced him to Xavier Schnyder, an aristrocrat, poet and musician from Switzerland. Schnyder, who was then teaching music at the local secondary school, had also worked for a year with Pestalozzi and found in Froebel a man to his liking. Both were advocates of the new liberalism sweeping across Europe, both were concerned with education and both were innovators in their own fields. Schnyder invited Froebel to start a school in his unoccupied castle in Switzerland. Froebel accepted enthusiastically. In spite of early set-backs fuelled by poison pen letters against Froebel's person in the local press, the children he taught very soon convinced the adults that they could trust the rough and ready character from across the border. Numbers of pupils increased and the authorities provided Froebel with a larger school building in nearby Willesau. They also asked him to organise and lead training courses for which teachers were seconded on full pay.

As Froebel's reputation grew, so the authorities increased his sphere of influence. In 1835 he was asked to take charge of the new orphanage in Burgdorf. Never before had Froebel worked with so many children of pre-school age. His careful and detailed observations of these children laid the foundations of a slowly growing realization of the need for pre-school education, for the creation of the Kindergarten and for the means by which such an education could be achieved. Froebel became aware that the physical grasping of an object by a child preceded his mental understanding (grasping) of that object, just as much as the ability to re-tell a story preceded the successful mastery of the skill of reading, and as drawing preceded writing. Froebel recognised intuitively the importance of the notion, so familiar to modern child-psychology, that representation of objects and experience is vital to the proper understanding of them.

Froebel's ability to think and feel at the level of the children in his care, his empathy with their joys, fears and aspirations, was in stark contrast to an otherwise often unyielding and uncompromising nature. Children trusted him immediately and he, in turn, gave them his full attention with unlimited patience. Recalling these days in a letter written to Mrs M. Schmidt, dated 21 March 1841, he says: 'I became the Founder and Director of an orphanage where I was introduced to the lives of very young children, their needs and demands as well as the ways of meeting these demands. From now on the care of early childhood became my life's goal; to achieve it, fate led me back to Germany'[1].

During all the time in Switzerland, Froebel's wife, Wilhelmine, had worked for the well-being of her husband and his many ventures. She did the cooking, washing and sewing, she mediated between parents, staff, the authorities and Froebel, and even worked in the gardens, although she never found physical work easy. Several minor illnesses were probably due to stress, and when news of her mother's death arrived, Froebel and Wilhelmine decided to return to Germany. For the next seven years Froebel's thinking was taken up with the problem of the education of pre-school-age children and the function of play in such a scheme. During this period he created the Kindergarten, the Gifts and Occupations, the Movement Games and *The Mother Song Book*. Wilhelmine continued to contribute to her husband's work in no small measure by discussion, suggestions and encouragement as well as discharging her domestic responsibilities. Unfortunately, she never really recovered from a lung infection which she had contracted in Switzerland. Before she died in 1839, she was able to provide suggestions for the construction of the Gifts and the workings of an institute in which they could be used.

Froebel spent over six months searching for the word which would accurately describe this new institution for the education of the very young. It certainly could not be called 'a school', because schooling implied teaching, it implied a method by which knowledge is gained from outside. But before a person can accept the knowledge of others, he has to be in the possession of some knowledge of his own, into which he can weave this new knowledge. This new institution was to provide an environment where children felt secure enough to try and match their inner life with the demands of the outside world, where opportunities existed for children to experiment through their play in areas not yet known but vaguely surmised. Such a protected and predictable environment was more like a nursery where the gardener tended his plants, provided water and air, and moved plants into the sunshine so that they could grow and flourish. It was going to be a garden for children, a Kindergarten.

The middle of the village was the correct place for the Kindergarten, where parents could bring and fetch their children easily and could also take part in the games, activities and lessons so that they would know how to work and play with their children at home. But a Kindergarten also needed enough ground to provide a garden in which each child looked after a small plot of land where he could sow and weed and reap and observe the effects of the seasons. This garden would also have flower - and vegetable - beds which were tended by all the children and where the produce benefited the community as a whole. (Cultivating these gardens helped children to acquire basic knowledge in the natural sciences and created situations where children learned to co-operate. It developed children intellectually as well as socially.)

Between thirty and fifty children attended the Kindergarten in Blankenburg daily. Their ages ranged from one to seven, although there were also some older children. These older children had brought their young siblings to the Kindergarten, but then stayed behind because life there was more interesting than in the school where they were supposed to be.

The Kindergarten was open from six in the morning until seven at night. Children brought their own sandwiches, which were collected and redistributed in such a way that the children of the rich and the children of the poor would have a chance to taste and enjoy the food of the others. Children whose parents were too poor to provide them with clean and mended clothes were provided with such from the collection kept in the Kindergarten. Teachers made sure that children were washed, combed and clean before they started in the morning and before they went home in the evening.

On arrival children were all given a box with the same number of wooden bricks in it, one of the Gifts. Children were encouraged to express with these bricks whatever was uppermost in their minds. If one of them produced a particularly successful construction, Froebel would ask the other children to look at it, discuss it and re-build it with alterations as envisaged in the discussion. The building of individual constructions was followed by task-orientated work as suggested by the teachers. Periods of sitting-still activities were interspersed with movement games and dance. Froebel avoided the teaching of numbers, poems, songs and even the telling of stories unless they were related to the free activities with which children had started the day. Froebel was reluctant to tell too many stories on the grounds that it left children inactive for too long.

To observe carefully and then utilise children's inclinations in the service of education was stressed in Froebel's training courses. When one of his trained Kindergarten teachers found herself wondering what to do with a group of children who were stamping their feet whilst sitting at the table and waiting for lunch, she 'used the natural movements (of the children), as she had learned to do' and transformed them into acceptable behaviour by making up verses about 'Stamping Feet', which provided a rhythm, a beginning and an end to the stamping. Froebel's idea of using children's inclinations for educational purposes included the notion that unacceptable behaviour could be modified for the better.

Above all, the Kindergarten provided time for exploration, time for experimentation and for verification. A child who picked flowers, then planted them in the ground and was given time to see them wilt, was confronted with a genuine problem. Froebel believed that the proper formulation of the problem was essential before a solution could be grasped even if the answer was provided by the teacher. The Gifts also had been designed with a view to encouraging problem-solving activities.

The basic idea underlying Froebel's Gifts is the attempt to provide children with three-dimensional objects with which they could discover and illuminate the laws of nature for themselves. Froebel starts with the assumption that nature and man are God's creation. The laws by which God's creation proceeds are natural laws based on the interaction of opposites, tempered by a mediator. If man wanted to understand God and to draw nearer to him, man, too, had to be creative.

The Gifts were to provide the means for young children to be creative, they had to illustrate the workings of opposites with the help of the mediators and they had to demonstrate the principle of unity. They were objects to help children to learn how to play, for, after all, play was not 'natural' as was generally believed, but had to be learned like any other human activity. Each Gift was introduced to the child with reference to the life he knew. The soft ball (Gift I, for the two year-old), for example, might be used to demonstrate how a cat jumps or a dog walks, while Gift VI for the twelve year-old (a wooden cube divided into many smaller cubes) might be used to illustrate the construction of a Roman arch. But the same Gifts were also to be used to demonstrate scientific principles. Pythagoras' theorem can be illustrated with Gift V, and Gifts I-IV can be used to help the understanding of scientific concepts such as time, space, causality and number, concepts involving relationships between past, present and future or movement, speed and impact, all leading to the consideration of cause and effect. But that was not all; a merely scientific education would create a lop-sided man indeed. Each Gift, therefore, had also to be used to develop a child's aesthetic awareness. Wooden bricks can not only be used for building a table and chairs, and for counting, but also for making beautiful patterns. Once the child had invented a pattern, he was encouraged to change this pattern into a different one, rather than destroy the old one before building a new one. By following Froebel's principle of progressive development, a box with nine bricks (Gift III) can yield over a hundred patterns. Once a pattern had been worked out with bricks, the child could now repeat it in his drawings, weaving, pottery or any of the other crafts.

Thus each Gift was to be used to help children represent objects and events which they had encountered in their own lives (Forms of Life), to explain these objects and events in scientific terms (Forms of Knowledge), and to foster an artistic awareness in them (Forms of Beauty). Because much of the work was based on group work, children learned to help and respect each other. No wonder Froebel's Kindergarten children grew into well-balanced people. Even while they were still attending the Kindergarten, parents noticed changes in their children and commented on their improved behaviour especially towards other children.

While the first Gifts were tried out in the recently established Kindergarten, Froebel began to collect songs and finger games, which he observed mothers using with their children in the village. These songs were eventually published in *The Mother Song Book* in which, in his words, he recorded the most important aspects of his educational theory. This is a reference to the use of the symbolic and the surmise in teaching.

The Mother Song Book consists of fifty songs and finger games which mothers are to use with their babies in arms. Froebel realized that the Gifts did not cater for the earliest stages of a child's development, the time when the child experienced his world primarily through his movements and through his limbs and senses. Each page has a verse printed in large letters to be sung by the mother and the child, and a verse in smaller print providing the mother with the deeper meaning of the song. Each song is illustrated with several beautifully executed line drawings, one of which explains visually the kind of hand and finger exercises which can be carried out with the song.

✗1   In his comments, Froebel explains that physical activity is the basis for mental activity especially when finger games are accompanied by the spoken word. A child is no longer tied to a perceptual awareness only, but can now see the connections between things and events. It is the ability to make comparisons and to draw conclusions which leads to logical thinking. But a rational appreciation of life is not enough. Just as the mind turns real objects into images, so images are eventually turned into symbols. And it is the symbolic which is used to illustrate abstract concepts such as honesty, truthfulness, perseverance, etc. It was, therefore, important to illustrate basic truth symbolically even when children were still very young.

However, a symbol like 'clear water' to illustrate truthfulness, as used in the book, only provides us with an approximation, a hunch, a presentiment of what we mean by truthfulness. And yet, this presentiment, this surmise, Froebel believed, was at the root of each piece of knowledge we acquire. Whatever man was eventually capable of knowing had to start as a surmise. Even the deeper meaning of life could only be explained in that way. Therefore, the fostering of the surmise, too, had to start as early as possible in the child's life. *The Mother Song Book* illustrates how it can be done.

The revolutionary unrest in 1848, leading to the consideration of the Basic Rights of the German People in the Frankfurt Parliament, also helped Froebel to spread his Kindergarten ideas. The discussions in Parliament covered issues relating to the freedoms of teachers and pupils and the running of schools. People became more susceptible to new ideas in education and Froebel used these years to spread his ideas by lecturing in Middle and North Germany. In Dresden, four Kindergartens were opened but Froebel refused the generous offer of a Government position as Trainer for Kindergarten Teachers because he wanted to be free to continue with his lecture tours. He now visited Hamburg where his ideas were greeted with great enthusiasm and where several of the political parties were putting the support for the Kindergarten idea into their election manifestos. Froebel had to work hard to make sure that it did not become a party-political issue.

In the meantime the Duke of Meiningen had offered Froebel his small castle at Marienthal for the purpose of training Kindergarten teachers. Froebel asked two of his young teachers to help him in his new venture, and in 1849, eight young ladies attended the first of these courses. Each course lasted a year so that students could experience the work which needed to be carried out with the children in each season. Nature itself provided the guidelines for the syllabus.

Reactions of the different German State Governments to the attempted revolutions were swift. Freedoms gained in 1848 were soon neutralised by new legislation. Education, too, came under scrutiny, and in August 1851, Froebel received the news, via a newspaper article, that all Kindergartens in Prussia were to be closed. The Prussian Government considered these institutions an essential part of 'Froebel's socialistic system of education which is designed to inculcate atheism in young people'.

Froebel, who had never before taken up the pen to answer his critics arguing 'if my ideas are right, they will stand the test of time, and if they are wrong, they are not worth defending', now wrote to the Minister of Education in Berlin. He asked for an interview, for the right to defend and justify his ideas. The Government, however, was not prepared to reconsider the matter. Institutions where children were encouraged to ask questions rather than to provide answers, where children were helping to make the rules rather than obeying the orders of others, where play was considered work and creativity and independent thinking more important than conformity, could not be tolerated by the State. Froebel died one year later.

It is ironic that the man who spent his lifetime trying to bring people to a love of Christ, if, at times, by rather unconventional means, should now be accused of preaching atheism. When a visitor once asked Froebel what he intended to achieve with his new kind of education, Froebel answered that his children, when adults, would be able to live in harmony with themselves, in harmony with their neighbours and their environment and in harmony with their Creator. Froebel knew only too well why the authorities kept a close eye on his work. In his biography he writes:

> ...had I planned my educational institution altogether differently, had I offered to train a special class, body servants, footmen or house-maids, shoemakers or tailors, tradesmen or merchants, soldiers or even noblemen, then I should have gained fame and glory for the usefulness and practical nature of my institution... and surely all men would have hastened to acknowledge it as an important matter, and as a thing to be adequately supported by the State. I should have been held as the right man in the right place by the State and by the world; and so much the more because as a State-machine I should have been engaged in cutting out and modelling other State-machines. But I, I only wanted to train up free, thinking, independent men.

We too, as we approach the end of the twentieth century, cannot help but be aware of an over-emphasis on an educational philosophy which equates education with competition and certification. Our belief in the value of technological progress to achieve a higher standard of living leads us to use educational establishments as a means for obtaining these ends. The pressure on schools, colleges and universities to produce people who are going to be useful to society in a narrow economic sense makes it more difficult for educators to provide a syllabus with a coherent, and in Froebelian terms, unifying and enduring content. Education then becomes an instrument for implementing political objectives. We are indeed in danger of becoming state-machines, unless we can muster the kind of understanding of children and the kind of commitment to their care as found in the lives of the young women whose story is told in these pages.

1. Froebel MsI/7/24

Madame Michaelis, late 1890s. One of the original founders of the Froebel Society and for thirty years one of the foremost exponents of Froebelian education.

Chapter 2

The First Fifteen Years

Therefore the present time makes upon the educators an inescapable demand - they must grasp children's earliest activities and understand their impulse to make things and to be freely and personally active; they must encourage their desire to instruct themselves as they create, observe and experiment. Friedrich Froebel

Without reference to educational practices and the treatment of children in general during the nineteenth century, it would be difficult to appreciate the Froebel Society's achievements. The history of childhood provides us with a disturbing picture of adults' ill treatment and misuse of those members of the community who due to their size, knowledge and intelligence were least able to look after themselves. Even though it is difficult to obtain a clear and coherent picture of the lives of children through the ages because of historians' preoccupation with battles and kings, there is sufficient evidence to show that too often children were considered as a burden rather than a blessing, and, especially girls, were used as cheap labour. They were ignored, beaten and starved. Like animals, they were subjected to violence, neglect and physical abuse. And in some parts of the world they still are today.

There have been, of course, in every century, adults who adored and cherished their children; and most of those who did not acted out of ignorance rather than malice. Historians believe that from the eighteenth century onwards a more humanitarian attitude emerged[1]. And yet, even in the nineteenth century, when the Froebel Society came into being, children endured practices which most people, today, would consider barbaric.

The social and economic changes brought about by rapid industrialisation affected both women and children as much as men and perhaps even more so. Changing from a life-style of seasonal work in the country to a time-regulated, supervised and machine-bound occupation demanded new forms of behaviour which many of the men looking for work in the factories found difficult to achieve. Many of those who succeeded performed their jobs grudgingly and under protest; those who did not became unemployed and had to be supported by their wives and children, whose wages were invariably lower than those of the men.

The earliest cotton mills at the beginning of the nineteenth century were largely operated by women and children. Working hours in some mills were from 5am - 8pm, with Sundays reserved for cleaning machinery. The Factory Inquiry Commission of 1833 reported that many factories were employing six and seven year-old children, some working eleven hours a day. Children who fell asleep were flogged to keep them awake and parents tolerated such treatment of their children because their labour kept the family above the breadline. Many of the boys and girls employed were pauper children who had been handed over to the mill owners by their guardians. Family life was not possible for them. They slept in shifts in barracks provided within the factory grounds.

But children working in factories might consider themselves lucky compared with those working in the mines. Stories are all too common of children aged eight or ten crawling on hands and knees pulling trucks or sitting for twelve hours in complete darkness and utter isolation in order to open and close a trap door. The Royal Commission's Mining Report of 1840 disclosed that one in ten of all the work-force underground were boys and girls under thirteen years of age.

Many children became permanently crippled because of accidents or cramped and often unnatural working positions. Curvature of the spine, twisted legs and shoulders, deformed hips and arms led to premature ageing and early death. In potteries boys were found stacking pots in drying rooms where the temperature never fell below 120 degrees. Those who dipped pots in lead glaze were soon crippled by lead poisoning. Many of the resulting injuries to children may not have been foreseen by the adults in charge, but there are too many reports, official as well as private, which indicate that in the last century adults considered the children of the poor to be an expendable commodity, scarcely worthy of attention, and certainly not of care. As late as 1864 the Third Report of the Children's Employment Commission records the following observations:

> Little boys and girls are seen here at work at the tip-punching machines (all acting by steam power) with their fingers in constant danger of being punched off once in every second, while at the same time they had their heads between the whirling wheels a few inches away from each ear. 'They seldom lose the hand', said one of the proprietors, 'it only takes off a finger at the first or second joint. Sheer carelessness'. (Robottom 1986:110)

There was nothing children could do to improve their condition, except to run away. But children on the loose faced hunger and cold. Dr Barnardo, in a paper delivered to the Social Science Congress in Liverpool in 1876, revealed that on a conservative estimate about 30,000 homeless and destitute children under the age of sixteen were living in London alone[2]. They were living on roof-tops, under tarpaulins and in cardboard boxes. And when an eight year-old boy was found stealing bread, he was sentenced to six months hard labour.

In defence of the courts which handed out such harsh treatment to children, it has to be pointed out that the huge increase of almost fifty per cent in the population between 1800 - 1831 had created a situation where children were roaming the countryside and running wild. How much the growth of elementary education in the nineteenth century was an attempt to keep children off the streets and how much a genuine desire to educate them remains debatable.

Until the French Revolution, educating a child had always been considered the prerogative of the churches and the parents. Parents who had the means to do so, sent their children to 'public schools', that is independent secondary schools, usually of the boarding type. These schools, though spartan in the treatment of the children, enjoyed a good reputation among the parents. But only a tiny percentage of children attended such schools. The children of the very poor received their education, if at all, in schools established by the churches. Churchmen certainly felt pity for those who were left to play in the gutters of the street, but it was also an attempt to make children into good Christian men and women by teaching them to read the Bible. The child of the middle classes attended private schools, for a small payment, run by respectable ladies of the community as well as men and women who could scarcely read or write. According to Matthew Arnold, the English middle-class child was the worst educated in Europe[3]. During the middle years of the last century, educational efforts in England, compared with those of several other countries in Europe were extremely poor.

There had, of course, been compassionate and courageous efforts by individuals like Robert Owen, Robert Raikes, Joseph Lancaster, Andrew Bell, Samuel Wilberspin and also by societies like the British and Foreign School Society (1807), the National Society (1811) and the Home and Colonial Society (1836) to awaken the nation's conscience by establishing schools in different parts of the country. But not until a general pressure by the newly created middle classes was felt, supported by reformers like Lovett and J.S.Mill, did Parliament begin to take the demand for popular education seriously. In 1833 the first ever Government grant for education was made available. £20,000 for the building of schools was allocated to local authorities which were prepared to pay half the cost, matching pound for pound. Needless to say this resulted in the creation of schools in comparatively well-to-do neighbourhoods rather than in the areas where they were most needed. The Factory Act, passed in the same year, laid down that children working in factories must attend school for two hours a day, but this was not enforceable, largely because schools did not exist in these areas in spite of a large input of charitable money by churches and landowners establishing schools where previously there had been none.

Twenty years later, little had changed. Matthew Arnold, Inspector of Schools from 1851-1886, records in his General Report for the year 1853:

> While more and more convinced that the present elementary schools sufficiently educate the children who frequent them, and while more and more convinced that the central institutions sincerely desire to promote the education of the poor, I remain of the opinion that in the schools which I visit, the children of the actually lowest, poorest classes in this country, of what are called the masses, are not, to speak generally, educated; that the children who are educated in them belong to a different class from these; and that, consequently, of the education of the masses, I in the course of my official duty, see, strictly speaking, little or nothing. (Arnold 1908:18)

Clearly something needed doing, and as a first step the Government created the Education Department in 1856 as the administrative instrument of the Committee of the Council for Education.

People concerned with education expressed misgivings about this move, as it seemed to indicate Government attempts to introduce compulsory state education. There were plenty of representatives of different denominations in both Houses of Parliament who were eager to convince the Government that education was safer in the hands of the churches, even though the demand for financial contributions from the state purse rose from year to year. In 1850 the Government spent £150,000 on education and in 1857 £541,233 and even though this is nothing compared to the £78,000,000 spent on the Crimean War, people were beginning to ask questions as to the value given by schools. To provide some of the answers the Government set up a Commission 'to enquire into the present state of popular education in England'. The Commission later known as the Newcastle Commission sat from 1858-1861, and its report indicated that of the two and a half million children attending school, about 300,000 attended endowed grammar schools and 'superior private schools', one million attended public elementary schools and half the country's children were educated in private schools which were neither assisted nor inspected by the Government[4].

The Commission concentrated on the public elementary schools and the uninspected and non-assisted private schools. They rejected the suggestion that education should be free or compulsory, but did advocate the continuation of state grants. Most worrying to them, however, was the quality of education provided in the private sector by untrained incompetent adults in, very often, most unsuitable premises. The report says

> None are too old, too poor, too ignorant, too feeble, too sickly, too unqualified in one or every way, to regard themselves, and to be regarded by others as unfit for schoolkeeping. Nay, there are few, if any, occupations regarded as incompatible with schoolkeeping, if not as simultaneous at least as preparatory employments. Domestic servants out of place, discharged barmaids, vendors of toys or lollipops, keepers of small eating houses, of mangles or of small lodging-houses, needlewomen who take in plain or slop work, milliners, consumptive patients in an advanced stage, cripples almost bed-ridden, persons of at least doubtful temperance, outdoor paupers, men and women of seventy or eighty years of age, persons who spell badly (mostly women, I grieve to say) who can scarcely write and who cannot cipher at all. When other occupations fail for a time, a private school can be opened, with no capital beyond the cost of a ticket in the window. Any room however small and close, serves for the purpose; the children sit on the floor and bring what books they please; while the closeness of the room renders fuel superfluous and even keeps the children quiet by its narcotic effects. (Peterson 1971:12)

In the Commission's view, the system was acceptable in principle, but it criticised both the high cost and the inefficiency. In an effort to tighten up on the effectiveness of the grants provided by the Government, Robert Lowe, the Vice President of the Education Department at the time, implemented the Revised Code of 1862 which introduced the principle of 'payment by results'. In future, the money to be allocated to a school was to be calculated on the number of pupils attending plus the results of an examination conducted by one of Her Majesty's Inspectors based on the three Rs. Each child of the age of six and in regular attendance would earn 12s. subject to a deduction of 2s8d for every failure in one of the three grant-earning subjects.

No doubt, there were benefits to be had from such a system. Every child would now have to receive attention from the teacher, not just the bright ones, if failure in the three Rs was to be avoided. It also helped to introduce reading books of a general kind apart from the Bible which hitherto had been the sole source of reading material in many schools. But on the whole, the Revised Code made matters worse rather than better. Children were increasingly subjected to drill rather than to the awakening of an inquiring mind, to a fear of teachers rather than a respect for educators and to a restricted curriculum rather than the widening of a child's horizon. There were some HMIs who supported the Code but many of them and especially two of the best known and most respected HMIs at the time, Matthew Arnold and the Revd R.H. Quick spoke out against it. The latter, who incidentally also became one of the first males to join the Froebel Society, considered the new system 'the greatest mistake possible' because it was changing education into an activity of grind and rote learning[5].

Even the Education Act of 1870 which paved the way for a national, free and compulsory system of elementary education did not improve the way education was handed out to children. Fifteen years after the introduction of the Revised Code and five years after the passing of the 1870 Education Act, when more and more children had been gathered into schools, things were getting worse rather than better inside these institutions, according to the inspectorate. Matthew Arnold blamed, above all, the Revised Code for the deterioration of standards in schools. He condemned the system of examinations on the grounds that it took away the teachers' and the pupils' spontaneous and creative approaches to teaching and learning. He particularly pointed out the harshness of the system when it is applied to the examination of seven year-old children[6]. However, he maintained his unfailing faith in the ability of teachers to beat the system.

> In the game of mechanical contrivances the teachers will in the end beat us; and it is now found possible, by ingenious preparation, to get children through the Revised Code examination in reading, writing and ciphering, without their really knowing how to read, write, or cipher.... (Arnold 1908:115)

Reports like these could not be ignored and the system was changed to include passes in subjects like history, geography, grammar, algebra, geometry and natural sciences as qualifying for government grants. But 'payment by results' was not abolished until 1897 when the yearly examination of each child was replaced by a general, periodic inspection of each school.

In spite of impressive efforts by the diverse voluntary organisations, especially the churches, to increase the provision of school places, there were considerable gaps in several parts of the country. The Education Act of 1870 was intended to fill these gaps and to supplement the voluntary system. The whole country was divided into school districts which were to be governed by school boards. Each school board was charged with the responsibility of ensuring that enough schools were available in its area so as to provide a place for each child of compulsory school age. The boards had the power to compel attendance by children between five and thirteen, but it was left to their discretion how far they used that power. Fixing the starting age at five compelled school boards to make provision for infant classes and infant schools. This was a definite step forward, but the vital question 'what happens to children when they get inside the schools' was not covered by the act. The regulations for infant schools adopted by the London School Board in 1871 indicates what was expected of teachers and infants. Teachers were asked to give instruction in a) the Bible, b) the three Rs, c) object lessons as outlined in the Kindergarten system, and d) music and drill. The emphasis was on the three Rs and the reference to the object lessons as outlined in the Kindergarten system indicated the extreme lack of understanding of Froebelian practice. But there existed a handful of young women who did understand. They were the founder members of the Froebel Society.

Ever since the Prussian Kindergarten Verbot of 1851, Froebel teachers had left their homeland to practise their trade and live their philosophy abroad. The first Kindergarten in England was established in 1851 at 32 Tavistock Place by Madame Ronge who had been a pupil of Froebel's in 1849, and had established several Kindergartens in Germany before she came to England. Charles Dickens recorded that the Kindergarten material exhibited at the International Educational Exposition and Congress in 1854, was demonstrated and explained by her.

Her Kindergarten was filled with children from French, German and Italian refugee families. Men and women in Europe had been asking themselves whether society could not be so organised that ignorance, poverty and oppression would become a thing of the past. The unorganised and isolated uprisings by these, often divided, social reformers had been a dismal failure all over Europe in the summer of 1848. The governments of Italy, France, Hungary, Prussia, Baden and Wurttenberg quickly brought events under control again and did not forget those who had been instrumental in the unrests. Many of them found their way to England. Manchester and London, particularly Soho, became their new home. Mostly of middle-class origin, often intellectuals of considerable standing, certainly idealists as regards human rights and individual freedom, a Froebelian Kindergarten must have been the ideal institute for their children's education. There were, of course, also children of British origin, especially as most of the immigrants were too poor to afford the fees. This would certainly have been true of Jenny and Karl Marx's children, who lived ten minutes walk away from the Ronge's Kindergarten and would have known of its existence.

Madame Ronge's deputy, Maria Boelte, was also an emigrée from Germany and so was Miss Doreck who later became one of the founder members of the Froebel Society. Miss Snell, founder of the Manchester Kindergarten Training College, later known as the Mather Training College, Professor Hoffmann, lecturer for the Home and Colonial Society, the Praetorious sisters who took over the Ronge Kindergarten when Madame Ronge moved to Manchester in 1857, had all left their homeland for a country which generously allowed them to practise what they believed to be of value and of importance. And in these early days, whenever they felt the need for another trained helper, they could always summon help from their homeland.

The Ronge Kindergarten existed well into the 1880s. The Praetorious sisters passed it on to Fanny Franks. Miss Franks had been trained by one of Froebel's students, Madame de Portugall, and as Principal of Camden House Training School for Kindergarten teachers and later as lecturer, examiner, and Vice President of the Froebel Society worked unceasingly for the movement until her death in 1920.

In Manchester, Madame Ronge's enthusiasm gave birth to the first Kindergarten Association in this country. She was also instrumental in obtaining the help and support of two of the most outstanding Froebelians from the continent, Madame de Portugall and Miss Heerwart. They both arrived in England in 1861. Madame de Portugall, having studied under Baroness von Marenholtz-Bülow, accepted the post as Principal of the Manchester Kindergarten for three years and then worked as the Kindergarten Organiser in Switzerland until 1884 when she became Principal of the Training College and Kindergarten in Naples.

Miss Heerwart, after completing her training in Keilhau, left Germany in the early 1850s and opened a Kindergarten in Dublin, and when called to Manchester accepted a post as Lecturer in Kindergarten Theory and Practice. From 1874–1883 she was responsible for the training of Kindergarten teachers in the British and Foreign School Society Training College in Stockwell. Towards the end of her career in this country it was said that the great improvements observable in infant school teaching were chiefly due to her work at Stockwell[7].

Some historians believe that the movement leading to the Education Act of 1870 originated above all in Manchester. In order to get more children into schools, the city fathers created the Manchester Education Aid Society (1864). Realizing that voluntary efforts alone could not meet demands, the Manchester Education Bill Committee was formed, aiming to improve educational provision in the city by educating people towards the realization that more public money was needed to achieve these improvements. It was this kind of pressure from cities like Manchester, and later Birmingham, which provided the impetus for the passing of the Education Bill of 1870[8], and it is probably more than a mere coincidence that the city which had spearheaded public opinion towards popular education was also the city where the Froebel Movement was strongest in the twenty years leading up to the passing of the bill.

Passing a bill compelling young children to attend school certainly got them off the streets, but it created new problems inside the schools. Rote learning, the method almost exclusively used in schools just did not seem to make much impression on five and six year-olds. Miss Doreck, the headteacher of Kildare Gardens had recently added a Kindergarten to the school and discovered the lack of suitably trained teachers. She contacted other young women with an interest in the care and education of young children for the purpose of forming a Kindergarten Association. On a late November evening, in 1874, they gathered in Miss Doreck's home at 63 Kensington Gardens Square. There were familiar names, familiar faces. Miss Heerwart from Stockwell Training College; Mrs William Grey, better known as Maria Grey and her sister Miss Emily Shirreff; Madame Michaelis, who later became the first Principal of the Froebel Educational Institute in Roehampton; Miss Emily Lord, the Principal of Notting Hill Kindergarten; Miss Steel, Principal of Stockwell Training College and later Principal of Saffron Walden Training College; Miss Caroline Bishop, the first lecturer on Kindergarten methods appointed to the London School Board; Miss Stoker, Lecturer at Stockwell Training College; Madame Althaus and Fräulein Roth from Germany; Miss Mary Gurney who was soon to publish *A Guide on Froebel's First Gifts*; Miss Manning who became a vice president of the Society after many years as lecturer, examiner and Honorary Treasurer; Miss Chessar and Miss Porter who both became examiners for the Society and, of course, Miss Doreck, who took the chair for this first meeting[9].

The meeting agreed to send a letter to people known to be interested in Kindergarten work, inviting them to become members of the Association. Miss Doreck was appointed President and Miss Manning Secretary and Treasurer. The object of the association was

to bring into communication all who were occupied or otherwise interested in Kindergarten work, and to extend a knowledge of the system both in its theory and in its practice. (FS Minutes 1874:3)

The association was named 'The Froebel Society for the Promotion of the Kindergarten System' and from the very beginning of its existence concerned itself with familiarising its members and the public with Froebel's educational principles, by means of lectures, conferences and exhibitions, and with the raising of standards of training for people engaged in the care and education of young children by providing examinable courses.

The lectures given to the members of the Society during the first two years concentrated on basic Froebelian principles like 'wholeness', 'the unity of education', 'unity in diversity' 'the interconnectedness of subject matter'. The main concern of schools at the time was the fulfilment of requirements laid down in the 1870 Education Bill, concentrating on the teaching of the three Rs. In these early days of popular education children went to school to learn specific things which they could not very well learn at home. To Froebelians, school should always be an extension of the home where children learned how to live rather than acquired specific skills or bits of knowledge. Thus, the first lecture given to members of the Society by Professor Payne of London University, who had joined the provisional committee within two weeks of its existence, suggested the extension of Kindergarten training beyond the ages normally accepted. During the discussion that followed Miss Heerwart agreed, pointing out that there was nothing new in Froebel's system and that Froebel did not claim to have invented anything novel, but simply used what was known in isolation and systematised it[10].

Miss Doreck took up Professor Payne's suggestion in her lecture on 'The Kindergarten in connection with the School' and showed how different school subjects had their origins in the Kindergarten. Her argument that Froebel's basic principle of 'harmony of development' needed to be used to examine the practices in primary as well as secondary education was supported by a paper from Madame de Portugall in which she emphasised that the Froebel system is based on the principles of natural development and that the education of children of all ages had to be seen and organised as a whole.

The unity of knowledge was also the theme of Madame Michaelis' lecture 'Kindergarten Games and Music'. She pointed out that Froebel's finger games and also the games for older children were not merely designed for children's physical development, but that they also made demands on the imagination and the intellect. She illustrated her talk by referring to 'the peasant game' which, apart from physical exercises to be carried out, taught children about the seasonal changes on the farm and the care of animals, thus stimulating body and mind as well as raising moral issues.

During the lecture on 'The physical education of young children', Dr Roth, a Wimpole Street physician declared that it was a mistake to treat all children of the same age in the same manner. Supporting this idea, Miss Heerwart spoke of the necessity of free spontaneous movement in a Kindergarten, rather than gymnastic exercises.

While Madame de Portugall's first paper sent to the Society concentrated on the concept of unity in Froebel's education, her second paper tried to explain how, according to Froebel, such unity needs to be looked for and can be found in the diversity of life. The paper was entitled 'The Law and relation of Contrasts'. Madame de Portugall wrote:

> Under this name Froebel announced his conception of the 'law pervading all things' by which order and harmony prevail in the universe, and unity is felt through the boundless variety of creation. There is perpetual change, perpetual action and interaction among the forces of Nature. In mental life there is also change and development - and in both it is through the perception of contrasts, of resemblances and differences that the sense of harmony is attained. So life is proof of levelling, dissolving and uniting of contrasts in an ever-changing relation of giving out and taking in, an eternal dying and reviving. All that is mutual and immutual, temporal and eternal, is brought into contact and united in life. All our knowledge is founded upon perceptions of resemblances and differences and thus Froebel, following out the universal law of Nature, bases his system on the gradual development of childish faculty in apprehending these relations, and guides the child's first efforts to work, to invent, and to combine by attending to those contrasts which result in harmony. Froebel considered this method the foundation of all artistic production. (FS Minutes 1874:28)

Because very few of Froebel's writings had been translated into English at that time, the members of the Society had to rely heavily on papers sent by Madame de Portugall or talks from members like Miss Heerwart who read and understood German. During her lecture on 'Reading and Preparation for it in the Kindergarten' Miss Heerwart advocated that children should not be taught reading until they were at least six years of age. She believed that the teaching of reading was usually undertaken when children were too young and that Froebel had always wanted any new learning to bring joy. The phonic and the look-and-say methods of teaching reading were discussed and Miss Heerwart advocated 'the teaching by sound without regard to spelling'.

Some of the infant school inspectors commented on the harm done by prolonged and too early instruction in reading, especially when reading was a matter of deciphering 'from a card some such monosyllabic morality as this: Sit on a sod and nod to me. A cat sits on a sod and nods to a lad...Am I to sit on a sod?' The same inspector continues: 'The gallery is under the control of one or two pupil teachers. If there are two, one invites attention to an alphabet card, while the other fitfully maintains order with blows and threats.'[11]

Corporal punishment was also discussed by members of the Society after a lecture by Miss Bailey, Principal of the Doreck Kindergarten, on 'Order and Discipline in the Kindergarten and the School.' Most members were opposed to its use under any circumstances, but a few urged that in certain extreme cases and for children 'in a low state of moral development' it might be necessary. However it was agreed that in Kindergartens such punishment need never be applied.[12]

While members of the society were thus trying to improve their own practices in the classroom and in their schools by attending lectures and participating in discussions, they were also eager to improve conditions for children in schools managed by people who, in the society's opinion, had not been adequately trained.

As early as April 1875, the committee discussed a six monthly scheme for the training of children's nurses. It was suggested that such a course might consist of instructions on various subjects connected with the care of children, daily practice in a creche under supervision and a two-month residency in a children's hospital like Great Ormond Street. Minimum age of entry for students would be sixteen and course fees £5 per student of which £3 would need to be paid to the hospital for two months' residency. When this scheme was put before the members of the Society, it was considered to be too elaborate and a considerably reduced course was proposed and accepted which from a financial point of view was probably also more realistic. This led to the formation of the first Committee for the Examination of Kindergarten Teachers.

In 1875 it was decided that candidates would need to pass a preliminary examination before acceptance for training, covering the following subjects: reading, writing, arithmetic, English grammar, literature, geography and history, unless candidates could produce a certificate from a recognised examining body. It was also resolved that candidates taking the Certificate of the Froebel Society would be examined in the following subjects: (a) Reading, writing, arithmetic, grammar, geography, history, English literature; (b) Theory of education, history of education, physical education, Froebel's books, geometry, stories, poetry, gymnastics, singing, physiology, elements of physics, zoology, botany, geology, hygiene, Kindergarten occupations and practical teaching. Kindergarten teachers were expected to have 'a good general culture so that they may be able to teach on the basis of philosophical principles and out of a full mind ... and urged on this ground that those who wish to prepare for Kindergarten work should allow themselves full time for training'.

Reports relating to the training of teachers during the last century do not make inspired reading. At the middle of the century about thirty colleges provided training courses lasting from between one to three years, and with the possible exception of the two British and Foreign School Society Colleges, Stockwell and Borough Road, concentrated on providing an advanced general education for their trainee teachers. Students were asked to study more of what they had started to learn in school; more arithmetic, algebra, English, geography, history, grammar, composition, religion and maybe some astronomy, land surveying and mechanics. Yet, as early as 1856, the Revd F.Temple, later Archbishop of Canterbury, in his report on Church training colleges was pointing out that as the schoolmaster's task was 'not so much to teach as to make children learn' students needed much more preparation in the science of education and method of teaching than a repetition, even if at a deeper level, of what was already known.[13]

A belief that education is a matter of filling empty heads with facts inevitably leads to the imparting of mere facts to students; and what better way to do this, than to lecture at them. But lecturing to trainee teachers results in young teachers lecturing to children. Matthew Arnold, in his reports referred to the grave limitations which such a method of teaching produced. Applied to the education of children of infant school age, the consequences can be devastating.

According to the Newcastle Commission Report of 1861, only one college, the College of the Home and Colonial Society, was providing a course for the training of infant school teachers. The examination paper set for 'Female students in Training Schools' in 1854, consisting of nine papers with about 150 questions, had but one question in it which referred to the work done in an infant school[14]. Considering the fact that examinations governed the curriculum, one must doubt whether any worthwhile knowledge about infant education was forthcoming during the general training of teachers. The more credit is due to the British and Foreign School Society for its attempt to introduce Kindergarten methods in its Practice School at Stockwell College as early as 1864, even if the results, due to a lack of a real understanding of Froebelian principles, were not very promising until Miss Heerwart took over ten years later. Members of the Froebel Society had good reason to be impatient to get their training courses under way. They had been in existence for four years when, in 1878, the first ten candidates presented themselves for examination together with the students trained at Stockwell College by Miss Heerwart. An inauspicious beginning and, yet, the first step towards the significant changes in infant education which eventually also affected teaching methods in junior schools, the training of teachers and educational philosophy in general.

Within a year of its existence the Society was able to record the membership of eminent people like the Revd A.Bourne from Stockwell College, Dr Roth, the Wimpole Street physician, Mr Sonnenschein, the publisher; but there also had been losses. Miss Doreck, the first President, who had called the first meeting less than a year before, died in June 1875 and Professor Payne a year later. Emily Shirreff was elected President of the Society and because of her many travels abroad, her sister, Mrs Maria Grey, frequently took the chair in her absence, as Vice President.

While the major efforts of the Society's members during the first two years had been directed towards the clarification of their own philosophy by examining Froebel's educational principles in lectures and discussions, they devoted much of their time during the next three years to the establishment of a training college for Kindergarten teachers, the formation of an inspectorate for the inspection and registration of Kindergartens, and the examination of candidates for the Froebel Society Certificates.

The need for the creation of a 'Central Kindergarten and Training College' in London was discussed as early as November 1877. Though most members of the Committee were for the establishment of such an institution, funding proved difficult. Most of the money towards this new venture was raised through drawing-room meetings. The first such meeting attracted over seventy people, mostly ladies. Members of the Committee explained the Kindergarten system, exhibited children's work and provided reasons for the establishment of a training institution for Kindergarten teachers. Many more such meetings were held in London, and members' untiring efforts facilitated the opening of 'The Kindergarten Training College' on 3 May 1879 at 31 Tavistock Place with ten students and Miss Bishop as the first Principal.

The Society's efforts to improve conditions in existing Kindergartens led to the formation of an inspectorate for the examination of Kindergartens. Inspectors were instructed to report on the manner of teaching, the curriculum, buildings and equipment. Adverts in the educational press as well as notices to principals announced the

Society's willingness to inspect Kindergartens periodically so that they might be placed on a register of approval. In 1877 three Kindergartens were placed on the register. Miss Heerwart, Madame Michaelis, Miss Snell and Miss Bishop, all members of the Council, were appointed inspectors. Difficulties arose when requests were received to inspect Fanny Franks' and Emily Lord's Kindergartens, as both were members of the Council themselves. The problem was solved by inviting Monsieur Braun, the Inspector General of Belgian schools, to carry out the inspection. Certificates granted lasted for three years only, after which time Kindergartens had to be inspected again if they were to remain on the register. During 1888, five Kindergartens were inspected and passed: Mrs Fearson's at Birkenhead; Miss Lord's at Nottinghill; Miss James' at Stamford Hill; Miss Franks' at Baker Street and Miss Fisher's at Warwick High Street, but several others failed to get recognition.

When, in 1880, Anthony Mundella was appointed Vice President of the Education Department, the Manchester Kindergarten Association believed the time to be right to press for a universal introduction of Froebel's system of education into all government infant schools and requested the Froebel Society's support in sending a deputation to Mr Mundella at the Education Office in Whitehall. After all, Mr Mundella had already expressed his interest in the Kindergarten work during his visit to Stockwell College and Froebelians had always been concerned that the new education should be available to all children in the country, not just those whose parents could afford the fees. Miss Davenport-Hill, a member of the Froebel Society Committee as well as the London School Board expressed anxiety about interfering with the infant schools on a large scale, but nevertheless promised to seek the support of members of the London School Board.

The deputation to Mr Mundella consisted of members from the Manchester Kindergarten Association, The London Froebel Society, The Stockwell Kindergarten Training College, The Stockwell Training College, The London Kindergarten Training College and the Teachers' Association: Mrs Schwabe, Miss Shirreff, the Revd A. Bourne and Miss Heerwart were part of the deputation. Mr Mundella replied to their proposals by stating that changes could not be made rapidly. He had visited Kindergartens in Germany and had also seen Miss Heerwart's work at Stockwell with the liveliest satisfaction. He promised to acquaint the Lord President with the delegation's view and to see whether anything could be done officially to encourage the system.

Even if not all the delegation's expectations were fulfilled, they must have been pleased to note that the Code of 1881 showed some modifications as regards infant schools. In order to qualify for the merit grant, they now had to include 'simple lessons on objects and the phenomena of nature and common life' and varied and appropriate occupations. The writers of the accompanying circular to the Code must have had Froebel in mind when they said:

> The Code assumes that besides suitable instruction in these elements (reading, writing and arithmetic) and in needlework and singing, a good infants' school should provide a regular course in simple conversational lessons on objects and on the facts of natural history, and a proper variety of physical exercises and interesting employments..... It should be borne in mind that it is of little service to adopt the gifts and mechanical

occupations of the Kindergarten unless they are so used as to furnish real training in accuracy of hand and eye, in intelligence and obedience. (Lawrence 1953:56)

The Froebel Society was well aware that many teachers regarded 'Kindergarten' as just another subject on the timetable, rather than as a principle which should permeate a child's daily life. To help teachers to make use of the opportunities the new Code offered, the Society now also arranged evening lectures for teachers generally, apart from the courses and lectures for its members. However successful these meetings were at the beginning, by 1882 attendance figures had dwindled alarmingly for both types of meetings. So much so, that Miss Manning, former Secretary and now Vice President of the Society read a paper to the Monthly Meeting questioning the Society's ability to justify its existence. When finally she suggested that the Froebel Society combine with the Education Society, she met with strong opposition from members like Miss Shirreff, Madame Michaelis and Miss Heerwart. Miss Heerwart urged members to spend more time studying the works of Froebel and also to provide direct support for teachers who were having difficulties with ignorant parents.

Whatever Miss Manning's intentions, and judging from her past record it is doubtful that she was serious in her proposals, she certainly succeeded in stinging members into action. The AGM which followed a month later was well attended and resolved to increase the Committee to eighteen members. Mr Picton from the London School Board gave the address and must have had the new Committee sitting on the edge of their chairs when he too examined the present position and the future of the Froebel Society. He pointed out that the Society dealt mainly with private schools which only affected fifteen per cent of the population. Until Froebel's principles had taken hold in the public elementary schools, little or nothing would have been done to affect the course of education in this country. The Society could not congratulate itself upon what it was doing until Froebel's principles were intelligently applied in what were our national schools.[15]

Although there was enough enthusiasm among the members to bring about such changes, the means for doing so were lacking. While the Monthly Meeting, for example, passed a resolution to celebrate the centenary of Froebel's birth by establishing a free Kindergarten for the poor children in London, the Committee, two weeks later, had to put on record that it could not see a way of carrying out such a scheme. The financial situation of the Society in 1883 was such that when the Kindergarten Training College in Tavistock Place asked for financial support, the Society could not help and the College had to close.

The unsatisfactory state of finances of the Society led to the resignation of the Secretary at the beginning of 1884. The Committee resolved itself into a Council with the addition of several people, among them Mr Claude Montefiore, a young man of twenty-eight who for the rest of his life committed a large part of his intellect, energy and material wealth to the Froebelian cause. Within two months of his election to the Council he became its Secretary. The Council now created an Organising Committee whose business it was to prepare and arrange the work of the Council and also act as Finance Committee. Subscriptions and examination fees were raised, drawing-room meetings to cover other parts of the country arranged, Emily Lord was sent on a lecture tour covering Durham, Leamington, Sheffield, Scarborough, Leicester and Hawick. A register of employers and Kindergarten teachers, on the same lines as the Teacher Registration Society, was opened; Kindergarten teachers conferences were organised and lecture programmes extended. When in 1885 the Manchester Kindergarten Association suggested joining the Froebel Society to form a National Kindergarten Union, the Society was in a strong position to wait until acceptable terms had been agreed upon.

Consultations between the Manchester Kindergarten Association and the London Froebel Society regarding the question of united action in the issue of Kindergarten Certificates and the recognition of approved Kindergartens had been going on since March 1885. When the Manchester proposal for a National Kindergarten Union was examined in detail, the differences between the two examining bodies became apparent. Manchester objected to the London Society's requirement of a Preliminary Examination for candidates as well as to the syllabus with its many subjects and the Society's failure to require candidates to attend a training college.

Further discussions followed until in 1887 a Special Council Meeting passed the resolution to set up a Joint Kindergarten Examination Board which was to consist of members elected by each society in the proportion of one member for every fifty subscribers. The first meeting of the Joint Board of Examination of the Froebel Society and Manchester Kindergarten Association took place in the same year and was chaired by the Revd A. Bourne, Principal of Stockwell Training College.

The Joint Board considered the revision of the syllabus for the Elementary Certificate 1888 and recommended to students *Sully's Handbook on Psychology for Teachers* and von Marenholtz-Bülow's *Hand Work* as basic reading. It was also agreed that in future the certificates were to be titled 'The Elementary Kindergarten Certificate' and 'The Higher Kindergarten Certificate', 'awarded by the Joint Board of the Froebel Society and the Kindergarten Association Manchester'.

In the meantime the Bedford Kindergarten Association also had approached the Froebel Society regarding the basis of an amalgamation, suggesting 'a more liberal view of the training and examination of Kindergarten Teachers'. Its subsequent formal proposals were discussed at the meeting of the Council in April 1886 and rejected. Claude Montefiore's resolution that 'any union of the Froebel Society with other societies or colleges is not desirable if it involves any lowering of the present value of the Society's Certificates' was accepted.

The Secretary was instructed to write and inform Mr Philpotts from the Bedford Kindergarten Association, that 'the Council is not prepared to hand the granting of certificates to any other body, and to request him to state what modifications in the syllabus the Council of the Bedford Kindergarten Training College were prepared to suggest'. Another two years passed before another letter was received from Miss Sim expressing the desire of the Bedford association to join the Joint Board of Examiners. This was granted on 8 May 1888 and as the Bedford Association had a membership of 150 people, three representatives from the Association were invited to serve on the Joint Board. Bedford elected the Revd D.Poole, Headmaster of Bedford Modern School, Mr J.S. Philpotts, Headmaster of Bedford Grammar School, and Miss Sim, Headmistress of Bedford Kindergarten and later Principal of Bedford College.[16]

Exactly one year later, Miss Snell, the Manchester representative, was withdrawn from the Joint Board because of the differing views held on the content of the syllabus and on the examinations. Once more the Society was at pains to define the objective of the Union, stating that the main purpose was to establish a uniform standard of examination and a joint certificate to replace those given individually by the bodies represented on the Board. The Froebel Society requested its representatives on the Joint Board to express their hopes that the union should be fully carried out. The three Bedford representatives gave the assurance that: 'The Bedford Centre, as long as it is united with the Joint Board, agrees to admit no external students but those who sit for the Union Examination'.[17]

Thus much of the Society's time and energy between 1885 and 1890 was spent on unification. Yet the basic work of informing itself and spreading the 'New Education' continued. Lectures to the Society during this time were given on: The Study of Children; Our Children: their Growth and Development as illustrated by plant-life; The Training of the Imagination; Pestalozzi and Froebel; Gifts and Occupations; Zoology; Botany.

Members of the Society provided lectures on Saturday mornings for elementary school teachers and Kindergarten teachers which aimed at helping them to prepare for the Elementary Certificate. Topics included: Froebel's view on Character, Conduct and Religion; The Culture of the Imagination; Teaching of Natural History in the Kindergarten, Transition and School Classes; Drawing in the Kindergarten: What the teacher can do; Zoology; Kindergarten in India; Fundamental Principles of Froebel's Teaching; Kindergarten methods as applied to Training Class; Natural Science and Blackboard Drawing. Classes were well attended and parallel classes were considered when attendance topped sixty.

In 1888 the Council proposed to hold classes for the instruction of mothers and to provide a course for children's nurses. They believed that they could not 'better carry out the teaching of Froebel than by introducing his principles to the notice of mothers, whom he recognises as the child's first educator'.[18] Members of the Society gave lectures on 'Froebel and the Kindergarten' in Richmond, Croydon, Hampstead, Glasgow and Deal. The more Froebel's ideas became known, the more the demand for written information grew. The Sonnenschein Publicity House provided the Society with copies of *The Kindergarten in relation to School* and *Stories in the Kindergarten* for distribution at half price. The Society was now also considering producing their own publications, although finance was still a stumbling block.

The gradual lengthening of compulsory school life effected by the Education Acts of 1870, 1876 and 1880 involved the Government in increasing expenditure and elicited searching questions from those who represented the interests of voluntary or church schools. Little was known about what was happening in the schools which were constantly expanding and using up more and more of the country's financial resources. On educational grounds too an inquiry was overdue 'into the working of the Elementary Education Acts, England and Wales'. The Royal Commission of 1886, under the chairmanship of Sir Richard (later Lord) Cross gathered evidence on all aspects of elementary education, from buildings to staffing, from the content of the syllabus to children's health. The Froebel Society too responded to the Commission's request for information but kept its reply strictly to matters which were of the Society's concern, namely infant schools, the training of teachers and inspections. The Society recommended:

> That timetables in infant schools and infant departments should not be signed by Government inspectors unless the main part of the time is given to games, occupations, and other exercises suitable for the imagination and the senses of the children. That in the Infant Department the desirability that there should be, whenever feasible, as much floor space as bench space, should not be ignored.

> That no examination be held in reading for children under six years of age.

> That in training colleges more time be allowed for the principles of teaching and the art of early education.

> That the inspections carried out in schools should include the hearing of lessons given, and that the inspectors should attach particular weight not so much to the results of the teaching as to the methods of teaching.

Unfortunately however, the final report of the Commission makes almost no mention of infant schools and the education of the very young, but concentrates on the upper end of elementary education, especially the children in the higher standards.[19] Such omissions were based on extreme ignorance about the importance of children's education in their early years, as well as lack of knowledge about how to educate them. An infant school mistress's recollections about her work in a London school illustrate clearly the adults' limitations in dealing with young children.

> Every movement, whether of body or tool, the downsittings and uprisings, the goings out and comings in, were all performed automatically to numbers.... Step into lines 1,2. Standing position - 1,2. Sitting position - 1,2. Pens up, dip, write! Imagine a class of sixty children doing thimble drill for one hour. Sixty solemn little infants. Sixty solemn little thimbles. No one moves 'til all is ready.... When I explained to an inspector who complained ... of the way in which the children held their needle that I had too little time to teach them to sew, she was horrified. 'But you surely have not been teaching them to sew! This is the class where they learn to hold the needle'. (Raymont 1937:255)

Even if members of a Government Commission, or, for that matter, inspectors could not comprehend the world of the infant, their abilities, limitations and needs, the London School Board, which was involved in the day-to-day running of infant schools and infant departments, knew a great deal about the problems facing infant teachers. They had started their own Kindergarten Training Centre under Miss Lyschinska, a Froebelian of considerable standing, and now asked the Froebel Society to nominate an examiner for the examination of their students. Not only was the Society eager to oblige because of the influence this would have on the syllabus of the Training Centre, but it also strengthened the Society's hands when it urged the School Board no longer to recognise Kindergarten certificates issued by teachers not connected with the Froebel Society. The Society had spent a considerable amount of time and energy revising the syllabus for the training of Kindergarten teachers between 1885-1888 and standards had risen accordingly. Its efforts were spoilt by pseudo-qualifications bearing the names of Froebel or Kindergarten in the title, issued by teachers who had neither the knowledge nor the qualifications to do so. The London School Board readily agreed to the Society's request.

Passing the Kindergarten Certificate seems to have been a considerable hurdle for many teachers. The results for 1887 read:

18 Lower Certificates   11 passed
21 Higher Certificates (Part I) 14 passed
15 Higher Certificates (Part II) 12 passed.

The Joint Board considered that the Higher Certificate was to be aimed at by all those who wished to take full charge of a Kindergarten while the Lower Certificate was primarily intended for assistant mistresses and teachers in elementary schools or for work in private families.

When students at Bedford, who had now joined the Froebel Union, were examined by the Joint Board for the first time (1888), the results were not much better. Twenty-four students were examined in Class Teaching, the obligatory paper and The Gifts and Occupations, and sixteen were passed. London was no longer the only examination centre and provided at least fifteen students sat the examination, the Society was prepared to make local arrangements. In 1888 examinations were held in Manchester, Cheltenham, Bedford, Plymouth and Shrewsbury apart from several centres in London.

Just as the demands for regional examination centres grew, so did the demand for the formation of local Froebel Societies. On affiliation to the parent society in London, members of local branches were eligible to vote at the Society's Annual General Meeting. The objective of these local branches was to 'spread the knowledge and practice of the Kindergarten system and of maintaining a high standard of efficiency among Kindergarten teachers'.[20] To achieve this, local branches met for discussions, arranged drawing-room meetings, lectures and public meetings.

The Society's attention was also drawn to the plight of children in hospitals, especially longstay patients, who suffered from lack of educational opportunities or even playtime supervision. The Society's concern resulted in a scheme to carry out Kindergarten work in hospitals. Particularly useful work was being done in hospitals like the Alexandra Hip Disease Hospital for Children, 'where a regular course of work can be carried out as the children remain many months in the ward'.[21]

Kindergarten teachers have always considered themselves to be educators and not playleaders, as is often assumed by the public. They were educators who needed a certain minimum time with children if their efforts were to be of value, rather than child-minders looking after children's physical needs and providing interesting occupations for them.

All these varied activities, arranging public lectures, organising courses for teachers, keeping an eye on what was happening to young children in schools, inspecting Kindergartens and communicating with outside bodies concerned with education and the welfare of young children, demanded more and more time and energy of members of the Council and the Organising Committee. To share the load more evenly three sub-committees were created so that financial details, the arrangements and supervision of examinations and the planning of propaganda work could be dealt with outside Council meetings. As the work load grew, so did expenses and though the deficits each year were never large, lack of finance was a recurring problem. Members' subscriptions, examination fees and fees from public lectures covered the greatest part of the expenses, but had it not been for the generous help of members of the Council and donations from friends, the deficits would have been much larger.

The 1880s did not see many improvements in the education of young children. Whatever small achievements the Society was able to claim were due to idealists who, like Froebel, considered their efforts towards the improvement of the conditions of young children their vocation. Those efforts demanded not only their time and energy, but often also financial sacrifices. It would be invidious to mention particular individuals, but the 1878 Committee[22], by introducing a system of examination for Kindergartens and by creating the first Kindergarten training college, even if it did not survive for very long, provided the signposts for those who followed.

1. Mause, 1976, p1
2. Williams, 1953, p80
3. Peterson, 1971, p21
4. ibid, p11
5. Burnett, 1982, p150
6. Arnold, 1908, p97
7. Murray, nd, pp65-78
8. Birchenough, 1938, p101
9. FS Minutes, 1874, p2
10. ibid, pp11-20
11. Raymond, 1937, p245
12. FS Minutes, 1874, p98
13. Birchenough, 1938, p379
14. Raymond, 1937, p205
15. FS Minutes, 1876, p161
16. ibid, 1882, p102
17. NFU Minutes, 1887, p36
18. FS Minutes, 1887, p39
19. Board of Education, 1926, p21
20. FS Minutes, 1887, p6
21. ibid, p39
22. The 1878 Committee consisted of:
    Miss Shirreff, President
    Mrs Alfred Bailey
    Revd A. Bourne, Stockwell College
    Mrs William (Maria) Grey, Vice President
    Miss Heerwart
    Miss E.A.Manning
    Madame Michaelis
    Dr Roth
    Miss Sharwood, Girl's College, Southampton
    A. Sonnenschein, Esq.

*Froebel advocated in 1838 that each Kindergarten teacher be trained for
at least one year, so that she would be able to view the four seasons
in terms of what they had to offer to a child's learning
Froebel students at the turn of the century.*

Chapter 3

The Turn of the Century

Froebelian principles have revolutionized the work of our Infant Schools. Sir George
Kekewich, Permanent Secretary of the Education Department. 1899.

During the 1960s students at the Froebel Educational Institute in Roehampton were in
the uncomfortable position of studying for three years without sitting for any examinations before the final exams at the end of their training. Uncomfortable, because a
lifetime of tests and examinations, class-position and rank-orders had conditioned these
young people to such an extent that they found it very difficult, at least in their first year,
to go through life without constantly being told how well they were doing. The staff of
the college, under its Principal, Molly Brearley, had decided that as constant evaluation
focuses students away from the real task of education - that of acquiring knowledge -
to that of passing examinations, lecturers would provide detailed comments on work
done by students, but refrain from giving grades or providing rank-order lists. After
students had survived the initial shock, they preferred this system of working as it
allowed for greater freedom of expression and experimentation. It took away the fear
of failure and encouraged a more creative, open and truthful approach to the solving
of problems. There was no need to beat the system, indeed there was no opportunity
to do so.

This is a typically Froebelian approach to education. Froebel had much to say about
how we acquire knowledge but very little about tests and examinations, probably
because they have nothing to do with education. And yet, much of the Society's work,
especially in the 1890s, was taken up with examinations and the granting of certificates.
Was this a peculiarly English obsession? After all, Miss Heerwart commented in her
autobiography that 'examinations are a daily occurrence in England' implying that it
is exceptional compared with other countries in which she had worked[1]. We have to
remember that she is referring to a time when the Revised Code of 1862 was the
regulatory instrument of elementary education.

The Code of Payment by Results undoubtedly created more problems than it solved,
but in fairness to the architects of the Code it has to be said that their intentions were
not only to simplify an untidy system of grant allocation, but to change the system so
as to benefit the children of the working classes. Children in private schools had always

had a system of examinations. Robert Lowe, Vice President of the Committee of Council dealing with education, who was largely responsible for the Revised Code, believed that examinations would compel teachers and governors of schools to pay more attention to the essentials in a curriculum and thus improve public elementary education.

Few people would object to examinations which are designed to determine competency in carrying out a particular task or examinations leading to professional qualifications. The creation of examinations which are designed for the purpose of placing children into rank-orders or are intended to 'improve standards' is a much more dubious practice. Members of the Froebel Society could not escape the examination debate. Even though the Code did not require tests to be carried out on children below the ages of seven, it affected children and teachers in infant schools and infant departments seriously, because of the strain on them to get children ready to pass into standard one, and this involved the testing of infants to which Froebelians were strongly opposed. Yet, their own examinations of student-teachers were rigorous and demanding because they were dealing with the issuing of professional qualifications.

The examination of students for the Froebel Certificate had been the responsibility of the National Froebel Union since its inception in 1887. Candidates had to sit and pass preliminary examinations before being admitted to take the National Froebel Union Certificates. Preliminary examinations for the Lower Certificate of the National Froebel Union consisted of papers in arithmetic, English language, English history and geography. Exemptions were granted to those candidates who had passed some recognised public examinations such as those held at the College of Preceptors, Oxford or Cambridge University as well as certificated teachers in public elementary schools and pupil-teachers who had gained a Second Class in the examination for the Queen's Scholarship. The preliminary examination for the Higher Certificate of the National Froebel Union consisted of papers in English literature, a language paper in either Latin, French, Greek or German, Euclid and algebra, and one of the following papers: physiology and laws of health, botany, zoology. Exemptions were granted to those who could produce a certificate in evidence of having passed one of the following: the London University Matriculation, Oxford and Cambridge Joint Board Higher Certificate, the local examinations of the Scottish universities, First Class College of Preceptors, the Maria Grey College Entrance, the Elementary Teacher's Certificate of Merit awarded by the Education Department, and to those who held the NFU Joint Board's Lower Certificate.[2] Possession of the Cambridge Teacher's Certificate and the London University Teacher's Diploma did not qualify a candidate for exemption from the preliminary examination of the NFU Higher Certificate. Quite clearly, the Joint Board of the NFU did not hold these two qualifications in high esteem.

In 1892 ninety-six candidates took the preliminary examination for the Lower Certificate of whom forty-nine passed and, of the twenty-six entrants to the preliminary examination for the Higher Certificate, fifteen passed. Comparable figures for 1898 were 131 of which 75 passed and 49 with 33 passes. Such low pass marks are not really surprising when one reflects on the examiners' comments that

....in most cases the arithmetic was deplorably inaccurate and unintelligent; the analysis of English was not much better. The geography was worse than it had been for years -

East confused with West; 'the two river mouths in England are the Hull flowing in the Indian Ocean and the Thames into the Pacific Ocean', while the maps were even more astounding. ..... In all the subjects there was a good deal of bad spelling. (NFU Minutes 1895:72)

Training colleges all over the country were reporting similar shortcomings in would-be students. As late as 1876 a Government report described students on entering college thus:

The average candidate can work the ordinary rules of Arithmetic, but no problems involving rules; he can write out a proposition of Euclid by memory, but cannot employ it intelligently; he knows just enough Algebra to be confused; he can parse an English sentence fairly, and has a very fair knowledge of the bare facts of geography and history; he has a slight smattering of a French or Latin vocabulary; he knows the ordinary forms of schoolkeeping. (Rich 1972:211)

And yet, teacher training had come a long way since the beginning of the nineteenth century when students were trained by attending monitorial classes, supplemented by instruction of a practical and theoretical nature from the teacher in charge. The academic superficiality which such a system created, together with an inevitable paternalism towards the trainee teacher, was to bedevil teacher training until the middle of the twentieth century. Kay Shuttleworth's attempt, in the 1840s, to move away from the monitorial system by establishing the well-known Battersea Institute introduced the idea of a continuous training by which a trainee teacher was able to attend his institute for one, two or three years after working as a pupil-teacher from age thirteen to eighteen. Before a candidate was accepted for training as a pupil-teacher he was required to be able to read fluently, to write neatly and spell correctly, to have an elementary knowledge of geography and be able to repeat the catechism if teaching in a school connected with the Church of England. In other schools the state of religious knowledge had to be certified by the managers. Girls were also required to be able to sew neatly and to knit.

By 1889 about 6,000 boys and girls completed their pupil-teacher apprenticeship each year, while the training colleges could not admit more than about 1,600 of them per year. At the beginning of the 1890s over half of women teachers in inspected schools and over a quarter of the men teachers had had no college training. The introduction of the pupil-teachers' centres in the later part of the nineteenth century helped to improve matters, and above all, they were instrumental in altering the balance of training given. So far the emphasis had always been on the teaching element, by the turn of the century this was no longer true. The instruction provided, however, was very elementary, especially as officially only certificated staff of the school to which pupil-teachers were allocated, were allowed to teach in the centres. Thus, by the beginning of the twentieth century the work of these centres was taken over by secondary schools which were able to provide a more rigorous academic programme.

The Cross Commission, which had been asked to review progress made in elementary education up to 1888, showed a marked difference of opinion with regard to pupil-teacher training. Some of its members thought that the pupil-teacher system was the weakest link in the educational chain. Yet the majority of the Commission were in favour of retaining the scheme as the most reliable source of supply of teachers in spite of strong criticism by several of the witnesses called. Miss Trevor, for example, then Principal of Bishop Otter College, answered well on 300 questions put to her and never wavered in her condemnation of the practice. When asked: 'To what do you attribute this lamentable failure of the pupil-teachers who come to you in the knowledge of history and geography?' she answered:

> I do not see how they can possibly learn them; I think it would be a miracle if they did know them. They go in at the age of fourteen when they are too young to have acquired much knowledge, and they then teach for five hours a day, not knowing how to teach. Of course it is a terrible strain on a girl who does not know how to teach, when she is at once put in charge of a lot of children whom, somehow or other she must teach and keep in order. It looks beautiful on paper; the syllabus that is given for pupil-teachers is, to look at, everything that we would wish, but they do not do it. Girl after girl whom I have questioned has told me that they have never, during the four years of pupil-teachership, answered a question in history or geography. If they can do sums they will pass through their pupil-teachership, and they can all do those.... (McGregor 1981:112)

The training colleges had outgrown the restricted curriculum imposed upon them in 1862 and were now providing a much wider range of subjects. Students who entered colleges via the pupil-teacher training scheme found it much more difficult to succeed than those who completed their education in secondary schools. In the best of these colleges students were able to prepare for the degree examinations of London University. The successes of these colleges persuaded the Cross Commission to introduce the idea of university day training colleges. By the turn of the century there were sixteen such colleges in existence. Their close links with the universities, many of which established Chairs which were filled by eminent educators, brought about a more serious approach to educational theory. This, however, still only affected the teachers who eventually worked with older children. The Cross Commission scarcely mentions infant schools. It is only in the minority report that some attention is paid to the work done in these schools and it is suggested that the Department encourage 'the special training of mistresses of infant schools and secure that their preparation shall be as complete and thorough as for other departments'[3].

There certainly were differences between the training given to Froebel teachers and those who took the general Teachers' Certificate, differences which related to the philosophy of education and to the wholeness of the total educational process in the classroom, both of which influenced the kind of topics or subjects to be offered to students. Training colleges in general simply provided opportunities for studying subjects to a more advanced level which were generally taught in schools. Their only concessions to professional training were the lectures given by the Method Master, providing detailed instructions about how to organise a class of children, how to teach a subject and keep discipline. In the 'Syllabus of Lectures in Psychology and in the Method Used in the Practising School at Chester College' of 1885, students are asked to conduct a reading lesson as follows:

1. Teacher reads; 2. Class reads in unison;
3. Teacher corrects; 4. Teacher reads again;
5. Class imitate again; 6. Individual reading
by poorest readers; 7. Children and teacher
correct; 8. Class are questioned on the passage

with closed books. (Bradbury 1975:157)

The psychology section of the same syllabus, advanced for its time, suggests that the processes of thinking are best investigated by concentrating on the study of:

1. The Mind; 2. Attention; 3. Sensation;
4. Perception; 5. Memory; 6. Imagination;
7. Conception; 8. Judgement; 9. Reasoning.

Character formation, based on the study of the work of Thomas Arnold was the culmination of the course.

The syllabus for the training of teachers taking the Froebel certificates changed frequently, but in general was always based on the educational philosophy of Froebel and therefore on the study of children by direct observation. The study of Froebel's philosophy provided students with the long-term objectives, while the study of children indicated to them how best to achieve these aims. The rest of the syllabus was based on these two overriding considerations. The examination of the Froebel Elementary Certificate of 1902 covered the following subjects:

1. Biographies of Froebel and Pestalozzi, their principles and methods and their application of these to the teaching of elementary subjects.
2. Nature Knowledge. A general knowledge of plants and animals familiar to English children.
3. Kindergarten Gifts and Occupations.
   a) Oral Examination, b) Papers.
4. Music and Singing.
   a) Paper, b) Practical skill.
5. Class Teaching.
   a) to tell a story, b) to conduct a game and give some simple gymnastic exercises,
   c) to give a lesson choosing one subject from each of the following sections:
   I) Gifts and Occupations
   II) Arithmetic; Reading; Singing; Writing; Natural Objects; (Children had to be aged between 3-7)
6) Blackboard Drawing. a) from memory; b) from Nature; c) illustrating a story, poem, game, work.
7) Knowledge of Child Nature; Elementary laws of psychology; practical observation and knowledge of Child Nature; simple conditions of a healthy body.
Optional subject:
8) Practical Geometry. Descriptions of the chief plane figures, methods of drawing them with help of mathematical instruments and other methods of drawing them suggested by Froebel's Gifts and Occupations. Construction of angles, parallels, perpendiculars etc.[4]

The Higher Certificate of the National Froebel Union consisted of two parts and was awarded as a First or Second Class Certificate. The Part I examination consisted of the following subjects: history of education; Kindergarten Gifts and occupations; geometry; music and singing; and two of the following: physiography, physics, chemistry of common life, botany, zoology. Part II of the examination covered: the theory of education; Froebel's principles; organisation and methods of education; physical education; (physiology and hygiene; simple physical exercises); class teaching;

blackboard drawing. A First Class Certificate was awarded to candidates who had obtained a mark of 65% and over in each of the following: class teaching and Gifts and occupations; Froebel's principles and the theory of education, provided an average mark of 60% had been achieved in all other subjects[5].

Considering that in the first year of the National Froebel Union's existence (1888) students were examined only in class teaching, natural science, Kindergarten subjects, the biographies of Froebel and Pestalozzi and the theory of music and singing, trainers became increasingly anxious about their ability to provide adequately for their students within the two-year course. The period of training for the higher certificate was therefore increased to two and a half years in 1899[6]. Elementary school teachers engaged in their school work during the day also found it extremely difficult to give sufficient time to the study of all these subjects in their spare time. The Association of School Boards approached the National Froebel Union with the request to establish a more elementary certificate for teachers in Board Schools, but this was rejected by the Joint Board on the grounds that as half of the elementary school teachers who had entered for the examination had obtained their certificate in that year (1895), it was clear that they could do the work demanded of them.

The assessment of practical teaching created special difficulties as examiners were paying attention to different aspects of a student's performance. After several meetings and lengthy discussions the examiners agreed (1895) on the form for assessing marks in class teaching:

Maximum Number of Marks: 100 (Pass Mark: 40)

Teacher - personal qualities	40	
Teaching - Lesson, Methods etc.	60	
Maximum Marks: Teacher -		
Manner, Language		6
Power to instruct		10
Power to control		10
Force, precision in teaching		7
Resource and tact		7
Lesson -		
Subject, choice, arrangement, notes	11	
Method: Induction,Deduction,Questions	14	
Training: Intellectual		10
Moral		10
Physical		5
Illustrations		5
Value of facts taught		5
		100

Examiners in practical subjects were encouraged to refer, in the case of any doubtful student, to the trainer and not finally to decide against the student, until the report had been received from the trainer.

In the year before the creation of the National Froebel Union as an examining body, seventy-five students were examined by the Froebel Society. Twelve years later almost seven hundred students were admitted for examinations. At first examinations were held in London only, but the steady increase of candidates necessitated the opening of examination centres in the provinces and in Ireland. To the main centres in London, Bedford and Manchester were soon added Croydon, Plymouth, Edgbaston, Chelten-ham, Ipswich, Shrewsbury, Liverpool, Sheffield, Cork, Leicester and Dublin. Applications were received at various times from India, Australia, Canada and the Cape Colony for examinations to be held there, but the Joint Board of the National Froebel Union could not see their way to grant such requests, mainly because of the great difficulty of examining in practical subjects. In 1898, however, the Joint Board agreed to hold the written part of the certificate examinations in the colonies but without granting a certificate. Candidates who passed the papers were given a written statement to that effect and encouraged to complete the examination when a satisfactory opportunity offered itself.

The syllabus as well as the examinations were constantly revised and attempts at raising standards not only resulted in the greater number of subjects to be examined, but also in a shift of emphasis from practical work to the passing of papers. Mrs Walter (Emily) Ward, a former pupil of Madame Michaelis and now Principal of the Norland Place Kindergarten and Training Centre, was well aware of this and in order to initiate change, she circulated a printed proposal under the title 'Manual Training Examina-tion' for the consideration of members of the Froebel Society[7]. She pointed out that 'during the past twenty years the standard of the examinations now held by the National Froebel Union has been raised. Several intellectual subjects, moreover, have been added, but the amount of manual work since Fräulein Heerwart's time has been enormously decreased'. She concluded that 'the whole subject of manual training is ripe for revision'. A sub-committee was set up to study the matter and make recommenda-tions to the Joint Board, but nothing more was heard of it. Emily Ward resigned from the Joint Board one year later, in 1896.

A much more serious and fundamental criticism of the examination system was made by Professor Findlay from Manchester University, a member of the Council of the Froebel Society since 1894. During a Council Meeting in 1895 he put before the Council a paper entitled 'An alternative plan for awarding the Froebel Teacher's Certificate'[8]. Professor Findlay argued that the then prevailing mode of awarding certificates was not Froebelian in character. He criticised the fact that the teaching was divorced from the examinations and that the 'simultaneous' printed paper required every trainer and every candidate to pursue each branch of study on similar lines and within the same limits. He believed that the system aimed at producing uniformity and that uniformity was especially unfortunate in this current state of knowledge of the theory of education. In this subject, independence of treatment and method were essential and simultaneous examination forbade independence. There might be little harm in imposing a common paper of questions in algebra or arithmetic, but the case was different with many Froebel Certificate subjects. The best results could not be achieved without diversity. Professor Findlay, therefore, put the following proposals to the Council which, after discussion were submitted to the Joint Board.

1) That students of <u>Approved</u> Training Colleges or Training Departments not be required to present themselves for the present examination, unless they desired it. But that

2) The Joint Board Certificate should be granted to students of such approved colleges on a) the report of the principal or the student's course of training; b) the result of the examinations conducted jointly by the college staff and an inspector or inspectors of the Joint Board.

3) That the approved Training Colleges obtain such approval from the Joint Board on the report of Joint Board inspectors that the course of training is satisfactory. This report should be based on:
   a) Unexpected visits to lectures and classrooms;
   b) Inspection of time-table and syllabus for each branch of study;
   c) Presence at lessons given by students;
   d) Inspection of written and practical work done by students.

The most forceful and coherent objection to this plan was submitted by Mr Courthorpe Bowen, the former Principal of Finsbury Training College for Secondary School Masters and Director of Examination and Chairman of the Joint Board from 1890-1908. He argued that the proposer entirely ignored the purpose for which the Joint Board was established: The creation of *one* certificate (of two grades) instead of many - a clear definite certificate which should win the confidence of the public, instead of the various and vague certificates which formerly existed. The special aim of the proposal was to do away with uniformity and to give each college the power to grant its own certificate under supervision.

Mr Courthorpe Bowen pointed out that the success of such a plan rested on inspection, and wondered whether Professor Findlay had counted the cost of inspection and examination. The practical examination at the Froebel Institute, for example, took a fortnight and cost £25, before travelling expenses and hotel bills. Mr Courthorpe Bowen estimated that the total bill for such a scheme would be between £750 and £1,000, in which case only larger colleges could contemplate joining. It was a matter of fact that much the greater part of examination candidates came in twos and threes from small Kindergartens generally attached to schools - with one trainer, often not certificated and a headmistress who knew nothing about the examinations. Were they to be awarded certificates under supervision? Candidates' fees in such cases would have to be doubled. And what about students in a college which had been pronounced unsatisfactory by the inspectors? Were they all to be denied certificates however efficient they might be individually? At any rate, one of the effects of the proposed plan would be the closing of all small Kindergartens, for they could not exist without their students in training and no inspector would report their system of training as satisfactory in itself[9].

When the proposal was finally discussed by the Joint Board, Claude Montefiore, Madame Michaelis, Principal of the Froebel Educational Institute, and Fanny Franks, Principal of Camden House Training School for Kindergarten Teachers, spoke for accepting the proposal, while Mr Courthorpe Bowen, the Revd J.B. Armstrong, Principal of the Home and Colonial Society, Emily Ward, Principal of Norland Place Kindergarten and Miss Penstone, Examiner, spoke against it. The plan was rejected by three votes to two, with the Chairman, Mr Courthorpe Bowen, and Claude Montefiore abstaining from voting. A year later Professor Findlay resigned from the Joint Board because of ill health, but remained a member of the Froebel Society.

The National Froebel Union was, of course autonomous in its decision-making as regards the syllabus and examinations, and yet, the opinions expressed by members of the Froebel Society could not be ignored. The introduction of several new subjects into the Higher Certificate course was probably responsible for the dropping of the 'Froebel's Principles' paper in the 1910 course. When the Society was informed about this particular change, its expression of disapproval was swift and couched in terms which left little room for argument. The resolution sent to the Joint Board of the National Froebel Union read as follows:

> The Council of the Froebel Society regrets that 'Froebel's Principles' are not to be an obligatory subject in the syllabus of the National Froebel Union for 1910, and requests that this be rectified in the syllabus in the future. (FS Minutes 1907:47)

It was implemented without any further discussion. Indeed, it is surprising that such a change should have slipped through at all, given that the Society's representatives on the Joint Board included people of the calibre of Miss Findlay, Miss Franks, Miss Lawrence, Miss Murray and Miss Vinter.

Mr Courthorpe Bowen, the Chairman of the National Froebel Union, resigned in 1909, having held this office from its inception. He died one year later. Under his stewardship such a change would probably never have been suggested. Mr Courthorpe Bowen was steeped in Froebelian philosophy, he himself had published books about Froebel and his untiring efforts whether for the National Froebel Union or as a member of the Council of the National Froebel Society guaranteed him a place of honour among the Froebelians of his time.

As early as 1890, the National Froebel Union received requests from Government training colleges and also from the London School Board for authorised examiners of the National Froebel Union to examine their Kindergarten students. Only on one occasion was such a request granted and even then it was with the proviso that the examiner acted in a private capacity and not under the auspices of the National Froebel Union. Such unofficial recognition of the Froebel Society's work prompted the Council to write to the Rt Hon. Mr Arthur Acland, Vice President of the Education Department, at the time when the Teacher Registration Bill was before the House of Commons (1891), asking him to take special cognizance of societies issuing certificates for teachers, especially certificates granted by the National Froebel Union. Two years later, the Education Department's Circular 322, issued to Her Majesty's Inspectors of Infant Schools dwelt at some length on the merits of the Kindergarten system[10] and set forth that holders of the certificates of the National Froebel Union were qualified to act as assistant mistresses in public elementary infant schools[11]. Such encouraging news, even though a National Froebel Union Certificate still did not qualify for a full Government Certificate, provided a greatly needed fillip to members of the Society at a time when its numbers were dwindling. The Annual General Meetings of 1893 and 1894 were not well attended, but by 1895 the Society was once more strong enough to invite evaluation of its work from an outsider.

Mr Field, one of Her Majesty's Inspectors was invited to speak to the AGM on 'The Froebel System of Education in Elementary Schools'. His observations throw light on an outsider's reaction to the Froebelians' insistence on the maintenance of certain principles which seem to have set them apart from elementary school teachers. His comments are therefore worth quoting in full, as recorded in the minutes[12].

Mr Field said the subject on which he had asked to be allowed to speak was a rather debatable one, namely, the establishment of the Froebel System in Elementary Schools. There were many difficulties in connection with it. He would consider them under two headings: the removable and the irremovable. Under the first he would place the supply of thoroughly trained teachers and the conditions of examinations. As regards the teachers, he thought in the district which he inspected, there was a certain number of teachers who had a thorough grasp of Froebel's System, and whose tact, originality and enthusiasm were beyond praise. But there were also many teachers who stumbled along, many who had studied Froebel's principles and taken up Kindergarten Occupations with no knowledge of their scope and aim, and with no results, so far as the children were concerned, which could be called satisfactory. He did not blame the teachers. It was quite obvious that we were only just emerging from darkness into light on the subject. It was only recently that official sanction had been given to the Froebelian System. There were no facilities, or practically very few, for obtaining a thoroughly good Froebel Certificate. There were absolutely no positive requirements of a Froebel Certificate of any sort for an infant teacher.

The first requirement was a large number of teachers with really good Froebel Certificates, a certificate which showed that the holder of it had gone through a thorough training in the principles and practice of Froebelian teaching. He wished every effort could be made to establish centres throughout the country, not only in towns, for it is in country places that the classes are small. In towns are the large classes, which are supposed to be so unmanageable. We need centres where the Froebel Certificate training can be cheaply acquired. At present the training is expensive and the difficulty in getting it is almost insuperable.... These were the removable difficulties.

Then came the irremovable - the difficulties which arose from the fixed conditions of the elementary schools. One of these was the size of classes, the other the early age at which children leave school; some leaving at eleven, practically all at fourteen. Many ardent admirers of the Froebel System had a horror of large classes. Looking at it from a practical point of view, Mr Field would say that it was impossible with the already heavy rates to provide a teacher for every twenty children. It would be nearly impossible to build a school which would satisfy these conditions. He would like to ask anybody who thought it impossible to manage the large classes to visit a good Infant School and see how 150 or 200 children, taken from the gutter, were in a very short time got into perfect order, and were proud to belong to the school which sometimes became to them something even better than their own homes. In the schools the children were occupied by drilling, singing, object lessons, and other collective work, Kindergarten Games included - though for the games the children were taken out. In drawing the children were taught together, and drawing was a subject capable of enormous development. Children in a well taught class could not only draw from a copy, but from memory, and afterwards colour the drawing with considerable taste. This was good work done, because it did not consist in cramming the child, but in training its faculty so that originality had full play.

Everything might not be perfectly orthodox, but there was nothing in any way in conflict with the spirit and essence of Froebelian teaching.

The great points were the training of the faculties rather than the imparting of mere knowledge, the training of the body as well as the mind..... The debatable question of reading, writing and arithmetic must be defended on the grounds of necessity, though he was not concerned to say much about arithmetic and writing, so long as they were not turned into drudgery. Reading he would defend on its own merit. Of all subjects of instruction it seemed the most cultivating. Children learnt it at their mother's knee. Their mothers read to them and they asked questions and soon wished to read the stories for themselves. And so it was in the Infant Schools. The d-o-g, dog, c-a-t, cat mode was done away with long ago. He himself had no misgivings at all about the future success of Froebelianism in England. But he did think the Froebel Society might show a little more willingness to admit them within the pale of Froebelianism, even though they *did* teach reading and though their classes *were* large.

No doubt, Froebelians attending the AGM had questions to ask, as they usually did, and were ready to give reasons why they were so reluctant to compromise on the issue of teaching reading to children of Kindergarten age, but there are no records concerning audience reaction.

While the creation of the National Froebel Union, as the official agency for examining Froebel-trained students and for awarding certificates, attracted more and more candidates and thus greatly improved that body's financial position, the Froebel Society, providing the courses and lectures for training, was once again struggling financially. In spite of appeals to several City companies for donations to the Society, which resulted in gifts of £20 from the Clothworkers' Company and £10 from the Drapers' Company, the Froebel Society showed deficits at the end of 1891 and 1892. Saturday lectures, which had been making a loss for several years, were now suspended. Morale was low. For the first time in the history of the Society the minute books record Council meetings in 1893-1894 where no business could be transacted because there was no quorum. The AGM in 1893 was so poorly attended that the Council took the President's advice and agreed to organise the AGM in 1894 as an internal affair only[13].

It was Emily Shirreff's outstanding example which in part provided the impetus for the Society's recovery. Her personal involvement and efforts in collecting £46 from new subscribers, together with her own personal donations, seem to have provided sufficient encouragement to the Council to organise lectures again and initiate conferences which, from all accounts, proved once more successful. The Society showed a profit of £57 in 1895 and of £70 in 1896. Yet, a year later the old pattern was repeated; and it was Claude Montefiore this time who came to the rescue to wipe out the deficit.

It was therefore not surprising, that when the balance sheet for 1897 was presented to the AGM in 1898, the Chairman added a few paragraphs to his report putting forward, at some length, the reasons for and against the Society's continuing existence as a separate body. The question was discussed as to whether the work now done by the Society was of sufficient value to justify its existence as a separate organisation. Several members expressed the opinion that affiliation with some larger body might, under the circumstances, be desirable. Fanny Franks, Principal of Camden House Training School for Kindergarten Teachers, on the other hand, was strongly of the opinion that there was still much work which the Society could do, even with its present limited income. It was finally decided that for the present no change should be attempted in the constitution of the Society and that their attention during the current year should be turned, in particular, to two important issues. First, to make the Society better known in the provinces and secondly, to aid in the diffusion of Froebelian knowledge among qualified elementary school teachers. Yet even this optimistic attitude did not prevent five of the eight retiring members of the Council from refusing to stand for re-election[14].

But those were not the only blows which the Society had to withstand. Baroness von Marenholtz-Bülow, one of Froebel's personal friends and disciples, who had been in London as early as 1854 to demonstrate and lecture on Kindergarten methods and who had been a constant supporter and adviser to the Froebel Society, died in 1893. Miss Sim, Principal of the Bedford Kindergarten and Training College who had been a member of the Froebel Society since 1875 and an untiring worker for the Movement since her Southampton days, followed her in 1895. But hardest to bear was the loss of Emily Shirreff who died in 1897, having presided over the Society's affairs for nearly twenty-two years.

Miss Emily Shirreff, together with her younger sister Maria, later Mrs Maria Grey, devoted her life to a crusade for female education. Maria's marriage to the nephew of the second Earl Grey, Prime Minister 1830-34, opened the doors for both women to the society of reform-orientated Liberals like Lord Aberdare, Anthony Mundella, and Lord Cavendish[15]. The English Liberals' notion of freedom for the individual and especially the liberation of women from social bonds, harmonised well with Froebel's ideas on education. Once the Foster Education Act, sponsored by a Liberal Government, had established a national system of elementary education, the road was clear for the propagation of the Kindergarten system. But Emily Shirreff saw in Froebel's Kindergartens not only the means for educating young women, but realized the difference between 'instruction' as practised in schools generally and 'education by self-activity' as advocated by Froebel. Miss Shirreff's writings demonstrated her powers of interpreting Froebel's ideas in such a way as to make them intelligible and accessible to English teachers. In a special Council Meeting, the then Chairman, Mr Montefiore, recorded:

> From the date of its first establishment to the close of her active life, Mrs Shirreff gave to the Society constant thought and increasing devotion, putting freely at its disposal, in addition to many material gifts, her time, her knowledge and her literary powers and skill. The position which the Society has achieved, the full recognition now generally accorded to the truth and value of Froebel's principles, and the wide diffusion of his methods in Great Britain, are all mainly due, directly or indirectly, to her ability and zeal, to her writings and speeches, to her influence and personality. (FS Minutes 1896:63)

It was clear to members of Council that it would be difficult to replace their President with somebody of an equally high social standing who at the same time also understood the principles of the new education and cared sufficiently to devote time and energy towards achieving the aims and objectives of the Society. This was probably the reason why the Society changed the constitution so that in future the President was elected annually and was eligible for re-election for a second year only.

The Council approached many eminent people: Mrs Creighton from the Bureau for the Employment of Women, who was the wife of the Bishop of London; Lady Frederick

(Lucy) Cavendish, the first female recipient of an honorary degree from Leeds University and President of the Yorkshire Ladies Guild, who was a friend of the Shirreff sisters; Mr Sidgwick, an academic; Lady Farrer; Lady Battersea and others - but none accepted. After six months of unsuccessful searching, Miss Ward proposed that Madame Michaelis, the Principal of the Froebel Educational Institute, should allow her name to go forward for nomination. Madame Michaelis, probably the most informed interpreter of Froebelian education at the time, accepted and was elected President in the spring of 1898. She was a formidable lady whose caring attitude, modest demeanour and intellectual integrity made her a favourite among children, students and teachers alike. By the end of the year membership had increased by 30 per cent to number 478. Saturday classes were started again and once more courses and lectures provided urgently needed profits for the Society.

Yet in spite of the Society's financial vicissitudes during the last decade of the century, the majority of its members never faltered in promoting Froebel's educational principles within the means available. To achieve this, the Society provided two different types of lectures: The Saturday classes which consisted of a series of lectures on one particular topic to the benefit of teachers and others to help them to prepare for the Elementary Certificate Examination, and the monthly lectures, aimed at the general public as well as members of the Society, dealing with different topics in each lecture.

Saturday classes often provided courses of ten lectures each on topics like: the Gifts, the Occupations, paper folding and stick-laying, the theory of Kindergarten games, blackboard drawing, brushwork (painting), child nature (child development), nature knowledge, and lectures on Froebel and Pestalozzi. Classes were usually held at St Martin's School, Charing Cross and might begin on Friday evenings rather than Saturday mornings. The programme of lectures for the autumn 1898 was as follows:

Fridays: 6.30 - 7.30 Child Nature: illustrated by principles and methods of Froebel
and Pestalozzi.
7.45 - 8.45 Nature Knowledge.

Saturdays: 10.30 -11.30 Gifts and Occupations
11.45 -12.45 Blackboard Drawing

Courses on blackboard drawing were popular, not only because the Froebel Certificate demanded that students had to prove their ability to illustrate their lessons on the blackboard and to illuminate poems and stories by simple line-drawings, but also because it seems to have encouraged the blossoming of latent talents of which adults had not been aware, thus demonstrating Froebel's ideas about 'creative activity' in a very practical way. Most of these courses were staffed by principals of Kindergartens who were also trainers of students for the National Froebel Union Certificates and by lecturers from Froebel training colleges.

Monthly lectures had a twofold purpose. They were, in the main, a vehicle for informing members of the Society, as well as the general public, of new or little-known ideas in education, but also to provide an open forum for discussion of these ideas. Lecturers were drawn from the medical profession, from philosophers, historians, psychologists, but above all from the ever-increasing number of Kindergarten principals. Topics ranged from historical lectures on Herbart, Comenius, Pestalozzi and Froebel to philosophical concepts like 'justice' and 'freedom', from practical issues like 'the teaching of reading', 'physical education', 'the best way of questioning children', 'hygiene for schools', to basic Froebelian notions like 'the connectedness in Kindergarten work' and 'how to combine history and geography in the teaching of junior classes'. 'New Education Movements in France', 'Contemporary Kindergarten Development in Germany', 'Sonnenschein's Mathematical Apparatus' and lectures on 'The New Modelling' kept Froebelians up to date and challenged them to rethink their own theories and practices. Similar lectures were now also provided in Yorkshire, Dover, Lewisham, Kidderminster, Bristol and other cities. But when the University of Durham requested a course of lectures on 'How to amuse my Children', the Council decided that no lecturer could be spared for a course on the subject mentioned, not even for payment. If an understanding of Froebelian education had not gone beyond 'amusing children', the ground for planting further ideas was certainly not yet prepared. Appeals to the Society for lectures in the provinces became more frequent, but even worthy requests like the one from the School for the Blind in Liverpool for provision of a course of lectures on Froebelian subjects was still beyond the means of the Society[16].

Froebelians were not only called upon to lecture during term-time, but were also in demand during the holidays to staff conferences and holiday courses. The yearly day conferences usually took place during the week before the autumn term started for the benefit of Kindergarten teachers and trainers, but were also for teachers of the lower age-groups in elementary schools. Lectures on reading, writing, numbers, music, nature knowledge, Kindergarten games, the occupations, literature for children up to twelve, were usually supported by exhibitions and demonstrations with classes of children. The successes of the day conferences in 1894 and 1895 persuaded the Council to restart their holiday courses, usually of a week's duration. The course which took place in January 1896, providing five lectures on Froebel's and Pestalozzi's educational principles, followed by a practical demonstration of Kindergarten teaching with a class of children in the morning and a course of lectures on the occupations and nature knowledge in the afternoon seems to have been particularly successful. Over a hundred participants signed a vote of thanks 'to the Froebel Society for having organised the course' and expressed their hopes that they might have the privilege of attending a similar course soon[17]. No doubt, it was the practical nature of the course which promoted such praise, for the Council decided that 'the next Holiday Course should largely consist of demonstrations'. Unfortunately these good intentions did not materialise because of lack of demonstrators. The course in 1897 and in 1898 consisted mainly of lectures only and the Society, once again, had to carry the losses.

Exhibitions provided one other venue for spreading Froebel's principles. Though the Society declined an invitation to exhibit at The World Fair in Chicago in 1892, they accepted an invitation to contribute to the Paris Exhibition of 1900, even if the exhibition space allowed was rather small. The Victorian Era Exhibition at Earl's Court from May - October 1897 however provided greater opportunities and enough space to furnish a room as a model Kindergarten in which Kindergarten lessons could be given and a space for demonstrations with larger groups of children.

Lectures, conferences, courses, exhibitions and public demonstrations kept Froebel's name in the public eye. More and more parents were sending their children to Kindergartens. Requests increased for inspection and recognition of Kindergartens by the Froebel Society. Examiners were paying attention to buildings, space provided per child, ventilation, light, furniture, sanitation, children's attendances, staffing and qualifications of staff, to methods used, to availability of apparatus, animals, gardens, out-of-door activities, Froebel's Gifts and occupations, collections made by the children, to games, gymnastics, free play, and to order, appearance, behaviour and tone. No wonder that more Kindergartens failed this inspection than were successful. By 1890 the following Kindergartens were registered:

Rock Ferry Kindergarten, Rock Ferry,
Notting Hill Kindergarten, Norland Place
The North Hackney High School for Girls and KG, Stamford Hill
The Camden House KG and Training College for Teachers, Baker Street
The North London Collegiate Preparatory School & KG, Camden Road
The King's High School for Girls (Kindergarten), Warwick

During the next ten years only four more Kindergartens achieved recognition:

The High School (KG) Sidney Place, Cork
The High School (KG), Chiswick
The Hampstead Kindergarten, Carlinford Road
The Lewisham Kindergarten, Lewisham.

Kindergartens on the Register were inspected every three years and recognition withdrawn if the examiners found that standards had not been maintained. Only abbreviated reports were sent to the principals, giving reasons for judgements made and if in the view of the Council it had been a near failure, principals were encouraged to have the Kindergarten re-inspected. Only Kindergartens with at least twelve children in attendance qualified for inspection. The years from 1890 to the turn of the century had been a turbulent time for the Froebel Movement: moving from near financial collapse to comparative stability, from curtailing weekend courses and monthly lectures to extending them to include holiday conferences, from examinations taken by fewer than a hundred students in London to providing examination centres in the provinces and in Ireland to cater for seven times that number. When Madame Michaelis gave the address on the twenty-fifth anniversary of the Froebel Society on the 4 November 1899, she could rightly look back with gratitude upon the work achieved. After giving accounts of the contributions of the Society's most active members, she continued:

> The work which we endeavoured to do was to promote Froebel's educational principles and to create a high standard of Kindergarten teaching. The aim was not an ambitious one for a Society which bears the name of Friedrich Froebel, yet it has had hard struggles to accomplish it. It has had its moments of financial depression; yet, then, as now, it found kind and generous people who contrived somehow to square the accounts at the end of the year. The Society had its adversaries within and without, but, through bad and good

report, it firmly has pursued its aims, and today it can look back upon good work done, upon great things achieved.

Let me for a moment glance at the result of the twenty-five years of work of our Society. Hundreds of well-trained and efficient teachers work in Kindergartens, private and public; the Education Department accepts in the elementary schools teachers possessing the National Froebel Union Certificate; India and the Colonies establish Kindergartens for children; and there is hardly any school in this country, secondary or primary, which does not adopt Froebel's System for its younger classes. Associations are formed similar to ours to promote Froebelian principles and teaching, and although these are still few in numbers, there is every hope that they may increase. Froebel's own works are translated into English, books of reference are at hand for our students in their own language, and many institutions exist which bear Froebel's name and which are animated by his spirit. The Society has its own Magazine, which is a connecting link between friends in town and country, between England and its colonies. Froebel's name has become a household word, and Froebel's principles are not any more a dead letter for many. (*Child Life* 1900:42)

This may sound like an exaggerated account to be expected from the President of the Society on such an occasion. Yet it was endorsed by an outsider. Sir George Kekewich, Permanent Secretary of the Education Department said, in the same year:

Those who have seen the Infant Schools of 30 or 40 years ago will agree with me that 'those early attempts of educating children was something little short of cruelty'. - It is the influence of Froebel, and of his system, which lives after his death in the work that he has created, and in the happiness that he brought to the lives of our children, that has changed all that. (*Child Life* 1900:57)

We cannot possibly overrate, I think, the work that this Society has done. It is not too much to say that Froebelian methods and Froebelian principles have in these later years revolutionized the work of our Infant Schools. (*Child Life* 1899:163)

Such comments needed to be brought to the attention of members of the Society and the means for doing so had occupied the minds of members of Council for many years. As finances were not available for the publication of their own journal, the Society used *Child-Life. A Kindergarten Journal* published by Messrs Philips & Sons from January 1891 - December 1892 as the medium for communication among the subscribers of the Froebel Society. The Society, however, took in no way responsibility for the content of this publication. The Journal ceased to be published in December 1892 and from then onwards *Hand and Eye* became the Society's mouthpiece until they took over the publication of *Child Life*, a magazine of the Michaelis Guild of the Froebel Educational Institute. This magazine appeared as a quarterly publication from January 1899 and became the official journal of the Froebel Society.

One other success for Froebelian ideas falls into this period. Eglantyne Jebb, the founder of the Save The Children Fund, also bears the marks of Froebelian influence. She was born into a well-to-do family in Shropshire, distinguished by its efforts in the field of social work. Her own affluent up-bringing, surrounded by twelve servants, contrasted sharply with her later experiences at the Bethnal Green Settlement in the East End of London.

Although her Oxford degree qualified her to teach in the private school system, Eglantyne Jebb decided to become a national school mistress, a teacher of the poor, and for this, Oxford had not prepared her. On the advice of her aunt she decided on Stockwell Training College for her training as a teacher. This was a most unusual step to take. Very few young ladies from wealthy homes, especially those with a university degree, considered a training college a suitable place to study. But then Stockwell, together with a very few other training colleges was offering a different philosophy of education, a different attitude towards children and a different way of teaching them. Its close connection with the Froebel Society dated back to the time when Miss Heerwart and Miss Stoker worked at the College as lecturers and were founder members of the Froebel Society. At the time, Eglantyne Jebb started her training as a teacher in 1898, Miss Manley was Principal of the College. She too was one of the pillars of the Froebel Society, serving on its Council for almost twenty years and also on the Joint Board of the National Froebel Union. Eglantyne Jebb mentions Miss Manley in her letters to her mother and talks about the close link which existed between the College and the practising school where Froebel methods were in use and where 'the connection with the College leads to the constant influx of the latest ideas.'[18]

These latest ideas, Froebelian in character, led Eglantyne Jebb to keep careful records of the children in her elementary school in Marlborough. She also tells about her work with children, which includes handwork, spinning and weaving, about her visits to the children's homes, and her contact with some of the children's poverty-stricken parents - all activities which only very exceptional teachers would consider part of their daily tasks.

Ill-health and her mother's move to Cambridge forced Eglantyne to give up her post at Marlborough. But her teaching career was not over. Her maternal uncle's children, then aged seventeen and thirteen, required a new governess. A German governess was employed, but Eglantyne took on the teaching of history and literature. The course she designed for them linked both subjects in a mutually complementary way. Each term's work culminated in an educational tour to illustrate the readings of the previous months. The older of her two cousins, G.E.M. Jebb, later Principal of Bedford College, London, wrote:

> ... illustrating pre-Conquest history, Eglantyne drove us in her high dog-cart... up and down the slopes of Berkshire and Wiltshire downs visiting the sites of Alfred's victories over the Danes and the relics of Roman and British civilisation. After nearly half a century these downs still have for my sister and for me a special quality derived from that expedition...[18]

G.E.M. Jebb's sister, Eglantyne Mary Jebb, became the Principal of the Froebel Educational Institute in Roehampton for 1932-1955, and was also Vice Chairman of the Save The Children Fund from 1946-1963. Children who experienced genuine Froebelian practices in their childhood very often carried the quality of their experiences well into adulthood. The Froebelians of Stockwell College have good grounds to be proud of their successes.

1. Heerwart, nd, p313
2. NFU Minutes, 1900, p3

3. Raymont, 1937, p254
4. NFU Minutes, 1900, p5
5. ibid, 1890, p18
6. ibid, 1895, p67
7. FS Minutes, 1892, p96
8. ibid, p116
9. ibid, p125
10. ibid, p49
11. NFU Minutes, 1890, p56
12. FS Minutes, 1892, p103
13. ibid, p35
14. ibid, 1896, p90
15. Ellsworth, 1979, p5
16. FS Minutes, 1896, p121
17. ibid, p1
18. Wilson, 1967, p84

Claude Montefiore, Chairman of the Froebel Society from 1892-1938.
'We salute him in his passing as a scholar, a philosopher and a leader, but we shall
ever treasure in our hearts the memory of his gracious personality and the gladness
which his friendship brought.' The Froebel Society, 1938.

Chapter 4

A Time of Expansion

We feel that a Froebel Society is a mere parody of itself while it remains exclusive and small. Only when its branches reach far and wide, only when it includes multitudes of children within its pale, is it worthy of the name of its master. Margaret McMillan,1909

In spite of recognition and praise of the Society's work by education authorities and voluntary bodies, concern persisted in Council discussions that the Society might have to close down or amalgamate with another education association because of lack of financial support. Even the most optimistic members of the Froebel Society who spoke in favour of the Society's continued existence as a separate body during the Annual General Meeting in 1898, could not have foreseen the influence the Society's work was to exert on primary education in this country during the next ten years. The two resolutions passed at that meeting, to make the Society better known in the provinces and to aid in the diffusion of Froebelian knowledge among qualified teachers, led to the establishment of fifteen local branches in different parts of the country, to an increase in membership from 562 in 1899 to over 2,600 members by 1910, and to an ever-extending programme of consultation with the Board of Education, Local Education Authorities, education societies, training colleges and schools. The Society's efforts to improve the conditions of children in school would now include older children, even though the emphasis was still on the under-sevens.

The problem of recognition by the Board of Education that the Froebel Certificate was comparable with its own Parchment Certificate, was still not resolved by the end of the first decade of the century. At the Annual Meeting of the Association of Education Committees in 1910, the Executive Committee expressed the opinion that the Higher Certificate of the Froebel Union was a suitable qualification for teaching infants[1]. The Board of Education recognised the National Froebel Union Higher Certificate as being equivalent to a degree when applied to teachers employed in secondary schools but did not feel able to equate it with the one-year Elementary School Teacher's Certificate, essential for teaching infants. Teachers trained in the institutions leading to the Elementary School Teacher's Certificate, however, became increasingly aware of the inadequacy of their training as regards infant methods in comparison with students trained in Froebel colleges. The demand for lectures and courses provided by the

Froebel Society therefore increased rapidly in many parts of the country, leading to the formation of local branches of the Froebel Society. Once a branch had been established, membership increased quickly, in many cases to well over a hundred.

The authority of the Council of the Froebel Society was based on the support of practising teachers. Many of the issues raised by the Council with the Board of Education and local authorities were not resolved in these ten years, but from then onwards they were not allowed to be ignored by the authorities. Local authorities responded more quickly and with greater understanding than the Board of Education. There were some exceptions, especially among the inspectors of infant and primary schools and their efforts were much appreciated by the members of the Society. To understand why and how the influence of the Society increased so rapidly between 1900 and 1910 one has first to examine the ways and means by which the Society was able to publicise its aims.

The dawn of a new century brought with it new aspirations for the future. To substantiate its ideas of progress late Victorian society had to demonstrate past achievements and current practice. Exhibitions illustrating the arts and sciences were held all over the world. Education played a considerable part in these world exhibitions and the Froebel Society received requests to contribute to several of them. These came from the English Education Exhibition, the Cambridge University Education Syndicate Exhibition, the International Education Congress in Paris, the Glasgow International Exhibition and the Japanese Exhibition.

Limited resources prevented the Society from contributing to the exhibition in Japan, but it managed to send a representative with some exhibits to the Paris one. The most rewarding efforts were recorded at the London Exhibition. Specimens of children's and students' work from Kindergartens and colleges throughout the country were used. Examples of Kindergarten work included illustrations of history lessons, drawings from nature, paintings of flowers, clay geography models, illustrations explaining Froebel's connected occupations, brushwork designs and specimens of sand-geography. There were models made from cardboard, clay and cane, buildings made with The Gifts and with plasticine. Students' work came from Stockwell College, Bedford College, Maria Grey College, Blackheath Training College and The Froebel Educational Institute. Several of these exhibits were selected by the Royal Commission for the Paris Exhibition.

While the exhibition was taking place, the Society had also arranged a three-day programme of demonstration lessons with children aged from four to eight years. Children were to work under the guidance of their own teachers. Visitors observed lessons in geometry in connection with geography, nature lessons and modelling with plasticine, songs and drills, English language lessons, biology, botany, reading, painting, marching and dancing, arithmetic, story-telling and stick-laying, building with the Gifts, ball exercises and Kindergarten songs and games. *Child Life* records that attendance at these demonstrations filled the hall to its utmost capacity on each occasion[2].

Many of the specimens used in the London Exhibition were incorporated in the Glasgow Exhibition in August 1901, where members of the Society again gave lectures. When the formation of local branches got under way, they covered the Midlands and the North of England exclusively. The first of the local branches to be formed was in Bedford in 1899, followed by branches in Bradford in 1901, Durham and North Riding in 1904, Nottingham in 1905, Wakefield in 1906, Derby in 1907, Sheffield in 1908, and then in Rotherham, Leeds, Norwich, and Northampton all in 1909.

The Manchester Society, formed even earlier in 1898, cannot be included because it refused to affiliate with the Froebel Society on account of the 2s 6d affiliation fee per member, demanded by them. Manchester also objected to the rules drawn up by the parent society, relating to local branches. When in 1902 the Manchester Society asked to have its Annual Report published in *Child Life*, permission was refused on the grounds that it was 'a rival society'. Considering that the Manchester Kindergarten Association was well established by the time the Froebel Society came into existence in 1874, it is not surprising that Manchester Froebelians found it difficult to recognise the London Society as the ultimate authority in matters Froebelian. The relationship between these two groups, over the years, is one of disagreement, reconciliation and renewed strife. There can be no doubt that the Manchester Society embraced an active body of people. In 1903 they ordered eighty copies of *Child Life* per issue. In general about one third of members subscribed to the magazine and on that reckoning Manchester had about 250 members.

The same spirit of independence is also evident in the relationship between the Bedford and the London Society. The Bedford Branch of the Froebel Society was formed on 1 November 1899 with the objective 'to spread the knowledge and practice of the Froebel System, as applied to education by giving public lectures and holding meetings, and by the formation of a library for the use of members'[3]. When in 1903 the Bedford branch of the Froebel Society gave notice that it was to change its name to the 'Bedford Froebel Society' because it believed that 'the expansion of the work now being carried on for the common cause in the Midlands will best be furthered by independent action', the parent society objected to the new title on the grounds that it would create confusion among the public. In January 1904 the Bedford branch reconstituted that branch as a new and independent organisation under the name of the 'Bedford Froebel Association'. The new association intended to work on the same lines as before and wished to remain in alliance with the Froebel Society but did not affiliate[4].

In the autumn of 1900, Miss Wragge, Principal of the first Free Kindergarten in Woolwich, lectured to 160 infant mistresses and school inspectors in Bradford on behalf of the Froebel Society. The discussion after the lecture indicated a keen interest in Froebel's principles and a desire to have closer contact with the Froebel Movement. Fifty people joined the Bradford branch at its inaugural meeting in February 1901. Three years later, for the first time in the history of the Froebel Society, its annual conference was held outside London. Bradford was chosen because of the branch-members' keen interest in the Society's work. The conference was organised in conjunction with the Bradford Education Authority and the West Riding Branch. In the same year the branch laid a memorandum before the Bradford Education Authority recommending:

1) That children under five years of age should not be inspected with regard to their attainments;

2) that a woman attendant should be attached to each infant school, her duties being
   a) to scrub out the babies room every week, b) to properly dry the children's
   clothes in wet weather, c) to assist the teachers in attending to the physical
   condition of the children and the formation of good habits;
3) that special care be taken to keep the sanitary arrangements in good condition.

Requests for lectures received by the Society were increasing rapidly and the success of the Bradford branch provided sufficient impetus to support these propaganda lectures financially. The first public meeting of the Durham and North Riding branch attracted two hundred people. The Nottingham branch, founded in 1905, recorded over two hundred members within a year and the Froebel Society recognised the enthusiastic work of the branch by holding its annual conference there which was attended by 350 people. This branch was particularly successful in working together with the local Education Committee and the University. All three bodies contributed in equal parts towards the expenses of lectures organised by the branch and therefore were able to attract excellent speakers. By 1910 the membership had increased to almost eight hundred people. No wonder they felt confident enough to challenge the practice of coaching little children to read lists of words introduced into Nottingham elementary schools by government inspectors.

The Froebel Society's newly adopted practice of holding its annual conferences away from the capital was continued in 1907. The Wakefield branch, founded a year earlier, took on the task of organising it and managed to obtain support from the Mayor and Mayoress who opened the Conference with a reception in the Town Hall[5]. The inaugural meeting of the Derby branch was held at the local training college (1907) and Miss Longdon, the chief organiser of the branch and its first chairman, was also a member of the Derby Education Committee. It was due to her efforts that the branch received a grant from the Parents' National Education Union which provided the basis for an extensive library[6].

Froebel's aim that education societies should cater for parents and teachers alike seems to have been achieved most successfully by the Sheffield branch. Their records show that they were particularly successful in obtaining the support of parents and male teachers. Reading circles for the study of educational books were formed, various classes for teachers and parents were held and a branch library established. In 1909 they recorded over three hundred members.

The Leeds and the Northampton branches enrolled seventy-eight and fifty-five members respectively within the first year of their existence, while Norwich, which had the support of the Very Revd Russell Wakefield, Dean of Norwich, attracted 137 members within a few months of its inauguration. The Dean accepted the Presidency of the local branch and later became Chairman of the Board of the National Froebel Union.

No such enthusiasm for Froebel's ideas was displayed in Scotland. Letters had been sent to teachers and others in Edinburgh, Glasgow, Aberdeen and Dundee as to the advisability of the Council's having propaganda lectures delivered in those places. Only Edinburgh and Dundee responded. In the estimation of the Council 'in Dundee opinion seemed scarcely ripe for a branch', though the replies from Edinburgh were more encouraging. Margaret McMillan was asked to lecture in Glasgow, Edinburgh and Aberdeen in the autumn of 1909, but still a year later no local branch in Scotland had registered with the Froebel Society in London[7].

And yet it is in Scotland that we find several of the first Free Kindergartens which came into being at the beginning of the century. It had always been a matter of great unease to Froebelians that Kindergartens were not available in the areas where they were most needed, among the poor. The establishment of a Free Kindergarten in the worst areas of large cities needed more than an enthusiastic and compassionate young woman. It demanded a room, a garden if possible, equipment, food, soap, clothes; it needed money. The first Free Kindergarten in England was established in January 1900 in one of the dirtiest parts of Woolwich. The second one opened in Edinburgh in 1903 in the Canongate, the wide road leading to the castle, which once housed the Scottish nobility but then gave shelter to the poorest in the city. Three more Free Kindergartens were opened in quick succession in Edinburgh. One of these was managed by the Provincial Committee for the Training of Teachers as a demonstration school for Froebelian principles. A scheme of penny dinners was in operation as four-fifths of the children came from homes where mothers were out at work all day. Birmingham had two Free Kindergartens by 1907, a few more were opened in London and one in Salford[8].

Many of the leading Froebelians were now committed to providing support in the provinces, yet the evening lectures of the Society in London, usually three lectures per term in the autumn and spring, were maintained. The following list of lecture titles throws light on the means the Society adopted to try to influence the teaching of certain areas and to win over the uncommitted.

The Teaching of Natural Science to Children.
The Foundations of Music and How to Teach Them to Children.
The Teaching of Drawing to Children between the ages 6-12.
A Froebelian View of the Educational Value of the three Rs.
Teaching the Elements of Arithmetic.
The Beginnings of the Teaching of History.
The Choice of Books for Children.
The Distinction between Work and Play.
The Teaching of Local History, with special reference to London.
Old English Games.
Westminster Abbey.
The Kindergarten Movement in America.
Froebel's Influence on the Secondary Schools.

Apart from lectures these programmes also included demonstration lessons of Kindergarten games and visits to Kindergartens. A debate on 'The Beginnings of Arithmetic Teaching' attracted an audience of 180 people. By 1906 these lectures were becoming so popular that latecomers had to be turned away because not even standing room was available. 'The Use and Abuse of Games and School Festivals,' a lecture given in 1910 by Miss Phillips, one of the Society's Kindergarten Inspectors, attracted an audience of over five hundred.

The Society also provided ten-week courses on subjects like nature study, the Gifts and occupations, blackboard drawing and the educational principles of Froebel and

Pestalozzi. These classes were primarily intended for teachers taking the Higher Certificate of the National Froebel Union and were held on Friday evenings and Saturday mornings. Attendance dropped considerably in 1901 and 1902, mainly due to the competition of lectures provided by the University Extension Programme at extremely low fees, so that the Society's courses were discontinued for these two years. Yet in 1907 an extended programme was operating which included courses in modern methods of teaching, handwork, brushwork, literature, games and practical geometry in addition to courses mentioned above.

The quarterly journal *Child Life*, which had become the official publication of the Froebel Society in 1899, became now a more definite part of the Society's work. The magazine, under the co-editorship of Miss Murray, for the Froebel Society, Lady Isabelle Margesson, for the Sesame Club, and Miss Yelland, for the Michaelis Guild, very quickly found a respectable place among educational periodicals, registering a circulation of 940 copies sold in 1906 and doubling the issues per year from four to eight in 1908. Yet there were anxious times when it seemed as if publication would have to cease, especially during the first four years when yearly deficits made it impossible to pay contributors. The editorial board was always searching for cost-cutting measures. But when in 1910 they considered tenders for publication from three printers and felt inclined to accept the lowest offer, the Chief Editor was instructed first to visit this particular firm 'to make sure that the Smith Publishing Company did not deal unjustly with its employees'.[9] The Smith Publishing Company did not get the contract. True to their Founder's example, Froebelians cared about mankind in general. Even if children occupied a special place in this concern, to obtain a bargain at the expense of those who produced the goods would have been unthinkable to anyone who professed Froebel's philosophy.

Old Froebelians, of course, were well informed about Froebel's philosophy, newcomers had to rely on information from lectures and above all from books. The demands on the Society's library grew from year to year. Requests for loans of books not only came from members in London but also from those in the provinces. Local branches also had to be considered and were allowed to borrow fifteen books each which could be exchanged every three months. In May 1909, the library contained 2,500 volumes, 600 books were circulating in various parts of England. The readership in London had increased considerably and the Society set aside one of its offices as a Reading Room[10]. By 1912 the library was receiving sixty-five English and American educational magazines, weeklies, monthlies and quarterlies, some of which were bought on subscription, but most of them were obtained in exchange for *Child Life*. The library now also opened all day on Saturday, apart from official office hours during the week. Nine hundred members subscribed to the Library, although that number was halved again by 1920.

Apart from providing members with books and periodicals containing the latest in educational thinking, the Society began to print its own pamphlets and books. The first pamphlet consisted of two papers given to the Montessori Meeting in 1913 by Miss Lawrence and Miss Solomon. The papers dealt with 'Modern Froebelianism'. The second pamphlet consisted of extracts from Professor Dewey's *Elementary School Record* and the next two were written by Professor Findlay and Miss Murray. Articles printed in *Child Life* which had received popular approval were sometimes also reprinted as pamphlets, (e.g. *The Psychology of Play* by Mrs Meredith, 1913).

This publicity work was also furthered by the Kindergartens which had been placed on the Society's Directory. The inspections of these Kindergartens were carried out as rigorously as before. Considerably more inspections resulted in failure than in success. The examiner's comments of an inspection carried out in 1900 provides some information as to the criteria used. The examiner found 'the Kindergarten lacking in connectedness. The children had not sufficient freedom and opportunities of self-expression and far too many school subjects were introduced into the time-table'. 'Too much drilling'[11] though mentioned in the report which was sent to the Principal of the Kindergarten inspected, did not by itself necessarily result in failure, while 'serious defects with regards to discipline and curriculum' were not acceptable. Before an inspection was granted the Principal of a Kindergarten had to supply the following information:

i) School   1) Name and Address 2) Name of Principal;
           3) Distance from nearest Railway Station;
           4) District from which pupils are drawn;
           5) How long established.

ii) Staff   1) Name; Regular/Visiting; Qualifications; Experience; Time per week
            spent teaching;
           2) Student Teachers: a) number b) examination for which they are being
            prepared.

iii) Pupils   1) Day pupils - number of; 2) Boarders-number of;
           3) Average daily attendance for the last term;
           4) Distribution of children: Kindergarten children under six; Transition
            classes (over 5 and under 8 years); School classes (over 8 years)

iv) Curriculum   1) Scheme of Work for the year (to be appended)
                2) Time-table for the Term (to be appended)
                3) Are pupils prepared for External Examinations?

v) General Remarks[12]

In January 1909 forty-nine Kindergartens and Training Colleges appeared on the Society's Directory. Thirty-one were located outside London[13].

Its many activities during the first ten years of this century increased the Society's standing to such an extent that schools, colleges, education authorities and voluntary organisations often requested its opinion on educational matters. The Coventry Education Committee, for example, asked for suggestions as to the mode in which the infant school curriculum for the reception class might be improved. A committee was appointed to consider the matter and to report to the Council. The answer produced was well received and eventually published in the January issue of *Child Life*, 1905. The

Northamptonshire Education Committee ordered 300 reprints of this article to be distributed among the headteachers of all their infant schools.

Even more successful was the Society's report on 'Existing methods of dealing with children under five'. Most of the material for this report came from Kindergarten practices abroad. It eventually appeared as 'The Froebel Society's Report on Foreign Infant Schools' as an Addendum to the Board of Education Report 1908[14].

The Froebel Society was by then well known to the Board of Education. They had received several deputations from the Society on varying matters. In 1905 a deputation urged that children in infant schools ought to be entitled to the same amount of grant as provided for the older children. In the same year another deputation urged the Board that, as measures had been taken to exclude all children under five from public elementa. / education, some other provision should at once be made, especially for children in the poorer neighbourhoods of town. When the 1907 Education Bill was discussed in the Houses of Parliament, the Froebel Society proposed an Addendum to the Bill in regard to Medical Inspection of Children and suggested that

> These powers and duties shall be administered under the supervision of the Board of Education and for the purposes of Subjection a Medical Department shall be constituted at the Board of Education to advise the Minister of Education directly and to report annually. (FS Minutes 1907:7)

The Act, when passed, laid upon all education authorities the duty of providing for the regular medical examination of schoolchildren by properly qualified inspectors. A Medical Department of the Board was also formed. The report in *Child Life*, October 1907 concludes:

> The long sick-list is to be drawn up; and instead of disquieting surmise, we shall have facts and figures which will be more appalling, perhaps, than even the present nightmare of our fears. But, even so, there will be no going back. An evil measured is an evil ripe for cure; and sooner or later, we shall come to realize that the best and the cheapest method of curing the symptoms is to prevent the cause.

Margaret McMillan was the prime mover of the addendum and the most influential enthusiast for the introduction of preventive medicine in the country. It all started with her experiences, as a Labour Councillor, of the School Board in Bradford, where an estimated 6,000 children attended school each day undernourished and some of them starving[15]. Margaret McMillan's argument that it was a waste of money to try to teach a starving child brought about, in spite of strong opposition from other councillors, the provision of food for children in schools and eventually the introduction of the school meals service. But physical illness was also rampant among these children. Believing that the health of a child needed to be recognised as a community responsibility before other educational endeavours could succeed, she worked unceasingly for the establishment of a school health service. The Education Act of 1907, which laid the foundations of the country's school medical service, provided for the medical inspection of children when entering school. When the then Secretary of Education, Sir Robert Moran, issued the circular drawn up for the local education authorities, he wrote to Margaret McMillan:

> This is the first clear proof of the first Annual Report of the first National System of School Medical Inspection that this country has known; and I cannot resist giving myself

the pleasure of sending it, in confidence, to yourself; for you are to me the person who most signally and most successfully embodied in a private individual the best enthusiasm and the most warming faith both in the possibilities of a Medical Inspection and in the potentialities of a real honest preventive conscience in the state and in the people. (Raymont 1937:329)

The children's clinic which she and her sister Rachel opened in 1910 in Deptford treated thousands of children each year, but did not cure them. Only better housing could do this. Unable to change matters in that direction, they created the open-air nursery school providing a garden, fresh air and sunlight. But this was not merely a day nursery with an emphasis on health and hygiene, but an institute where equal importance was given to a child's mind. Teachers in charge were usually Froebel-trained[16] and Margaret was also a member of Council of the Froebel Society. She was instrumental in introducing remedial and preventive medicine into the field of education and thus influencing it profoundly.

The welfare of young children was also raised with the education authorities of the London County Council when teachers reported that no provision was made by the LCC for children to sleep at midday. The Education Officer replied that no provision was as yet made by the Council itself implying that individual schools probably did. Within a few months reports were received that 'some provision is now being made by the Council'[17].

When the Froebel Society organised visits to Kindergartens for elementary school teachers, they found that it would take years to accommodate all the applicants, as, of course, they were only free to attend on Saturday mornings. The Froebel Society approached the LCC with the request to give their teachers leave of absence for the purpose of visiting other schools. Within two months the Society received the reply that the LCC had decided to adopt the Froebel Society's suggestion with regard to granting facilities to their teachers to obtain leave of absence in order to visit other schools and that a notice to that effect would appear in the *London Education Gazette*. Before the year was out, over five hundred LCC teachers had applied to the Society for permission to visit Kindergartens[18].

In 1909, the London County Council's Education Department received two deputations from the Society. The first one was concerned with examinations in infant schools. The Council of the Froebel Society urged the LCC that any written examination tests to infants before they proceed into the upper school should be abolished as being harmful to the children's education. The second deputation concerned itself with the inspection of infant schools. They dwelt on the necessity to appoint persons as inspectors 'who had not only sympathy, but actually some knowledge and experience of children'.[19] Members of the Society felt so strongly about this matter, that the Council instructed the Propaganda Committee to do all in its power to influence the LCC to make more careful appointments in future, more especially by bringing influence to bear on various members of the appointing Committee.

In spite of the respect shown to the Froebel Society by local authorities, it did little to persuade the Board of Education to recognise the three-year course leading to the Froebel Certificate as being equivalent to the one-year course provided by Government and church training colleges leading to the Elementary Teacher's Certificate. Even the support given by the Association of Education Committees and the Association of Headmistresses did not bring this long struggle to an acceptable conclusion.

The renewed efforts by the Society for recognition of the Froebel Certificates started in 1902 when a Draft Order of Council was before the House of Commons regulating the manner in which a new register for teachers should be formed and kept. As no provision was made for the registration of Kindergarten teachers and the Froebel Certificates were not recognised as qualifying for registration, the Society contacted the Secretary of the Consultative Committee dealing with the new Government register who invited a delegation of the Froebel Society to appear before the Committee. At the subsequent meeting the training of Kindergarten teachers and the examinations they had to undergo before becoming qualified, were discussed. After the discussion the Committee agreed to write to the Joint Board of the National Froebel Union to ask for statements concerning the constitution of the governing body, the appointment of examiners etc. with a view to including the Higher Certificate on the register.[20]

A letter was subsequently received by Claude Montefiore from the Secretary of the Consultative Committee saying that the question of the position of Kindergarten teachers on the register was being thoroughly examined by the Committee and it was hoped that they would arrive at a satisfactory conclusion. They demanded, however, that the National Froebel Union become an 'Incorporated Company' to give it legal status.

As no further communication was forthcoming from the Board of Education, a further memorandum was sent by the Society in 1904. In the meantime information circulated that the new register had been formulated in such a way that elementary and secondary teachers appeared separately. The Teachers' Guild objected to such 'unnecessary and invidious' arrangements and invited the Froebel Society to join them in their representation to the Board. The Teachers' Guild would at the same time support the Froebel Society's claims.

The deputation was received in June 1904 and one month later the Society received a reply from the Board of Education stating that the Consultative Committee were unable to find means for the desired inclusion of the Froebel Certificates 'either by alteration of the qualifications for the Teachers' Register or by the creation of a Supplementary Register'.[21]

Neither the Teachers' Guild nor the Froebel Society accepted this as a final answer. The Guild set up a committee to frame their own regulations for such a register and put the new scheme to the public by means of press and meetings. In 1907 the Government set up the 'New Registration Council' because of dissatisfaction expressed with the register by diverse organisations concerned with education. The Society applied for representation on the new Registration Council which was supported by the Council of the Head Masters' Association. The scheme originally put forward by the Teachers' Guild and now supported by thirty-seven Teachers' Associations was accepted by the Board of Education. This scheme gave the Froebel Society the opportunity to provide one representative on the Registration Council. The new Registration Council, however, met rarely and nothing had changed by the summer of 1910. At the Annual Meeting of the Association of Education Committees the matter was discussed again. The extract from their Annual Report reads:

The Executive Committee have had before them the question of the qualifications of certificated teachers in public elementary schools. With regards to teachers of Infants, it is felt that the Higher Certificate of the National Froebel Union is a satisfactory and suitable qualification. This certificate is held in high repute by educationalists, and, moreover, is accepted by the Board of Education, in the case of teachers in Secondary Schools, as equivalent to a degree. The Executive Committee has therefore urged the Board of Education to recognise the Higher Froebel Certificate as an alternative in infants' schools to the Elementary School Teacher's Certificate. This representation has only been made recently, and at the time of issuing this report the result of the Committee's action is not known. (FS Minutes 1907:56)

No results were forthcoming and the Froebel representative on the Teachers Registration Council, serving on the Secondary Teachers Panel, had little influence in the matter. It may seem odd not to have appointed the Froebel representative to the Elementary School Teachers Panel, and yet it was quite logical, since holders of the National Froebel Union Higher Certificate could obtain certification only by teaching in a secondary school. When, in 1918, the Froebel Society sent yet another deputation to the Board of Education, approval of the Higher Certificate was expressed as one of high academic standing, but as it could be obtained without training in a recognised college, it could not be equated with the parchment given to elementary school teachers. It was pointed out to the deputation that in respect of National Froebel Union Certificates gained in a Froebel college, the College should apply directly to the Board of Education for the recognition of their students for elementary school teaching. As at that time members of the Registration Council were also in favour of the recognition of the National Froebel Union Certificate for Elementary School Teachers, they brought the matter to the attention of the Education Committee of the National Union of Teachers and both bodies joined in a direct approach to Sir Edmund Phipps of the Board of Education. Two years later the problem had still not been resolved. On 15 May 1920 the Conference of Representatives of the National Association of Teachers passed the resolution that:

> All Froebelian teachers who have satisfied the requirements for registration as regards attainments and training should be eligible for work in elementary or secondary schools as certified teachers. (FSCM 1906:277)

Several more years were to pass before this became a reality.

To support these 'unrecognised' Kindergarten teachers and to assist them in their search for suitable employment, the Froebel Society had set up their own Registry as far back as 1898. To be placed on the Registry teachers had to provide evidence of suitable training and experience in teaching. The agency also accepted registration of vacancies and then sent details of available Kindergarten teachers to the employers. In 1901 the Registry recorded 'eighty-six disengaged teachers and four vacant posts', while in the summer of 1904 eighty-four vacant posts were available with ninety-two teachers on the books.

In the same year regulations for employers were discussed by the Council. It was proposed that 'no vacancy can be entered on the Registry with a salary of less than twenty-four pounds resident or forty pounds non-resident'. The Secretary reported that as little as fifteen pounds a year had been offered by employers and she suggested the new regulation in order to raise the status of the Registry and to safeguard the interests of the teachers. The Council, however, decided that it would be undesirable to make any such limiting regulations as a minimum salary might be regarded by some persons as the Council's notion of adequate payment. To save employers from inconvenience it was also proposed 'that Teachers should be required to state on their application forms to what religious denomination they belonged'. This too was rejected by the Council.[22]

Requests for Kindergarten teachers were by now also being received from abroad. A letter from the Johannesburg Kindergarten Association (1901) indicated that as soon as the war was over, many Kindergarten teachers might be required in the Transvaal where many schools had been started by the Association. It was suggested that the Council of the Froebel Society in London might be of considerable help in selecting suitable teachers and sending them out to South Africa, where they would be made welcome and be looked after by a committee of ladies appointed by the Johannesburg Kindergarten Association. The Council responded by assuring their cooperation whenever needed.[23]

In 1903 the Commissioners of National Education in Ireland were considering the appointment of an Organiser of Kindergarten Instruction for the National Schools under their control. They asked for the Society's help in finding such a person at a salary of £150 per annum and an allowance of ten shillings per night when absent from Dublin on business. The Council of the Society responded by stating that they would have much difficulty in finding a lady with the necessary experience who would undertake such work at the salary mentioned. However, several names were put forward and an appointment was duly made at the salary mentioned.

Requests for affiliation from overseas branches were also increasing and applications were received from Wellington, New Zealand (1899), and from Calcutta in 1908. Hospitality was provided and visits to Kindergartens arranged by the Society for Russian Teachers in 1909 and for American Teachers in 1911. Clark University, Mass. ordered *Child Life* in 1907 and also requested back numbers of the journal published. Contacts with Froebelians in other parts of Europe were also established.

The Articles of Association drawn up when the Society was incorporated in 1891 allowed for 500 members; now there were 2,580 of them. No provision was made in the articles for the establishment of branches and their representation on Council, now there were branches at home and abroad. Not even the name, 'The Froebel Society of Great Britain and Ireland' was any longer true and correct. The amendments which twenty years of steady progress had necessitated were approved by a members meeting in December 1910 and from then on they were registered as 'The Froebel Society'.

This chapter cannot be closed without mentioning the death of two outstanding Froebelians in the early part of the century. Miss Manning, a member of the Joint Board of the National Froebel Union and a member of the Council of the Froebel Society, died in 1905. She was the last active founder member. But the greatest, and in the estimation of the Council, the 'irreparable' loss to the Society was suffered by the death on 30 December 1904, of Madame Michaelis. The Annual Report of the Society recorded:

> She had been for thirty years, ever since her arrival in this country, one of the foremost exponents and champions of the principles and cause of Froebelian Education. She was one of the original Founders of the Froebel Society, and has ever since been a member

of the Council.... She was President of the Society in the years 1898 to 1900....Soon after her arrival in England, she became the head of a Kindergarten at Croydon, where she also undertook the training of students. Through her training work then begun and continued for twenty-five years, she practically revolutionized the teaching of young children in England, for she and her disciples have trained by far the greater number of Froebelian teachers in this country, and through her the Kindergarten system has spread far and wide. Her inspired talks with her students will never be forgotten by those who heard them.... ' *Child Life 1905:63*

One of Madame Michaelis' former Kindergarten pupils wrote:

She gauged so perfectly the individual character and capacity of every child she met, and showed herself so entirely in sympathy with it, that all our best efforts were called forth in response to the demand made by such a friend.... *Child Life 1905:64*

And, of course, she is also remembered as the first Principal of the Froebel Educational Institute, of which Mrs Salis Schwabe was the founder. She retired from this post four years before her death but maintained her active interest in Froebelian teaching, visiting most of the great provincial cities, either to deliver lectures or to hold examinations. She died in a small cottage in Rotherfield in Sussex, and at her own request was cremated at Golders Green.

1. FS Minutes, 1907, p56
2. *Child Life*, 1900A, p124
3. FS Minutes, 1898, p55
4. ibid, 1904, p7
5. *Child Life*, 1907, p153
6. FS Minutes, 1904, p119
7. ibid, 1907, p44
8. Murray, nd, p116
9. FCSM, 1906, p61
10. FS Minutes, 1907, p41
11. ibid, 1898, p84
12. GPCM, 1892, p156
13. *Child Life*, 1909, p31
14. FS Minutes, 1907, p25
15. Van der Eyken, 1973, p155
16. Raymont, 1937, p332
17. FS Minutes, 1907, p60
18. ibid, 1904, p71
19. ibid, 1907, p51
20. ibid, 1898, p155
21. ibid, 1904, p30
22. ibid, 1904, p48
23. ibid, 1898, p738

Competence in blackboard drawing was an essential part of the Froebel Certificate.

Chapter 5
The Future Looked More Promising Than Ever

The boundaries of citizenship are not determined by wealth.
Herbert Fisher, President of the Board of Education, 10 August 1917.

The years just before the First World War were characterised by the expansion of the Society's work as much as the inter war years were to be fraught with difficulties leading to contraction. The establishment of the Froebel Summer Schools, the continued growth of local branches, the increasing demand for the Froebel Certificate and the persistent requests for Froebel Society members to serve on committees of professional and voluntary associations indicate that Froebel thinking, comment and philosophy was held in high esteem. The Society's struggle during the war years was not one for survival, but one of trying to meet too many demands made on too few volunteers. It was also a time of experimentation in education generally.

In 1920 Miss Alice Woods, Principal of Maria Grey Training College from 1892-1913, member of Council of the Froebel Society for many years and its President from 1913-1914, published a book under the title *Educational Experiments in England*. She presents us with a colourful picture of practical innovations in our schools in the 1920s. The 'new education' was no longer confined to the Kindergarten. The advantages of self-activity, of freedom from unnecessary restraints, of the provision of light and space and a garden as an essential ingredient for healthy living of children, of communal play and work as a means for a child's social development, all so well demonstrated in the Kindergartens, were now challenging established practices in other educational institutions.

Bedales, J.H.Bradley's school at Petersfield, added a new dimension to the meaning of progressive education by offering a curriculum with more arts and crafts subjects than usual, disregarding school uniform, encouraging freer personal relationships, establishing a school council on which pupils served and introducing co-education into a boarding system.[1] A different idea of the school as a community was introduced by the Caldecott Community which provided a boarding school for children of working people, while Homer Lane's self-governing community of mostly delinquent boys and girls aimed at healing emotional disabilities by providing love, care, security and freedom for children to reject futile and false ideas themselves.

This was also the time when the 'sloyd' system of manual instruction was introduced into secondary schools and Montessori methods into infant schools. Uno Cygnaeus, a Finnish teacher, inspired by Froebel[2] had worked out a detailed scheme by which to introduce handicrafts to boys and girls of secondary school age. Advocating practical work in preference to verbal learning, the method was also applied to cookery, needlework and gardening. But it was wood-sloyd, eventually leading to the teaching of wood-work in most secondary schools, which had the greatest impact.

The influence of Dr Maria Montessori's methods on nursery and infant schools was also considerable especially after the publication, in this country, of her book *The Montessori Method*, in 1912. Because writers on the history and also on the philosophy of education often mention Froebel and Montessori in one breath with an emphasis on what they have in common, it is important that some of the differences, which are considerable, are highlighted. True, both educators believe that education should be centred on the individual child and that it should offer opportunities for native powers of growth, but they start from a different child psychology and they aim at different objectives.

To understand the Montessori method's characteristics, especially its psychological foundations, one needs to know its origin. Maria Montessori worked as a doctor in a psychiatric clinic in Rome where she had opportunities to observe mentally retarded children in the city's mental institutions. During that time she became familiar with the methods of Seguin, Pinel and Itard for dealing with these children. Concentrating on the one particular organ, or function of an organ, which was least developed in a person, exercises were invented to strengthen that particular organ. Dr Montessori developed and extended these exercises, after careful observations, with considerable success. She argued that as those exercises made such a difference to mentally retarded children, how much more effective might they be with normal children. She found a way of trying out her apparatus and exercises in a normal school and again met with great success.

Up to that point, Dr Montessori had not considered the education of the pre-school child. Dr Montessori only began to concern herself with the training and education of pre-school-age children when approached by a Roman architect to help him equip some nursery rooms in his newly created council housing blocks, so that the new buildings might be saved from ravage by roaming children not yet old enough to attend school. In 1907 the first 'Casa dei Bambini' was opened in San Lorenzo and became a pedagogical and psychological research institute under her guidance. This institute used the same apparatus as had been devised for mentally disabled children and which had been improved after trials with ordinary children. Dr Montessori wrote:

> If a parallel between the deficient and the normal child is possible, this will be during the period of early infancy *when the child has not the force to develop and he who is not yet developed* are in some ways alike. (Montessori 1915:44)

Froebel started off by studying philosophy and the sciences. Having sorted out, for himself, his own philosophy, he decided that his vocation in life must lie in changing mankind for the better. As, in his opinion, it was too late to do anything about adults, he had to concern himself with children and so he became a teacher. The style and content of what a person taught depended on his belief about the nature of man. Froebel's ideas about the nature of man were based on the philosophy of the romantics, especially Schelling and Krause. The unity which was to be found in the sciences, in religion and in the philosophies needed also to be made explicit in education. The principle of unity and interconnectedness governed all his educational decisions. The education of the pre-school-age child should not be a matter of providing something extra for a select group of children but should be an essential part of every child's life. And of course, it should not stop at the level of the Kindergarten but should extend to and include the education of the child on his mother's knee. According to Froebel a child had the force to develop himself from the day he was born. He found his evidence for this idea in careful observation of the birth of a baby.[3]

Froebel's child begins his education by interacting with his environment using the tools with which he has been endowed: looking, hearing, grasping, making vocal noises and bodily movements. Montessori's child begins to educate himself when he has been provided with pieces of apparatus which will train his senses. Froebel's child achieves independence by means of his own actions while Montessori believed that 'the first form of educational intervention must tend to lead the child towards independence'[4]. Montessori devised techniques which aimed at the acquisition of scholastic subjects while Froebel advanced a philosophy which placed the emphasis on the development of the creative powers in the child. Montessori's children were acquiring that which was already known, Froebel's children were discovering that which, at first, was only a surmise.

Many of these differences are easily demonstrated when one compares Montessori apparatus with 'Froebel Gifts'. Montessori's apparatus, created with a view to training the senses, were of a simple design and self-corrective. The tying of shoelaces, the buttoning-up of a coat, the arranging of wooden rods according to length or tablets of one colour according to their different shades, or hollow cylinders filled with sand or stones according to the varying shades of sounds they produce, provided the children with a variety of occupations which besides teaching simple skills also stimulated and trained the senses of touch, smell and hearing. Serial arrangements and classifications led to the teaching of the three Rs, again by means of self- education and self-correction. All this, so Montessori said, would lead to the habits of discipline and obedience.[5] These, of course, are also the objectives of schooling as generally implemented, though probably by different means. Froebel's Gifts (see chapter 1), at least from Gift 3 onward, can be used to represent objects and events as experienced in a child's life so that he may recall those events and objects and reflect on them. The same Gift can be used to demonstrate the rules of mathematics and the geometrical relations of lines, surfaces and solids. And yet it can also be used to create patterns and shapes of beauty exploring, imitating and extending the aesthetic qualities to be found in the environment. While each piece of Montessori apparatus can be used for the purpose for which it has been intended, Froebel's Gifts are devised to encourage and develop the creative powers in a child and by so doing Froebel places the emphasis of his educational aims on the investigation of that which is not yet known.

During the 1920s, Montessori training courses of about four months duration provided teachers with an easy solution to the problem of how to occupy children.[6] To use Froebel's Gifts, teachers not only had to study Froebel's educational theory, but had to be inventive if they wanted to succeed in helping children to use the Gifts creatively.

The introduction of the Montessori method into nursery and infant schools provided yet another experiment in working with children and it also encouraged members of the Froebel Society to re-examine the use of the Gifts. In 1910 the Parkstone Toy Factory had been asked by Local Education Authorities to supply them with thousands of boxes of Froebel's Gifts, which formerly had always been bought from Germany. Being aware of the harm done to children by the regimented use of the Gifts by untrained teachers, the Society considered the means by which to make known their opinion that bags of bricks of various sizes would be a more appropriate educational aid than the Gifts. At the same time the Council of the Society also considered the educational uses of 'Group Toys, Dramatic Toys, toys about Trades, caravans and dolls and animals made of soft materials'.[7] Arnolds of London and the Board of Trade were consulted and eventually a factory was found willing to produce such toys from samples made by members of the Society and students in Training Colleges. The factory concerned went out of business in 1917 and for some time toys were produced at the Society's offices at Bloomsbury Square.

Probably the most innovative move by the Froebel Society was the creation of summer schools, where practising teachers could attend courses in school subjects but were also made aware of the latest ideas in educational thinking. These courses were usually held in schools and training colleges in pleasant surroundings where the environment could be used for historical, geographical and natural history explorations. They were residential and mostly of two weeks' duration.

The first summer school, which took place in 1913 at Broadstairs, provided classes for 196 students, of which 150 were from secondary schools and the remainder from elementary schools. Classes were held in nature study, eurythmics, handwork, geography, literature and educational theory. Grants to teachers with payments of fees were provided by several education authorities. In spite of the outbreak of war, the summer school in 1914 was again successful, but by 1915 attendance had shrunk to eighty-four students. The Board of Education's Inspectors had visited the summer school and having been favourably impressed, the Board promised a grant towards expenses for 1915, which in fact was never paid, but which 'in view of existing circumstances', the Society hardly expected the Board to honour.[8]

When the 1916 summer school, at Westfield College, Hampstead, attracted only forty students, the Council decided to suspend activities for the following year. Summer schools were, however, successfully resumed in 1918. The inspector's positive reports encouraged the organisers to widen the scope of the courses provided for 1919 to include gardening and music as well. There were lectures by Homer Lane on 'Self Government in Education' and 'The Little Commonwealth', lectures dealing with very practical issues like 'The first year of a Nursery School', 'The new Curriculum', 'The essentials of Religious Education', 'The training of Nursery School Superintendents', 'Ideals in the physical development of children', and those of a more theoretical nature like 'Man the Creator' and 'The life and reality in education'. Of the ninety-three teachers who attended only thirty-five were members of the Froebel Society. There were twenty-eight elementary school teachers, of whom ten were headmistresses and eight headmistresses from private schools, and fifty-seven Kindergarten and lower school mistresses from secondary schools.

In 1920 the location of the summer school was once more moved to a seaside town, this time Eastbourne. Professor Kilpatrick from Columbia University, New York City, gave a course of nine lectures on 'The Foundations of Methods, with special references to the Place of Purpose in the Learning Process'. The handwork course included spinning, weaving, basketry or clay modelling and pottery, and there was also a course on the art of story-telling. There can be no doubt about the popularity of these summer schools. Teachers attending came from all over the country thus it is not surprising that the years between 1910-1920 were especially marked by the continuous growth across the country of local branches of the Froebel Society.

Local branches of the Society in Bradford, Derby, Leeds, Norwich, Northampton-shire, Nottingham, Rotherham and Sheffield which were in existence by 1910, were soon joined by branches in Northumberland, Durham and North Riding (1911), Cambridge (1912), Bristol (1912), Stafford (1913) and Leicester (1914).

In the years just before the First World War, local branches reported their greatest increases in membership, courses and extensions of libraries. Norwich, for example, recorded 144 members in 1910, and 269 members in 1911. It had its own library and attendance at lectures arranged by the branch frequently attracted over two hundred teachers. It enjoyed not only the support but also the presidency of the Dean of Norwich. The membership in Derby rose from 170 in 1910 to 253 in 1911; Nottingham added 264 books to its own branch library in 1912 and Leeds also extended its library extensively in that year. Calcutta produced its own *Child Life* magazine and reported ninety-three new members in 1911.

The Central Society kept in touch with its branches by sending copies of Council Meeting Minutes as well as the 'London Letter' which gave fuller information on topics under discussion. Each branch was allowed to send one representative to the Central Society's Council Meetings and all members of branches were entitled to borrow books from the Central Library, which according to Mary Miller Allan, Principal of Homerton (later Chairman of the Cambridge branch) was one of the chief appeals which led to the formation of the branch in Cambridge.

Opposition to the annual capitation fees of one shilling per member, which were demanded from branches by the Central Society resulted in various efforts to form closer links between the two. Council members offered themselves as speakers at branch meetings and special Branch Council Meetings in London were arranged twice a year. Yet, much of the enthusiasm witnessed before 1914 seemed to abate with the outbreak of the war. No new branches came into existence in 1915 and 1916. Indeed, 1916 saw the suspension of branch activities in Norwich, Rotherham, Bristol and Northumberland, Durham and North Riding. There were some exceptions to the general decline. The Sheffield branch, for example, remained very active and passed a strong resolution in 1916 protesting against the employment of unqualified teachers in infant schools and a year later was again in touch with the Board of Education via the Central Society about improving a child's passage from one department in school to the next. They urged joint meetings of infant departments with other departments where teaching methods could be discussed.

The first signs of renewed interest in the movement came at the end of 1917 when teachers in Birmingham created a new branch, with the Bishop of Birmingham as its

President, and then in 1918 when Stoke- on-Trent enrolled one hundred members at its inaugural meeting and the West Kirby branch sixty members.

All the branches which had suspended their activities in 1916, renewed their work in 1919. The revised 'Rules and Regulations for the formation of Local Branches of the Froebel Society' drawn up in 1920, once more stated the objectives of the local branches:

These shall be the objects of the Froebel Society which are:

a) To educate the public mind in all the matters concerning the welfare of children.

b) To promote efficiency and welfare of those engaged in the teaching of young children.

c) To bring together and promote a better understanding between teachers (of all grades), parents, doctors, officials and all others interested in education. (FSCM 1906:260)

The letter heading of the Froebel Society in 1919 included the following branches: Bradford and District, Bristol and District, Cambridge, Derby, Hull, Leeds and District, Leicester, Northamptonshire, Northumberland, Durham and North Riding, Norwich, Rotherham, Sheffield, Stafford and District, Calcutta.

Although summer schools were not directly linked with the preparation of teachers for the National Froebel Union Certificate, many teachers considered them an additional help for obtaining their qualifications. Even though the Certificate was still not recognised for salary purposes by the Department of Education, more and more teachers presented themselves for the National Froebel Union Examinations. In 1911 fifty-six candidates sat for the Preliminary Certificate, of which twenty-four passed; 822 sat for the Elementary Certificate; 1,726 for the Higher Certificate Part I and just over 1,000 for the Higher Certificate Part II. Examinations were held in March, September and December in towns spread throughout the United Kingdom. In 1912 the following Examination Centres were used: Bedford, Belfast, Birmingham, Bradford, Bristol, Cardiff, Cheltenham, Edinburgh, Leicester, Liverpool, Manchester, Plymouth, Sheffield and Clapham and West Kensington in London. There were also examination centres in Moritzburg and Durban.

With between 200-400 candidates registering for their Certificate examinations each year, it is not surprising that the National Froebel Union was able to declare annual profits of between £400-500 in the years before the First World War. Comparing these figures with the Froebel Society's finances, which in many years were kept out of the red only by Claude Montefiore's generous donations, one can imagine how the Froebel Society felt. After all, it was the members of the Froebel Society who spent their time and energy on lecturing and carrying out the publicity work as well as organising and staffing the courses which prepared teachers for the National Froebel Union's Certificates. Yet theirs were not rewards measured in financial terms. The Society made a profit of £28 in 1910, losses during the middle war years and only just managed to get out of the red again by instigating an extensive membership drive in all the Froebel colleges. But it must be said that whenever the Froebel Society asked the National Froebel Union for contributions towards books, furniture or rents, the response was usually positive.

The work involved in preparing candidates for the Certificates was considerable. In 1915 the Froebel Society organised the following classes:

Principles of Education (24 Lectures), History (4 Lectures),
Practice of Education (24 Lectures), Maths (6 Lectures),
English (8 Lectures), Organisation (4 Lectures), Handwork including Drawing
(24 Lectures), Nature/Geography (8 Lectures), History of Education (18 Lectures)

The distribution of courses in different subjects varied from year to year, just as the content of the syllabus was re-examined and frequently modified. When, for example, after the turn of the century the study of 'The Education of Man' was changed to 'A critical study of Froebel's Education of Man', examiners soon complained to the Trainers that the work was not studied sufficiently in relation to modern developments and that the emphasis should be on the word 'critical'. More changes were introduced to bring this about, most notably the creation of the Trainer's Diploma in 1914, which in the years to come became the most highly regarded diploma in the education of young children in the country.[9]

Great concern was shown that subjects should be studied in relation to their use in the classroom and to children's understanding. The syllabus for literature, for the Higher Certificate, Part I (1910), reads:

> The object of this section is to ensure that Candidates have studied a variety of material from which to select what is suitable for children of varying ages. Critical examination of obscure or difficult passages and matters involving a knowledge of the History of Literature will be avoided. Attention will be directed chiefly to testing the Candidate's appreciation of Literature and Knowledge of methods of dealing with those parts of the subject which are suitable for children.

Suitability depended on children's level of understanding based on past experiences. Froebel's dictum that subjects must be conveyed in a practical way to students and linked to life outside school was carefully guarded. The syllabus for mathematics, of the same year, concludes:

> The treatment should chiefly be experimental and practical, including construction in paper, cardboard and other suitable material. The question proposed may also involve numerical calculations and easy applications to practical questions of every-day life.

The extensive lecture programme undertaken in the autumn and spring terms during the war had an abundance of lecture and course titles of a very practical nature: 'Children's writings after a fortnight in the country', 'Oral composition', 'Mathematical notions arising out of toys and games', 'The modern treatment of decimals', 'Practical arithmetic', 'A school journey', 'Nursery rhymes with musical illustrations'. And the Saturday morning demonstrations in conjunction with visits to nursery schools were always in great demand.[10]

Several of the teachers attending these courses were already in the possession of a London University BA Pass Degree which qualified them to teach junior and middle forms. In the opinion of the Society this was a most unsuitable qualification for teachers of young children. There were many others who thought so too. On 29 June 1918 a conference on the BA Pass Degree as a qualifying examination for teachers of junior and middle forms was held at which Miss Escott from the Froebel Society was in the chair. The following societies were represented: University of London Graduates Association, Association of University Women Teachers, Geographical Association,

Headmistresses Association, Mathematical Association, Modern Languages Association, National Union of Teachers, Froebel Society and the Historical Association.

The Chairman opened the meeting by stating that the Council of the Froebel Society was of the unanimous opinion that the BA Pass Degree of the University of London, neither by choice of subjects imposed on candidates, nor by the syllabuses of the said subjects, was an adequate academic preparation for the teachers of younger children. As it was to a great extent such teachers who took the Pass Degree, the Council considered the matter a serious one, and for this reason had called the meeting. The Froebel Society had drawn up certain resolutions of which the following ones were passed in an amended form by the conference:

1) That in order to make the examinations of the London BA (Pass) degree more useful for Teachers, certain alterations are advisable in the number of subjects required and the character of the syllabus.
2) That at the Intermediate Examination four subjects be taken, of which two must be languages, and one language must be English.
3) That at the BA Pass Examination, three subjects be taken, of which one must be language.

This resolution, together with explanatory notes regarding the kind of modification desired in the syllabus, were sent to Senate in preparation for a suggested meeting, which for reasons unknown never took place.[11]

. The major concern of the Froebel Society in these years, however, focused on the lack of provision for children under the age of ten and for those of Kindergarten age in particular. In 1915 the Council of the Froebel Society was discussing the lack of Kindergartens, a lack apparently not just confined to the London area according to the reports from the branches. The Society was considering the possibility of opening Kindergartens in suitable areas and the advisability of applying to the Board of Education for grants to such schools. In the same year the London County Council began economising by increasing numbers of children in classes and excluding the under-fives altogether, and yet, as numbers of women working for the war-effort were steadily increasing, the need for nursery provision became more urgent. In 1917 the Froebel Society busied itself drawing up schemes 'for the training of the new type of teacher needed for the Nursery Schools which would soon be opened in all parts of the country'.[12]

The Nursery School Conference of 1917, which was called to make sure that the teachers' advice would be heard before the ratification of the new Education Bill then before Parliament, agreed on submitting the recommendations that if nursery schools were to be built, they ought to be small and have close contact with the homes of the children. The conference also pleaded for ample space for nursery schools, gardens, and a position which provided ample sunshine and fresh air. It also expressed the hope that nursery education might be extended up to the age of six.

When the then Minister of Education, Mr Herbert Fisher, introduced the Education Bill to the House of Commons, he referred to the social solidarity which had been created by the war. He pointed out that when conscription demanded the lives of the poor and rich alike, one began to realize that the boundaries of citizenship were not determined by wealth and neither should the boundaries of educational opportunities.[13] He believed that the success of raising and training an army at such short notice was due to the discipline and influence of the elementary school. The bill to be introduced was a measure to advance secondary as well as primary elementary education. When the bill was eventually accepted by the House and became the Education Act of 1918, it abolished fees in elementary schools, provided for the attendance at day continuation schools of all young people up to the age of eighteen and empowered the local education authorities to provide nursery education for the two to five year-olds and encouraged the authorities to attend to the children's health, nourishment and physical welfare. Teachers of the very young had achieved yet another of their goals.

The London County Council's quick response in establishing nursery provision created problems of policy and organisation. In response to requests for guidance, the Froebel Society set up a Nursery Schools' Conference in 1920. It recommended that no nursery should contain more than thirty children of all ages and that it be supervised by two adult helpers in addition to the superintendent. Even a nursery unit attached to an infant department would need at least two rooms, a cloakroom and a separate playground. Superintendents would have the power to safeguard the children from too early promotion based on proficiency in school subjects alone, but would use as their criterion the child's development in general. Inspectors of these nurseries would be women who had undergone special training for this work. Mothers meetings and closer co-operation with the home would be encouraged. The conference stressed that groups of children had to be small so that the superintendents would be able to work without harassment and provide opportunities for observing the children carefully in order to be able to select the right materials and toys for them.[14]

These different conferences demonstrate that although many educational organisations were aware of the need for the establishment of nursery education, few were able to foresee the problems involved let alone recommend strategies. Froebelians were well ahead in their thinking and their actions compared with the rest of the community. No wonder that organisations dealing with education, welfare, women, children and social issues, such as the National Union of Women Workers, the Child Welfare Bureau and the British Institute of Social Services, frequently asked representatives from the Froebel Society to serve on their committees.[15]

Regular attendance at these meetings, however time-consuming to members, helped the Froebel Society to spread their aims and objectives in a very direct way. The Froebel Society's concern for the lack of educational facilities for children under ten, for example, culminated in a conference on Junior Schools which was attended by representatives from the Headmasters' Conference, The Headmistresses Association, The Headmasters' Association, The Parents' National Educational Union, The Association of Preparatory Schools and The Private Schools Association.

The problem under discussion related to the lack of sufficient places for children in public elementary schools and the shortage of good preparatory schools in the private sector. The Conference wanted the Board of Education to take on the inspection of private schools for children under ten or twelve years of age on the grounds that 'at present young children who do not attend the public elementary schools are being in many cases exploited and that it is the duty of the Board of Education to protect an ignorant public and helpless children by seeing that every child in the community has at least a fair elementary education in a proper building and under competent teachers'.[16]

On request, members of the Board of Education met a delegation from the Conference informally. It was agreed to compile a list of good junior schools and a list of places where such schools were needed. Although such a list was eventually published, showing that the South-Eastern District of London most lacked good junior schools, little progress was made at the time. Yet the Froebel Society felt so strongly about the lack of proper education for the under-tens that in 1917 they changed the title of the Society from 'The Froebel Society' to 'The Froebel Society and Junior Schools Association', thus providing a continuous focus on those aspects of English education which needed most improvement.

By the end of the war Froebel colleges were still not recognised by the Board of Education. The Board inspected the Froebel Educational Institute in 1918 at the College's request. As long as the College examinations were external ones only, the Board maintained its position and was not prepared to recognise the College as a certified college. The Froebel Society took up the matter with the Board of Education and asked whether the Board would recognise the National Froebel Union as the external examining body of certain Froebel colleges if they were certified by the Board of Education. The reply was favourable and colleges were asked whether they would like internal examinations. The majority of colleges expressed a wish for internal examinations.

Quite clearly, the National Froebel Union had no intention of relinquishing overall supervision of the syllabuses nor the examinations. The Board of Education's attempt to change examination procedures must have created genuine anxieties about lowering standards in the Froebel colleges. After all, the governors of the National Froebel Union still insisted that candidates trained for two years in a Government training college and wishing to omit Part I of the Higher Certificate had to be trained for the third year in a Froebel college, not a Government college, thus indicating that the latter were not providing an adequate training for teachers of young children. Candidates who had already obtained a degree, however, were excused Part I of the examination for the National Froebel Union Higher Certificate.[17]

There was possibly also a feeling that Board of Education interference was on the increase. Many educators, at the time, believed that the principles outlined in the Whitley Report on Industrial Councils should also apply to the decision-making processes in education. The resolution passed by the College of Preceptors and endorsed and supported by the Froebel Council on the reconstruction of the Board on more representative lines deserves detailed attention.[18] The first resolution notes the successful establishment of industrial councils on the lines suggested by the Whitley Report and predicts the imminent necessity of comparable councils in education. The second resolution then summarises the principle of the Whitley Councils, that is that representatives of employers and employees should meet on equal terms to negotiate wages, output and working conditions. Resolutions three and four deal with a suggested make-up of the proposed council for education. On the employees side, the Committee suggested suitable representation of all types of teaching work was to be found in the Teachers Registration Council. The position of the employer was harder to define, since

in Education the real employer and paymaster is the public. Hence it follows that the joint body contemplated cannot consist of officials of the Board of Education acting with teachers, but should be made up of a body representative of the public, of whom in this instance the officials of the Board of Education are merely the paid agents.

The solutions suggested was a Standing Committee of the House of Commons (as the public's representatives) to meet with representatives of the Teachers Registration Council as a National Education Council (or Board of Education). The decisions of this new Board of Education would be carried out by its officials, but would be subject to parliamentary scrutiny. The President of the Board would be the Chairman of the new joint board. The resolutions conclude:

6. Your Committee further suggests that as an immediate step the Ministry of Labour and the President of the Board of Education should be informed that the College of Preceptors desires to see a Joint Educational Council set up on the lines of the Whitley Report, such Council to consist of a Standing Committee of the House of Commons acting with an equal number of representatives of the Teachers Registration Council.

The re-examination of man's relationship to man, as expressed in this document, was born in the sufferings and the comradeships of war. Only hope in a better future could overcome the pain experienced when millions of young lives were lost on the battlefields of Europe. Such hope was above all to be found in a new kind of education. An education which ceased to place the emphasis on material rewards for success, but which valued knowledge for its own sake and which provided the means for a fuller and richer life. Such aims were well expressed by a resolution passed by the Parents' National Educational Union and endorsed by the Froebel Society to which it had been sent for support. The resolution formulated in April 1919 reads:

This Council enters a protest against the prevalent tendency of exploiting education, by lowering and cheapening its objects by holding out material rewards for success, and by appealing to the baser desires of human nature, such as avarice, ambition and emulation, rather than the natural desire to know. It desires to further any scheme of liberal education, such as those put forward by the Parents' National Educational Union and the Workers' Educational Association, which will give all classes of the Community the power of full living and of employing wisely, profitably and joyously their increased opportunity for leisure. (FS 1970:202)

The Froebel Society was working hard at such a scheme of liberal education, which it was convinced would come into existence after the war. Such a scheme, as far as the Society was concerned, had to start at the bottom of the educational ladder. The common aim of the branches and the Central Society was the provision for children under six and the establishment of nurseries and nursery schools after the war. They discussed in detail the need for co-operation with parents, the advantages of formal and informal teaching, the question of simplified spelling, the qualifications needed for nursery school teachers, the training of such teachers and the position of headteachers of nursery schools. The war years had created problems for the Society, yet the future looked more promising than ever before.

1. Castle, 1970, p169
2. Curtis & Boultwood, 1962, p227
3. Froebel Ms18/4/7
4. Montessori, 1915, p95
5. ibid, chap.21
6. Curtis & Boultwood, 1962, p229
7. FSCM, 1906, p190
8. FS Minutes, 1907, p181
9. NFU Minutes, 1911, p83
10. FS Minutes, 1907, p199
11. FS Minutes, 1907, p211
12. ibid, 1907, p196
13. Maclure, 1968, p173
14. FS Minutes, 1907, p255
15. ibid, p103
16. ibid, p175
17. ibid, p208
18. ibid, p224

Milbank Infant School, 1907.
Children using Froebel's Gifts but not as intended by their inventor.

Chapter 6

Set-Backs In The 1920s

Play is the highest phase of human development at the stage of childhood, because it is the spontaneous expression of what is within. A child who plays thoroughly, with spontaneous determination, persevering till physical fatigue forbids, will be a thoroughly determined man, capable of self-sacrifice for himself and others. Play is not trivial, it is highly serious and of deep significance. Friedrich Froebel

The hopes and aspirations created by the Fisher Education Act of 1918 were short lived. The boom years just after the war were followed by a slump in trade and manufacture, by unemployment and a financial crisis leading to the formation of the Geddes Committee which was charged with reducing government expenditure by £100m. Cuts imposed on the different departments also affected education, and nursery education in particular.

Paragraph eighteen of the Fisher Act had given local authorities the power to establish nursery schools at the public's expense. The Board of Education issued regulations for the administration of nursery education in 1919, expressing preference for the creation of separate schools rather than additions to existing day nurseries or nursery classes in infant schools. When the Geddes Committee recommended the reduction of education grants by one third, nursery schools shared the fate of all social ventures which involved new public expenditure. Local authorities were extremely reluctant to proceed with the provision of nursery schools especially when the notorious Circular 1371 of 1925 forced local authorities to trim their educational expenditure even further, virtually putting a surcharge on having children under five in schools.

Many nursery schools and preparatory schools, some of excellent repute, had to close. The Froebel Society was concerned about the estimated three million children who by 1928 were being educated in badly staffed and poorly equipped private schools,[1] but also about the unemployment this created among Froebel-trained teachers. Summer schools continued their successful run for the most part of the 1920s and lectures arranged by the Society were now extended to include study groups for mothers and fathers. Membership remained between 600 and 800, even though several new branches were opening during that time. The Board of Education's Circular 1371, published in

1925, was probably the most devastating blow the Froebel Society had had to suffer so far, though it all started well before that fateful year.

In the spring of 1922, the then Minister of Education, Herbert Fisher, stated that he was in favour of economising on the staffing of the infant schools.[2] He suggested that the headteacher only, with one or two assistants, should be trained and certificated and that the rest of the staff could be untrained and uncertificated young women. In response to a private letter written by Claude Montefiore, Herbert Fisher replied that good work had been done by such women during the war in infant schools. Mr Montefiore pointed out that it did not follow that it would be possible to secure equally capable women in time of peace. The Council of the Froebel Society therefore decided to send an official letter to Mr Fisher stating their misgivings about the provision for the education of young children.

The Council urged that in the education of the children of the nation - the younger no less than the older - there was no place for the untrained. The old notion that anybody could 'mind babies' could no longer be supported, knowing how important those early years are in a child's development. How frequently had his Majesty's Inspectors stated that the infant department was the best department of the elementary school. The Council appealed to the Board of Education to allow the standard to be kept up for the sake of the children, and to remember the great and increasing importance attached by modern psychologists to the impressions made in the early years of childhood.

But such pleading was to no avail. The Minister replied that 'we have never yet been able to staff our schools entirely with trained or certificated teachers'. As the country generally had to retrench, the question was where could savings be effected with least harm. He continued: 'The alternatives before us were either the exclusion of children from school until they reach the age of six, or a reduction in the cost of their education and supervision before that age. The government has decided (and I think rightly decided) to adopt the latter alternative'.[3]

More correspondence followed between the Council and the Minister, some of which was made public in the educational press, but it did not materially change the situation. It did however alert the Teacher Registration Council which, in its resolution, strongly deprecated the increasing practice of employing untrained teachers and strongly opposed the practice of laying upon registered teachers the obligation to take part in the wholly inadequate form of training for such women during a three-month period.[4]

The implied promise by the Minister of Education in his letter to the Society, dated 3 May 1922, not to exclude the under-sixes from schools because of government cuts, was broken, at least in parts, by Government Circular 1371, three years later. The circular envisaged the exclusion of the under-fives from all state education thus virtually closing all nursery schools and nursery classes.[5] Lord Gorrell, who had been elected President of the Froebel Society in 1926 used his Presidential address to attack government policy. He suggested that every member of his Majesty's Government ought to be given Froebel's *Education of Man* to make them aware of what teachers were trying to do in schools and what 'Education' was really about.[6] There were other national associations which protested against the circular and one member from the Board of Education Inspectorate arrived at the Froebel Society's offices urging the

Council to do its utmost 'to educate popular opinion on the great evil contemplated by excluding the child under five from school'.[7]

The Council decided to send letters to all its branches encouraging them to protest in every possible way and to educate public opinion. The Council also took in hand the reprinting of an article which had appeared in *Child Life* in October 1916 on the environment of the slum child before he goes to school, indicating in their Foreword that the article had a fresh and immediate application to present conditions.

These attacks on the education of the young child created greater solidarity than ever before among those who cared. An amalgamation between the Froebel Society and the Nursery School Association was first considered in June 1925. In order to create an even more formidable front, The Child Study Association, The Parent Association and The Educational Handwork Association were also approached. Though all these organisations agreed on some form of amalgamation, especially as regards lectures and the magazine[8], trying to accommodate sectional interests made it an uphill task. The question of a common library and the financing of it also produced difficulties. The outcome of eighteen months deliberations finally established The Federal Lecture Board, a committee which tried to arrange lectures of common interest. Because several organisations shared expenses, the Board was able to choose from a wider selection of prominent speakers and people like Emmeline Pankhurst, J.A.Hadfield, H.G.Wells, Arnold Bennett and Julian Huxley were approached to contribute to the lecture programme. But over the years dissatisfaction was expressed with the choice of topics provided, many of them not relating at all to educational issues.

The Society's efforts to minimise the effect of lack of finance on the education of young children led it to the consideration of encouraging the formation of 'Small Group Schools'. Government cuts in grants to the private sector forced many of the secondary schools to close their preparatory departments. A well-briefed deputation consisting of representatives from the Froebel Society, The Froebel Union, The Association of Head Mistresses, The Headmasters' Conference and The Assistant Masters Association was received by the Board of Education on 1 June 1921. Everybody was agreed that the ideal form of national education was attendance at primary school till the age of eleven and then secondary school. As this was not possible at the time, financial support of the preparatory departments by the Government was essential if one wanted to avoid 'cheap private schools of doubtful and probably depreciating efficiency'.[9] As preparatory departments did not exist in many LEA schools, or were being closed, primary education could only be obtained in overcrowded elementary schools, private schools or from governesses. Even if the last two ways were efficient they were different in kind from that produced by the elementary schools. No longer was there a place available for the intelligent child to be helped to meet the demands of public examinations. Not to tap and develop the intellectual resources of these children was an irreplaceable loss to the nation. But the arguments of the delegation in no way succeeded in influencing the Government's course of action.

The Association of Head Mistresses then suggested to the Froebel Society the setting up of a scheme where three or four families might employ one trained teacher for the education of their children. After careful consideration of the deliberations of a Special Committee of the Froebel Society, the Council agreed that the time was right for the starting of 'Small Group Schools'. It was envisaged that support for these schools, or classes, might be given by the headmistresses of the local high or secondary schools who had no preparatory departments. It was suggested that parents should form a committee and write to suitable agencies asking for a certificated teacher and guarantee an initial salary of not less than £150-£170 irrespective of the number of children attending. This sum divided between four families would be less than the salary of a private governess. The rent of the room should also be guaranteed by the Parents' Committee. The teachers would provide their own private accommodation.[10]

The scheme was reported by some of the daily papers but as 'Small Group Schools' are not mentioned again in the Society's records, one has to assume that they never became a reality.

Government cuts not only affected children. The New Code of Regulations for elementary schools and the new regulations as to payment for Deficiency Grants in respect of secondary schools not maintained by Local Education Authorities also resulted in staff reductions so that a considerable number of teachers leaving colleges in 1922 were unable to find teaching posts.[11] The situation became worse in the following year. According to an article in *The Teacher's World* (4 June 1923) it was estimated that about 1,000 newly qualified Kindergarten teachers would leave the Froebel colleges of whom a large number would be unable to find employment. In addition teachers holding the Higher Certificate of the National Froebel Union, which hitherto had been accepted by secondary school headteachers, found it increasingly difficult to stay in employment. Because of the great pioneering work of Froebel teachers among young children, the National Froebel Union Certificate came increasingly to be considered as a qualification for teaching the lower age-ranges only. The problem was well illustrated in a letter to the Froebel Society written by the Inspector of Secondary Schools for the West Riding, dated 28 October 1925.

> I am afraid that there is nowadays so large a supply of graduates that teachers possessing the National Froebel Union Higher Certificate are not likely to obtain posts except as Kindergarten Mistresses. The day of the non-graduate assistant teacher in a Secondary School is over, except so far as teachers of special subjects are concerned. I do not see what remedy there is for holders of the National Froebel Union Higher Certificate, unless they can persuade the Burnham Reference Committee and the Board of Education to recognise them as equivalent to Graduates. For such recognition the minimum requirement would be the passing of a matriculation examination before entry upon the training course, and an approved course of training for at least three years. But even were these conditions satisfied I doubt very much whether the Reference Committee or the Board would agree to give graduate recognition. Moreover even if graduate recognition were accorded, Secondary School Heads would probably still prefer for Junior Forms the Graduate who has taken a training course in teaching after graduation. I am afraid this is not very hopeful, but seems to me to point to the need for instituting a degree course which includes work suitable for those who intend to teach young children, and still feel that this might be done by the addition of another alternative to the existing courses. (FS Minutes 1920:199)

Attempts by the Froebel Society to create such a degree for junior school teachers, date back to 1918. The Society then invited other interested bodies to co-operate in a conference on the subject of degrees for mistresses of junior forms. This Conference appointed a committee which drew up suggestions for a Pass Degree suitable for teachers of Junior Forms and these suggestions were forwarded to the University of London. Nothing resulted from this action and in 1923 the Froebel Council was considering alternative possibilities. Mr T. Raymont, who was Warden of Goldsmiths' College in London at the time and also a Governor of the National Froebel Union and Vice President of the Froebel Society, suggested that a delegation might be favourably received by Professor Strong of Leeds University, who seemed to be in sympathy with the establishment of such a degree.[12] London University was also approached again in the same year. Neither University responded positively, probably, because there was already a surplus of Kindergarten teachers.

The Society was frequently called upon to support teachers in their efforts to achieve a salary commensurate with other professions. It received a constant stream of letters from teachers urging the Society to present their grievances at the appropriate places. To members there seemed to be no justification for placing graduate teachers in secondary schools on a higher scale than a specialist non-graduate, teaching in the same school, nor did it make much sense to differentiate between graduates and non-graduates when paying the cost of living allowance in London so that graduates were paid thirty pounds more. In a letter dated 31 January 1921, to the Viscount Burnham, who headed the recently formed Standing Joint Committee on teachers' salaries, the Society pointed out the anomalies created by a scale which paid pass graduate teachers (untrained) a salary between £275 - £440 and a three-year trained teacher between £210-£360. Yet even this scale was a rather optimistic guideline. The actual salary paid to non-graduate teachers, as averaged from application forms for grants towards the cost of the Froebel Society's summer schools, amounted to £210 for non-resident teachers and ninety pounds for resident teachers. (In comparison, the Secretary of the Froebel Society was receiving a salary of £275 at that time). When government cuts in education were biting hardest, some teachers found their salaries cut by half and in such cases the Society negotiated with the school or directly with the Local Education Authority concerned on the teacher's behalf.[13]

Teachers who lost their jobs altogether were encouraged to register with the Scholastic Agency of the Society. For a small fee, teachers who were looking for employment were matched with schools who had written requesting Froebel-trained teachers. The agency usually had between 250-400 teachers on roll, between 200-350 vacancies on offer and were able to place about sixty teachers per year on average.

Ever since the Board of Education Regulations of 1907, which insisted that private secondary schools in receipt of Government grants had to provide twenty-five per cent of their places each year free for children from elementary schools, many children's education was tied to a syllabus governed by scholarship examinations. After the publication of the Hadow Report *Education of the Adolescent*, 1926, which introduced two types of secondary schools, 'Grammar' and 'Modern', the problem of how to prepare children to pass examinations at the end of their primary school career increased. In order that they should benefit from this new type of post-primary education, it was necessary to discover in each case the type of school most suitable to a child's ability. Children had to undergo written and oral examinations at the age of eleven plus and the report recommended psychological testing for borderline cases. This was bound to affect primary education considerably.

While the Froebel Society supported the schools' efforts to get children over the hurdles of public examinations, the Society was always alert to the harm done to children by the pressures put upon them. True to Froebel's spirit, they condemned competition. In March 1925, the Froebel Society called a meeting to consider the effects of 'Scholarship Tests for Children from the Primary Schools'. Representatives from the London Headteachers' Association, The Association of Assistant Masters, The National Union of Women Teachers, The National Union of Teachers and The Association of Assistant Mistresses attended. Speaker after speaker criticised or condemned the system yet there seemed to be no solution as long as there were not enough secondary school places available.[14] At their next meeting, three months later, only the London Teachers' Association and the Assistant Masters' Association had each sent one representative. But this did not stop the Froebelians on the Committee getting down to the details of the problem. They argued that scholarship examinations taken at ten plus or eleven plus were bound to affect the curriculum of the primary schools and often also the work in the infant schools. They looked at examination questions and came to the conclusion that only rote-learning could produce the desired results and ventured to suggest that children's health was also at risk. But there was no evidence available to support any of these ideas. It was therefore decided to draw up an extensive question-naire to be sent to 'Members of Council, the Hon. Secretaries of the Branches, Members of the Society who are Head Teachers, the National Union of Head Teachers, the London Head Teachers Association, the London Teachers Association, the National Union of Teachers, the National Union of Women Teachers, the Assistant Masters' Association, the Assistant Mistresses Association, the Head Mistresses' Association, and the Head Masters' Association'. Over 3,000 questionnaires were sent out but fewer than forty replies were received. The questions asked and the summarised evidence were as follows.

1) Do you consider the present system of scholarship tests for secondary schools satisfactory? If not, what improvements can you suggest?

Opinions were divided almost equally for and against them. On the whole headmasters viewed them with much more favour than headmistresses. All would approve of more intelligence tests and of more weight being given to the head teacher's report and the school record. No other improvements were suggested.

2) Do the children appear to have been forced in any direction in preparing for the examination? If so what effect had this had on the successful child and on the unsuccessful candidate in the senior and in the junior school?

Many heads of girls' schools considered there was much forcing in preparation for the examination, but this was generally attributable to difficulty in home conditions and was not seen by heads of schools in prosperous districts. Very few were able to compare the after-effects on successful and unsuccessful children. But a few noted evil effects on the successful child, such as loss of nervous energy and consequent slow development, in the secondary school.

3) How does the subsequent work of the children who fail compare with that of the child who succeeds in getting to the secondary school?

Many recorded difficulties found by scholarship children in adapting themselves to the different kind of work in the secondary school and some note the possibility that this was due to the cramming which has hindered the children's power of reasoning. Very little evidence was produced.

4) What was the opinion of teachers, invigilators and psychologists as to the apparent or probable effects on young children of working for three hours continuously at four papers?

Several answers noted the fact that the examinations were far too fatiguing for the children who entered and some speak of fear beforehand, so that the test became one of emotional and nervous powers rather than of knowledge or intelligence. It is noticeable that evidence of fatigue seems to have struck the teachers of girls but hardly at all teachers of boys. One writer noted that a three-hour paper is far too great an effort for most children.

The report concludes by stating that, on the basis of many private conversations and from letters received, the Society has come to the conclusion that:

a) There are special classes for scholarship work which writers do not admit to be the case.
b) That children are sometimes frightened by being told that there is no second chance.
c) That promotion of teachers does largely depend on the number of scholarships gained in their schools.
d) That there is a general disinclination to rouse sleeping dogs in this matter.[15]

Others might well be disinclined to consider the matter, the Froebel Society persevered and called more meetings in the following year and also succeeded in getting the Chief Examiner of the London County Council to attend a Round Table Conference. The assurances given by the Chief Examiner, 'that there is no need for any kind of pressure in Junior and Infant Schools, nor for the omission of any methods which make for real intelligence, for it is intelligence only which the examiners seek to find', failed to convince the members of the Froebel Council that the effects of competitive examinations on the teaching of young children in schools were anything but disastrous.[16]

It was certainly not beyond the capability of teachers to organise a school successfully without competition and handing out prizes. Two of the school inspectors had said so quite clearly in their report after the inspection of the Froebel Educational Institute Demonstration School at Colet Gardens on 15 and 16 June 1927. And this was achieved in spite of the fact that this school served as a demonstration school as well as a preparatory school. It exemplified modern educational thinking so that visiting students were able to observe the practical outcome of Froebelian principles studied in college. At the same time teachers prepared their pupils for their diverse secondary schools which in most cases demanded the passing of entrance examinations. The inspectors commented on the fact that as these two functions were evidently not incompatible it said much for the structure of a curriculum which was at once generous and concise. As regards competition, they recorded: 'The school deliberately dispenses with marks, prizes and the competitive spirit. They simply are not needed'.[17]

The Froebel Society's opposition to some of the Government's policies and some of the practices in schools did not seem to diminish the high standing of the Society in the eyes of the Board of Education. In 1927 they asked the Society for help with a list of suitable books for primary school children and a year later requested a delegation to appear before a Consultative Committee of the Board, which was considering courses of study suitable for children in elementary schools. The delegation, true to Froebelian philosophy and principles, introduced their evidence by referring to the needs of childhood, stressing that each stage of childhood was a complete whole in itself. They emphasised the great danger of letting the next stage overshadow the present one. Children at this stage in their lives were inquisitive and enthusiastic people who needed to be taken out of school to explore their immediate environment at first hand. Science, mathematics and the use and development of language was an integral part of such a scheme. They stressed again that the use of a standardised and competitive examination at the end of such a period of education could never be considered a good yardstick for estimating future potential.[18]

Efforts to spread Froebel's educational ideas also among parents involved the Society in the arrangements of a lecture programme for mothers and teachers in 1924. It proved so popular that attempts were made to involve fathers as well, but with less success. Topics discussed related to the developments of the total child and covered areas like day-dreams, co-education, play and health. But it also included subjects which are usually part of a child's curriculum in school, like number work, reading, story-telling, dramatic work, musical and physical education, poetry, formal and free handwork and needlework. Topics examined in the lecture programme for teachers were of a more professional nature: intelligence tests, individual methods in history and geography, speech defects, life and literature, the project method, the three Rs and the future of the nursery school. But in spite of much publicity work, membership of the Society remained static over the years.

MEMBERSHIP:	1921	1922	1923	1924	1925	1926	1927	1928	1929
Members	750	752	626	659	696	702	697	719	784
Members using Library	444	389	330	383	366	370	348	337	346
Members taking *Child Life*	270	362	322	335	349	334	344	340	360

These figures are not surprising when one considers the vicissitudes of the branches. New branches were opened in Cheltenham, Darlington, Eastbourne, Liverpool, Stockton and Middlesbrough in 1920, Newport in 1922, and Bolton and Manchester in 1925, while branches in Rotherham and Northumberland closed in 1922, Cambridge in 1925 and Birmingham, Derby, Stoke on Trent and Norwich severed their connection with the parent society in 1926. Some of these branches later affiliated to the parent society for a small fee, but their members no longer counted as members of the Froebel Society. In January 1927 the Froebel Society had branches in the following towns: Bolton, Bradford, Bristol, Chesterfield, Eastbourne, Hull, Leeds, Manchester, Middlesbrough, Newport, Northampton, Sheffield and affiliated branches in Cheltenham and Norwich.

One of the main avenues used by the Society to disseminate their ideas was the magazine *Child Life*. When its readership had sunk below the three hundred mark it produced losses of twenty pounds per year. The Council discussed whether it would be possible to produce the magazine more cheaply and to include more practical help for the uninitiated. It was shown that magazines which provided tips for teachers were already on the market and that *Child Life* could not be produced more cheaply without altering the policy of the magazine. The Council decided that the magazine was worth the loss it sustained each year. Even when in 1925 the deficit of the magazine reached the fifty pounds level, the Council still argued that 'the more educationally valuable the magazine, the less likely it was to pay its way'. Something had to be done to cut costs and a new editor was appointed. The subsequent improvements led to the decision to produce the magazine four times a year as from 1929, instead of three times as before.

The credit for sustaining the magazine probably belongs to Claude Montefiore. In 1920, for example, the balance sheet of the Society showed outgoings of £659, while income amounted to £424. Even when the profits of the summer school had reduced the deficit considerably, there were still fifty pounds to be found. If it had not been for Mr Montefiore's generous donations, the Society would again have been in the red. In the following years the Society usually broke even and sometimes produced gains, but this was mainly due to the extremely good profits gathered from the ever-popular summer schools.[19]

The success of the summer schools was probably due to the careful balance which was maintained between the theoretical and the practical presentation of old and new ideas. There were practical courses in eurythmics, geography, needlecraft, pottery, art, Froebel's occupations, country dancing, spinning, weaving, drama, music for young children, nature exploration and scriptwriting. Lectures were given on : Music in relation to play, New Methods in Education, Scripture Teaching in the Light of Today, Handwork for Young Children, Speech Training, The Nursery School of Today (by Margaret McMillan), Drawing and Free Expression, Experimental Psychology and Measurement, Schoolroom and Playground Games, Aspects of Child Psychology, Good Handwriting and How To Develop It, World Citizenship, Education for Peace, English and Story-Telling, The Teaching of Arithmetic, The Use of the Gramophone in Schools, Spinning, Weaving and Basketry. There were assistant teachers, headteachers, governesses, lecturers from training colleges and inspectors from the Board of

Education and they came from England, Scotland and Wales, from India, China, Canada, Egypt, Jerusalem, Ireland, South Africa and Tasmania.

The report of the 1927 summer school, which was held at the Froebel Institute in Roehampton, provides a glimpse of the enthusiasm which prevailed among students and lecturers alike.

The 1927 Summer School was attended by fifty-four full-time resident students, four full-time non-resident and twelve part-time students. It was a smaller school than usual but a remarkably friendly one and very representative. (+)

We had training college lecturers, a representative from the BBC, a good number of tired but keen headmistresses from infants' schools, a group of very young and about-to-become headmistresses of private schools, and many assistant mistresses from government schools, high schools and private schools.

The success of the School owed much to the beauty of its setting. There were glowing tributes from all to the beauty of the house and the grounds, the delight of rowing on the lake and sitting about in the evenings in such surroundings.

The informal opening, a recital of folk songs selected by Miss McClure, struck just the right note. Miss McClure's introductory talk about folk songs, her very beautiful rendering of them, and her friendly talk with the Students afterwards over coffee in the Common Room did much to make everybody feel at home and to get rid of the inevitable shyness incident to the collection of sixty-five teachers of varying ages from twenty to sixty and from very different environments.

There was great keenness over the lectures, which were extraordinarily well attended. The staff were called upon for extra lectures, informal talks on their subjects and for advice about books. Much time was also spent voluntarily by the students in carrying out experiments suggested by Dr Dale in her practical psychology lectures.

From the spontaneous remarks of several of the students it was obvious that Miss Hamilton's lectures were delightful, refreshing and stimulating. Two more poetry readings were given in the evenings by popular demand.

We were fortunate to have for the all-too-short geography course Miss Fleming, who not only had many practical suggestions to offer, but who held the broad view on the teaching of geography to young children that it can further the understanding and peace of the world.

The full meaning of Miss Payne's unique course, 'Handwork growing out of Play', was not grasped by all students at first, but their final appreciation of it was voiced by one student who said that her whole outlook on children's education had been altered by her realization of the possibilities opened out to her by Miss Payne's suggestion.

Perhaps one of the pleasantest sights of the whole fortnight was that of numbers of arms and legs and trunks, gropingly performing what should be skilled movements in Miss Spafford's delightful physical exercises and children's games, and that of the delight on the faces of the performers and onlookers in the wealth of new suggestions for their work in the coming year.

One of the most valuable opportunities offered by the Summer School was the Publishers' Library. About 600 volumes had been collected, and the students were very grateful for the opportunity of seeing the best text books, readers and reference books bearing on the subjects of their lectures.

Since the library was in constant use it speaks well for the students that no book was missing at the final checking. The 200 books kindly lent by the Society were also in great demand. This year, as in 1925, the evenings were left free and again it was found to be very successful. Some students read or discussed in groups, some investigated in the Publishers' Library, some worked in the grounds, some in the craft rooms and there were general meetings for progressive games, community singing and country dancing on the lawn, all organised by the students.

Miss Lawrence was her kind hospitable self. Her generosity brought one very enthusiastic student to the School, and provided a lavish supply of ices on the memorable evening when the staff gave a variety entertainment for the students, and on the last day she sent many students away with armfuls of flowers.... (FS Minutes 1920:179)

(+) Attendance at Summer Schools was as follows:

1920 1921 1922 1923 1924 1925 1926 1927 1928 1929

  95 98   97   80   ?   76   ?   54   70   42

While summer schools provided the means to spread Froebelian ideas among teachers and while Froebel colleges provided professional training for those prepared to spend three years in a college, there was another large group of young women available for training who did not fall into either of these categories. Those were the young women who, having left secondary school, wanted help with preparation for their future work with children whether as mothers or social workers. A year's course in child welfare with an examination set by the Board of the National Froebel Union might fill an important year usefully, between leaving school and starting a life's vocation. Such a course would fit girls for work in clubs, play centres, nursery schools and children's clinics. If such a course were structured and carried out by the Froebel Society it might also improve candidates' educational chances if later they wanted to enter a training college.

Less than a year later, in 1927, a sub-committee had worked out the details. It was to be a course for thirty students where lectures included child hygiene, child psychology and social history with special reference to the development of agencies for child welfare. The practical work was to be carried out in nursery schools, infant welfare centres, play centres, Sunday schools and by visits in connection with the Invalid Children's Aid Association and the Children's Care Committee. There were going to be classes in singing, handicraft, folk-dancing, and story-telling, from the point of view of helping the girls to adapt what they knew to the requirements of children. The United Girls' School Settlement in Camberwell was approached regarding accommodation for students and lecturing facilities. Although at first very interested, no agreement could be reached with the United Girls' School Settlement and nothing more was heard of the scheme.

In contrast, the training course for the National Froebel Union Certificate set up in 1929 got quickly under way and became a well-attended and popular course. This course was designed for qualified, Government and college-trained teachers and for untrained teachers who had taken Part I of the National Froebel Union Certificate privately. This two-year part-time course of six terms of ten weeks each, covered the following syllabus on the two evenings of two hours per week:

Year 1:
    2 hours Handwork
    1 hour History of Education
    1 hour Principles of Education and General Method

Year 2:
    2 hours Special Method (to be taken by specialists)
    1 hour Principles of Education
    1 hour Discussions in smaller groups (with teaching supervisor)

Teaching Supervision:
    Most important part of course and to be arranged for throughout the course and to consist of:
    a) supervision of teaching and teaching notes ⎤ dealt with by a panel
    b) demonstration lessons   ⎦ of supervisors
    c) school visiting

It may not look much of a syllabus, yet the demands made on students were high. The average attendance for the first year,1929, was forty-five students per evening of whom thirty-three sat for the first-year examinations and only fourteen passed in both subjects and teaching practice. In spite of these stringent demands the course flourished for many years.

One of the Society's highlights at that time took place in 1925, when members celebrated its fiftieth Jubilee and very fittingly, elected Claude Montefiore to be their President. A 'conversazione' was held on 23 May at the Froebel Educational Institute in Roehampton which was attended by 250 people. For the morning, visits had been arranged to see children at work at:

The Preparatory Department, The High School, Clapham Common,
F.E.I. Demonstration School, Colet Gardens, West Kensington,
Maria Grey Training College, Brondesbury, NW6,
Notting Hill Nursery School,
Camden House School, 118 Baker Street, W1,
The Rachel McMillan N.S.Training Centre, Deptford,SE8,
The Richmond High School, East Twickenham,
Craven Hall, The Whitfield's Institute, Tottenham Court Road.

In the afternoon, tea was served in the grounds of Grove House and Sir Michael Sadler, Master of University College , and Mr Montefiore addressed the visitors. The day was concluded with an eurythmic demonstration on the lawn.

But it was not only a time for celebrations, it was also an opportunity for examining the successes and shortcomings of the Society and for evaluating present policy. A lengthy discussion by the Council early on in the Jubilee Year raised the question why one could now find so many infant teachers who were in ignorance of the work of the Society. It was felt that a few years previously the Society had been a more lively and powerful force, especially when it broke away from the literal interpretation of Froebelian philosophy and began to proclaim the liberal interpretation of Froebelian views, but unfortunate results had ensued. One could now observe a retrograde movement in infant schools, where the three Rs, taught formally, had come back into their own and even children under five were taught them. Sometimes these lessons took the whole morning, and a good part of the afternoon. The old-fashioned object lesson had come back in the form of 'Sense' training. To see dolls' houses as storage space for apparatus was symbolic of a general attitude. There was little attempt to appreciate the spirit of play, too many teachers worshipped efficiency and results. A revival of the spiritual and more Froebelian side of education was required. Was the Jubilee Year not a good time to make the Society better known, to correct false ideas too often held by outsiders as to what Froebel had taught and above all to proclaim its future policy and aspirations?[20]

These discussions led to the production and printing of 3,000 copies of the Jubilee pamphlet *Then and Now*, which in its introduction gave an account of the work of the Society and the debt the education system owed to Froebel. This was followed by a chapter each on The Nursery School, The Primary School, The Junior Department of the Secondary Schools, The Froebel Training Colleges and was concluded by showing hopes and aims for the future. The pamphlet emphasised that many of Froebel's ideas had not yet been implemented, especially those on religion, play, handwork and the work in nursery schools in general.

It seemed essential that members of the Society had to reflect from time to time on the origin of their very existence if they were not to lose their direction. The President of the Society, Mr T. Raymont, used his Presidential address in 1928 to remind his audience of 'England's Educational Debt to Froebel'. He began by stating that the Froebel Society was one of the oldest educational societies in existence. Its views were sought and respected wherever the right kind of training for young children was in question. He then quoted from the educational writings of Susannah Wesley, Isaac Watts, Samuel Wilderspin and Thomas Arnold and showed how even kind people were mislead by the apparent need to exorcise sin and to justify 'the fear of the rod' even in one year-olds. He compared these writings with Froebel's comments on childish faults:

> When we look for the origin of these shortcomings we find a double reason, first the complete neglect of the development of certain sides of human life; secondly, early misdirection, an arbitrary interference with the natural course of development. At the bottom of every shortcoming in man lie crushed, frustrated qualities, or tendencies suppressed, misunderstood, and misguided.

Mr Raymont pointed out that even if one could not accept that statement as a complete explanation of human waywardness, one can accept it as suggesting an infinitely more hopeful method of dealing with childish faults than that which is based upon the notion of an innate depravity to be exorcised by force.

There were other areas where Froebel was marching out on his educational journey in exactly the opposite direction from the commonly trodden path. While it was commonly held that children should be seen and not heard, Froebel said:

> The child, your child, ye fathers, follows you wherever you go. Do not harshly repel him. Show no impatience about his ever recurring questions. Every harshly repelling word crushes a bud on his tree of life. Question upon question comes from the lips of the boy thirsting for knowledge - How? Why? When? What for? and every satisfactory answer opens up to him a new world.

Mr Raymont continued that a corollary to the assumption of innate depravity was the assumption that a child who prefers play to doing algebra, is fair set to grow up an idle person. As play is a child's natural bent, so the argument goes, play must be wrong. It is Froebel who set going the train of thought which led to the belief that the highest and noblest forms of work are those which, because they engage one's whole mind and soul, most closely resemble play. In one of the wisest and most significant passages in his writings Froebel says:

> The plays of childhood are the germinal leaves of all later life, for the whole man is developed and shown in these...and ...Play is the highest phase of human development at the stage of childhood, because it is the spontaneous expression of what is within. A child who plays thoroughly, with spontaneous determination, persevering till physical fatigue forbids, will be a thorough determined man, capable of self-sacrifice for himself and others. Play is not trivial, it is highly serious and of deep significance.

Mr Raymont believed that Froebel's doctrine of play led him to a new emphasis upon manual and constructive activities. His doctrine of self-activity and self-expression, though perhaps needing to be freed from metaphysical difficulties, was practically sound, and led him to a new emphasis upon such activities as drawing, painting and singing. His clear perception that school ought to be a bit of life, led him to a new emphasis upon the cultivation of social relationships during childhood. And his aesthetic values in education led him to a view of nature study, and an appreciation of schoolgardens, which placed the Kindergarten immeasurably in advance of the old-fashioned infant school. It was Froebel who most helped to put down the radically false notion that education merely means putting a child 'to his book'.

The President pointed out that the lucky accident that infant schools never came under the system of payment by results meant that progressive infant school teachers enjoyed greater freedom to experiment than the teachers of older children. The School Boards encouraged their infant school teachers in the study of Froebelian principles, and the publicity work of the Froebel Society and the examinations of the National Froebel Union had for many years past been instrumental in spreading the Froebelian gospel among teachers of the elementary infant schools. The general conditions of infant school work, however, still constituted a formidable obstacle to progress, and the best that an experienced and sympathetic observer was able to say was that, whereas the infant school of the past was worse than the average home, the infant school of today was better than the average home. If that was the case the result was mainly to be ascribed to the fact that the trainers of the younger generation of infant school teachers in the training colleges had themselves practically all been trained under Froebelian auspices.

And the President concluded:

I have heard it said - sometimes, I regret to state, by people of position and influence who ought to know better - that Froebel's ideals so far as they are valid have now been achieved, that it is time to cease harping upon the Froebelian string, that a teacher trained definitely on modern Froebelian lines is not different from a teacher trained otherwise, that our educational system, and in particular our Infant school system, has absorbed into itself all that is best in Froebel and rejected the rest - in short that, for practical purposes, as distinguished from historical interest, we have done with Froebel.

In a sense I heartily wish this were true. I wish the Froebel Society and the National Froebel Union could put up their shutters and confess that the cause for which they came into the world had been won. It would indeed be a proud confession. But existing facts are utterly against such a step. Froebel cannot yet be relegated to history, and regarded only from the historical point of view. Let me tell you why.

So long as one of our greatest and most progressive educational authorities can put forward a scheme under which, whilst forty older children are supposed to be enough for one teacher, forty-eight young children are supposed not to be too many; and so long as the ideas underlying that formula are accepted as valid - we have not done with Froebel.

So long as the national conscience remains dormant about the nation's little children, and especially about the little children of the slums; so long as the nation, though able to afford many things less important, cannot afford nursery schools - we have not done with Froebel.

So long as we have a scholarship system, which really means that competition begins in the Infant schools, that the old emphasis upon the premature grind in the 'three Rs' is reappearing, and that all that you Froebelians have done for the wise training of children of tender years is in danger of being undone - we have not done with Froebel.

And finally, so long as it can happen that in this England of ours, in the year of grace 1927, young boys can be sent to prison, can be made into juvenile gaol-birds, for the crime of playing football in the streets, when they have absolutely no other place in which to play football, Froebel, who stands alone among the modern prophets of education in seeing the high significance of play, who stands alone among them in demanding, not only a place in a school but also a place in a playing-field for every child in the land, is not a back number.

Much still needed to be done. How unfortunate then, that this was also the time when the Society had to record the loss of their principal founder member. Miss Fanny Franks, Principal of Camden House School, Trainer of Kindergarten teachers, Member of Council of the Froebel Society from 1881-1914, Member of the Examination Board of the National Froebel Union from 1894-1914 and Vice President from 1914-1915, died in October 1920. Her friends collected over £200, £20,000 in 1990 terms, and handed the money over to the Froebel Society to create a fund 'for the use of the Society in the education of the young'. Enthusiastic and committed young teachers were ready to carry on with the work started fifty years previously.

1. FSCM, 1920, p295
2. FS Minutes, 1920, p50
3. ibid, p57
4. ibid, p72

5. ibid, p206
6. *Child Life*, 1926, p7
7. FS Minutes, 1920, p214
8. ibid, p196
9. FSCM, 1920, p24
10. ibid, p60
11. FS Minutes, 1920, p79
12. FSCM, 1920, p74
13. FS Minutes, 1920, p118
14. ibid, p137
15. FSCM, 1920, p200
16. ibid, p216
17. Owen, 1927, p5
18. FS Minutes, 1920, pp256, 305
19. ibid, pp84, 129
20. ibid, p172

A more creative use of Froebel's Gifts at Southfield's Infant School, 1906.

Chapter 7
Froebelian Practices Enter Junior Schools

...the curriculum is to be thought of in terms of activity and experience rather than of knowledge to be acquired and facts to be stored. Board of Education, 1931

The educational set-backs of the 1920s, however severe, especially regarding the education of the young child, could not and did not stop or even retard the development of progressive educational thinking. The years after the First World War witnessed the growth of a new humanism based on justice, the world over. Teachers were questioning an education based on mechanical obedience and were looking to Rousseau, Pestalozzi, Froebel, Herbart, Tolstoy, Dewey and Freud for guidance. This led to further educational experimentation which, in several different ways had already been started at the beginning of the century. The New Education Fellowship founded by Beatrice Ensor and Dr Adolphe Ferriere in the early 1920s, investigated and reported on new methods of teaching in its journal *The New Era*. There were reports from the USA, France, Switzerland, Belgium, India, Germany and Great Britain. The efforts of Decroly in Belgium, Dr Claparede in Switzerland, Tagore in India, Steiner in Germany, Dewey in the USA, and Neill, Susan Isaacs and the Elmhirsts from England were carefully studied by teachers. The promotion of individuality, education as an end in itself rather than a preparation for adulthood, learning by doing, were no longer ideas exclusive to Froebelians.

Underlying this new approach to education was the growing interest in child psychology. Melanie Klein's use of play techniques in 1923 provided evidence on the importance of family life in early childhood. Freud's study of the unconscious increased the surmise that unresolved experiences in early life can still influence behaviour in adulthood. Piaget's study of the development of concepts as published in his first major work *The Language and Thought of the Child*, 1923, first published in English in 1926, demonstrated that even very young children ordered their environment by careful comparison and logical thinking.

As knowledge about children's behaviour grew, so did the awareness that wronged children might benefit from careful guidance. Birmingham recognised the value of the contribution child psychologists could make to the welfare of children early on, and though not one of the richest boroughs in the land, opened the first Child Guidance

Clinic in 1932. By 1945 there were seventy-nine such clinics in the country providing one of the supports on which the Children's Act of 1948 was based which established a nationwide child care service.

Even though progressive methods of teaching for older children were still mainly restricted to those in a few private schools, they gained ground in the public elementary schools via the Kindergartens, the nursery schools and the infant schools. Creative activities and informal ways of learning became increasingly attractive to many parents, teachers and inspectors. Even the Government now gave support to these new ideas in their *Report of the Consultative Committee on The Primary School*, 1931. At the request of the Consultative Committee of the Board of Education, the Froebel Society submitted a memorandum on 'Courses of Study suitable for Children from Eight to Eleven'. The memorandum stressed that there should not be a break in the continuity of the child's experiences in the infant and junior school. The junior school was to be regarded as giving children time and scope for general development prior to later instruction in definite subjects and should not become the forcing ground for selective schools. The aim of such a school was to unite school experience with life experiences and teachers should therefore not feel obliged to follow a fixed time-table. The Society recommended the careful keeping of records of 'The tools of learning': English and Arithmetic. There were detailed suggestions for schemes of projects worked round children's interests but above all the emphasis was on gaining experience by doing. The questions put to the representatives of the Froebel Society by members of the Consultative Committee in response to the memorandum indicate the difficulties people experience when faced with such liberal aims of education and revolutionary methods of achieving them. On the one hand members of the Consultative Committee expressed doubts about the wisdom of using a child's interest as the guideline for his/her learning rather than a fixed curriculum and on the other hand the Chairman of the Committee expressed his surprise at the literature the Froebel Society had suggested as not only possible but appreciated by children under eleven. Were those books not far too difficult for these children? The Froebel Society's representative replied that they spoke from experience with children who had not been taught to read too early and who had from the beginning been introduced to real books rather than 'primers'.

The Committee which had listened to teachers, lecturers and inspectors were above all influenced by the evidence given by child psychologists, especially by Cyril Burt from the London County Council. Intelligence tests had revealed the wide range of children's intellectual differences and there was therefore a strong case for teaching children in groups of similar ability, a way of teaching which was eventually introduced into schools under the name of 'streaming'. But the one sentence which educators eventually picked out as the most revolutionary statement to be printed in any Government report on education was to be found in Chapter seven which dealt with the primary school curriculum. The sentence reads:

...the curriculum is to be thought of in terms of activity and experience rather than of knowledge to be acquired and facts to be stored. (Board of Education 1931:93)

Activity methods had at last been given the official seal of approval. This author has been told by Miss A.L. Murton, former Chief Inspector for Primary Schools, that the exact wording of this sentence created considerable difficulties during the discussion.

The committee intended the sentence to read '...the curriculum is to be thought of in terms of activity and experience *and* of knowledge to be acquired and facts to be stored'. To give equal value to learning by doing and to the storing of facts would leave the door wide open for teachers to carry on as before. The two members on the committee who had been most impressed by the evidence presented by the Froebel Society's representatives argued their case for two hours before agreement was reached to substitute the 'and' with the 'rather than'. It made all the difference to the primary schools, especially during the exciting and inspiring 1950s and consolidating 1960s.

But it still needed lectures, courses and books which provided the reasons for activity methods and the philosophy underpinning it. Equally it needed competent teachers to demonstrate the know-how. With the publication of the Primary School Report, the demands on the services of the Froebel Society increased.

Membership in the 1930s never quite reached the thousand mark, yet the Society's main activities: the library, the summer schools, evening classes, lecture courses, the employment agency and the *Child Life* quarterly were not only maintained but extended. *Child Life* became a monthly publication. The printing of pamphlets as a means for disseminating information was increased. Lecture courses now also covered the education of junior school children and evening classes prepared teachers, not only for the Teacher's Certificate, but also for the Handwork Diploma for those who wished to specialise in handwork, the Trainer's Diploma for those who wanted to take up training college work, the Nursery School Diploma for superintendents in nursery schools[1] and the Natural History Diploma for those who intended to specialise in the natural sciences. The considerable increase in the volume of work handled by the secretaries demanded extended office accommodation. The small and familiar rooms at Bloomsbury Square were no longer adequate.

In November 1932 the Society's offices were moved from 4 Bloomsbury Square to 29 Tavistock Square. Bloomsbury Square had been the Society's home since 1896. Here the English conception of what Froebel meant was born. The rooms were full of the memories of those early pioneers of child-centred education. Of the twenty-four members of the Council at that time only two or three were now still alive. The then President, Miss Shirreff, who died in 1897, had been President since 1877. Madame Michaelis, who became President after Miss Shirreff, was appointed the first Principal of the Froebel Educational Institute five years later. One also has to recall the indefatigable Miss Bayley, the Secretary and initiator of *Child Life*, also Maria Findlay the outstanding lecturer who had worked with Professor Dewey in Chicago, Miss Manley, Principal of Stockwell Training College and Agnes Ward, Principal of 'Maria Grey', both members of Council at that time. Of the male members of the Council, Mr Courthorpe Bowen became the first Chairman of the National Froebel Union which was founded in 1878. The only member of Council of 1896 who was still a member in 1932 was Claude Montefiore.[2]

The new premises at 29 Tavistock Square were part of the Bedford Estate though owned by the New Education Fellowship. The Nursery School Association and the Home and School Council were already in residence when the Froebel Society joined them on the ground floor.[3] There was now enough space available to open a 'Book Room' which allowed the Society to sell books and pamphlets and to display specimen copies for inspection by teachers. Even though permission for the establishment of the Book Room had been given by the owners, the Agents of the Bedford Estate objected and eventually the Froebel Society had to look for new accommodation. In July 1936 they moved to 28 Little Russell Street.[4]

The idea of a permanent Book Room was born after the successful exhibition of Kindergarten materials at the Conference of Education Associations in January 1933. Members of Council were well aware of the importance of keeping educational issues constantly in the public eye. They arranged exhibitions of children's drawings at London University, responded to the BBC's request for advice on talks about present-day methods of education and, on request, contributed to a conference on 'Films for children'.[5] Topics for discussion with the BBC included: 'The Organisation of Education into Nursery Schools, Kindergartens and Junior Schools', 'How children are taught to read and write', 'Learning by activity and experience' and 'The new non-subject approach to the curriculum'.[6]

The new non-subject approach to the curriculum was also being discussed in relation to the junior school curriculum. But change was slow. For this reason the Society approached Mr Pym, the Chief London County Council Inspector of Schools, with a view to discussing the need for more enlightened methods of teaching in junior schools as well as the provision of Froebel training for male teachers. After the meeting with the Froebel Society in 1934, the Chief Inspector responded by asking all the District Inspectors to call meetings of headteachers of the junior schools in their areas at which the subject of methods in junior education should be discussed. He invited the Froebel Society to submit a list of speakers who would be willing to open and take part in such discussions. The outcome of these discussion groups was the publication of a list of junior schools which were prepared to receive visitors anxious to study good junior school methods. Also a club for junior school teachers was founded which registered eighty members at its first meeting in September 1936. Male teachers, for the first time, were registering for the Froebel Teacher's Certificate.

This change of focus in the Society's activities from the infant school to the junior school can also be observed in the evening lecture programmes. While at the beginning of the 1930s lectures dealt with nursery schools, story-telling, handwork and art, during the second half of the 1930s lecturers examined 'The opportunity of the Junior School', Discipline and Punishment' and 'Approaches to Life in the Junior School'. The latter consisted of a series of lectures and had been developed from the theme 'Education as an approach to various aspects of life'. The lectures started off by exploring man and his environment in the present, then concentrated on the history of mankind, language and scientific progress and closed with an examination of man's spirituality using nature study as its vehicle.[7] It is interesting to note that when Froebel worked out the different uses for his Gifts, he grouped them in exactly the same way; namely 'Forms of Life' where children were encouraged to build replicas of objects which they found in their own environment (chairs, tables, houses, gates, churches, etc.); 'Forms of Knowledge' where children could explore the mathematical and scientific base of their environment by learning about halves, quarters and eighths; addition, division and multiplication; squares, oblongs, hexagons and rhomboids; lines, areas and volume; and 'Forms of Beauty' where children were able to demonstrate for themselves the unity of things and see the divine in the symmetry of the flowers which they were asked to re-construct in the mosaics of wooden bricks. One wonders whether the members of the Lecture Committee were aware of Froebel's three categories of ordering knowledge when they structured their courses. However, be that as it may, junior school teachers, probably for the first time, were made aware of the Froebelian principle that all good teaching starts with the child and his environment and develops in such a way that it takes care of all the child's needs, his physical, mental as well as spiritual.

The Froebel Society's approach to its evening lecture programme, though essentially designed to provide its members with new ideas in the field of education was never narrow nor insular. 'Psychological Aspects of Juvenile Delinquency' and 'The Meaning of Failure to the Child' were as much part of the programme as the lectures on 'Education for Peace' in 1939. Contributors like A.S.Neill and Lady Astor were joined by Kurt Hahn from Germany and Dr Buhler from Austria, and when the Council approved a scheme of organising visits to museums and nature rambles as part of the monthly lecture programme they did no more than implement their own belief and Froebel's dictum that 'Life educates'.

Because Froebelians believed that the educating life of a good school was no more than an extension of the educating life of a good home, it was crucial that parents needed to be involved in the life of the school. Members of the Society were aware that much energy was wasted and good work spoilt owing to a lack of understanding and co-operation between the teacher and the parent. A certain measure of diffidence on the part of the parent, who was often shy and constrained when dealing with someone considered to be intellectually superior, as well as a complete misunderstanding as to the teacher's objectives and methods used, led frequently to disharmony between the home and the school. Members cited instances of parents having said that they did not send their children to school to play or to be taken to the docks.[8]

The 'Parent-Committee' which was now called into existence proposed that the Society should encourage the formation of Parents' Associations on a local level and to support these by sending speakers and by providing literature. The following titles for the printing of pamphlets for parents were suggested[9]:

Child Development	showing the stages of growth and development
Behaviour Difficulties	obstinacy, untruthfulness, fears, rewards....
Hygiene of Childhood	food, clothes, habits....
Early Education	principles of teaching, educative play
Educative Toys	toys, games, playmaterials....
Books for Children	graded according to ability and understanding
Drama for Children	lists of plays
Children's Questions	including sex education....
First Lessons	reading, number....
A Child's Religion	prayers, stories....

Many of these pamphlets were completed and some published. But as the Home and School Council had already started publications of a similar kind, the Froebel Society agreed to let its own pamphlets appear in the Home and School Council series.[10]

There was also an awareness, however slight, of the value of co-operation between home and school in the Government *Report of the Consultative Committee on Infant and Nursery Schools* published in 1933. Even though the Froebelians who gave evidence to the committee must have mentioned the pioneering work they were doing in this respect, their success in convincing the committee of the importance of parents' groups working with teachers was minimal. The report carried one paragraph on the 'Co-operation between Parents and the School'. But there were many other areas in the report where the Froebelian influence was marked.

The introduction to the report indicates that the core-issues of the education of the young child are dealt with in chapter six. It furthermore mentions, by way of a summary of what the report is going to say, namely that 'formal education, generally speaking, has been begun at too early an age in England' and that the committee endorses the view that 'this early formal education has received so large a share of the school time that other activities of equal importance to the young child have been starved'. One might almost think that this paragraph had been written by a Froebelian, especially when one reads its concluding sentence: 'Reading is but another way of looking at pictures, writing but a variety of drawing, and elementary operations in number are associated with most of his childish occupations'.[11]

Chapter six deals with 'The Training and Teaching of Young Children in the Infant and Nursery School'. This chapter provides many references to Froebel, his philosophy and educational ideas. The committee is encouraging nursery and infant schools to consider Froebel's principles regarding creative activity, the unity of knowledge leading to topic work and the realization that the child, not the class is the real unit of instruction. In consequence, the report says ' school procedures must be so modified that each child should have liberty to grow his own way, and to learn by doing'. And adds that those are Froebel's 'enduring contributions to educational theory'.[12]

Froebelians would not have expressed it in those terms for it might give the impression that children were left free to develop without guidance. But it was a reasonable approximation to what Froebelians were hoping for.

Unfortunately, the report gives only little guidance as regards the training of nursery and infant teachers, and none at all when it refers to the training of superintendents for nursery schools, except to say that the training should be the same as for infant teachers.[13] The more credit needs to be given to the Froebel Society's creation of the Nursery Diploma Course in 1931, two years before the Infant and Nursery Schools Report was even published.

This diploma gained the reputation of not being available to ordinary mortals. Only teachers who had already undergone an approved course of training in a training college and who had had at least three years of teaching experience, were accepted. An applicant also had to provide evidence of having undergone practical training in a nursery school for at least two terms, preferably three, and of having attended a children's hospital, or similar institution, for at least six weeks so that a candidate could recognise such signs of poor health as malnutrition, nasal catarrh, adenoids, enlarged tonsils, rickets, rheumatism and infections of the eyes, ears, teeth, skin and hair. Candidates also had to have had opportunities of observing the organisation and management of other nursery schools and classes before commencing the course.

The diploma was intended for those who were hoping to be employed as nursery superintendents. At the end of the course, candidates were examined in child psychology and hygiene, with special reference to the child over seven, in the history of the infant and nursery school movement and the planning and the organisation of nursery schools. A thesis on an approved topic to be suggested by the candidate had also to be submitted. These extended pieces of work had to deal with educational issues relating to the pre-school-age child. They could be either critical reviews of educational problems or accounts of educational experiments, or original work carried out by the candidate, but, of course, it had again to relate to the pre-school-age child. Candidates also had to produce a record book of relevant experiences observed in nursery schools and medical centres.[14]

The practical test took the form of supervising a group of children in an approved nursery school during a whole morning's session. One needs to compare this with the general practice of examining student teachers trained in colleges or institutes of education in the universities who were usually seen for one lesson by the examiners.

When the National Froebel Union printed their 'Regulations for the Award of the Nursery School Diploma', the introduction concluded by inviting 'suggestions for the improvement of the scheme from local authorities, teachers and others interested in the problems of the Nursery School'. Suggestions and criticisms were received, but they usually related to requests for making the course requirements less arduous, which the Society refused to do.

The first examinations for the Nursery School Diploma were held in 1932. By October 1936 fourteen candidates had entered for the examination, and of these eight had gained their diploma. Several hundreds of applicants had been refused admission to the examination on grounds of insufficient practical experience.[15]

The Froebel Society's offices were now also receiving an increasing number of requests for book lists and information on project work from teachers. In order to rationalise time spent on the dissemination of information it was decided to meet this need by way of issuing pamphlets on topics frequently under discussion. The writing and printing of pamphlets became an important activity of the Society. Pamphlets on how to use puppets as an educational aid and publications on project work like *The Chelsea and Harrods Store Project*, *The Zoo*, and *A Dramatic Project* based on the Old Testament seem to have been particularly popular. Two thousand copies of *Froebel's Letters* were also reprinted as a pamphlet in the early 1930s. In the meantime, *Child-Life*, the Society's quarterly publication was once again facing a difficult time. Miss Ostle, the retired Secretary of the Society, had accepted the editorship for one year because of lack of volunteers from within the Society. After the resignation of Miss Ostle, the Society succeeded in obtaining the services of Mrs Macfarlane, a former lecturer who had edited the Piers Ploughman Histories. After editing two numbers of *Child Life* quarterly, Mrs Macfarlane provided an editorial policy statement to the Council for discussion. In it she observed that as teachers and parents showed a certain lack of interest in the teachings of Froebel, several articles in consecutive issues examining Froebel's relationship to modern thought might be appropriate. In view of the findings of the Primary School Report, teachers were anxious for more information on methods in junior schools. Method articles should therefore be devoted to 'The

Beginnings of each School Subject'. To attract more parents to read the magazine might prove difficult, but articles on children's interests outside school and general articles on the theatre the cinema and modern books for children might help.[16] Most of these ideas were put into practice but in spite of a general recognition that the magazine had improved, financially it was still not paying its way.

In 1934 a special sub-committee was set up to consider whether the magazine should be combined with the Froebel Bulletin, a monthly information sheet compiled by the Secretary mainly for members in the provinces, and whether the policy of the magazine should be altered in such a way as to put the emphasis on the junior school, its methods and problems. The Council agreed to the amalgamation of the Froebel Bulletin with *Child Life* quarterly but was less in sympathy with the suggestion to change the emphasis of the magazine from nursery/infant to junior school education, equal weighting being preferred. From January 1935 onwards *Child Life* appeared monthly. A new editor, Mr Marriott, was appointed in October, 1935. Although his idea to deal with one leading subject in each issue was at first approved, it was eventually considered to be too limiting. By the end of the financial year, the magazine was still recording a deficit and members felt uneasy about the content which had 'become too popular in an undesirable sense of the word'.[17] It was therefore decided to edit the magazine from within the offices, giving the Council more direct control over its policy. The responsibility of the magazine would be shared by an Editorial Board which would consist of inspectors of schools, psychologists, teachers, parents and the medical profession. A panel of specialists would be consulted on occasion, especially as regards the arts and crafts and mathematics. All of it was to be reviewed again in a year's time, in the summer of 1938.[18]

The evening classes leading to the Teacher's Certificate received similar critical treatment. To understand the difficulties facing the Society one has to recall the reasons for the changing of the Certificate course over the years. For a long period the normal extent of the course of training for the Teacher's Certificate was two years and a term. The examination of the Certificate was in two parts. Part I being taken in July and Part II in the December of the following year. In 1924 the Governors of the National Froebel Union decided to extend the course of training to three years. Examinations now fell into three parts, one part to be taken at the end of each year. Part I, as usual, consisted of academic subjects e.g. English, mathematics, history, biology etc. Part II was now to include child hygiene, history of education and handwork, and Part III principles of education, organisation and method and class teaching. This arrangement came into force in 1926. The reason for placing handwork, history of education and child hygiene in Part II was based on lecturers' and students' anxiety to get some subjects out of the way at the end of the second year. There were no sound educational grounds for dismissing these subjects in the middle of a student's professional training. In 1933 members of the National Froebel Union came to the conclusion that 'professional subjects taken in the second and third years of the course should form an interconnected whole, and should be steadily pursued together during the two years.' The idea of getting a subject 'over and done with' at the end of the second year was uneducational and wrong.[19] It was therefore agreed that Part II and Part III should be merged into a new and inclusive Part II and the examination should be taken at the end of that period of training. The memorandum sent to the six colleges taking the Froebel Certificate, outlining the new scheme, stated that in the third-year examinations three papers on education should be offered and that they should include a) principles of education, b) history of educational ideas, c) method and organisation, d) theory of handwork, e) hygiene, and that these papers should include questions on subject matter to ensure that the academic subjects hitherto examined in the first year, formed an integral and continuous part of the whole training.[20]

While it was comparatively easy to obtain the co-operation of the six Froebel colleges, many of the other institutions running courses for the Froebel Certificate were spread far and wide and more difficult to reach. Froebel courses were provided in public secondary schools, private schools, colleges, university departments, at Moray House, Jordanhill and St George's in Scotland, at Leeds High School, Bangor University and at evening classes for trained teachers in Liverpool and London.

The London evening classes were held at the offices of the Froebel Society and staffed by its members. The Secretary of the Society organised the classes, arranged for lecturers to visit students in their classrooms twice a term and organised demonstration classes on Saturday mornings. Criticisms of these classes had been rumbling for some time and when the Chief Inspector of the National Froebel Union, Mr Raymont, was called in for advice, his report blamed the Froebel Society in general for the shortcomings. Not only were premises inadequate and classes overcrowded, but there was also lack of central and individual responsibility for the organisation of classes. He recommended the appointment of a Director of Studies. Within a year of filling the post, evening classes were running smoothly and examination results improved. There were usually between thirty-five and fifty students in Year I, twenty-five to thirty students in Year II and fifteen to twenty students in Year III.

In 1935 the Secretary of the Society reported that a large number of enquiries had been received from the provinces asking for means of training in Froebel methods for those who were already teaching. Apart from the evening classes in Liverpool, the only other means of study open to such enquirers was by means of correspondence. It was recommended that steps should be taken to establish evening classes where they seemed to be called for, using as a means either branches of the Society or the training colleges already recognised by the National Froebel Union. In the autumn of 1936 evening classes in preparation for the Teacher's Certificate of the National Froebel Union had been started in Sheffield. The Education Authorities in Leeds and Manchester gave the matter sympathetic consideration.[21]

The spreading of the demand for the Froebel Certificate also led to the formation of several new branches. Liverpool, Durham, Paignton and Southampton opened in 1931, Epsom in 1935, Carlisle in 1937 and Bedford re-affiliated in 1932. According to the Society's letter-heading, the following branches were in existence in 1938: Carlisle, Liverpool, Chesterfield, Middlesbrough, Newport, Sheffield, Durham, Epsom, South Derbyshire and District with affiliated societies in Bedford, Bolton, Bradford, Hull, Leeds and Southampton. Concern was expressed that no branches existed in Scotland, especially as in the Society's opinion 'infant schools there are in a very bad state'.[22] Though no branches are recorded as being in existence in Eire and Northern Ireland, Froebel Certificate Examinations were held in 1934 in Victoria College Belfast, the

Dominican Convent in Belfast, Belfast Training Classes and Alexandra College Dublin.[23] In 1932 Froebel Certificate courses were also held in Kenya and New Zealand.

In spite of recruiting over 200 new members in each of the three years between 1932 and 1935, membership never exceeded the thousand mark. Financially the Society survived only because of Claude Montefiore's generous gifts and because of yearly contributions of between £200-£400 from the National Froebel Union, though, no doubt, the National Froebel Union had no difficulties in feeling generous to its parent society at a time when its own reserve fund amounted to £20,000. Froebelians, like Froebel himself, had very little sense of the importance of money, especially when there were so many more important issues to be discussed and to be acted upon: issues like examinations, corporal punishment, how to educate training college lecturers, teachers' salaries and the criteria for the recognition of schools.

The question of the examination system by which children were selected for promotion and for scholarships seemed to be a recurring topic for discussion at Council Meetings. The Government Report of 1932 on examinations for sixteen and seventeen year-olds provided the inevitable pointer to look again at selection procedures at eleven. A special committee was set up to consider the matter and to invite participation from different educational organisations like the Preparatory Schools Association, London Teachers' Association, London Union of Teachers, Independent Schools Association, London Headteachers' Association, Child Guidance Clinic, New Education Fellowship and the Home and School Council.

A year after the formation of the Committee the Council received a pamphlet entitled *Examinations - Before and After*, but as a Royal Commission was dealing with examinations at the time, the Society could not accept the responsibility of publishing the pamphlet. It did however publish a *Symposium upon the Scholarship Examinations* in *Child Life* in summer 1933, where two headmistresses, a parent and a psychologist from the East London Child Guidance Clinic expressed their misgivings about the prevailing system.[24]

Child Life also carried articles on the harm done to children by corporal punishment and about the distinction one needs to draw between discipline and self-discipline, topics where Froebelians have always expressed an independent view based on their founder's belief in the dignity of man and the freedom of man's spirit. Obedience given in fear was palpably ugly and evil and to be avoided at all cost according to the President of the Society in his Annual General Meeting address in 1937. He believed that:

> ...discipline of a military pattern, while it may be a necessary evil, is none the less very evil indeed. To see a company of free creative men compelled through fear to move as automata on the command of another will, is to witness a degradation of mankind. ...the aim of us all, whether we are parents or teachers or prison governors, is to set our charges free of their facile disciplinability and to turn them into original, inquiring, restless and adventurous men. (*Child Life* 1932B:75)

It is not surprising therefore that educators who were constantly challenging generally accepted values should also express their misgivings about the way Empire Day was celebrated and the kind of thoughts it would implant in young children's minds and to question 'a system and an ideal' which tolerated 'men dressed in pink jackets hunting little living things'.[25] Froebel's idea that children must be free to develop according to their own gifts and abilities, to learn to think for themselves and act in accordance with their own conscience, did not leave any room for coercive discipline, thoughtless expressions of flag-waving or the killing of living things in the name of sport. In 1935 members of the Society reminded themselves once again of 'The first principles of the Society'. These principles were later published as a manifesto, which included the following main points:

1) That the educational policy of the Society should stand for the full and free self-development of the child up to the age of twelve years - this development to be directed in such a way as to encourage the child to think and act as an intelligent individual in the community in which he lives.

2) That the *whole* personality of the child should be developed largely by means of experience and activity and according to sound psychological principles.

3) That the content of the school curriculum should be determined by the needs of the whole child.

4) That it is more important to stimulate a desire to know and to provide the opportunity for satisfying that desire than simply to provide information and knowledge ready made.

5) That the educational principles which had proved successful in infant schools should now be applied to junior schools where the curriculum was in need of reform.

6) That it should be remembered that such education was laying foundations for future development and that results should not be expected at too early an age. (FS Minutes 1934:115)

Evening classes, monthly lectures and *Child Life* all contributed to upholding these principles among Froebelians, as did the continuation of the yearly summer schools. The organisers of the summer school together with members of Council were continually looking for ways in which the summer schools could be used to fill special needs of teachers. The summer school in 1930, for example, concentrated on project work (centres of interest) where the tools of the three Rs were constantly used to explore children's environments, their past, present and future. Going shopping, baking buns, laying tables, eating and washing up, visiting the theatre and acting parts of Shakespeare's plays, making wheat into flour, visiting the railway station and following its line on a map after walking along it for some distance, visiting museums and handling primitive tools and then reconstructing them, were all activities used to help children to experience the past, find joy in the present and hope in a predictable future. Taking account of members concern about the state of Scottish infant schools, the Society arranged its 1935 summer school in Edinburgh. Attempts to do the same for Eire failed because of lack of suitable accommodation. A compromise was reached by holding the 1937 summer school in Bangor, North Wales. This summer school was recognised by the Ministry of Education for both Eire and Northern Ireland, giving leave of absence to teachers attending and thus doubling the usual attendance of about one hundred teachers.[26]

The most unusual summer school was held in 1932. It concerned itself with the training of the trainers, and the question of how best to educate teachers in junior and infant schools and Kindergartens. Representatives from the Board of Education and the

Training College Association had been invited to provide speakers and observers. Fifty to sixty people were expected, nearly one hundred attended.[27] The Froebel Society was probably unique in concerning itself with the training of lecturers. While teachers of children were expected to train for two or three years, teachers of students in universities and colleges were not asked for any further qualifications. The desire for further training, however, did not come from the colleges or the universities, but from teachers who had been appointed lecturers. Miss Catty, one of the Society's Inspectors of Schools, had provided classes for the Trainer's Diploma in her own home for some time, but from 1934 onward the Society took over the responsibility for the course. The course was of an advanced nature and prepared candidates for the Trainer's Diploma of the National Froebel Union. It was intended for lecturers in training colleges who had had at least three months' experience working in a training college.[28] The course usually lasted fifteen months and provided a minimum of thirty meetings. In 1934 eight students attended, three of whom completed the course successfully.[29]

A most important event, as regards the Froebel Movement in England, took place in 1938 when the Froebel Society and the National Froebel Union amalgamated to form the National Froebel Foundation. The relationship between the Froebel Society and the National Froebel Union as regards finance and a closer alliance was discussed as early as 1935. The need for such a discussion had arisen in consequence of the increased subsidy allotted to the Froebel Society by the National Froebel Union. The Froebel Society had also approached the National Froebel Union with the request to consider sharing premises after the Society's move from Tavistock Square in November 1936. The Governors of the National Froebel Union however felt that the two bodies should not share premises in order to avoid confusion between those who did the teaching and the propaganda work and those involved in the examination of that work. The Governors were however prepared to consider closer co-operation between the two bodies.[30]

After further discussions, a year later, on 25 March 1936, the Governors of the National Froebel Foundation passed a resolution approving in principle the amalgamation of the two societies.[31] The purpose of such an amalgamation was financial but also educational. Members believed that more could be achieved with the same expenditure, while at the same time two Societies working for a common purpose were, no doubt, stronger working together than separately. The common purpose was defined as: 'the discovery and development of the ways in which the young child may come to the full strength of his potential manhood'.[32]

A special meeting of the Council of the Froebel Society was held on 17 December 1937, recommending the voluntary winding up of the Society to its members so that the amalgamation could proceed. This was agreed by members at their Special Meeting on 7 February 1938. The Board of Education approved the scheme on 8 August 1938 and the first meeting of the Governors of the newly formed National Froebel Foundation took place on 3 November 1938.[33]

The very first act of the newly formed Foundation was to record and express the very great loss experienced by the Governors at the death of Claude Montefiore. Even though the final seal had not been fixed to the documents before Dr Claude Montefiore died, he lived long enough to see the amalgamation of the two societies practically completed. As a young man in his twenties, Dr Montefiore had taken part in founding the National Froebel Union as an examining body, retaining for the Froebel Society, with which he had already identified himself, the propagandist part of the movement. In effect he had agreed that the Froebel Society should give up the remunerative business of examining and hand over that function to the newly formed National Froebel Union. In later years he regarded that transaction as one of the sad errors of his youth. He had been heard to refer to the Froebel Society as the poverty stricken mother of a wealthy and rather stand-offish daughter. No wonder that a few months before his death, when presenting the yearly report as Chairman of the Froebel Society for the last time, he appealed to members to continue and if possible to increase their support for the re-unification of the two Froebel Societies. This was the last meeting Dr Montefiore attended. He died, after a short illness, on 9 July 1938.

Claude Montefiore had been connected with the Froebel Movement since 1884. Elected to the Council of the Froebel Society, he became its Honorary Secretary in the same year and was made permanent Chairman in 1892, a post which he held for forty-six years. During his long association with the Froebel Society, both as Chairman and as its main source of inspiration, he gave unfailingly of his interest, encouragement and kindly advice, not to mention his constant and generous financial support.

The Froebel Institute, Training College for Teachers, had also benefited greatly from his generosity. He was one of the principle contributors to the fund launched in 1892 by Mrs Salis Schwabe for establishing in West Kensington a training centre and school based on the teaching of Froebel. Up till 1920 he served as Treasurer to the Institute and it was characteristic of the personal interest he took in all the workers with whom he was associated, that, every term, he would write a letter of gratitude to each member of the staff to accompany the salary cheque. It was said that his personal interest extended to the domestic staff and gardeners and never failed. He visited both school and college nearly every week.

But Claude Montefiore was also a great scholar. His particular service as a writer was to interpret Judaism as a religion, unfettered by its nationalism. His New Testament studies produced the outstanding book on *The Synoptic Gospels*. It had been said that no Jew has done more justice to the teaching of Jesus, from a Jewish standpoint, than Claude Montefiore.

There was much grief, but also gratitude for the privilege enjoyed by those who had associated with this great personality. The officers of the Froebel Society concluded their letter of condolences to his son, Mr Leonard Montefiore, by saying: - 'We salute him in his passing as a scholar, a philosopher and a leader, but we shall ever treasure in our hearts the memory of his gracious personality and the gladness which his friendship brought'[34]

Yet another great Froebelian had died only a few years previously. Elsie Murray, the former Vice Principal of Maria Grey College, member of the Council of the Froebel Society for thirty-four years, author of several books on the teaching of young children, died in 1932. She contributed many articles to *Child Life*, including the controversial essay 'Symmetrical Paper Folding and Symmetrical Work with the Gifts are a waste of time for both Students and Children', which appeared in the very first issue of the magazine in 1899. This was a most convincing document, which must have produced much indignation on the part of old Froebelians. In 1913 she went on study-leave to make herself thoroughly familiar with Montessori methods as taught and practised in Rome. Two years later, when Froebelianism was somewhat under a cloud and Dr Montessori occupied the stage, Elsie Murray produced her small but well researched study *Froebel as a Pioneer* in which she drew comparisons with leading experts of that time like James Ward and John Dewey and demonstrated Froebel's outstanding contribution to education in spite of his weaknesses which she was never afraid to face. It is interesting that after her careful study of Dr Montessori's methods, she scarcely finds room to refer to her in the book. The Council of the Froebel Society referred to Elsie Murray as 'one of the two or three outstanding Froebelian educationalists of her time'.[35] And the Governors of the National Froebel Union expressed their admiration and gratitude for 'her long and incessant labours in the cause she had at heart, her love for little children and her unique understanding of their ways and needs, her wide and beneficial influence upon the teachers of those children, and her clear vision of that which is essential in the doctrine of our master and founder, Friedrich Froebel, whose faithful though progressive disciple she remained to the end of her life'.[36]

The Society could ill afford these losses at a time when people in Europe were once again facing the possibility of another major war. Froebelians, with their belief in the goodness of man, fostering independent thinking in people and doubting the value of imposed discipline, must have felt such aberrations of the human mind particularly painful. They needed all the support and guidance from within their own group they could muster. How, for example, were they to respond to the war-games which children were increasingly enacting in school playgrounds? How were they to respond to the plight of the children in occupied Czechoslovakia? Was the Society right in appealing to its members, to its branches and to the Froebel training colleges to support the Czechoslovakian Children's Fund? How far could an educational organisation be involved in matters which at least in parts, were of a political nature? It seems that, as so often before, Froebelians made their decision on the rights and wrongs of the case rather than on any consideration of whether they might offend anybody because of the political issues involved. As early as December 1938, *Child Life* carried an article on the fate of Jewish children in Austria and Germany. The author not only describes the children's suffering in some detail, but also makes practical suggestions, encouraging individuals as well as schools to guarantee shelter to such a child for at least a year so that a British visa could then be secured for them.

But the crises also began to affect the children at home. Articles in the *Child Life* issues of 1938 provide the first glimpse of evacuating children from a London school. The account provides us with the atmosphere of an exciting school outing to distant hills and rushing streams. How quickly it was all to change.

1. NFU, 1932, p109
2. *Child Life*, 1933A, p12
3. FS Minutes, 1920, p429
4. ibid, 1934, p77
5. ibid, 1920, p425; ibid, 1934, p76
6. FSCM, 1936, p13

7. FS Minutes, 1934, p85
8. ibid, 1920, p424
9. ibid, 1934, p50
10. ibid, p110
11. Board of Education, 1933, XX
12. ibid, p140
13. ibid, p156
14. NFU, 1933A, p6
15. ibid, 1932, p46
16. FS Minutes, 1920, p470
17. ibid, 1934, p85
18. ibid, p109
19. NFU, 1932, p29
20. ibid, 1932, p35
21. FS Minutes, 1934, p86
22. ibid, 1920, p422
23. NFU, 1932, p69
24. FS Minutes, 1934, p63
25. *Child Life*, 1931A, p7
26. FS Minutes, 1934, p131
27. ibid, 1920, p435
28. NFU, 1932, p71
29. FS Minutes, 1934, p75
30. NFU, 1933, p33
31. FS Minutes, 1932, p134
32. NFU, 1933, p39
33. FS Minutes, 1934, p150
34. ibid, p160
35. ibid, 1920, p420
36. NFU, 1932, p8

'*The essential business of the school is not so much to teach and to communicate a variety and multiplicity of things, as it is to give prominence to the ever-living unity that is in all things.*' *Friedrich Froebel.*

Chapter 8
War And Educational Reconstruction

'...the nation has woken up to the deficiencies of its public educational system.'
The McNair Report, 1944

The war years imposed a considerable strain on the education services of the country. Many teachers had to leave their schools and serve in the Forces, thus increasing the numbers of children in each class to be taught by those left behind. Parental control of children was seriously affected by absent fathers and also by mothers going out to work. There was the disruption of ordinary life through air raids, the evacuation of schools and colleges and an increasing shortage of teaching space during the worst part of the bombing.

The evacuation of school children from London and other large cities considered to be the first targets of enemy air raids, had been well planned long before the scheme was set into operation during the first days of the war in September 1939. Although this was a most complex exercise, involving 750,000 children, it worked smoothly and successfully. The difficulties which subsequently arose were of a social nature rather than an educational one. Stories soon appeared in the press of lousy, dirty and badly behaved city children roaming the villages and destroying fruit trees, crops and gardens, stories of children who refused to get undressed before going to bed and others who preferred sleeping on the floor because that was the place where they usually spent the night. No doubt, there were children who were dirty and ill-fed, children who had not been introduced to the finer points of etiquette and children who never before in their lives had encountered apples on a tree ready for the picking. Yet it was also true that children from well-to-do homes with a high standard of living and behaviour found themselves in dirty and primitive surroundings with little sense of decency, though such stories are not so numerous. The scheme quite clearly had concentrated on fitting certain numbers of children into available classroom spaces rather than on considerations of placing children into homes compatible with their upbringing and backgrounds. This, however, had a most salutary effect on the nation. The public had, of course, known in a very general sense that large areas of poverty existed. But now, for the first time, several sections of the public experienced at first hand the effects of poverty on people and especially on children. Verminous children exhibiting low standards of behaviour and discipline 'so shocked the public conscience that there was a universal demand for a complete reform of the social services, and it was thought that it ought to begin with education'.[1]

The Government, quite clearly, was aware of the people's sentiments. In September 1941 the National Froebel Foundation received a 'Strictly Private' document published by the Board of Education entitled 'Education after the War' asking the Foundation for comments. Eager to gather views and facts from informed and interested parties, this 'confidential' document was so successfully leaked that it was widely discussed in the press, by the BBC and the Armed Forces. It produced an enormous amount of information some of which was eventually incorporated in the 1944 Education Act.

The education debate concerning a fairer deal for the children of the general public, also examined the effectiveness of teacher training. The outcome of this debate was enshrined in the McNair Report, also published in 1944. Here too the National Froebel Foundation was asked to give evidence and contributed a lengthy memorandum to both committees. Much of the evidence given in these papers and expanded orally by the National Froebel Foundation delegations became part of the 1944 Education Act and the McNair Report. At a time when the nation was involved in a struggle for survival, the Government found time to debate and introduce new legislation, at any rate in those areas which once again were considered of great importance, the social services and education. But before examining the details, one needs to look at the activities of the National Froebel Foundation during and immediately after the war. After all, the impact of events in the war also affected the work of the Foundation.

Most of the nursery schools had been evacuated by the summer of 1941. Nursery centres were now being established all over the country for evacuated children under five years of age. Local Authorities in reception areas were authorised to make provision for these centres at the expense of the Exchequer. The Child Welfare Council was willing to help people to prepare for emergency assistant posts in the nursery centres and anyone between the ages of eighteen and fifty-five could attend a short course of twelve weeks on child care which was being conducted by that body. This training was recognised by the Government as sufficient for assistant posts in nursery centres. The Froebel Foundation, however, was asked to provide names of teachers with experience who were considered suitable for the posts of organiser or superintendent.[2] In addition the Foundation, for the first time, approved a two-year teacher training course for students entering colleges in 1942, 1943 and 1944. The course was limited to forty-five students per year. Candidates had permission to return to college for a deferred third year in order to obtain the full certificate at any time within five years of demobilisation.[3]

The autumn term lectures in 1939 had to be cancelled as many teachers had left London. Some students were unable to complete their course of training for the Teacher's Certificate at a recognised institution and had to continue by private study. Survey work in history and geography initially started by students in Clapham had to be finished in Brighton because of the evacuation of London colleges. Bedford students doing survey work were no longer allowed to use maps or take photographs and Maria Grey Training College students who had been evacuated to Dudley were now being taught by two different sets of lecturers. An Emergency Committee, consisting of nine members was appointed to conduct the business of the Foundation in war time and all minute books and registers of the Foundation were taken to Bedford Froebel College for safe-keeping.[4]

The National Froebel Foundation Bulletins also reflected the problems of the times. There are articles on 'Psychiatric Treatment of Difficult Evacuees', 'Problems of the Social Background of Children', 'Studies of Froebelian Schools in War-Time', 'A Public School in Exile', and a report on 'Teaching soldiers to read', expressing concern about the number of illiterate men and women to be found in His Majesty's Forces and recording the efforts made to help. After the war, Froebel teachers were also involved in the teaching of reading to soldiers in the Army of Occupation in Germany. In 1944 the Foundation's activities included a week's lecture tour to the ATS, and the library was opened up to teachers who were then serving with the Allied Forces in England.[5] The realization of an acute teacher shortage after the war led to the creation of the one-year Emergency Training Courses. The first one started at Wall Hall Training College, Hertfordshire in 1944 and is extensively described by the Principal, Miss Balfern in Froebel Bulletin 41.

In May 1940 an informal meeting of a group of the younger members of the Froebel Foundation took place at 2 Manchester Square, the new headquarters of the Foundation since October 1939. The meeting had been called by two of the Governors to find out how one could harness the enthusiasm, creativity and intelligence of the 'group of outstanding personalities' who in the past had shown such an active interest in the work of the Foundation. Among those called were women who, after the war, played a decisive part in the shaping of educational thought in this country: personalities like Miss Atkinson, later Principal of St Gabriel's Training College, London, Miss Ault, Miss Baybrooks, Miss Bradley, later Vice Principal of Homerton College and subsequently Assistant Director of the Cambridge Institute of Education, Molly Brearley, later Principal of the Froebel Educational Institute, Roehampton, Miss Foster, Miss Gardner, later Reader in Child Development at the University of London Institute of Education, Miss Philips, later Principal of Shenston Training College, Miss Priestman, later Headteacher of an Independent School, Miss Sogno, later Principal Lecturer in Education, Miss Thornton, Dr Walters, later in charge of Teacher Training at the University of the West Indies, Miss Warr, later Headmistress of an Independent School, and Miss Whitwill, later Her Majesty's Inspector for Schools. They discussed the nature of educational meetings, lectures and evening classes, summer schools, the quality of contributions to the Bulletin, membership and how best to keep contact with affiliated societies. Their ideas, suggestions and recommendations greatly impressed the Governors so that they had no hesitation in agreeing to the proposal that these young people should form themselves into a Members Committee.

All through the war the Committee met on a regular basis, examined well-established practices and suggested improvements, produced pamphlets for parents and teachers, initiated changes in the syllabus of the Trainer's Diploma and organised several conferences, sometimes in conjunction with the New Education Fellowship, the Nursery School Association and the Association for Lecturers in Training Colleges and Departments of Education. If one considers that these young women were at the same time occupied with clubs and nurseries for evacuated children (many of whom had lost their parents in raids on London), with fire-watching at night and their normal jobs during the day, one begins to appreciate the quality of these people. In 1942 discussions took place on the 'policy which we as Froebelians are ready to support in regard to a common primary education'. The memo which resulted from these discussions was eventually presented to the Governors and shaped the Foundation's educational policy which later formed the basis for discussions with the Board of Education.[6]

The Members Committee also initiated the formation of branches of the Parents' Guild in other parts of the country. Originally created by the Foundation in London for the purpose of disseminating information about the upbringing of children, the Guild now concerned itself with the content of the White Paper going through Parliament. In order to be able to maintain an independent view, the Guild did not affiliate to the National Froebel Foundation nor any other association. Its independence was its strength and its weakness. It spread rapidly but did not survive for long.

The autumn term lectures, abandoned in 1939, were re-started in 1945. By popular demand, the Foundation initially concentrated on junior school issues in these lectures, but one year later was again catering for infant school teachers. The usefulness of these lectures can be measured by the attendance figures which rose from 150 for the first lecture to over 350 for lectures during the second year.[7]

Summer schools too ceased to operate during the war years, but once re-started attracted two to three hundred participants each year. The Members Committee, always concerned about Froebelians in the provinces, was instrumental in moving the venue of the summer school from the South to Sheffield in 1947 and to Scotland in 1949. Evening classes too were successfully opened up in the provinces and the 1948 Christmas vacation course in Derbyshire attracted an attendance of ninety teachers. Two-year part-time classes for qualified teachers leading to the Froebel Certificate were started in Bristol (1942), Essex and Manchester (1944), Middlesex and Birmingham (1947), and a full-time one-year Nursery Course at Homerton College, Cambridge (1942).

Some training colleges in Ireland were also providing courses leading to the Froebel Certificate which were examined by the National Froebel Foundation in London. The Alexander College in Dublin instituted a one-year Nursery School Course in 1943, which subsequently also counted as the first year of the Froebel three-year course. There were, however, serious misgivings about 'the defective work' done at the Victoria College in Belfast. Equally a request by the Dominican Convent in Dublin to be allowed to award Certificate A, as well as Certificate B (formerly called the Higher and Lower Certificate, see pp. 37 and 45), was refused on similar grounds. But standards improved quickly after Sister Simeon, a graduate who passed the one-year Froebel Certificate course, had taken charge of the training of students in 1948. This enabled the Governing Body of the Froebel Foundation to recognise the training department of the Dominican Convent as efficient and consequently able to provide courses leading to Certificate A.[8]

Approaches by the Colonial Office to help with the establishment of training colleges in the East African Territories (i.e. Kenya, Tanganyika [one part of modern Tanzania], Uganda, Zanzibar [also part of modern Tanzania]) and in West Africa on the Gold Coast (modern Ghana) involved the Foundation in exploratory work and the production of a detailed assessment of the situation in West Africa. Two Froebel

Colleges under the Foundation's supervision were established in Kenya in 1944, one for Europeans and one for Indians and the Government in Kenya laid down that in the new training centres for 'Native Women Teachers' students are to receive 'training in child-education from the beginning of the school career up to Standard III by Froebel methods'.[9] The Gold Coast asked for Froebel-trained school inspectors and the Froebel Foundation also supplied a governess for the young King of Iraq.

Work for the Trainer's Diploma continued throughout the war. The Governors expressed the hope of abolishing this external diploma after the war, believing that Government agencies would take over advanced courses of that kind. There were always sufficient numbers to warrant starting another course, but the number of teachers actually sitting for the examination was small and those passing each year could be counted on one hand. In those years it must have been easier to obtain a PhD than a Trainer's Diploma of the National Froebel Foundation.

	Number of students sitting for the Diploma:	Diplomas awarded.
1939	5	2
1940	3	1
1941	3	0
1942	2	2
1943	4	3
1944	4	2
1945	5	3
1946	8	0
1947	6	4
1948	5	0
1949	9	1
1950	18	3

The lack of success in obtaining the diploma was probably due to the wide-ranging demands made on teachers, rather than the grades of difficulties. Teachers had to attend Saturday morning lectures at Manchester Square for two to three years; give lectures to third-year students as well as take discussion groups in front of examiners and also teach a class of children in the presence of students and examiners. This was in addition to passing the usual written and oral examinations.

Ever since the amalgamation of the two Froebel Associations, the work to be done fell to the executive committees appointed by the Governors of the Foundation, even though the decision-making rested with the Emergency Committee. During the war the following committees continued to function:

The Finance Committee.
The Boards of Studies determining the courses to be followed by the students.
The Moderating Committee which oversaw the setting of examination papers.
The Editing Committee for National Froebel Foundation pamphlets and publications.
The Bulletin and Library Committee.
The Members' Committee. (The only Committee not appointed by the Governors.)

To most members, however, it was the Director and the Secretary who stood for the National Froebel Foundation. In 1927, on his retirement from the Wardenship of Goldsmith's College, Professor Raymont, who at that time was Chairman of the National Froebel Union, offered his services to act as its Director, i.e. to inspect the Colleges which trained for the National Froebel Union Certificates, and to be educational adviser to the Governing Body.[10] In 1935 Miss R.L. Monkhouse took over as educational adviser and in 1940 she was appointed Director to the National Froebel Foundation. It was during her term of office and at the beginning of the war that she suggested major changes to the curriculum of the six internal Froebel colleges. Miss Monkhouse's Committee's suggestions were considered by the individual colleges and at a representative conference of all six colleges. The conference emphasised three points in particular.

1) The need to preserve the special character of the Froebel Certificate with a stress on learning through practical investigation and experience as well as through books, and through the close study of children's needs and activities.
2) The importance of ensuring that all students at the completion of their training should have an adequate knowledge of the programme, curriculum, and activities of the different types of school in which young children are taught.
3) The need for keeping abreast of the recent developments in educational reform, both in the schools and in the colleges. It was felt that the present system and pressure of examination for the Certificate did not give sufficient opportunity to develop the special gifts and aptitudes of students. The colleges were strongly of the opinion that the number of examinations should be reduced, and that all students should be freed from the pressure of external examinations until the end of the second year.

The Conference then agreed an outline syllabus as follows:

First Year Work - Unexamined
An approach to the programme and curriculum of the nursery, infant and junior school based on the needs of children, to include a study of handwork, art, music, English, history, geography, arithmetic and nature study, as these subjects enter into children's interests and activities in school. The study to be closely related, as conditions permit, to the practice and observation of teaching. The handwork should be shown to include the provision for the 'play needs' of children and therefore the making and assembly of material and toys to challenge such play interests. (If a student's work was to fall below a certain standard, she should either be advised to discontinue the course, or repeat some or all of the first year's work.)

Second and Third Year Work
a) Professional Subjects:
The professional subjects to be examined by three papers relating to principles of education, method and organisation, and hygiene. Practice of teaching to be examined in the usual way. (The history of education to be kept in the curriculum as an unexamined subject.)

b) Special Subjects:

Three to be selected from the following list (a student taking an advanced course to select two subjects only):

a) Handwork including some art, or Art including some handwork.
b) Music
c) English literature
d) Geography
e) History
f) Mathematics
g) Nature study

Each College was to submit its own schemes and syllabuses as before to the National Froebel Foundation, but to keep within the general framework of these proposals.

When these proposals were put before the Board of Education in June 1940, the Board responded by saying that although it agreed with the general principles worked out in the scheme, it expressed reservations on two counts. The Board thought it important to avoid over-professionalisation of the course, which ought as a whole, to ensure, among other things, the continuity of the education of the students, independent of their immediate professional interest, and furthermore it could certainly not accept a scheme of reform which did not require the English language to be a compulsory subject for study and examination.[11]

After further consultation with the Board, English became one of the compulsory courses and students had to choose four of the special subject courses, instead of three, unless they took one subject at advanced level, in which case three subjects sufficed. Apart from these alterations, the scheme was implemented as proposed.

In the autumn of 1941 an informal meeting was held with the representatives of all the externally examined institutions in order to ascertain their wishes in regard to the revision of the course leading to the Teacher's Certificate. The conference agreed that the course as revised for the internal examination was also to be desired for their students.[12]

Within two years of implementing the new syllabus, requests were received from the colleges to reduce the special subject courses from four to three because of overloading. When the Governors put the new proposal to the Ministry, approval was granted on an experimental basis and made permanent three years later.

In 1946 the following colleges and training institutions were providing courses based on the new syllabus leading to the Froebel Certificate A:

Internal Colleges - 3 Year Course	Number of Students
Clapham & Streatham Hill Training College	149
Froebel Educational Institute	295
Maria Grey Training College	127
Rachel McMillan Training College	134
Bedford Training College	124

Internal College - 2 Year Course
Saffron Walden Training College   96

External Course - 3 Years
Convent of the Sacred Heart, London SW18   30
Coloma Training College, Croydon   39
Northfield School, Watford   5
Colston Primary School, Bristol   12
Westhill Training College, Birmingham   30
Jordan Hill Training College, Glasgow   9
Girls High School, Birkenhead   7
Moray House, Edinburgh   8
Victoria College, Belfast   43
Alexandra College, Dublin   31

Part-Time Classes for Qualified Teachers
Organised by:
National Froebel Foundation, London   36
Essex Education Committee   11
Manchester Education Committee   25
University of Durham, King's College   12
Bristol Education Committee   __12__
                                                      1235

Private Study, correspondence course
Number of students not known, but in 1946 twenty-two candidates entered the final examination.
Crescent College, Belfast   2
Dominican Convent, Dublin   2
Dartington Hall, Totnes   3
Qualified Teachers   9
Untrained Candidates   __6__
                                                       22

Of the untrained teachers, three studied through a correspondence course and three appear to have received no coaching whatsoever.[13]

There were other centres and colleges which the Foundation recognised and therefore by implication inspected, but which had not entered any candidates in 1946, such as the Aberdeen and Dundee Training College Centres. All the external training centres, except King's College, Newcastle, had their own school in which students did part of their practical training.[14]

In 1947 the Education Committee considered the future of Certificate B and agreed to recommend to the Governing Body that it should be abolished. It was argued that Certificate B lowered the whole standard of Froebel qualifications as it did not entitle the holder to Qualified Teacher status. Candidates taking Certificate B trained through private study, correspondence courses or through training centres which were not recognised by the Foundation. Students had no sure means of realizing what standards to achieve, especially in teaching method, nor could they obtain any effective help in reaching these standards. A great many of them failed in teaching and many were passed because examiners had not the heart to fail people who tried so hard, in such adverse circumstances. Candidates who were awarded Certificate B thought that once they had obtained a teaching qualification they were eligible to teach in all types of schools and considered themselves mislead when they found that they did not rank as qualified teachers. The Governing Body accepted the recommendation and no more Certificate Bs were awarded after 1953.

The Foundation's continued appraisal of its own different educational activities during the war years, especially the thorough revision of its teacher education programme, placed the Foundation in a most favourable position when, in response to popular pressure, the Government began to collect information in search of the ways and means to improve the educational system. The Board of Education's request to the National Froebel Foundation for comments on the pamphlet *Education after the War*, generally known as the 'Green Book', produced a ready response from the Governing Body of the Foundation. The memorandum which was drawn up embodying the main conclusions reached on that part of the 'Green Book' relating to the special interests of the Foundation covered teacher training, the education of children under eleven, nursery schools, refresher courses for teachers and religious education.

In the memorandum the Foundation welcomed the proposed extension of the Teacher Training Course to three years, as already carried out by all the Froebel Colleges, but criticised the indicated structure of the course which envisaged a break during the second year of training when students would be in schools. The Foundation insisted that the course had to be seen as a unified whole, consisting of interrelated theory and practice, where school practice under the supervision of College Staff was the pivot on which all the training turned. Their view of how this unity of training and practice should be achieved had been worked out by the six Froebel colleges in their new scheme of training recently approved by the Board of Education.

The second matter which was of serious interest to the Governors of the National Froebel Foundation was the education of children under eleven. The Governors considered that it was even more important to have small classes in infant and junior schools than those for children over eleven, and, generally, that primary education should be administered as far as amenities are concerned on at least as generous a scale as for children over this age. They proposed that nursery schools, Kindergartens and preparatory schools run for private profit be inspected and recognised if efficient.

As regards nursery schools, the Foundation strongly supported the Board's conclusions that it should be obligatory for Local Education Authorities to make provision for the 'physical and mental development' of children between the ages of two and five, but they argued that such provision should include the facilities for a full nursery school education, and not become a mere child-minding operation.

The Governors also approved the proposal for the provision of refresher courses for teachers. They pointed out that the Foundation already provided such courses by means of its diplomas and it was hoped that the Board would recognise these examinations and that a grant would be made available for teachers taking them.

On Religious Education, the memorandum stated that Froebelian principles of education are based on the recognition that the spiritual welfare of children is of paramount importance. From this it followed that an understanding of the significance of Religion in Education should form a vital part of the student's training as a teacher.

Finally, the Governors urged the appointment of a Royal Commission on education generally and asked for a special investigation into the training of teachers. Both recommendations were put into operation within three years. The deputation which presented the Memorandum to the Board of Education consisted of Dr Halliday, Chairman of the National Froebel Foundation, Mr Brooks, Treasurer, Professor Cavanagh, Miss Jebb, Principal of the Froebel Educational Institute, Miss Monkhouse, Director of the National Froebel Foundation, and Miss Spence, Principal of Bedford College.[15]

The most important provision of the 1944 Eduaction Act was that which established the principle of secondary education for all and which changed the old arrangement of 'elementary' and 'higher' education to a system which was to be 'organised in three progressive stages to be known as primary education, secondary education, and further education'.[16] It now became the responsibility of each Local Education Authority to provide sufficient schools for children of all ages, abilities and aptitudes and this time included children under the age of five years. For the first time in English education the provision of nursery schools and nursery classes was no longer an extravagant optional, but a recognised necessity for a successful public education system.

The Foundation also recommended in its memorandum of September 1941, the appointment of a committee to investigate all aspects of teacher training. Six months later a committee was set up under the chairmanship of Sir Arnold McNair with the task of investigating 'the present sources of supply and the methods of training teachers and youth leaders in the future' and in its report described how 'the nation as a whole has woken up to the deficiencies of its public educational system', and how it was demanding reform.[17] When the McNair Committee requested comments and observations from the National Froebel Foundation in this matter, members of the Foundation who had just spent three years of their time and energy looking at their own ways of training teachers, had little difficulty in forwarding a lengthy memorandum.

In the memorandum the Foundation expressed the hope that steps would be taken to raise the esteem of teachers by insisting on a recognised training and a professional qualification. It was argued that 'too many untrained teachers could still be found in the lower ranks and also at the top, as at Eton and other public schools'.[18] It was essential that the public should be convinced that training produced better teachers. There should also be ample opportunity for teachers to attend advanced courses and to obtain further qualifications, to be given sabbatical leave with pay and be encouraged to research into how children learn. Froebelians were acutely aware that too much teaching was based on tradition rather than on an understanding of how children acquire knowledge.

The memorandum also stated that it was unsound educational policy to have one type of basic training for all teachers, irrespective of the age of the children to be educated. There was no reason, however, why the teaching profession, though split functionally, should not be integrated socially and economically. Although the Foundation did not link a teacher's esteem with financial rewards in its submission to the McNair Committee, the Governing Body of the National Froebel Foundation quite clearly perceived a connection between the two. The National Froebel Foundation Employment Agency, for example, refused to negotiate residential teaching posts for schools which paid less than seventy pounds per annum in 1939.[19]

Once again Froebelians were insisting most strongly on a three-year course of training for teachers, especially for those intending to teach the younger children. They also advocated that all training be closely associated with work in school so that staff and students could respond to the needs of the community and the training be linked with the life of the people around them.

Many of the ideas expressed in the memorandum and given in evidence by the Froebel representatives, Dr Halliday, Miss E. Jebb and Miss Monkhouse, found a place in the McNair Report. Its recommendations included a three-year training course for students in all colleges, substantial increases in the payment of teachers, the abolition of different pay for teachers in 'elementary' and 'secondary' grades, the creation of a basic salary structure for all qualified teachers and the linking of colleges with universities in an attempt to improve the training of teachers and thus the standing of education in the eyes of the public. It was the latter, the re-organisation of the administration of the training institutions, as outlined in the McNair Report which had the greatest impact on the Froebel Colleges.

Teacher training colleges, education departments at universities and other training institutions were grouped into an Area Training Service, each with a focus on a university. To secure enlarged provision for educational research and the maintenance and diffusion of a high standard of knowledge of the subject of education, in both its theoretical and practical aspects, steps were taken to bring into existence a school of education within selected universities in which all the approved institutions for the training of teachers were included. All 'approved institutions' (e.g. Training colleges, including those associated with the National Froebel Foundation, university departments of education and colleges of physical education) were offered affiliation to a school of education on terms that would secure to them the same kind of independence within the school, and of participation in its work and government, as the colleges of the university enjoy within the university.

The Froebel colleges, which so far had been the only truly independent colleges in the country, being neither under the auspices of a particular religious denomination nor a local education authority, were anxious not to lose their freedom to determine their own way of training students. To maintain this kind of independence it was important to preserve the right of the National Froebel Foundation to continue the examination of the students in their own colleges. Discussions with the Ministry and London University led to a compromise similar to that reached by Westhill Training College, Selly Oak with the Birmingham Institute of Education, where the college appointed its own external examiners subject to the approval of the university. The latter appointed assessors, who were members of the staff of other colleges within the School of Education, with the approval of the Froebel College. Examination papers and sylla-buses had to be approved by both the colleges concerned and the university; in London, by the Froebel Foundation and London University Institute of Education. Some independence had to be sacrificed for the advantage of a Certificate which bore the stamp of the University and which made available to students a greater range of educational resources.[20]

The establishment of primary schools as recommended in the 1944 Education Act led to the closure of primary departments in secondary schools. Members of the Froebel Foundation were most concerned about this new development. In Leicester, for example, there were three junior departments attached to secondary schools to be closed, which catered for 750 children. How were these children to be re-housed? As new schools did not exist, old secondary schools, very often the oldest ones in town, were allocated to form the new primary schools. Space was at a premium and classes housed between forty and fifty children, numbers far above those tolerated in secondary education. The Froebelians argued that the youngest children needed the greatest attention and therefore the best pupil/teacher ratio. Putting larger classes into older and less well-equipped schools was a retrograde step. One also had to consider that allowing a child to stay in the same school from seven to eighteen years of age provided better opportunities for recording a child's progress and aptitudes. At least some teachers would know the child all through their school life. These children were now also losing the best use of specialist teaching at the junior level. Froebelians were very alarmed, but even a well briefed deputation to the Ministry could not change matters. However, it became clear that civil servants in the Ministry too were worried about the way the Local Education Authorities were implementing the new Education Act. Quite clearly money had to be made available for a huge building programme of primary and infant schools. The Foundation lost no time in putting forward its ideas about plans for primary school buildings and its first letter on the subject to the *Times Educational Supplement* was published in October 1945.

Schools for younger children were no longer to be seen as buildings where they received instructions and absorbed facts, but as an environment in which they could actively learn, grow and develop. Why should classrooms be severely rectangular, with not so much as a recess in which a child can read quietly or a group of children discuss a project? Why must windows be uncurtained and desks be the only furniture in the room? Mats to sit on, space to play in, areas for painting, corners for books, furniture for display, cupboards for storage and floor coverings to accommodate sand- and water-play heralded a new era in primary school buildings and thus in primary school education. Froebelians were once again in the forefront of educational change.[21]

1. Curtis & Boultwood, 1962, p196
2. NFF, 1938, p118
3. NFFGBM, 1942, p29
4. NFF, 1938, pp58-118
5. NFFGBM, 1942, p33
6. NFF, 1938, pp100-116; NFFGBM, 1942, pp25, 60
7. NFFGBM, 1942, pp62, 82
8. ibid, pp21-150
9. NFF, 1938, p128

10. NFF Bulletin, No.30
11. NFF, 1938, pp122-5
12. ibid, 140
13. NFFGBM, 1942, p83
14. ibid, p93
15. NFF, 1938, pp122-7
16. Education Act, 1944, p4
17. Lawson & Silver, 1973, p415
18. NFFGBM, 1942, p6
19. NFF Bulletin, March 1946
20. NFFGBM, 1942, pp95-157
21. ibid, 32-62

'Music, the soul and the support of our spiritual life, can also be the core and the pillar of our ordinary life.' Friedrich Froebel.

Chapter 9
Creative Activities are an Essential Part of Primary School Education

In order to understand the Creator Man must be in a position to create after him. Man must himself be a Creator. Friedrich Froebel

After enduring the deprivations of six years of war, the survivors were ready to face the future with confidence, ready to absorb and explore new ideas in commerce, industry and leisure. The Festival of Britain of 1951 provided the means for the expression of such sentiments and the National Froebel Foundation contributed its ideas of a better future by mounting an exhibition demonstrating progressive education as seen in some of the country's primary schools at the time.

Space being at a premium on the Festival site itself, the Foundation managed to obtain the co-operation of Professor Judges from King's College and was able to hire rooms in the college along the Strand, close to the Festival site. The Foundation exhibited in the Great Hall and in four rooms. An infant classroom and a junior classroom were each equipped ready for work with thirty children. The other two rooms were showing supplementary material for each age-range.

In the centre of the Great Hall a miscellaneous collection of barrels, boxes, old bench-type desks, motor tyres and ladders were to be found, each piece labelled with information as to source, price and usage, where this was not obvious. It was suggested that a play-ground equipped with this kind of improvised play material would offer a more challenging and satisfying recreation time than could the bleak asphalt yards still only too prevalent.

On one side of the hall was the nature section containing much home-made equipment for nature study - bird tables, pond dipping gear, weather recording apparatus, rain-gauges and the like as well as observations made by the children and recorded by means of words, drawings and charts. One corner of the hall was arranged as a book corner and, by thoughtful arrangement of display screens, the effect of an almost enclosed room was obtained in which books could be comfortably and quietly examined. Among them was a set of children's books from the National Book League together with a variety of reference books suitable for junior age libraries and pictures and story books for all ages from five to eleven. This corner of the exhibition was particularly valued by visitors from the country and overseas.

Finally there was a music section, demonstrating that musical experiences and knowledge grow from the earliest experiments with sound made in the nursery school, from playing with tins filled with a variety of substances, striking horse-shoes, rattling shakers made from milk tops threaded on wire, tapping half-coconuts made into drums and from noticing the differences in pitch made by differing lengths of metal tubing. Visitors found it exciting to see how principles they had readily applied to other sides of infant school work could be worked out in practice in music.

The four rooms, two of which were arranged like workshops rather than classrooms and the other two as additional rooms exhibiting work in the infant and junior age-range respectively, elicited a keen interest from visitors. Both classrooms and the additional rooms, showing work from a wide variety of schools, provided evidence that the opportunities for study of wider interests also produced high achievements in the basic subjects. 'Life was their oyster and the treasures they had found included drama and literature, contemporary events ranging in complexity from playing out domestic life situations such as tea-parties and shopping, to elementary studies in town planning and the Kon Tiki expedition. The exploration of the environment likewise ranged from experimental play with water, wood and plastic material to organised trips to visit farms, places of historical interest, factories and the like.'[1] Froebelians demonstrated more clearly than ever before that education is above all a creative process in which the learner is actively involved, a matter of 'drawing out rather than putting in' as Froebel once expressed it. At the end of the week two thousand visitors had passed through these rooms. Though it is not possible to estimate the influence of such an exhibition, its value lay in its being a clear statement of Froebelian educational philosophy in a concrete form.

The concept of the 'class' as being the only viable arrangement for teaching was being challenged. Open-plan schools where classrooms were replaced by work-areas became popular. Family-groupings, so successful during the war-years, especially in the Bristol area, where enlightened infant and primary school headteachers kept evacuee children of the same family in the same class irrespective of age, was another growing feature in the 1950s and 1960s. The advantages of such an arrangement, where older children cared for and taught their younger siblings, were so obvious that more and more schools stopped grouping by age alone.

The primary school time-table was also under scrutiny and the arrangement of short lesson periods was changed in favour of providing blocks of time which encouraged children to concentrate for longer periods and would enable them to complete the task in hand rather than to stop at the sound of a bell. The Froebelian notion of helping children to be 'creatively' active, in preference to work involving rote-learning, also took a strong hold of primary school work at that time. Creative writing, poetry, the arts and crafts, making music, dancing and drama were blossoming as never before.

By the mid-fifties, the effects of the 1944 Education Act had also become more and more noticeable. A considerable amount of money had now been spent on equipping existing schools with new books, teaching aids and physical education apparatus. An extensive building programme had created many new schools and improved old ones, and Burnham Scale salaried teachers were providing an enthusiastic workforce. But such improvements in the state sector affected private schools adversely. Parents, especially in the middle classes, who hitherto had sent their children to private pre-prep schools until children were eight and to the preparatory schools until their children could take the Common Entrance Examination, providing entry into the public school system, were now comparing the two systems and very often finding the private sector wanting.

Many private schools could no longer keep up with the favourable ways state schools were equipped, nor with paying Burnham Scale salaries to their staff. This was particularly true of private Kindergartens and pre-preparatory schools, many of them being Froebel schools. Even the one great advantage which private schools were able to offer, namely smaller classes, was not sufficient to reverse the trend. Some parents, however, were beginning to have misgivings about the misuse of 'Activity Methods', 'Projects' and 'Free Discipline'.[2] While 'Froebelian principles' had become the basis of the educational philosophy of many state schools[3] the Foundation did not find it easy to provide an effective training for teachers so that the principles behind 'Activity Methods' were known, rather than just the method by itself.

Froebel training colleges had always recognised that just as children learn best through their first-hand experiences students too had to be provided with time for experimentation and personal discovery in all aspects of the training college course, so that they could experience for themselves the principles behind 'Activity Methods'. Such maturation and growth takes time and the Froebel colleges' third year of training allowed for such experience and consolidation. This was still not true of the rest of the teacher training in the country where courses lasted for two years only. The negotiations of the National Froebel Foundation with the Ministry of Education and with the University of London Institute of Education regarding the place of the Froebel colleges in the national scheme was to some extent a battle for the retention of the three-year course.

The establishment of the Area Training Organisations, where training colleges had to affiliate to their nearest university for course-approval and the granting of Teacher Certificates, limited the National Froebel Foundation's right to speak on behalf of all Froebel training colleges. Westhill Training College, for example, negotiated directly with the Birmingham University Institute of Education and Saffron Walden with Cambridge. The Director of the London University Institute of Education however negotiated with the National Froebel Foundation in respect of students of the Froebel Educational Institute, Maria Grey Training College and Rachel McMillan Training College who were candidates for the award of the Teacher's Certificate of the University and who, in accordance with past practice, were also candidates for the award of the Teacher's Certificate of the National Froebel Foundation.[4] These new arrangements started with students entering the colleges in September 1950 and lasted until 1962. Amicable arrangements were worked out regarding the examination of students. The examination in practical teaching, for example, was very largely an internal affair for the colleges which assessed their students on a five-point scale. External examiners appointed by the Institute of Education adjusted or confirmed marks by sampling in order to achieve a degree of standardisation within the Institute as a whole. As the Institute of Education was prepared to accept the colleges' internal assessment marks without question, the National Froebel Foundation equally accepted the agreed mark reached by the internal and external examiners and in borderline cases, the external examiners' marks as final.

Yet, the Froebel colleges' three-year training courses created problems for students and thus ultimately for the colleges themselves because of the Ministry of Education's refusal to provide full grants to three-year students while there were empty places in the two-year colleges. Coloma Training College, for example, decided to discontinue training for the Froebel Certificate 'as the refusal of the Ministry to give grant-aided status to Coloma students as long as they continue with an initial three-year course has deprived the college of many promising students'.[5] Bedford Training College and Philippa Fawcett Training College awarded the last Froebel Certificates in 1953 for similar reasons, even though the Ministry and the Institutes of Education approved of the three-year course in principle for all teachers.

Froebelians were not the only ones who pressed for a three-year course of training for all teachers. The standard for the two-year teacher's certificate course had been under criticism from many quarters for several decades and in the 1920s and 1930s was frequently equated with the Higher School Certificate. Not surprisingly, the McNair Report recommended the addition of an extra year of study in 1944. But the increased demand for teachers in the post-war period delayed the introduction of the three-year course for another fifteen years. The Emergency Training Scheme which was introduced to meet this demand, could only do so by operating a reduced course of one year's duration while at the same time lowering the standard of its entrance qualifications, thus implementing a teacher training scheme which had all the features of that which McNair had tried to change. On the other hand, many of the ex-servicemen and women who took part in the scheme had worked in industry or commerce before going into the forces. Thus, they were able to meet one of the main criticisms of teacher training, namely that teachers, having gone from school to training college or university and back into school, had no experience of the outside world and therefore no real qualification for educating their pupils for a life teachers themselves had never known. Within six years the scheme had produced 35,000 teachers and by the middle of the 1950s it became clear that the shortage of teachers would be over by the early 1960s and so in 1957 the Ministry announced that students entering teacher training institutions from 1960 onward would have to take a three-year course.

Another Froebelian aim had been achieved, yet a victory it was not, for as soon as the three-year training course became universal, the Froebel Certificate was no longer awarded for basic training, even though, according to the National Froebel Foundation, 'the training of students would continue on the same lines as before'.[6] Between 1950 and 1960, the National Froebel Foundation awarded, on average five hundred Froebel Certificates per year.

The implementation of the 1944 Education Act also affected the work of the National Froebel Foundation as regards its policy decisions. Negotiation between London University's Institute of Education and the National Froebel Foundation in respect of syllabuses and examinations in the London Froebel colleges demanded the creation of a new committee. The Education Committee of the National Froebel Foundation which hitherto had advised the Governing Body on matters of general policy connected with all sides of the Foundation's work including the conduct of the examinations, courses of lectures, summer schools, publications and public relations was changed to the 'Standing Committee' and the 'Standing Sub-Committee for the London Colleges'. The former was still responsible for general policy formation while

the latter concerned itself with syllabuses, regulations, examinations and appointment of examiners for the London Colleges. In May 1952 the work of the Foundation was carried out by the following Committees:
1) The Examination Committee,
   a) The Moderating Committee
   b) The Awarding Committee
2) The Finance Committee
3) The Bulletin and Library Committee
4) The Members Committee
5) The Standing Committee
6) The Standing Sub-Committee for the London Colleges.

While the influence of the National Froebel Foundation on policy-making in the Froebel colleges at home was diminishing, its influence on the training of Froebel teachers in Eire was increasing. In March 1950, the Dominican Convent in Dublin which hitherto had been providing courses leading to the Froebel Certificate B, applied for permission to train students for the Froebel Certificate A. At the end of the two- day inspection in June, the four examiners recommended provisional recognition of the Dominican Convent as a training centre for Certificate A because of 'the need of sound training for the Catholic Teachers of young children in Eire and the Order's keen desire to satisfy this need and partly because the work in the department had in the last two years shown a measure of progress which held promise for future achievement'. The inspectors 'paid tribute to the work of Sister Simeon, who had given a new vitality to the teaching' and were much impressed by 'the happy tone of the whole department where the relationship between children, students and trainers was one of confidence and respect'.[7]

The inspectors' expectations were fulfilled and final recognition was granted when the new syllabus worked out between the National Froebel Foundation and the Dominican Convent at Sion Hill was introduced in 1953. The Alexander College also accepted the new syllabus, even though the Department of Education in Dublin still did not recognise the Froebel Certificate as a valid teaching qualification in Eire. The Department's main objection was the omission of the Irish language as a field of study in the Froebel Certificate. When the Dominican Convent wished to introduce Irish into the syllabus in 1952, no-one at London University could be found able to examine the subject.[8]

Recognition by the Department of Education in Dublin was not granted until 1959 and yet the Ministry in London accepted from the beginning the certificate as valid for teaching in the United Kingdom. The work of the Dominican Convent's Assumpta Training Centre was considered of such a high standard by the National Froebel Foundation that when Sister Simeon, the Principal, submitted schemes for the introduction of a one-year full-time course for graduates and a two-year part-time course for qualified teachers in 1960, the Foundation's approval was given without the imposition of major changes.

The training of Froebel students in Northern Ireland however came to an untimely end in 1956 when the Victoria College in Belfast closed its Froebel training department and proposals by the National Froebel Foundation to continue the course at Stranmillis were rejected by the Ministry of Education at Stormont because 'all students at Stranmillis must take one of the courses leading to the Ministry's Teacher's Certificate and must take the Ministry's Final Examination'.[9]

The enthusiasm of the young teachers of the Members' Committee continued to provide the impetus for the Foundation's publicity work by means of summer schools, courses for teachers, lectures and the printing of pamphlets. The Saffron Walden Summer School in 1950, with 'Learning through Activity and Experience' as the theme, was led by the Principal of Shenstone Training College with assistance from lecturers from Fishpond Training College, Saffron Walden Training College and Washington Hall Training College. Educating teachers by concentrating on 'Learning through Activity and Experience' was no longer the prerogative of the Froebel colleges. The Foundation was increasingly able to staff their summer schools from training colleges all over the country; but this did not mean that the Froebelian practices in schools were adequately supported by Froebelian philosophy. When the Members' Committee discussed the Edinburgh Summer School of 1951, they also considered the organisation of a course for head teachers and country organisers as 'it had been felt that sound teachers would find more encouragement in their work on modern progressive lines if they had the sympathetic understanding of the headteachers and this understanding was not always given'.[10]

The Moray House Summer School held in Edinburgh under the title 'The Education of Children in the Primary School' and attended by one hundred and forty-four teachers, was organised along lines which eventually provided a blue print for several summer schools to come. Morning sessions concentrated on the dissemination of knowledge about the characteristics, abilities and needs of primary school children. Molly Brearley, then a lecturer at Birmingham University, provided the main course of lectures for the two weeks on child development followed by work in small discussion groups. The afternoon was kept free for students' own choice and practical courses in nature study, mathematics, music, English, handwork and arts followed in the late afternoons and early evenings. Teachers, inspectors and lecturers attended from the UK, Australia, Jamaica, Trinidad, Canada, Nigeria, The Gold Coast, Malaysia, Mauritius and Eire.[11]

The summer school held at Matlock Training College in 1952 attracted only sixty-three teachers and in the following year the summer school had to be cancelled because there were not sufficient bookings to make the school viable. The competition with summer schools held by Local Education Authorities, Institutes of Education and the Ministry, many of which were financially subsidised, led to consideration of whether non-residential courses during term-time might not be a more feasible venture. Thus in 1954 three non-residential courses were arranged which attracted over two hundred and fifty applications so that each course had to be duplicated. Non-residential courses, weekend courses and day conferences became very popular and were usually over subscribed. Courses provided covered topics like reading, physical education, weaving, needlework, numeracy, backwardness, art and craft, music and aspects of Piagetian thinking. When the Foundation organised the first non-residential summer school in London, in 1956, many course members expressed preference for residential courses. From then onwards all summer schools met both requests, providing residential as well as non-residential places on courses. Attendance at the summer schools in Oxford

(1957), London (1958), Brighton (1959), and again in London (1960) averaged ninety participants a year.

Some of the lectures given at these conferences were reprinted in the Bulletin and others extended and produced as pamphlets. The selection of articles for the bulletin and for the pamphlets fell to the Bulletin and Library Committee which continued to meet four times a year, reviewing educational journals, books, film strips and submissions for publication. Between 1950-1960 the following pamphlets were published by the Foundation:

Allen, G. *Scientific Interests in the Primary School*
Ash, B. and B. Rapaport *The Junior School Today*
Brearley, M. *Number in the Primary School*
Brearley, M.   *Backwardness in Reading*
Hutchinson, M.M. *From Seed to Seed*
Isaacs, N. *Early Scientific Trends in Children*
Judges, V. *Freedom: Froebel's Vision and Our Reality*
Langdon, M.   *Active Methods of Learning for LargeClasses in the Junior School*
Lawrence, E. *Froebel and English Education*
Nelder, N. *Art in the Junior School*
Parr, D. *Music in the Primary School*
Priestman, O.B.   *Froebel Education Today*
Rapaport, B. (Ed.) *Aspects of Language*
Stone, H. *Some Playmaterials for Children Under Eight*
Walters, E. *Activity and Experience in the Infant School*
Walters, E. *Activity and Experience in the Junior School*

Works published on some aspects of Piaget's research
1) *Child's Conception of Number*
   a) *Summary* - E. Lawrence
   b) *The Teacher and Piaget's Work on Number* - T.R. Theakston
2) *The Wider Significance of Piaget's Work* - N. Isaacs.
3) *Piaget and Progressive Education* - N. Isaacs

Increasing competition from Local Education Authorities in the field of part-time classes and refresher courses, but above all the loss of fees for examinations which had been taken over by the Institutes had curtailed the Foundation's income considerably. The huge deficit of almost £2,000 in 1953 perturbed the Governors greatly. The Foundation's future was once again under review. Of course it was possible to raise the examination fees, if the Ministry approved, and increase membership fees, but these were all short-term measures. The real question which needed to be answered concerned the long-term future of the Foundation. Professor Judges pointed out that as more and more people in the country accepted progressive methods as the correct way of educating children, the Foundation would cease to be in the vanguard and within fifteen to twenty years its functions might have to come to an end, however much one might regret to see the disappearance of an educational body of such standing. Even the

Foundation's increasing work load in Dublin and the success of its publications and sale of pamphlets did not alter the situation fundamentally.

After submitting a memorandum to the Ministry, carefully setting out the activities and income of the Foundation and asking for permission to increase examination fees, representatives of the Foundation had an informal meeting with the Ministry. The Ministry's officers pointed out that the Foundation's examination fee was already twice that of the Institutes of Education and that the Ministry could not agree to subsidising from public funds a fee of fifteen guineas. It seemed to them that the only way of raising the necessary money was to add five guineas to first-year students' entrance fees which were paid by the students themselves and did not qualify for a grant, and thus did not involve Government money.

These increases together with the increases in membership and course fees improved the financial position but did little to clarify the Foundation's long-term prospects. These prospects became even more nebulous after the introduction of the three-year course for all students in the country. With the cessation of the Froebel Certificate for basic training Froebel Certificates were awarded only to graduates who took the one-year course at Maria Grey College, to qualified teachers who took a one-year course in Scotland, to students in Eire who had completed a three-year course of initial training and to qualified teachers who attended part-time classes in London, not all of whom came under the aegis of the Institutes of Education in England. The functions of the National Froebel Foundation were thus further reduced.

Members of the Foundation were now asking themselves whether there were new lines of educational work which they could undertake? The idea of an 'Advanced Froebel Teacher's Certificate' was discussed over a period of two years. It was to be a course for qualified teachers with at least five years teaching experience, of one year's duration and full-time. The course would consist, in addition to the theory and study of education, of some experimental work in practical teaching and some consideration of aspects of educational and staff administration. When in 1958 the Ministry of Education was approached about the possibilities of recognition for such a course, the Ministry's officers expressed the opinion that an Advanced Froebel Certificate would be rather superfluous having regard to the post-graduate and other courses then being offered by the Institutes of Education. The Ministry would certainly not be able to consider giving grants for such a course. The officers of the Ministry wished the Foundation well and hoped for the successful continuation of its activities. A further meeting with the Ministry in 1960 also elicited sympathetic concern for the Foundation's future, but there was nothing the Ministry could suggest in terms of practical help.

Was this going to be the end of a society which for three-quarters of a century had been spearheading the advancement of education, especially of primary school children? Its help and services had been available - and widely used - for the same good cause in the Commonwealth and other countries. The Froebel Certificate had acquired a prestige which was recognised by educational and appointing authorities in many different parts of the world. The Foundation now drew its membership from all over the world with members in Rhodesia (modern Zimbabwe), Nigeria, Natal (South Africa), Kenya, the Gold Coast (modern Ghana), Sierra Leone, Uganda, Nyasaland (modern Malawi), Argentina, Australia, Canada, Ceylon (modern Sri Lanka), China, Cyprus, Egypt, Eire, Germany, Holland, India, Iraq, Madagascar, Malaysia and

Singapore, New Zealand, Norway, Pakistan, Portugal, Sudan, Switzerland, Syria, Trinidad and the United States of America. And yet its usefulness seemed to be drawing to a close.[12]

This may well have been the case had it had not been for the appearance of Piaget's work dealing with the importance of a child's own action as a means for the establishment of intelligence. Because Piagetian research was providing scientific evidence of the correctness of much of Froebel's intuitive thinking as regards how children learn best, the Foundation explored, supported and disseminated Piagetian ideas earlier than probably any other single body in the United Kingdom. In the early and mid-fifties the National Froebel Foundation Bulletin published three articles by Dr Lawrence on Piaget's study of the 'Development of Children's Ideas of Number', followed by T.R.Theakston's and Nathan Isaacs' two articles on 'The Teacher and Piaget's: *The Child's Conception of Number*' and Nathan Isaacs': 'Piaget's Work and Progressive Education'.

In 1959 and 1960 one-day conferences were held for invited guests under the leadership of Dr Lawrence and Nathan Isaacs, discussing aspects of Piagetian thought. In October 1960 Piaget gave a lecture to the Froebel Foundation, at the end of which Nathan Isaacs was congratulated on his brilliant translation of the lecture. Three more articles were published in the Bulletin in 1960 and several pamphlets followed. Lecturers at the Froebel Educational Institute were particularly keen to structure their courses around Piaget's developmental ideas and it was not surprising that for a long time the Froebel Educational Institute became known as the 'Piaget Institute' among students and educators in London.[13.]

The concentration on Piaget's work put the Foundation once more in the forefront of educational thought. Membership, which had gone down during the early fifties, once more topped the thousand mark by 1959. Almost two thousand copies of the June Bulletin were printed and sold in the same year. There were 224 life members, 1,175 ordinary members and forty-one branches and affiliated societies. Financially too there was a real turn around. Deficits of up to two thousand pounds a year from 1949-1955 were changed in the late fifties into profits of one and a half thousand a year. It had been a difficult time, and yet, there was hope.[14]

1. NFFGBM, 1950, p53
2. NFF Bulletin, April 1956
3. ibid, June 1956
4. NFFGBM, 1950, p6
5. ibid, p68
6. ibid, p307
7. NFFIS, 1941, pp41-9
8. NFFGBM, 1950, p94
9. ibid, pp108, 115
10. NFFSSC, 1940, pp78-80
11. NFF Bulletin, October 1951
12. ibid, October 1954
13. NFFMCM, 1957, pp1-30
14. NFFGBM, 1950, pp197, 216, 300, 344

Story time at Grove House School in the 1930s.

Chapter 10
The Last Chapter of the Froebel Movement
may yet have to be Written

*The dogmatic and scholastic education of our time leads children to indolence
and laziness, a vast amount of humanpower thereby remains underdeveloped
and is lost.* Friedrich Froebel

Reading through the Froebel Movement's records which constitute the last chapter in
its one-hundred year history, one is struck by the members' uncompromising adherence
to Froebelian principles in the face of hardships and set-backs. It would have been easy
for the Froebel Foundation to provide in pamphlets and articles, and in summer schools
and weekend courses a popular interpretation of current educational issues. Instead we
find that every topic examined by members of the Foundation has the unmistakeable
stamp of educators who are concerned with the child as well as the subject, with the
child's total growth as well as his mastery of skills, with the worth of the individual as
well as the importance of the community. Here is but one example.

The first record we possess of Friedrich Froebel as a teacher describes his efforts
to explain the concept of erosion to three junior age children. We find him wading
through the village stream and, together with his three pupils, building a dam, forcing
the flow of the water around a sharp bend. Froebel's axioms that we learn best through
our own actions and that life itself, in the immediate environment, is the best schoolmaster are well illustrated by this example. Froebel-trained teachers will always try to
take nature and the child's direct environment as their starting point for learning,
irrespective of whether they are encouraging a child to weave a rug, make a pot, write
a poem, or observe in order to explain and predict. No wonder that Froebel Teachers
often held influential positions in the School-Nature-Study Union, frequently wrote
about environment studies' and published pamphlets on children's scientific interests
in the primary school long before they became national issues.[1]

When in the late fifties, the Soviet Union launched the first Sputnik into space,
politicians in the West, anxious not to be left behind in the space-race, began to examine
the teaching of science in schools. Here in England, it resulted, among other initiatives,
in the publication by the Ministry of 'Science in the Primary School' in 1961, followed
by the Nuffield Science Project. In March 1962, the National Froebel Foundation
arranged a symposium on 'Science in the Primary School' to which were invited a

number of professional bodies concerned with the teaching of science, science advisers from the Local Education Authorities and inspectors from the Ministry, teachers known to be doing interesting work in this field and representatives from industry. The discussions centred around the 'how and why' of science teaching rather than 'what' to impart. The account of the symposium was published by the National Froebel Foundation's Science Sub-Committee, which had its objective 'to encourage teachers to handle the introduction of science into the Primary School along educationally right lines'.[2] Between twenty and thirty teachers took part in a newly devised three-year project under the supervision of science advisers and with the support of the Foundation. Teachers submitted termly reports about their work which at the conclusion of the project were published as a pamphlet entitled: *Children Learning: Through Scientific Interests*.[3]

Throughout the project the Foundation held fast to the idea that science 'must not become another "subject" formally taught', but that 'the right approach at the Primary School level, is to start from children's own experiences that will arouse questions'; and then to help them to discover how to find their own answers. It was argued, that 'this approach follows from the Froebelian conception of education generally'. [4]

Clearly, it would have been much easier to ask the experts to produce a 'syllabus', a 'core-curriculum for science' and provide teachers with a blueprint of what to teach. Teachers who were following the Froebelian approach, were in a very real sense 'out on a limb'. They, like the children, had to experiment, improvise and discover the best ways of steering children's own active interests in the world around them into an appreciation both of what science is and how it comes into being. Friedrich Froebel even at the level of teaching the one year-old child, explains to mothers that 'only a creative mother (teacher) is able to encourage creativity in the child'. This dictum too, still held true for members of the Foundation in the last years of its existence.

It is possible to argue that the approaching demise of the Foundation was due, at least to some extent, to a rejection of these principles by the public on the grounds that only exceptionally gifted teachers, and exceptionally hard-working teachers could operate such a system. It is more likely, however, that, as many of Froebel's principles were now accepted in the educational world generally, the need for the continuation of the Foundation had diminished.

Finance, of course, also played an important part in this. Ever since the Government had increased teacher training courses from two to three years and had also taken away, via the area training organisation, the three-year Froebel Certificate courses, the Foundation had lost its main source of income, which came from registration and examination fees. A deficit of £100 in 1961 increased to a deficit of almost £2,000 in 1963. An appeal to the Ministry of Education in 1962, for a grant, was politely refused. Even though the Ministry appreciated that:

> The Foundation has made an important contribution towards the understanding of problems concerned with the education of young children, and has played a leading part in establishing standards in the education and training of teachers.... the Minister has reluctantly decided that he would not be justified in offering the Foundation financial assistance to maintain such services in being.

The letter concludes:

It is a matter of real regret that the Foundation's activities should now be curtailed through lack of funds. But there is surely also great cause for congratulation upon the success with which it has carried out its purposes. There must indeed be few institutions concerned with the education of young children today which do not owe something to the early pioneer work of the Foundation. The thanks of the Ministry are due to all who have, over the years, given so much of their time and energy to the Foundation's work. (NFF GBM 1961:26)

The Foundation's efforts to obtain grants from other educational societies and trusts were more successful. Apart from some smaller contributions from several sources, the Foundation received a yearly grant of £2,000 from the Godfrey Mitchell Trust between 1962-1967. It became clear that after 1967 the Foundation would be running at a minimum loss of about £2,000 a year. The Foundation could, however, draw on capital of about £18,000 and could therefore continue, if it were so decided, to run for up to nine more years, after 1967.[5]

The 1966 deficit of over £2,000, in spite of the Godfrey Mitchell Trust Grant, forced the Foundation to increase membership, course and examination fees as well as rents for lettings at Manchester Square. But even then, the deficit for 1967, the first year without any support from grants amounted to about £3,000. The library was no longer viable and therefore closed down in 1967. One hundred guineas were paid by the Froebel Institute College of Education in Roehampton for a special collection of Froebel books. Manchester College of Education took about 850 books for the sum of forty pounds and the remaining books were collected, free of charge, by the National Central Library. The large Georgian bookcase realized £200 through sale by auction. The contraction of the Foundation's activities had begun in earnest.

In addition to these financial difficulties, the Foundation was also faced with the problem of accommodation. The lease of 2 Manchester Square was to run out in 1977. It was thought that the work of the Foundation might continue until 1973 in its present premises. It would then appear that 1971 would be the last year for accepting students for Froebel training in Manchester, Scotland and Ireland. The transfer of examinations in Manchester and Scotland would present no difficulties. The Scottish examination would be taken over by the Scottish Education Department and the Manchester examinations by the Local Education Authority. Maria Assumpta in Dublin would have to consider alternative plans for the future. As the Irish Department of Education in Dublin was also moving towards a three-year training system, Maria Assumpta would probably become part of the State system.[6]

In the event, the move from Manchester Square took place earlier than planned. The Froebel Educational Institute in Roehampton had been approached about the availability of a room where the work involved with the *Froebel Journal*, the Trainer's Diploma, short courses and membership could be continued. The Froebel Educational Institute very generously offered two rooms at a low rent and by the autumn of 1971 the move from Manchester Square to Roehampton had been completed.

Because of pressure from Manchester, the Scottish Colleges and Dublin, the Foundation continued to take responsibility for examinations until 1975 for Manchester and the Scottish Colleges and until 1978 for students at Maria Assumpta in Dublin. The last edition of the *Froebel Journal* appeared in the Autumn 1974 and the final meeting of the Governors of the National Froebel Foundation took place on 10 November 1975.

These are the bare facts of the Foundation's last years, but they do not convey anything of the members' untiring efforts, until the very end, to work for the ideals so close to their hearts. The National Froebel Bulletin provides us with a comprehensive perspective of their efforts and the educational issues under consideration in these days.

The early sixties saw an impressive growth in membership and yet it became increasingly difficult to persuade members to contribute articles to the Bulletin. After extended discussions, the Committee decided to discontinue the two-monthly Bulletin and replace it by the one-termly *Froebel Journal* as from March 1965. The issues discussed, though always topical, never lost the Froebelian flavour.

The Foundation's three one-day conferences on Piaget's work, in the early sixties, led to articles on 'The Relation between Perceptual and Conceptual Development', 'Providing for Number Readiness in the Reception Class based on Piagetian Investigations', and discussions and conferences on children's thinking about their environment to articles on the teaching of science and the 'Finding Out' articles. In the mid-sixties members of the Governing Body were heavily involved with the evidence the Foundation was asked to give to the Plowden Committee, investigating primary education. The issues raised in the Plowden Report inevitably raised questions of teacher training and also the education of children with special needs. Articles followed on teacher training and the mentally handicapped, the maladjusted, educationally sub-normal and cerebral palsied children. The child as creator and the creative aspect of education featured large in several issues, including an article on 'The Discovery Methods of the Teaching of Reading'. It is significant too that the last but one issue of the Journal dealt at great length with 'An Individual Study of a Child'. 'All I know I have learned from the children', Froebel used to say. His followers too, until the very end, did not fail to make sure they were on the right lines, by carefully observing individual children as a means for formulating policy.[7]

Many of the topics discussed in the *Froebel Journal* were also dealt with in the pamphlets published by the Foundation. The sale of pamphlets rose considerably in the middle sixties and by the early seventies many titles had to be reprinted, especially those dealing with children's scientific interests, e.g. *Practical Nature Study in Town Schools, Children Learning Through Scientific Interests, Discovering Man's Habitat, Scientific Interest in the Primary School, Early Scientific Trends in Children.* The popularity of these articles reached well beyond the boundaries of local teachers and orders were received from colleges, schools and teachers abroad.[8]

Throughout the Foundation's existence, and of course also before 1938 when the Froebel Society and the National Froebel Union were still two separate bodies, the Froebel pamphlets, bulletins and journals provided the movement with the means to conduct a dialogue between teachers on the curriculum and function of the primary school, in stimulating research into children's ways of learning and in fostering educational experiments in the light of new knowledge.

Such dialogues, very often, had their beginnings in the summer schools organised by the Foundation. Themes like the following gave expression to the Froebelian notion of wholeness and unity in education:

'Learning and Living', Cambridge, 1961
'Children and the Arts', London, 1962
'Children Discovering Their World', Coventry, 1963
'The Enrichment of Learning', London, 1964
'Mathematics and Science and their setting in the Primary School', Chichester, 1965
'Learning through Discovery', London, 1966

Letters of appreciation sent to the Foundation after the completion of such courses often indicated how little emphasis was placed on the learning of facts but rather on the path of discovery which was followed and the attitudes which were formed on the way. This does not mean that the teaching of subjects and skills were neglected. Subjects like history, geography, poetry, arithmetic, reading and writing were covered in short-term and weekend courses. There were usually three courses per term, but by the early seventies they had shrunk to one or two courses per year. The last of these courses was held in 1973.

The sixties also witnessed a complete re-organisation of the two-year part-time course leading to the Froebel Teacher's Certificate. Up till then, the course catered for qualified teachers with a two-year basic training. Now, when three-year training had become universal, it seemed wise to try to extend the range of the course, to offer a suitable piece of further education to teachers with two- or three-year training and to graduates working in primary schools.

Such a change inevitably entailed some fundamental alterations in the content of the course and in the form of the examination. A course tutor was appointed to co-ordinate all the student's work. Art, craft and music ceased to be treated as special subjects and more weight was given to the whole of the primary school curriculum. The practice of meeting once a week for thirty weeks a year was discontinued and replaced by two or three weekend courses per term plus a full week's residential course per year. These longer periods of time were intended to give students the opportunity to follow a number of interests, including, among other topics, arts and crafts and music. Such a plan would enable all teachers to see the work of the rest of the group and to learn from each other. Throughout the course it was hoped that all the work undertaken by teachers would follow the same principles as those which can be applied to the education of children. In other words, they would learn as they hoped to teach.

After several years of planning, the course was started in April 1968 under the title 'The Froebel Advanced Certificate for Teachers'. The course was held in different centres, all centres offering different opportunities and facilities for one term in each year.

Miss Murton, who had become the Foundation's Organising Director in 1963, was largely responsible for the re-structuring of the two-year part-time course. She applied the same rigour of re-examining the course structure, to the Trainer's Diploma. As a former Chief Inspector for Primary Education in the Ministry of Education, she was well aware of the value of the Trainer's Diploma to the country. In one of the first meetings of the Governing Body which she attended, she remarked that without this particular course it would have been very hard to staff the extra education courses during the period of expansion of training colleges throughout the land. She had looked at the register of this diploma and was interested to see that it contained the names of some of the most distinguished teachers and training college lecturers in the country.[9]

But it would be wrong to give the impression that towards the end, the Foundation's work was mostly done by the Organising Director. As always, the Foundation drew its strength from a great variety of people, working as a team. The successful continuation of the Trainer's Diploma, in the sixties, for example, was largely due to the efforts of women like Molly Brearley, Honor Southam, Elizabeth Hitchfield, Joan Tamburrini, Jean Johnson and Chris Athey, who so generously gave of their time on Saturday mornings with enthusiasm and for little financial reward. There were also Miss Nightingall, the Secretary who had been with the Foundation since 1940 and retired in 1963; Dame Joyce Bishop who was elected Chairman of the Governing Body in 1964 after the retirement of Eglantyne Mary Jebb; Nathan Isaacs, one of the Governors who contributed so much to the Foundation's work by his brilliant intellect which he brought to bear on the problem of children's thinking with which Froebel teachers were forever wrestling. And there was the little known Jewish refugee from Germany, Dr Ingeborg Gurland who served on several committees and who contributed one of the first articles on Piagetian theory as observed in children's play; a classic, used extensively by lecturers and students in the sixties and seventies to illuminate difficult theory in terms of children's behaviour. Miss Faithfull, Dr Howarth, Dr Evelyn Lawrence, Barbara Rapaport and Beryl Ash all distinguished themselves by their unfailing support for the Foundation's work. These pioneers were not only to be found in London. Miss Bradley, from Bedford contributed greatly to the work of the Members' Committee and Froebelians in the branches in Birmingham, Bolton, Liverpool, Manchester, Sheffield and the North East (Newcastle and Durham), were active until the Foundation ceased to function in the mid-seventies.

The history of the Froebel College at Sion Hill in Dublin cannot be told without reference to Sister Simeon, Sister Jude and Sister Marian. The Dominican School, Ballyfermot, in Dublin, with 4,000 pupils was the largest primary school in Europe at the time (1958), and offered excellent opportunities for Froebel students to demonstrate that Froebelian principles can also be applied in overcrowded and poorly equipped classrooms. The then Principal of the Froebel College, Sister Simeon, considered it a 'grand challenge' and the Principal of the Infant Department at Ballyfermot, Sister Jude, looked at 'those students as pioneers who began to spearhead the way towards a more abundant life for the children in Ireland. They began, indeed, to inject into the national system, in an unofficial way, the "new ideas" which would be officially recognised in our schools within a little more than a decade'.[10] In 1971, the Irish Department of Education published *CURACLAM BUNSCOILE*, two fully illustrated volumes which incorporated Froebelian principles in a positive and practical way.

The training of teachers in Ireland for the Froebel Certificate had really started in the Alexandra College in Dublin in 1918 and continued without a break until the re-organisation of the training of teachers in Ireland closed the College in 1970. The Froebel College in Sion Hill, though a much smaller college, survived the re-organisation and has continued the training of teachers for primary schools until the present, even though students are no longer given the Froebel Certificate. A two-year part-time course leading to the In-Service Froebel Teacher's Certificate is still in operation. The Certificate is no longer under-written by the Froebel Foundation, yet one of its former examiners still gives help and advice and carries out the examinations. Such is the high esteem of this particular course with the Irish Department of Education that it offers teachers an extra increment on the successful completion of the course. The credit for ensuring that the College's work was accepted and integrated into the state system belongs to Sister Marian and the credit for the successful continuation of the work to Sister Maura, both enthusiastic champions of Froebelian principles.

The sixties also witnessed an upsurge of Froebel courses in Manchester and some of the Scottish colleges. The Local Education Authority in Manchester was actively encouraging the Froebel Certificate by paying the salary of the staff of those who were running the courses. The two-year part-time course was so successful that eventually two courses were running side by side. A Trainer's Diploma Course was also in action.[11]

In the early sixties three new colleges of education were established at Ayr, Falkirk and Hamilton and these colleges together with Notre Dame in Glasgow began to develop Froebel courses, so that by the end of the decade the number of candidates for the Froebel Certificate had been doubled. Sir Henry Wood, the former Principal of Jordan Hill College of Education believed that Scotland gained from these courses in four significant ways:

1) Two to three thousand teachers trained in the Scottish tradition of class teaching had opportunities to understand and practise another concept of the teaching process and to appreciate more fully than ever before the importance of self-directed activity, the value of Music, Art and Craft to the young child and the application of theory to the real world of the school.

2) Administrators concerned with teacher training had opportunities to recognise the value of courses conducted in small groups by experienced tutors who were not only very gifted teachers but who could also relate theory and practice to an extent not realised on any other course in the training system.

3) Staff of Colleges had opportunities to appreciate the value of External Examiners - not only as a means of achieving and maintaining high standards but as a source of advice and encouragement....

4) The expansion of Froebel training meant an inevitable extension of the teaching practice.... This, and the contribution of the Froebel members of the Committees which produced 'Primary Education in Scotland' and 'Before Five'.... has undoubtedly helped to change the situation in Scottish Primary Schools. (*Froebel Journal* Autumn 1974)

In England too the change brought about in the field of primary education in the sixties and seventies were monumental. Froebel teachers in a struggle lasting a century had paved the way. Many of their ideas and much of their philosophy became eventually enshrined in the Plowden Report of which Molly Brearley, the then Principal of the Froebel Educational Institute, was a member, and to which she made a substantial contribution.

The committee's report 'Children and their Primary Schools' published in 1967, endorsed progressive methods which had already spread to many of the country's primary schools. The committee based its recommendations on the most recent research into child development and welcomed 'the trend towards individual learning' and the 'unstreaming in the infant school ... [hoping] that it will continue to spread through the age groups of the Junior School'.[12] It encouraged 'learning by discovery' which 'in a number of ways resembled the best modern university practice' and condemned the widespread notion that the teaching of the Arts is a 'frill' rather than 'a fundamental and indispensable part' of children's education.[13]

For the first time in educational thinking the idea was expressed that 'equal opportunity in education' means an unequal distribution of resources in favour of the children of the poor. The Plowden Committee which had been asked to consider primary education in all its aspects, was faced with plenty of evidence that the least well-equipped schools were to be found in the poorest areas of the country. The children who lived in the slums, also attended the oldest and most decrepit schools. Not surprisingly, these schools also did not attract sufficient teachers so that understaffing was also acute in these areas. It was a vicious circle of deprivation which was bound to affect a child's educational chances. J.W.B. Douglas' book *The Home and the School*, published in 1964 which was based on a research project involving 5,000 babies born in 1946 who had been followed throughout their childhood and adolescence, also provided convincing evidence that even a well intended 'equal opportunity' scheme did not eliminate the wastage of educational potential among the children of the poor.

To break this chain of injustice inherent in our society, the committee elaborated criteria by which certain areas could be identified as being in need of a greater share of the available resources and designated them 'Educational Priority Areas'. Schools in such areas would be entitled to additional teachers so as to improve the pupil-teacher ratio and they would be able to claim a greater share of educational equipment and receive preferential treatment in the nation's school building programme.

Knowing how much parents' attitudes influenced children's educational achievements, the committee recommended a much closer co-operation between parents and teachers and encouraged the participation of parents in school activities. Parents were to be made welcome in schools and not just tolerated.

The committee's definition of a good primary school is given in paragraph 505 of the report. Comparing the aims and objectives of such a school as expressed in this paragraph with those given in evidence by the National Froebel Foundation, one is struck by its many similarities. Paragraph 505 of the Plowden Report reads:

> A school is not merely a teaching shop, it must transmit values and attitudes. It is a community in which children learn to live first and foremost as children and not as future adults. In family life children learn to live with people of all ages. The school sets out deliberately to devise the right environment for children, to allow them to be themselves and to develop in the way and at the pace appropriate to them. It tries to equalise opportunities and to compensate for handicaps. It lays special stress on individual discovery, on first hand experience and on opportunities for creative work. It insists that knowledge does not fall into neatly separate compartments and that work and play are not opposite but complementary. A child brought up in such an atmosphere at all stages of his education has some hope of becoming a balanced and mature adult and of being able to live in, to contribute to, and to look critically at the society of which he forms a part. Not all primary schools correspond to this picture, but it does represent a general and quickening trend.

How often had Froebel and his disciples maintained that a good school provides each child with the means to complete successfully the stage of development in which he finds himself rather than the means to prepare him for the stage to come. How often had Froebel and his disciples insisted that children can develop at their own pace, through their own creative activities and first-hand experiences. How often had Froebel and his disciples proclaimed that it is the child's own interests which determine the focus of his learning, rather than a compartmentalised syllabus imposed from without. How often had Froebel and his disciples suggested that only children who had been given opportunities for creative work and lateral thinking, for working with others, for choice, for making judgements would eventually develop into adults capable of critically assessing and, if found wanting, changing the society in which we live. Now it was all contained in one paragraph of the Plowden Report. How similar this paragraph is to part of the evidence given to the committee by the National Froebel Foundation, which reads:

> The aim of Primary Education should be to give children the experience of delight in learning and of success in working with others so that they can go forward with confidence to the next stage of education. This aim involves the cultivation of each child's potentiality both for feeling and thinking, the provision of an environment in which full development can be achieved and the acquisition of relevant skills which enable a child to tackle new situations and to feel at home in his own world. Equally important will be the cultivation of curiosity, imagination and inventiveness through individual and group work interests enabling the child to understand more and more of a widening range of things, people, feelings and ideas. It follows that in a good primary school the children are actively involved in learning rather than passively accepting the instruction of a teacher, however able. (*Froebel Journal* March 1965)

The product of such an education is more likely to grow into a person able to think for himself, to make up his own mind and act accordingly than somebody brought up to 'accept instructions'. Such people may not always be to the liking of those in power. The Prussian Government, for example, considered such education too subversive and its Kindergarten Verbot of 1851 closed all Froebel schools within its borders. More recently, efforts by governments to use education to impose the kind of citizenship it desires are aimed at the control of the curriculum. To make sure that teachers are carrying out their duties, regular testing of pupils becomes part of such a scheme.

Froebelians have always seen learning as a series of creative acts in which subject and object, the known and the unknown are linked in such a way as to produce the breathless moment of discovery. To them, each act of learning is unique and one more step towards the enlargement and growth of the total person. And because such learning is an activity carried out by each person individually, it needs the appreciation, by the teacher, of the individual learner's freedom to explore, to observe, to reflect. As each learner has to do this at his own speed and in his own time, an educational philosophy which expects children to absorb the same material, at the same speed at the same time, does not fit into an education as envisaged by Friedrich Froebel. His followers have achieved much in these hundred years. Schools have become more interesting places, children are happier pupils, teachers better educated and qualified for the job. Unless they remain vigilant, much may get lost again. The last chapter of the Froebel Movement may yet have to be written.

1. NFF Bulletin, August 1962
2. NFFGBM, 1961
3. ibid, p114
4. *Froebel Journal*, March 1965
5. NFFEFC, 1958, A77
6. NFFEFC, 1958, p131
7. *Froebel Journal*, March 1965-Summer 1974
8. NFFEFC, 1958, p149
9. NFFGBM, 1961, pp98, 101
10. *Froebel Journal*, Summer 1974
11. NFFGBM, 1961, p142
12. Board of Education, 1967, pp96, 100
13. ibid, pp669, 681

Bibliography

Manuscript sources
Froebel publications

Child Life

Vol.I No.3 (15.7.1899)	No.152 (Autumn 1930)
Vol.II No.5 (15.1.1900)	No.153 (Spring 1931)
Vol.II No.6 (1900A)	No.154 (Summer 1931)
Vol.V No.18 (April 1903)	No.156 (Spring 1932)
No.25 (January 1905)	No.158 (Autumn 1932)
No.26 (April 1905)	No.159 (Spring 1933)
No.35 (July 1907)	No.159 (New Series)
No.36 (October 1907)	(Summer1933)
No.45 (January 1909)	(No Number)(August 1938)
No.136 (March 1926)	(No Number)(October 1938)
No.142 (Spring 1928)	(No Number)(November 1938)
No.151 (Summer 1930)	(No Number)(December 1938)

Froebel Society Minutes

I	1874-1876	VI	1892-1895
II	1876-1882	VII	1896-1898
III	1882-1887	VIII	1898-1903
IV	1887-1889	IX	1904-1907
V	1889-1891		

Froebel Society Council Minutes

X 1907-1920
XI 1920-1934
XII 1934-1938

National Froebel Foundation Board Minutes 1938

Froebel Society Committee Minutes
1 1906-1920
2 1920-1929

Froebel Society Executive Committee Minutes 1936-1938

General Purpose Committee Minutes 1892-1906

National Froebel Foundation Bulletin (NFF Bulletin)

(Nov 1944) No.30	(June 1956) No.100
(March 1946) No.38	(February 1958) No.110
(Oct 1950) No.66	(June 1961) No.130
(Oct 1951) No.72	(April 1962) No.135
(Oct 1954) No.90	(Aug 1962) No.137
(April 1956) No.99	(December 1962) No.139

Froebel Journal   March 1965-Autumn 1974

National Froebel Foundation Executive & Finance Committee (NFFEFC 1958) 1958-1971

National Froebel Foundation Governing Body Minutes (NFFGBM)
>   (1942)   1942-1950
>   (1950)   1950-1961
>   (1961)   1961-1972

National Froebel Foundation, Inspection of Schools (NFFIS1941) 1941

National Froebel Foundation Members Committee Minutes (NFFMCM)
>   (1940)   1940-1949
>   (1949)   1949-1956
>   (1957)   1957-1965

National Froebel Foundation Summer School Committee Minutes (NFFSSC 1940) 1940

NFU (1887)   Joint Board Minutes 1887-1890
>   (1890)   1890-1895
>   (1895)   1895-1902

NFU (1907)   National Froebel Union Minutes Book 1907-1911
>   (1911)   1911-1920

NFU (1906)   National Froebel Union Committee Book 1906-1913
>   (1913)   1913-1924
>   (1932)   1932
>   (1933)   1933

NFU (1900)   Syllabus and Examination Papers

NFU (1933A) Regulations for the Award of the Nursery Diploma 1933

TD   (1914)   Trainer's Diploma 1914

Books

Armytage, W.H.G.	*Four Hundred Years of English Education* Cambridge: Cambridge University Press, 1970
Arnold, M.	*Reports on Elementary Schools 1852-1882* London: HMSO, 1908
Birchenough, C.	*History of Elementary Education in England and Wales* London: University Tutorial Press Ltd, 1938
Board of Education	*The Education of the Adolescent* London; HMSO, 1926
Board of Education	*Report of the Consultative Committee on the Primary School* London: HMSO, 1931
Board of Education	*Report of the Consultative Committee on Infant and Nursery Schools* London: HMSO, 1933
Board of Education	*Education Act 1944* London: HMSO, 1944
Board of Education	*Children and their Primary Schools* London: HMSO, 1967
Borer, M.C.	*Willingly to School, A History of Women's Education* London: The Lutterworth Press, 1976
Bradbury, J.L.	*Chester College and the Training of Teachers 1839-1975* Chester: Chester College, 1975
Burnett, J.	*Destiny Obscure* London: Allen Lane, 1982
Castle, E.B.	*The Teacher* Oxford: Oxford University Press, 1970
Curtis, S.J. & M.E.A. Boultwood	*An Introductory History of English Education since 1800* London: Universal Tutorial Press, 1962
Ellsworth, E.W.	*Liberators of the Female Mind, The Shirreff Sisters* Westport, Connecticut: Greenwood Press, 1979
Finlay-Johnson, H.	*The Dramatic Method of Teaching* London: James Nisbet, nd
Final Report	*Final Report of the School Board for London 1870-1904* London: King and Son, 1904
Froebel, F.	Manuscript: Kasten I Mappe 7 Folio 24 Berlin: Deutsche Akademie der Wissenschaften, ms
Froebel, F.	Manuscript: Kasten 18 Mappe 4 Folio 7 Berlin: Deutsche Akademie der Wissenschaften, ms
Gordon, P. and J. White	*Philosophers as Educational Reformers* London: Routledge & Kegan Paul, 1979
Gosden, P.H.J.H.	*Friedrich Froebel, Die Entwicklung seiner Erziehungsidee* Eisenach: Verlag von J.Bachmeister, 1875
Healey, E.	*Wives of Fame* London: Hodder and Stoughton, 1986
Heerwart, E.	*Funfzig Jahre im Dienste Froebels* Eisenach: Hofbuchdruckerei Kahle, nd
Holmes, E.	*What is and what might be* London: Constable, 1911
Holmes, G.	*The Idiot Teacher* London: Faber and Faber, 1952
Hyndman, M.	*Schools and Schooling in England and Wales* London: Harper and Row, 1978
Lange, W.	*Friedrich Froebel's Gesammelte Schriften, Band I* Osnabruck: Biblio Verlag, 1966
Lawrence, E. (Ed)	*Friedrich Froebel and English Education* New York: Philosophical Library, 1953
Lawson, J. & H. Silver	*A Social History of Education in England* London: Methuen, 1973
Maclure, J.S.	*Educational Documents, England and Wales 1816-1968* London: Methuen Educational Ltd, 1965
Mause, L. de (Ed)	*The History of Childhood* Norwich: Fletcher and Son, 1976

McGregor, G.P.	*Bishop Otter College and Policy for Teacher Education 1839-1980* London: Pembridge Press, 1981
Montessori, M.	*The Montessori Method* London: Heinemann, 1915
Murray, E.R.	*A Story of Infant Schools and Kindergartens* London: Sir Isaac Pitman and Sons Ltd, nd
Owen, G. & H. Ward	*Froebel Educational Institute Demonstration School. Report of an Inspection* No Publisher, 1927
Peterson, A.D.C.	*A Hundred Years of Education* London: Duckworth, 1971
Raymont, T.	*A History of the Education of Young Children* London: Longmans, 1937
Rich, R.W.	*The Training of Teachers in England and Wales during the Nineteenth Century* Bath: Cefric Chives, 1972
Robottom, J.	*A Social and Economic History of Industrial Britain* London: Longmans, 1986
Smith, F.	*A History of English Elementary Education 1760-1902* London: University of London Press, 1931
Ternent, A.T.	'Ahead of Her Time,' Unpublished thesis submitted for the Teacher's Certificate, University of Southampton, 1971
Van der Eyken, W.	*Education, The Child and Society* Harmondsworth: Penguin Education, 1973
Williams A.E.	*Barnardo of Stepney* London: The British Publishers Guild Ltd , 1953
Wilson, F.M.	*Rebel Daughter of a Country House* The Life of Eglantyne Jebb, Founder of the Save The Children Fund, London: Allen and Unwin, 1967

Index